PENGUIN BOOKS

The RULING CLASS

Also by Jennifer Lynn Barnes

The Inheritance Games Saga

The Inheritance Games
The Inheritance Games
The Hawthorne Legacy
The Final Gambit
The Brothers Hawthorne

The Grandest Game
The Grandest Game
Glorious Rivals
Coming next: *The Grandest Game 3*

Games Untold
The Same Backward as Forward

The Debutantes
Little White Lies
Deadly Little Scandals

The Fixer
The Ruling Class
Lessons in Power

The Lovely and the Lost

The RULING CLASS

JENNIFER LYNN BARNES

PENGUIN BOOKS

PENGUIN BOOKS

UK | USA | Canada | Ireland | Australia
India | New Zealand | South Africa

Penguin Books is part of the Penguin Random House group of companies
whose addresses can be found at global.penguinrandomhouse.com.

www.penguin.co.uk   www.puffin.co.uk   www.ladybird.co.uk

First published in the USA as *The Fixer* by Bloomsbury Children's Books 2015
Paperback edition first published in the USA by Bloomsbury Children's Books 2016
This edition published in the USA by Bloomsbury YA and in
Great Britain by Penguin Books 2025
001

Text copyright © Jennifer Lynn Barnes, 2015
Illustrations copyright © Jim Tierney, 2025

The moral right of the author and illustrator has been asserted

Penguin Random House values and supports copyright.
Copyright fuels creativity, encourages diverse voices, promotes freedom
of expression and supports a vibrant culture. Thank you for purchasing
an authorized edition of this book and for respecting intellectual property
laws by not reproducing, scanning or distributing any part of it by any
means without permission. You are supporting authors and enabling
Penguin Random House to continue to publish books for everyone.
No part of this book may be used or reproduced in any manner for the
purpose of training artificial intelligence technologies or systems. In accordance
with Article 4(3) of the DSM Directive 2019/790, Penguin Random House
expressly reserves this work from the text and data mining exception.

Printed and bound in Great Britain by Clays Ltd, Elcograf S.p.A.

The authorized representative in the EEA is Penguin Random House Ireland,
Morrison Chambers, 32 Nassau Street, Dublin D02 YH68

A CIP catalogue record for this book is available from the British Library

ISBN: 978–0–241–76307–0
SCHOLASTIC ISBN: 978–0–241–79766–2

All correspondence to:
Penguin Books
Penguin Random House Children's
One Embassy Gardens, 8 Viaduct Gardens, London SW11 7BW

Penguin Random House is committed to a
sustainable future for our business, our readers
and our planet. This book is made from Forest
Stewardship Council® certified paper.

For Allison, sister-in-law extraordinaire

CHAPTER 1

As far as I could tell, my history teacher had three passions in life: quoting Shakespeare, identifying historical inaccuracies in cable TV shows, and berating Ryan Washburn. "Eighteen sixty-three, Mr. Washburn. Is that so hard to remember? Abraham Lincoln signed the Emancipation Proclamation in eighteen sixty-*three*."

Ryan was a big guy: a little on the quiet side, a little shy. I had no idea what it was about him that had convinced Mr. Simpson he needed to be taken down a notch—or seven. But more and more, this was how history class went: Simpson called on Ryan, repeatedly, until he made a mistake. And then it began.

As Mr. Simpson railed on, Ryan stared at his desk, his head bowed so far that his chin gouged his collarbone. Sitting directly to his left, I could see the tension in his shoulder muscles, the sweat starting to bead up on his neck.

My grip on my pencil tightened.

"Where is that *incredible promise* I hear my colleagues chatting about in the teachers' lounge?" Mr. Simpson asked Ryan facetiously. "You have a lot of fans at this school, Mr. Washburn. Surely they can't all be mistaken about your intellectual capacity. Perhaps the emancipation of every enslaved human being in this country is simply not significant enough to merit a student of your *remarkable* caliber taking note of the date?"

"I'm sorry," Ryan mumbled. His Adam's apple bobbed.

Something inside me snapped. "It wasn't all of the slaves," I said evenly.

Mr. Simpson's eyes narrowed and flicked over to me. "Did you have something to share with the class, Ms. Kendrick?"

"Yes." I'd long since shed the Southern accent I'd had when I'd moved to Montana at the age of four, but I still had a habit of taking my time with my words. "The Emancipation Proclamation," I continued, at my own languid pace, "only freed slaves in the Confederate states. The remaining nine hundred thousand slaves weren't freed until the ratification of the Thirteenth Amendment in eighteen sixty-*five*."

A muscle in Mr. Simpson's jaw ticked. "'The fool doth think he is wise,' Ms. Kendrick, 'but the wise man knows himself to be a fool.'"

I'd been up working since five that morning. Beside me, Ryan still hadn't managed to raise his gaze from his desk.

I leaned back in my seat. "Methinks the lady doth protest too much."

"Want to tell me why you're here?" The guidance counselor scrolled through my file. When I didn't provide an immediate answer, she looked up from the computer, folded her hands on the desk, and leaned forward. "I'm concerned, Tess."

"If you're talking about the way Mr. Simpson victimizes his most vulnerable students, I am, too."

The words *victimize* and *vulnerable* were guidance counselor kryptonite. She pressed her lips together in a thin line. "And you think *inappropriate backchat*"—she read the phrase off the slip Mr. Simpson had written me—"is the most constructive way of expressing your concerns?"

I decided that was a rhetorical question.

"Tess, this time last year, you were on the girls' track team. You had nearly perfect attendance. You were, by all reports, sociable enough."

Not *sociable*, but *sociable enough*.

"Now I'm getting reports of you falling asleep in class, skipping assignments. You've already missed five days this semester, and we're not even three weeks in."

I shouldn't have stayed home when I had the flu, I thought dully. I'd given myself two days to recover. With absences racking up, that was two days too many. *I should have kept my mouth shut in Simpson's class.* I couldn't afford to draw attention to myself. To my situation. I knew that.

"You quit the track team." The guidance counselor was relentless in her onslaught. "You no longer seem to associate with any of your peers."

"My peers and I don't have much in common."

I'd never been popular. But I used to have friends—people to sit with at lunch, people who might ask questions if they thought something was wrong.

And that was the problem. These days, friends were a luxury I couldn't afford.

It was easy enough to make people give up on you if that was the goal.

"I'm afraid I have no choice but to call your grandfather." The guidance counselor reached for the phone.

Don't, I thought. But she was already dialing. I gritted my teeth to keep from reacting and tipping my hand. I forced myself to breathe. Gramps probably wouldn't answer. If he did, if it went badly, I already had a stack of excuses ready to go.

You must have caught him getting up from a nap.

It's this new medication his doctor has him on.

He's not much of a phone person.

The fifteen or twenty seconds it took her to give up on someone answering were torture. My heart still pounding in my ears, I pushed back the urge to shudder with relief. "You didn't leave a message." My voice sounded amazingly calm.

"Messages get deleted," she said dryly. "I'll try again later."

The knots in my stomach tightened. I'd dodged a bullet. But with Gramps the way he was, I couldn't afford to sit around and wait for round two. She wanted me to talk. She wanted me to *share*. Fine.

"Ryan Washburn," I said. "Mr. Simpson has it in for him. He's a nice kid. Quiet. Smart." I paused. "He leaves that class every day feeling stupid."

It shouldn't have been my job to tell her this.

"Do you know what we do out at my grandfather's ranch? Other than raise cattle?" I caught her gaze, willing her not to look away. "We take in the horses no one else wants, the ones who've been abused and broken and shattered inside until there's nothing left but *animal anger* and *animal fear*. We try to break through that. Sometimes we win." I paused. "Sometimes we don't."

"Tess—"

"I don't like bullies." I stood to leave. "Feel free to call my grandfather and tell him that. I'd say it's a good bet he already knows."

CHAPTER 2

My gamble appeared to have paid off. The phone didn't ring that night. Or the next. I kept a low profile at school. I got up early, stayed up late, and held my world together through sheer force of will. It wasn't much of a routine, but it was mine. By Thursday afternoon, I'd stopped expecting the worst.

That was a mistake.

Standing in the middle of the paddock, my feet planted wide and my arms hanging loose by my sides, I eyed the horse channeling Beelzebub a few feet away. "Hey now," I said softly. "That's not very ladylike."

The animal's nostrils flared, but she didn't rear back again.

"Someday," I murmured, my voice edging up on a croon, "I'd like to meet your first owner in a dark alleyway." Behind me, the sound of creaking wood alerted me to the arrival of company. I half expected that to send the horse into another fit, but instead, the animal took a few hesitant steps toward me.

"She's beautiful."

I froze. I recognized that voice—and instantly wished that I hadn't. *Two words.* After all this time, that was all it took.

My chest tightened.

"I'll be a while," I said. I didn't let myself turn around. This particular visitor wasn't worth getting riled up over.

"It's been too long, Tess."

Whose fault is that? I didn't bother responding out loud.

"You're good with her. The horse." Ivy didn't sound the least bit angry at being ignored. That was the way it was with her—sugar and spice and everything nice, right up to the point when she wasn't.

Go away, I thought. The horse in front of me gave a violent jerk of her head, picking up on the tension in my body. "Hey," I murmured to her. "Hey now." She slammed her front hooves into the ground. I got the message and began to back away.

"We need to talk," Ivy told me when I reached the outer limits of the paddock. Like her presence on the ranch was an everyday occurrence. Like talking was something the two of us did.

I jumped the fence. "I need a shower," I countered.

Ivy could not argue with my logic. Or more likely, she chose not to. I had the sense that the great Ivy Kendrick was the kind of person who could successfully argue just about any point— but what did I know? It had been almost three years since the last time I'd seen her.

"After your shower, we need to talk." Ivy was nothing if not persistent. I deeply suspected that she wasn't used to people telling her no. Luckily, there were benefits to being the kind of person known for taking my time with words. I didn't *have* to say no. Instead, I walked toward the house, my stride outpacing hers, even though she had an inch or two on me.

"I got a call from your guidance counselor," Ivy said behind me. "And then I made some calls of my own."

Her words didn't slow me down, but my gut twisted like a wet towel being wrung out and then wrung out again.

"I talked to the ranch hands," Ivy continued.

I climbed up on the front porch, flung open the door, and let it slam behind me when I'd stepped inside. There was a time when slamming a door would have drawn my grandfather's attention. He would have called me a heathen, threatened to scalp me, and sent me back out onto the porch to "try again."

Not anymore.

Ivy's been asking questions. I escaped to the second floor but couldn't get away from the certainty bubbling up inside me. *She knows.*

"Enjoy your shower," Ivy called after me. "Then we'll talk."

She was like a broken record. And she *knew*. I'd tried so hard to keep this secret, to take care of my grandfather, to do this one thing for the man who'd done everything for me, and now . . .

I wasn't sure exactly what Ivy did in Washington. I didn't know for a fact that she still lived there. I couldn't have told you if she was single or dating someone—she might have even been married. What I *did* know—what I was trying very hard *not* to know—was that if Ivy had deigned to fly out to Montana and grace the ranch with her presence, she'd done so for a reason.

My sister was a mover, a shaker, a problem solver—and right now, the problem she'd set her sights on solving was *me*.

CHAPTER 3

I gave myself three minutes to shower. I couldn't afford to leave Ivy alone with Gramps for longer than that. I shouldn't have left them alone at all, but I needed a moment. I needed to think.

I hadn't seen Ivy in nearly three years. She used to make it out to the ranch every few months. The last time she'd come to visit, she'd asked me if I wanted to move to DC and live with her. At thirteen, I'd worshipped the ground my sister walked on. I'd said yes. We'd had plans. And then she'd left. Without any explanation. Without taking me with her.

Without saying good-bye.

She hadn't been back since. *If I can convince her that Gramps and I are okay, she'll leave again.* That should have been comforting. It should have been my glimmer of hope.

I wasn't thirteen anymore. It shouldn't have hurt.

I tossed on a pair of sweats and a T-shirt and towel-dried my devil-may-care, too-thick hair. Ivy and I were bookend brunettes, my hair a shade too light to be considered black and my sister's a fraction too dark to be blond.

She met me at the bottom of the stairs. "You ready to talk?" Her voice sounded like mine. She spoke faster, but the pitch was the same.

I felt a familiar rush of anger. "Did you ever think that maybe I don't want to talk to you?"

Ivy's mask of pleasantness faltered, just for a second. "I got that general sense when you didn't return my last three phone calls," she said softly.

Christmas. My birthday. Ivy's birthday. My sister called home exactly three times a year. I'd stopped picking up at approximately the same time that my grandfather had started forgetting little things like keys and names and turning off the stove.

Gramps. I willed myself to concentrate on what mattered here. *There's a situation. It's my job to get it under control.* I rounded the corner into the kitchen, unsure of what I would find.

"'Bout time, Bear." My grandfather greeted me with a ruffle of my hair and a cuff to the shoulder.

He knows me. Relief washed over my body. *Bear* had been his nickname for me for as long as I could remember.

"Look who's finally come to visit," Gramps said, nodding toward Ivy. His voice was gruff, but his hazel eyes were sparkling.

This is good, I thought. *I can work with this.* I'd been covering for my grandfather's lapses for the past year. More frequently now than a year ago.

More frequently now than a month ago.

But if today was a good day, Ivy didn't have to know that. If there was one thing experience had taught me, it was that she wouldn't stick around to find out.

"I know, Gramps," I said, taking a seat at the rickety wooden table that had been falling apart in my grandfather's kitchen for longer than I'd been alive. "I can't believe we actually merited an in-person Ivy checkup."

My sister's dark brown eyes locked on to mine.

"Ivy? Who's Ivy?" My grandfather gave Ivy a conspiratorial grin before turning back to me. "You got an imaginary friend there, Bear?"

My heart skipped a beat. I could do this. I *had* to do this. For Gramps.

"I don't know," I replied, my fingers digging into the underside of my chair. "Is 'imaginary friend' what they're calling perpetually absent siblings these days?"

"You're the one who stopped returning my calls," Ivy cut in.

Good. Let her focus on me. Let her get mad at *me*. Anything to keep her from realizing that whatever she'd managed to glean from talking to my guidance counselor and the ranch hands—it wasn't even the half of it. Nobody knew how bad things were.

Nobody but me.

"I didn't return your calls because I didn't feel like talking," I told Ivy through gritted teeth. "You can't just check out of our lives and then expect me to drop everything when you finally decide to pick up a phone."

"That's not what happened, Tessie, and you know it."

Getting a rise out of Ivy felt better than it should have. "It's Tess."

"Actually," she snapped back, "it's Theresa."

"For goodness' sakes, Nora," my grandfather cut in. "She's only here for two weeks each summer. Don't get your panties in a twist over a few missed calls."

Ivy's face went from frustrated to gutted in two seconds flat. Nora was our mother's name. I barely remembered her, but Ivy was twenty-one when our parents died. The age difference between the two of us always felt massive, but the fact that Ivy had spent seventeen more years with Mom and Dad—that was truly the great divide. To me, the ranch was home, and our grandfather was the only real parent I'd ever known. To Ivy, he was just the grandpa she'd spent two weeks with every summer growing up.

It occurred to me, then, that when she was little, he might have called her *Bear*, too.

He thinks I'm Ivy, and he thinks Ivy is Mom. There was no covering for this, no barbed comment I could toss out that would make Ivy brush it off. For the longest time, she just sat there, staring at Gramps. Then she blinked, and when her eyes opened again, it was like none of it had ever happened, like she was a robot who'd just rebooted to avoid running a program called "excess emotion."

"Harry," she said, addressing our grandfather by his first name. "I'm Ivy. Your granddaughter. This is Tess."

"I know who she is," he grunted. I tried not to see the uncertainty in his eyes.

"You do," Ivy replied, her voice soothing but no-nonsense. "And you also know that she can't stay here. You can't stay here."

"Like hell we can't!" I bolted to my feet.

My grandfather slammed his palm into the table. "Language, Theresa!"

Just like that, I was me again, if only for the moment.

"Give us a minute, Tess," Ivy ordered.

"Go on, Bear." My grandfather looked old suddenly—and very, very tired. In that instant, I would have done anything he asked. I would have done anything to have him back.

I left them alone in the kitchen. In the living room, I paced as the minutes ticked by. *Five. Ten. Fifteen.* Around the furniture, in little figure eights, from one side of the room to the other.

"You used to do that when you were little." Ivy appeared in the doorway, hovering there for a moment before taking a seat on the couch. "You'd do loops around Mom's feet, the coffee table. Other babies learned to walk. You learned to pace." She smiled slightly. "It drove her nuts."

Ivy and I had only lived in the same house for that one year, when I was a baby and she was a senior in high school. I wished sometimes that I could remember it, but even if I could, she'd still be a stranger—one who threatened everything I'd worked so hard to protect.

"You should have called me when things got bad, Tess."

Called her? I should have picked up a phone and *called her*, when she couldn't even be bothered to visit?

"I'm handling it, Ivy." I cursed myself, cursed the guidance counselor for making the call. "We're fine."

"No, sweetie, you're not."

She didn't get to come here, after *years*, and tell me I wasn't fine. She didn't get to insert herself into our lives, and she didn't get to call me *sweetie*.

"There's a treatment center in Boston," she continued calmly. "The best in the country. There's a waiting list for the inpatient facility, but I made some calls."

My stomach twisted sharply. Gramps loved this ranch. He *was* this ranch. It wouldn't survive without him. I'd given up everything—track, friends, the hope of ever getting a good night's sleep—to keep him here, to keep things running, to take care of him, the way he'd always taken care of me.

"Gramps is fine." I set my jaw in a mutinous line. "He gets confused sometimes, but he's *fine*."

"He needs a doctor, Tessie."

"So take him to a doctor." I swallowed hard, feeling like I'd already lost. "Figure out what we need to do, what *I* need to do, and then bring him *home*."

"You can't stay here, Tess." Ivy reached for my hand. I jerked it back. "You've been taking care of him," she continued softly. "Who's been taking care of you?"

"I can take care of myself."

The set of her jaw matched my own. "You shouldn't have to."

"She's right, Bear." I looked up to see Gramps standing in the doorway. "Don't you worry about me, girlie," he ordered. He was lucid—and intractable.

"You don't have to do this, Gramps," I told him. My words fell on deaf ears.

"You're a good girl, Tess," he said gruffly. He met my sister's eyes and something passed unspoken between them. After a long moment, Ivy turned back to me.

"Until we get things settled, I want you to come back with me." She held up a hand to cut off my objections. "I've talked to a school in DC. You start on Monday."

CHAPTER 4

"I'd tell you that you can't stay mad forever," Ivy commented, "but I'm pretty sure you'd take that as a challenge."

I hadn't spoken to my sister once since we'd checked my grandfather into the facility in Boston. She kept telling me how nice it was, how highly thought of the specialists were, how often we could go to visit. None of that changed the fact that we left him there. *I* left him. He would wake up in the middle of the night, disoriented, and I wouldn't be there. He would frantically start looking for the grandmother who'd died before I was even born, and I wouldn't be there.

He would have good days, and I wouldn't be there.

If the silent treatment was getting to Ivy, she showed no sign of it as we navigated the DC airport. Her heels clicked against the tile as she stepped off the escalator and glided into the kind of graceful power walk that made everyone else in the airport look twice and get out of her way. She paused for an instant when we came to a row of men in black suits holding carefully lettered signs. *Chauffeurs*. At the very end of the line was a man wearing a navy blue T-shirt and ripped jeans.

There was a hint of stubble on his suntanned face and a pack of cigarettes in his left hand. In his right hand he, too, held a carefully lettered sign. But instead of writing his client's last name, he'd opted for: PAIN IN THE *%$&@.

Ivy stalked up to him and handed him her carry-on. "Cute."

He smirked. "I thought so."

She rolled her eyes. "Tess, meet Bodie. He *was* my driver and personal assistant, but as of five seconds ago, he's fired."

"I prefer 'Jack-of-All-Trades,'" Bodie interjected. "And I'm only fired until there's a female you can't sweet-talk or a law you won't br—"

Ivy cut him off with an all-powerful glare. I mentally finished his sentence: *I'm only fired until there's a female you can't sweet-talk or a law you won't* break. I darted a glance at Ivy, my eyebrows shooting up. What exactly did my sister do that she needed a chauffeur willing to break laws on her behalf?

Ivy ignored my raised brows and plowed on, unperturbed. "Now would be a good time to get our bags," she told Bodie.

"You can get your own bags, princess," Bodie retorted. "I'm fired." He rocked back on his heels. "I will, however, help Tess here with hers out of the goodness of my heart." Bodie didn't wink at me or smirk, but somehow, I felt as if he'd done both. "I'm very philanthropic," he added.

I didn't reply, but I did let him help me with my bags. The cigarettes disappeared into his back pocket the moment my duffels came into view. Muscles bulged under his T-shirt as he grabbed a bag in each hand.

He didn't look like anyone's chauffeur.

Ivy's house loomed over the pavement, boxy and tall, with twin chimneys on either side. It seemed too big for one person.

"I live on the second floor," Ivy clarified as she, Bodie, and I made our way into the house. "I work on the first."

It was on the tip of my tongue to ask Ivy what *work* entailed, but I didn't. My sister had always been mysteriously close-lipped about her life in Washington. Asking for details now would be taken as a sign of interest.

I'm not interested.

Stepping into an enormous foyer, I concentrated on the sight in front of me: dark wood floors and massive columns gave the expanse the look of a ballroom. To my left, there was an alcove lined with bay windows, and behind that, a hallway lined with doors.

"The closed doors go to the conference room and my office. Both are off-limits. The main kitchen is through there, but we mostly use it for entertaining."

We? I wondered. I didn't let myself get further than that as I followed Ivy up a spiral staircase to what appeared to be a sparsely decorated apartment. "The kitchen up here is more of a kitchenette," she told me. "I don't cook much. We mostly order in."

Bodie cleared his throat and when she didn't respond the first time, he repeated the action, only louder.

"We mostly order in, and sometimes Bodie makes pancakes downstairs," Ivy amended. I took that to mean that Bodie was definitely part of Ivy's *we*.

"Do you live here, Bodie?" I asked, darting a sideways glance at Ivy's "driver."

He choked on his own spit. "Ahh . . . no," he said, once he'd recovered. "I don't live here." I must have looked skeptical, because he elaborated. "Kid, I worked for your sister for a year and a half before she even invited me up here, and that was only because she broke the plumbing."

"I did not break the plumbing," Ivy replied testily. "It broke itself." She turned back to me. "Your room is through here."

My room? I thought. She spoke so casually, I could almost believe that I wasn't just some unpleasant surprise that fate and Alzheimer's had dropped in her lap.

"Don't you mean the guest room?" I asked.

Ivy opened the bedroom door, and I realized that the room was completely empty—no furniture. Nothing.

Not a guest room.

The room was mostly square, with a nook by the window and a ceiling that sloped on either side. The floors were a dark mahogany wood. A series of mirrors doubled as sliding doors to the closet.

"I thought you might like to decorate it yourself." Ivy stepped into the room. If I hadn't known better, I would have said she looked almost nervous. "I know it's a little on the small side, but it's my favorite room in the house. And you've got your own bathroom."

The room was beautiful, but even thinking that felt disloyal. "Where am I going to sleep?" I asked.

"Wherever you put the bed." Ivy's reply was brusque, like she'd caught herself caring and managed to put a cork in it.

"Where am I going to sleep *until I get a bed*?" I asked, checking the impulse to roll my eyes.

"Tell me what kind of bed you want," Ivy replied, "and Bodie will make sure it gets here tonight. I've got some furniture catalogs you can look at."

I stared at my sister, wondering if she realized just how ridiculous that plan sounded. "I don't think furniture companies do same-day delivery on a Saturday night," I said, stating the obvious.

Bodie set my bags against the wall and then leaned back against the doorjamb. "They do," he told me, "if you're Ivy Kendrick."

CHAPTER 5

The next morning, when I woke up in the bed I'd selected more or less randomly from one of Ivy's catalogs, there was no escaping the physical reminders of where I was. And where I wasn't. The bed beneath me was too comfortable. The ceiling above wasn't my ceiling. Everything about this felt wrong.

I thought of Gramps, waking up in Boston and staring at a strange ceiling of his own. Pushing back against the suffocating wave of emotion that washed over me just thinking about it, I got up, got dressed, and pondered the fact that the mere mention of my sister's name had been enough to make furniture appear within hours of being ordered. Back on the ranch, she'd managed to have herself declared my legal guardian and obtained our grandfather's power of attorney almost as quickly.

Who *did* that? And more importantly—who could?

I should have known what my sister did for a living. I should have known Ivy. But I didn't. Making my way out of the bedroom, I found the loft empty, a visceral reminder that it had always been my sister's choice not to know me. She was the one who'd left. She was the one who'd stopped answering my calls.

Whoever she was, whatever she did—she'd chosen this life over me.

The muted sound of voices rose up from downstairs. At the top of the spiral staircase, I paused. The female voice was unmistakably Ivy's. The person she was talking to was male.

"You don't think that this was, just possibly, a little bit impulsive?" The mystery man's tone of voice made it quite clear that he thought *little bit* was an understatement.

"Impulsive, Adam?" Ivy shot back. "You're the one who taught me to trust my instincts."

"This wasn't instinct," the man—*Adam*—countered. "This was guilt, Ivy."

"I'm not debating this with you."

"Evidence would suggest you are."

"Adam"—I could practically hear Ivy clenching her teeth—"if you want me to look into your little friend at the DOJ, you'll stop talking. *Now*."

For several seconds, there was silence, followed by a grunt of frustration.

"What do you want me to do, Adam?" my sister asked finally, her voice soft enough now that I had to strain to hear. "Things were bad in Montana. I'm not sending her back, and I am not shipping her off to some boarding school. And don't give me that look—you were the one who told me to bring her here three years ago!"

Realizing that they were arguing about me turned my body to stone. And what did Ivy mean that *Adam* was the one who had suggested she invite me to live with her the first time around? Who was this guy? Why had she listened to him?

Why had she changed her mind?

Some memories were like scars. This one had never healed right. Just hearing Ivy talk about it ripped off the scab.

"Three years ago, bringing Tess here might have been the right call." Adam's voice was terse. "But things change, Ivy. Three years ago, you were on speaking terms with my father."

I shifted my weight from one foot to the other, and the stair beneath me creaked. The voices below went suddenly quiet. They'd heard me. I had a split second to decide on a course of action. I went with "pretend you weren't just eavesdropping and walk down the stairs."

"Ivy?" I called out. "You down there?"

Ivy met me at the bottom of the steps. Her light brown hair was loosely coiffed at the nape of her neck. She wore a formfitting blazer as comfortably as most people wore sweatshirts. Even her jeans looked expensive. If she saw through my innocent act, she didn't call me on it. "Good," she said. "You're up."

I had an excellent poker face, refined by years of playing actual poker with gruff old men. "I'm up."

Ivy smiled, gleaming white teeth covering for the fact that she didn't look happy in the least. "Adam," she called out, her voice so pleasant my teeth ached from the sugar in her tone. "Come meet Tess."

I had two seconds to wonder what the man would look like before he rounded the corner. He was a couple of years older than Ivy. If I'd had to guess, I would have put his height at exactly six feet. *No more. No less.* His posture was perfect; every muscle in his face was tightly controlled. His eyes met mine, and that control wavered. Just for a second, this stranger looked at me the way Ivy had looked at our grandfather when he'd called her by Mom's name.

The expression was gone from his face in an instant. "Tess," he said, holding out his right hand, "I'm Adam Keyes. It's nice to meet you." His words sounded genuine. He looked like an honest enough guy. But given that *Adam Keyes* thought bringing me here was a mistake, I somehow doubted he was all that pleased to meet me.

I took his hand. "Yeah," I said. "You, too."

He waited, like he thought I might elaborate, but I didn't say anything else.

"Ivy tells me you'll be starting at Hardwicke tomorrow," Adam said, trying to make conversation. "You'll like it there. It's a great school." He raised an eyebrow at the expression on my face. "Not a big fan of school, I take it?"

"School's fine." Again, he waited, and again, I left it at that.

"But you'd rather be outside," Adam elaborated on my behalf. I glanced over at Ivy, wondering what she had told him about me—wondering how she even knew that about me, when the two of us were practically strangers.

"My brother was like that," Adam said, clearing his throat. "IQ off the charts, but his favorite subject was recess."

"And how'd that work out for him?" I asked, trying to decide whether or not I'd just been insulted.

A small, fleeting smile passed over Adam's face. "He joined the army the day he graduated from high school."

Bodie announced his presence by slamming the front door. "Somebody call for pancakes?"

The smile hardened on Adam's face. Apparently, he wasn't as fond of my sister's driver as she was. "I should go," Adam said stiffly. "I need to stop by the office."

"On a Sunday?" Ivy pressed.

"Like you're one to talk," Adam retorted. "You never stop working."

"I do now," Ivy said, folding her hands in front of her body. "Sunday is the day of rest. This is me, resting. I thought Tess and I might go shopping this afternoon, get some clothes for her first day at Hardwicke."

Shopping? With Ivy?

Bodie let out a bark of laughter at the expression on my face. "Hate to tell you this, princess, but the kid looks like she'd rather rip out her own thumbnails and use them to gouge out her eye than go shopping with you."

Ivy wasn't deterred. "She'll adjust."

Adam's phone rang. He excused himself, leaving me staring down my sister, and Bodie watching the two of us with no small amount of amusement.

"Have you heard from the doctors in Boston yet?" I asked Ivy.

"Not yet." For a second, I thought that might be all she was going to say, but then she elaborated. "They'll be doing a complete diagnostic assessment in the next few days."

Days. I swallowed, unable to keep my mind from latching on to the word. *Days. And weeks. And months. And none of it good.* I forced my expression to stay neutral. I couldn't let myself go down that road. I couldn't think about Gramps. I couldn't think about the future.

Adam walked back into the room. "Ivy." His tone was low, serious.

Ivy turned to look at him. "Everything okay?"

Adam glanced at Bodie and me, as if to say, *not around the children*.

"Let me guess," Bodie drawled, poking at Adam like someone taunting a bear with a stick. "The Pentagon?"

"That wasn't the Pentagon," Adam said curtly. "That was my father."

His father—the one Adam had said Ivy was on good terms with three years ago. The one she presumably was not on good terms with now.

"And?" Ivy prompted, in a tone that told me that there was always an *and* with Adam's father.

"And," Adam said, his face devoid of emotion, "he was calling to tell me that Theo Marquette was just rushed to Bethesda General. Heart attack. They're not sure if he's going to make it." He let that sink in for a second before continuing. "They've got a lid on it for now, but the press will know in a matter of hours."

Ivy took a beat to absorb that information, then locked her hand around Adam's elbow and pulled him to the side of the room for a hushed conversation. In less than a minute, Ivy was on her phone, barking out commands.

Glancing back over her shoulder at me, she lowered her voice. "Sorry, Tess. Something's come up. When I have an update on Gramps, I'll let you know. In the meantime, Bodie can take you shopping for anything you need."

I should have been grateful for the reprieve—but really, it was just a reminder that Ivy could and would ditch me at the drop of a hat. I might not have known what my sister's job was, or why news of some guy's heart attack had sent her into hyperdrive, or even why the name *Theo Marquette* sounded vaguely familiar in the first place. But the one thing I *did* know was that Adam was right—Ivy never should have brought me here.

It was only a matter of time before she dropped me for good.

I didn't say a word when Ivy shut herself in her office, or when she left the house, power walking like the devil was on her heels. I let Bodie make me pancakes. It wasn't until later, after I'd eaten four of them, that I realized suddenly where I'd heard the name *Theo Marquette* before.

Theodore Marquette was the chief justice of the United States Supreme Court.

CHAPTER 6

Ivy was still in crisis mode the next morning, but—lucky me—she managed to carve half an hour out of her schedule to take me to school. In the back of my mind, I'd expected the illustrious Hardwicke School to look like Hogwarts. Needless to say, I was severely disappointed. The Upper School—because heaven forbid they call it a *high school*—looked like nothing so much as a granola bar turned on its side.

"The facilities here are just fantastic," Ivy told me as we walked down a stone path toward the historic home that served as the administrative building. "The Maxwell Art Center has one of the largest auditoriums in the city. The Upper School just added a state-of-the-art robotics lab. And you should see the new gymnasium."

I gazed out at the nearby playing fields. The wind sifted through my hair, lifting a few strands upward, and for a moment, looking out at the massive stretch of green in front of me, I could almost forget where I was.

"Now or never." Ivy's voice brought me back. "And you're not allowed to say never."

"You don't have to come with me," I told her, hooking my thumbs lazily through my belt loops. "I'm sure you have more important things to do."

As if to accentuate the point, Ivy's pocket began to vibrate.

"It can wait," Ivy told me, but I could practically *see* her fingertips twitching to answer it.

"Go ahead." I gestured to the phone. "Maybe there's an update on Justice Marquette's condition. Or maybe the president has a head cold. You get calls for that, too, right?"

Ivy looked up at the sky. I wondered if she was asking God for patience. "That moment," she said under her breath, "when you realize that sarcasm is hereditary."

Before I could formulate a suitable reply, the door to the administrative building opened, and my sister and I were ushered inside.

"Ms. Kendrick." The headmaster's assistant had suburban-soccer-mom hair. She was wearing a peach twinset, and I couldn't shake the feeling that she was about to offer us lemonade. Or cookies. Or possibly both. "And you must be Theresa."

"She goes by Tess," Ivy said, as if I were five years old and incapable of speaking for myself.

"Tess it is, then," the woman replied gamely. "We were so sorry to hear about your grandfather, dear."

I couldn't help feeling gut-punched. I'd spent the past year hiding my grandfather's condition. Ivy, apparently, had taken out a billboard announcing it to the world.

"But we're very happy you'll be joining us here at Hardwicke," the woman continued, oblivious to my train of thought. "I'm Mrs. Perkins. If you'll wait just a moment, Headmaster Raleigh will be—"

A compact man with dark hair and a beard made his way around the corner. Mrs. Perkins cut off her previous sentence with a smile. "And here he is now."

"Ivy." The headmaster greeted Ivy by name and reached both of his hands out to take hers.

"Headmaster Raleigh," she returned, in a tone that made me think that under typical circumstances, she'd leave the *headmaster* off. "I appreciate you making this happen."

"Yes, well . . ." Headmaster Raleigh plucked his glasses off his face and began polishing them against his shirt. "We think that you—and Tess—will fit in with the Hardwicke family quite well."

"I know my way around Hardwicke," Ivy replied, in a tone that made me wonder what experience she'd had with the school—and why the headmaster looked uncomfortable with the reminder. "This is the right place for Tess."

"And, of course," the headmaster added, "you can expect us to respect your sister's privacy. Just as we respect the privacy of *all* of our students."

There was subtext there—a warning.

"What happens at Hardwicke stays at Hardwicke," Ivy said smoothly. "Believe me, I know."

"Am I early?" a voice piped up from the doorway. I turned to look at the girl who stood there. Ivy and Headmaster Raleigh kept their eyes on each other.

"You are right on time," Mrs. Perkins told the girl cheerfully, ignoring the tension in the room. "Tess, this is Vivvie Bharani. Since you girls are in most of the same classes, she's going to be showing you around today."

Vivvie was an inch or two taller than me with dark brown skin, a round face, and wavy black hair that she wore pulled into loose pigtails. She offered me a hopeful smile. "I know," she said apologetically. "This whole 'hey, new girl, go with the total stranger' thing is kind of cliché, but don't think of me as your school-assigned buddy." Her smile brightened. "Think of me as your travel guide to a strange and bewildering country, where the locals are always restless and the bathrooms are impossible to find." There was an energy to Vivvie, an earnestness that made her very hard not to like.

"And as your travel guide," she continued, bringing her right hand to her heart, like she was pledging allegiance, "I am morally obligated to tell you that if we don't leave now, the Hut will be totally sold out of everything bagels by the time we get there." She paused to let what I could only assume was the seriousness of that sink in. "You cannot possibly be prepared for your first day at Hardwicke with only *some* things in your morning bagel."

I glanced over at Ivy and the headmaster, who'd finally ended their friendly little staring match. Then I turned back to Vivvie. "After you."

CHAPTER 7

The Hardwicke Hut was essentially a student-run coffee shop that didn't serve coffee.

"Two everything bagels," Vivvie ordered, with the air of a fairy godmother granting a most elaborate wish. "And do not tell me you're out," she told the boy behind the counter. "You are not out of everything bagels. The world would not be so cruel."

"We're not out," the boy replied. "But there's only one left. The world is a little bit cruel."

Vivvie put on a brave face. "In that case, Tess will have an everything bagel, and I'll have—"

"Half of mine?" I suggested. I would have given her the whole thing, but I wasn't sure she'd take it.

"I knew I liked you!" Vivvie beamed. As we slid over to await our order, a trio of girls started making their way to the counter. Vivvie mistook my registering their presence as a sign of interest.

"The one on the left is Maya Rojas," Vivvie told me, like this was some kind of nature documentary and she was narrating. "She's a three-sport captain. As a junior." Apparently, at Hardwicke, that made Maya a person to know. "The one next to her, with the white-blond hair?" Vivvie continued. "That's Di. She's from Iceland."

"Di?" I repeated. "As in Diana?" That didn't exactly sound Icelandic to me.

"Errr . . . no. It's actually short for something else." Vivvie tried and failed to sound inconspicuous.

"What's it short for?"

Vivvie hesitated. "It's Di as in *D* period *I* period. And it's short for *diplomatic immunity*." Vivvie had the decency to look a little sheepish. "Di's father is an ambassador, and her real name is pretty much impossible to pronounce. Plus she never turns down dares. Like, ever."

A teenage girl with diplomatic immunity and a fondness for dares. *That won't end well.*

That just left the third girl. Vivvie didn't get the chance to tell me anything about her, because a second later, the girl in question spotted us. She cut across the Hut like a homing pigeon.

"Vivvie, aren't you going to introduce me to your friend?" Without waiting for Vivvie to respond, the girl plowed forward. "I'm Emilia Rhodes."

"Tess," I said. For a moment, Emilia and I studied each other. She was tall, with strawberry-blond hair and eyes that walked the line between green and blue. She wore almost no makeup, except for a light gloss on her lips. "So you're Ivy Kendrick's sister," she said finally. "I thought you'd be taller."

"I'll get right to work on that."

Emilia cracked a very small smile. "Hardwicke almost never accepts midsemester transfers," she said. "Your sister must have pulled some very impressive strings."

I shrugged. "I wouldn't know."

Emilia might have continued cross-examining me, but Vivvie pulled her attention away. "I saw the news about Justice Marquette online," Vivvie told her. "Have you heard from Henry at all?"

Emilia gave a brief shake of her head. "Neither has Asher. Henry Marquette isn't really one for communication. Or sharing. Or the outward display of human emotion of any kind." Coming from Emilia, that didn't sound like a criticism. "We'll hear what happens from the papers before we hear it from Henry."

Having placed their orders, Maya and Di appeared behind Emilia, like an athletic angel and an Icelandic devil on her shoulders.

"My mom's already running numbers," Maya commented. "The president wasn't expecting to appoint a justice this term. It could be a game changer."

"Maya," Emilia interjected, cutting off that topic of conversation completely. "Di." She looked from one girl to the other. "Meet Tess Kendrick."

"Ivy Kendrick's little sister?" Maya raised an eyebrow. "Remind me to stay on your good side."

"Who's Ivy Kendrick?" Di asked. Her hair was so pale it practically gave off light. Her accent was sharp—and impossible to ignore.

"Remember the time you got *me* arrested, Miss Diplomatic Immunity?" Maya shot back.

Di tilted her head to the side. "This sounds vaguely familiar."

Maya gave Di a pointed look, and after a long moment, a realization settled over Di's face. "Oh," she said. "*That* Ivy Kendrick. Is she the one who . . . that thing with Grant?"

Emilia nodded. "I don't even want to know what she has on the members of the board," she added, her gaze darting over to me. "Like I said, Hardwicke almost never admits students midsemester."

I shrugged. "Just lucky, I guess."

Emilia stared at me for three or four more seconds, then gave up on pumping me for information. "We should go," she decided with the force of a monarch declaring law. "I have Latin first period. *The Aeneid* waits for no man."

As quickly as they'd descended upon us, the three girls were gone.

"Emilia's angling for valedictorian," Vivvie said almost apologetically. "I'm pretty sure she's been angling for valedictorian since we were about four. She comes on a little strong sometimes." Vivvie took a tiny nibble of bagel, then changed the subject. "I'm guessing you heard that Justice Marquette is in the hospital. It was all over the news this morning."

I nodded but didn't mention that I hadn't gotten my information from the news.

"It's so sad," Vivvie said softly. "His grandson Henry is in our grade, and I hear they're actually pretty close. But even Henry's friends aren't thinking about Henry. Or his grandfather. I mean, Maya's mom works for the White House, and they're already talking about replacements."

I felt a pang for this Henry Marquette and tried not to think about grandfathers—Henry's or mine.

"What exactly does Maya's mom do at the White House?" I asked. Vivvie had said the phrase *White House* the way that kids at any other school might say *City Hall*. From the lack of emphasis Vivvie gave it, Maya's mom might as well work at the local mall.

Vivvie blinked several times. I could practically see her reminding herself that I was new—not just to the school, but also to DC. "Mrs. Rojas is a pollster. She analyzes numbers and statistics, does surveys, that kind of thing."

I hadn't even realized that was a job.

"What about Emilia?"

Vivvie tilted her head to the side. "What about her?"

"Di's father is an ambassador. Maya's mom crunches numbers for the president. What do Emilia's parents do?"

Vivvie thought for a moment. "I think they're dentists."

Emilia did have remarkably good teeth.

"One more question," I told Vivvie.

She made a finger gunning motion. "Shoot."

"What," I said slowly, "*exactly* is it that my sister does?"

Vivvie's eyebrows disappeared into her hairline. "You don't know?"

I gritted my teeth. "I know that everyone around here seems to know her name," I said finally. "I know that she apparently got Maya out of being arrested. I know that Headmaster Raleigh is a little bit scared of her, and I know that she got a call yesterday morning about Justice Marquette."

I hadn't meant to say that last bit out loud.

"Your sister," Vivvie said delicately, "is, shall we say . . . a problem solver. When important people in Washington have problems, she makes them go away."

"What kinds of problems?" I asked suspiciously. With a description that vague, Ivy could be a hit man.

Vivvie's shoulders moved up and down in an exaggerated shrug. "Money problems, legal problems, PR problems—you go to Ivy Kendrick, and—*poof*—no more problems. She fixes things."

I thought of Ivy swooping onto the ranch like she owned the place, packing my whole life up in a matter of days. "You're telling me that my sister is a professional problem solver?" I asked tightly. "She just goes around, solving other people's problems? How is that even an occupation?"

"Supply and demand?" Vivvie suggested. "Around here, we call them fixers."

CHAPTER 8

"Are you okay?" Vivvie asked me for maybe the fifteenth time in the past six hours.

That's one word for it, I thought. A better word might have been *irked*. Or possibly *overwhelmed*.

I'd traded American History with Mr. Simpson for Contemporary World Issues with Dr. Clark. We were currently broken into pairs, discussing the effects of internet censorship in East and Central Asia. Or at least that was the assignment. I had a feeling most people were actually discussing Contemporary Hardwicke Issues. Namely me. And my sister. Who apparently fixed problems for a living.

"I'm fine," I told Vivvie. Her brow furrowed. Clearly, she was less than convinced.

"Would you feel better," she said seriously, "if I recapped my favorite horror movie and/or romance novel for you?"

"All right, people!" Dr. Clark clapped her hands. "I'm going to assume the sound of chattering means you have strong thoughts on the issue of governments limiting access to information—thoughts that you'll back up tonight with a five-hundred-word essay analyzing the content of a major news site and the effects of denying access to that content."

I'd made it through English, Spanish, physics, math analysis, and an elective called Speaking of Words. If it hadn't been for a free period in the middle of the day, I might not have survived this long.

The second the final bell rang, I slipped out of my chair. Automatically, my brain began thinking ahead. *Check the feed. Put in orders. Make sure Gramps eats something. Call—*

Reality hit me a moment later. I didn't need to *do* anything. There was nothing for me to do. *And Gramps—*

I cut the thought off at the knees.

"Are you *sure* you're okay?" Vivvie asked. "The offer about the romance novel still stands."

My lips took a stab at a smile. It probably looked more like a grimace. *Get it under control*, I told myself. *It was just a stupid Pavlovian response. Hear bell, go home.* But I wasn't going home. *Home* didn't exist anymore. Not without Gramps.

"I'll be right back," I told Vivvie. Ducking into the hallway, I pushed through the crowd and made a beeline for the bathroom. I just needed a second. I needed to breathe.

The bathroom door closed behind me. I walked over to the sink and turned on the faucet. I closed my eyes and, just for a second, let myself listen to the sound of running water.

And that was when I heard it—a hitch of breath.

I turned off the water and waited, and there it was again. I looked back at the stalls. Only one was occupied. I could picture its occupant, hand over her mouth, trying to stifle the sound of a sob.

It's none of my business. I made it halfway to the door, but couldn't make myself keep walking.

"Hey," I said, feeling about as awkward as I sounded and wishing I was the type of person who could leave well enough alone. "You okay?"

Oh God, I thought, realizing how much I sounded like Vivvie. *It's catching.*

There was another ragged breath on the other side of the stall door, and then: "*Go. Away.*"

Whoever was crying in that bathroom stall would have wished me off the face of the planet if she could have. It wasn't the anger in her voice that crawled beneath my skin and stayed there—or the deep and cloying sadness. It was desperation: wild, violent, spiraling out of control.

"I said *go away*," the girl repeated, her voice hoarse.

I almost did, but as my hand brushed the door to the bathroom, I couldn't bring myself to do it. I couldn't just *leave*.

"Not a big fan of *away* right now," I said instead. No response. I leaned up against the wall and crossed one foot over the other. The seconds ticked by in silence. Finally, the stall door opened. The girl inside was doe-eyed and baby-faced—and not a graceful crier. Everything about her screamed *freshman*.

"You're the new girl," she said, her eyes swollen from crying, her voice dull.

"Tess," I supplied.

She didn't tell me her name, and I didn't ask.

"I've had a really long day," I told her. "You?"

The girl looked down at the ground, then walked over to the sink. She turned on the faucet and washed her hands. Again. And again.

"I did something stupid." Her words were almost lost to the sound of the water. She was taller than me, but bent over the sink, scrubbing at her hands like she could wash away this entire day, she looked very small. Very young.

"How stupid?" I asked softly.

She should have told me it was none of my business, possibly with a few colorful modifiers thrown in for emphasis. She didn't. Instead, she turned off the faucet. The edges of her lips trembled. "The kind of stupid that involves pictures?"

I slammed out of the girls' bathroom. Vivvie was waiting for me.

"Just out of curiosity," I asked her serenely, "where is the boys' bathroom?"

"Down the hall and to your left," Vivvie replied. "Why?"

I was already striding down the hallway. "No reason."

If Vivvie had known me for longer than a few hours, she would have been concerned. Very concerned. I reached the boys' bathroom, put my hand on the door, and shoved it inward.

"Tess!" Vivvie said. I glanced back at her. She studied me for a moment and then shrugged. "Godspeed."

A ghost of a smile pulled at the ends of my mouth, but as I stepped into the guys' bathroom and the door shut behind me, the expression hardened on my face. Three boys stood nearby, passing a single phone between them.

"No, *this* one is my favorite. Totally this one. The expression on her face!"

"Fresh meat, man. You should have heard her. 'Are you sure? Do I look okay?'"

Fury worked its way through my body as I sidled up behind them. The phone was passed from hand to hand, and inadvertently, they passed it to me. The third boy's eyes registered my presence just as my hand locked around the phone. He attempted to pull it back, but I twisted. Hard.

"What the—"

I tucked the phone into my waistband. They all stared at me like I had just announced an intention to set myself on fire.

"This is my phone now." I let the weight of my words sink in. The biggest of the three boys took a threatening step toward me.

"Yeah, right," he scoffed. "Hand it over."

I hated bullies, and I'd had a very long day. I stared at him for several seconds, daring him to come closer. Somewhere inside that empty skull of his, an alarm should have been going off.

It wasn't.

"That's private property," he grunted, towering over me. He reached for the phone, and I caught his wrist. He was bigger than me. Stronger than me. But my hands were calloused, and he'd probably never worked a day in his life.

"There are a lot of ways to castrate a bull," I said, my words deliberate and slow. "You can band the balls off so they shrivel up and die. Or you can take a knife and slide it just so." I demonstrated with my free hand. "I grew up on a ranch. I know a lot about castrating bulls."

There was a moment of stunned silence.

"Are you threatening me?" the boy asked. His friends glanced uncomfortably at each other. In my experience, it was pretty much impossible for the male of the species to be comfortable while listening to someone reminisce about castration.

"No," I said, my eyes locking on to the ringleader's. "If I were threatening you, it would sound more like this." It took everything I had not to ball my hands into fists. "She's fourteen. Ever heard of Andrew Stinson? That case got some press, didn't it? If I remember correctly, they found pictures on his phone, too. And you know where you can find good old Andrew now?" I could see the wheels in the boy's head turning. "I'll give you a hint: it's a registry, and it's not for weddings."

I took the phone out and scrolled through the sent texts, then through the e-mails. One of the boys tried to stop me, but a strategically placed foot and a tiny bit of applied pressure gave me the space I needed.

"You haven't sent them to anyone," I said. "That's good."

"You psychotic little—"

I didn't bother listening to the coarse insults that came pouring out of his mouth.

"I'm not psychotic," I said. "I'm just used to dealing with creatures a lot bigger and a lot meaner than you. This is my phone now. I suggest you get a new one."

I turned and walked out of the bathroom.

"You just made a very big mistake," one of the boys yelled after me.

I didn't bother turning around. "That's the only kind I make."

CHAPTER 9

Bodie picked me up after school. "Body count?" he asked as we pulled past the security gate and out onto the road.

"Very funny," I told him.

Bodie shrugged. "I can't help it if I recognize your true ruthless nature."

I had to remind myself that he didn't know me. He wasn't here for *me*. "Because my sister is infamous *fixer* Ivy Kendrick?" I retorted.

"No," Bodie replied with a generous roll of his eyes. "Because I'm an impeccable judge of character." He merged onto the highway and then glanced over at me. "And Ivy prefers the term *consultant*."

I would have preferred not to feel like I was the last person in the entire school—if not the DC metro area—to be clued into Ivy's occupation. I would have preferred if she'd asked me, even once, what I wanted before she'd packed up my life and swept me across the country like it was *nothing*. I would have preferred that my closest living relative not treat me like a fire that needed to be put out, or a situation that needed to be handled.

Like a job.

"You didn't answer my question about the body count." Bodie prodded me out of my thoughts, like he knew no good could come from letting me stew for long.

"No casualties," I informed him.

"But?"

I looked out the window so he wouldn't see the edges of my lips tick up as I thought about the dumbfounded look on the boys' faces when I'd confiscated the phone. "But what?"

The two of us rode in companionable silence until the car pulled into Ivy's drive. Bodie cut the engine, and I reached for the door handle.

"Wait," Bodie ordered sharply. He sounded nothing like the man who'd lazily tweaked me about my attitude. I followed his gaze to a dark-colored sedan parked across the street.

Bodie turned the car back on. "What are your thoughts on ice cream?" he asked, putting it in reverse.

"Normally, I'm in favor of it," I said, "but right now, I want you to tell me what's going on."

Before Bodie could evade my question—and I was sure that was what he was going to do—the front door to Ivy's house opened. An older man came out. He was tall with a shock of thick white hair and a face made for conveying his pleasure and displeasure from a hundred yards away.

My hand went to the door handle again.

"Don't even try it, kitten," Bodie warned. I paused but didn't draw my hand back as I tracked the older man's progress across the street.

"Who is he?" I asked, finally letting my hand sink back to my side. There was something familiar about the way the old man walked, the way he stood.

"Ask me again once you're old enough to curse like a sailor, and maybe you'll get an honest reply." Bodie's tone left no question about his distaste for the man. I was half tempted to tell him that I could curse like a sailor *now*, but instead, I watched the object of that distaste climb into the passenger side of the sedan and ride away.

Apparently, Ivy wasn't the only one with a driver—and that was when I realized who the man reminded me of.

"Adam," I said out loud. "That was Adam's father, wasn't it?"

You were the one who told me to bring her here three years ago! The argument I'd overheard the day before echoed in my mind. *Three years ago, you were on speaking terms with my father.*

Bodie didn't tell me I was right. He didn't tell me that Adam's father was a powerful man. He didn't have to.

"You're scary, you know that?" Bodie said. "And—I don't care if you glare at me—you *definitely* get that from Ivy."

"What?" I asked, before I thought better of it.

"That beyond-freaky ability to pull conclusions out of midair and sound so blasted sure of them."

I sounded sure because I *was* sure. I didn't know how I knew, but I did. "Who is he?" I asked. "Adam's father, what does he do?"

Bodie fixed me with another look. "That's need to know, and you don't."

Just like I hadn't needed to know that Ivy was a professional problem solver—or that Ivy's "driver" was a man who was used to assessing and responding to threats.

CHAPTER 10

"Did I or did I not make it clear what breaking that particular confidence would mean?" Ivy's voice—ice cold and sharp enough to draw blood—cut through the foyer. I could see her silhouette near the bay window, cell phone pressed to one ear as she paced. "I'm sure the senator would be *very* interested to know what you've been—"

She turned to pace back the opposite direction and her eyes caught mine. She cut off midthreat. "I have to go." She hung up the phone, and as she strode toward me, she schooled her face into a smile that almost reached her eyes.

"Tess." She glanced at Bodie, and a wealth of information seemed to pass between the two of them. "How was your first day?"

I stared at her. Was I supposed to pretend I hadn't overheard her putting the fear of God and Ivy Kendrick into the poor sod on the other end of that phone line?

"The seven hours and forty-two minutes you spent at school," Ivy clarified. "Good? Bad? Indifferent?"

"I'm *Ivy Kendrick's* little sister," I replied. "How could my day have been anything but good?"

Even a long-absent sister knew better than to take my syrupy tone at face value. "People talk," she said, shrugging off the way I'd said her name—the way *everyone* said her name. "Give it a few days, and things will settle down."

"Is that your *professional* take on the situation?" I kept my voice dry and caustic. This wasn't worth yelling over. It wasn't even worth a heated whisper.

"I never lied to you about what I do," Ivy said calmly. "I just wanted to give you some time to adjust."

"Consider me adjusted." I headed for the stairs. She didn't stop me, and somehow, that was worse—worse than having to ask Vivvie to clue me in on my sister's life, worse than the fact that the great Ivy Kendrick was acting like the stares and whispers I'd gotten all day at Hardwicke were no big deal.

I took the steps two at a time. I made it up the stairs and into the living room, and then I froze. On the coffee table, there was a plate of cookies, slightly burnt around the edges, laid out just so.

"I had a plan." Ivy's voice was soft as she followed me into the room. She kept her distance, hovering in the doorway. "I thought we'd sit. Talk. Eat cookies."

"You made me an afternoon snack?" I couldn't quite wrap my mind around that.

"It was a good plan," Ivy defended.

I picked up one of the cookies. Ivy took a single step forward, then paused, like I was a horse that might spook if she got too close.

"It might have been a better plan if I'd bought the cookies," she admitted grudgingly, eyeing the burnt cookie in my hand.

"You don't bake," I inferred. I meant to stop talking, but two more words escaped my mouth. "I do."

"You bake?" Ivy took another small step forward. "I wouldn't have called that one."

It was such a small thing—a tiny thing, really—to tell someone about myself, but the fact that I'd told Ivy anything felt like losing a protective layer of skin. I'd spent years building up my calluses. I hated that a stupid plate of burnt cookies could take them away.

Even as I clamped down on my emotions, Ivy saw through them. "Tell me what I can do, Tess. To make this better."

This as in the new life she'd shoved me into without a second thought? Or *this* as in *us*?

I couldn't let myself wonder. "You can tell me about Adam's father." I wasn't sure if I was trying to peel back one of *her* layers or testing her by asking for something I instinctively knew she wouldn't want to give.

"His name is William Keyes." Already, that was more than I'd thought Ivy would tell me. "I used to work for him," she continued, each word carefully measured. "We had a difference of opinion. Now I work for myself. He forgets that sometimes."

"What does he do?" I asked.

"He makes things happen." Ivy took her time with the reply, and I could almost understand how time had worn away at my grandfather's memory, blurring the lines between my sister and me. "Political things," Ivy continued. "He has a lot of money, and a lot of connections, and he's gotten used to calling the shots behind the scenes."

I wanted to ask her why Bodie had been so adamant about my staying in the car. I wanted to ask her why Adam had thought that Ivy having made an enemy of his father meant that I would be better off in Montana. I wanted to ask her why William Keyes had come to see her.

But *wanting* anything was dangerous when it came to Ivy and me. I set the cookie back down.

"Tess?" She shot me a questioning look.

I fixed my gaze on a spot just over her left shoulder. "I don't want to sit. I don't want to eat cookies. I don't want to tell you about my day."

When I was thirteen, I would have given anything for this Ivy. For after-school snacks and a bedroom in this house. For the phone to ring more than three times a year. I would have poured my heart out to her. I would have asked her everything I wanted to know.

"You can't make this better," I said, my throat tightening around the words. "You can't *do* anything."

"Tessie—"

"I'm not broken." My voice was low. "And whatever *this* is, you can't fix it. Not anymore."

CHAPTER II

The next morning, Bodie was the one who dropped me off before school. I made my way sluggishly to the Hut, wondering at the cruelty of a student coffee shop *that did not sell coffee*.

"I have a job for you." Apparently, that was the Emilia Rhodes version of hello. She'd appeared out of nowhere and waylaid me on my way to a bagel. When I didn't reply immediately, she arched an eyebrow. Clearly, she was expecting that eyebrow arch to engender some kind of response.

"Hello to you, too," I muttered. I hadn't slept well the night before, and it was too early in the day for this. I edged past her and toward the counter. She sidestepped directly into my path.

No bagel for me.

"You can pretend you're not interested," she told me, "but if you're smart, you'll bypass playing hard to get and jump straight to negotiations." For all the sense that Emilia was making, she might as well have been speaking Latin.

"I have literally no idea what you're talking about," I said.

Emilia pressed her lips together into an expression that was, at best, a distant cousin of a smile. "I have a problem."

"Yeah," I replied under my breath. "You have several."

"It's my brother," Emilia continued as if I hadn't spoken. "His best friend isn't at school this week, and that means he's bored."

Again, my response—or lack thereof—must have left something to be desired, because Emilia fixed me with a look.

"When Asher gets bored, things get broken. Laws, standards of decency, occasionally bones." She wrinkled her nose slightly. "There was an incident in his chemistry class yesterday—suffice it to say, he's skating on thin ice with the Hardwicke administration."

I wondered if the incident in chemistry class had involved an explosion, but figured that asking would only encourage her to block my bagel consumption for that much longer.

"I'm applying to Yale next year," Emilia continued, "and I am *going* to get in." Her tone strongly implied that she'd burn anyone and anything that stood in her way. "Unfortunately, Yale has an unofficial admissions policy on twins. Most of the time, either both twins get in, or neither of them do, and *my* twin seems intent on getting himself expelled." Emilia let out a huff of air, summoning her zen. "I just need someone to do damage control until Henry gets back. Three days, maybe four."

If I stood there long enough, she'd tell me what any of this had to do with me.

"You're going to make me say it again, aren't you?" She forced a smile. "Asher is a problem."

I waited. "And?"

"And," she said, as if she were talking to someone either very young or very slow, "you fix problems."

"I . . . *what*?" My voice rose up on that last word. All around us, people were beginning to stare.

Emilia hooked her arm through mine, like we were the best of friends. "You solve problems," she said again. "I have a problem. Ergo . . ."

"You have a job for me." This conversation was starting to make so much more sense. And it was becoming that much more an after-coffee kind of endeavor. "You're barking up the wrong tree here, Emilia."

"So you're *not* the Tess Kendrick that Anna Hayden is swearing is a miracle worker?" Another eyebrow arch. "Anna's not exactly sharing what the *miracle* was, but she's a big fan, and she has a big mouth."

"Hayden," I said out loud. "The girl I . . . *helped* . . . yesterday—"

"Hayden comma Anna." Emilia dropped my arm. "Freshman wallflower, beloved youngest daughter, and the only person at this school with a Secret Service escort?"

I flashed back to the day before. I remembered thinking that the crying girl had looked young and scared and vulnerable and *pissed*. The one thing I hadn't thought was that she looked *familiar*. She'd never told me her name.

Emilia snorted. "You honestly expect me to believe that you came riding to the rescue of the vice president's daughter with *no* idea of who she was?"

No wonder Anna had been freaking out—and thank God that jerk whose phone I'd confiscated hadn't e-mailed the pictures of her to anyone. I didn't even want to think about the kind of media storm it might have kicked up if he had.

"Believe what you want," I told Emilia. "I'm not a miracle worker. I'm not a problem solver. Whatever's going on with your brother—"

"Asher," she supplied.

"I can't help you," I said firmly.

"I'll pay you." Emilia clearly wasn't acquainted with the word *no*—but the two of them were about to get downright cozy.

"I don't want your money." I pushed past her—successfully this time—and she amended her offer.

"I'll *owe* you."

I wondered who or what I had offended in a previous life to end up in this position: sister of famed fixer Ivy Kendrick, endorsed as a miracle worker by the vice president's daughter.

"Sorry, Emilia," I said, almost meaning it. "You've got the wrong girl."

CHAPTER 12

About five minutes into my first class of the day, it became clear that Emilia Rhodes was not the only person who was operating under the impression that I was a chip off the sisterly block. Anna Hayden might not have told the entire school that I was *the* person to go to if you had a problem, but she'd whispered it in the right ears.

In a school the size of Hardwicke, word got around.

In English, one of my classmates attempted to retain my services to handle "rumor management" in a nasty breakup. In physics, I got a request that—as far as I could tell—had something to do with a show-choir rivalry.

I dearly hoped to never so much as *think* the words *show choir* again.

By lunchtime, I was nearing the end of my patience.

"Hypothetically speaking, should I be concerned that you look like you might throw that meatball sub at someone?" Vivvie popped up beside me.

I glanced over at her. "If I was going to throw something, it would be the bread pudding. Hypothetically."

"Don't throw the bread pudding," Vivvie objected vehemently. "It's got a butter rum sauce!"

She sounded so horrified at the idea that I managed half a grin.

"Here at Hardwicke, we take our baked goods very seriously," Vivvie informed me pertly. She hesitated just for a second. "Are you looking for someone to sit with?"

Across the room, Emilia met my eyes, then slid her gaze to an empty seat at her table, across from Maya and next to Di. Clearly that was an invitation.

I turned back to Vivvie. "I assumed I was sitting with you."

Vivvie broke into a smile the way other people broke into song and dance. It lit up her entire face.

"Where do you normally sit?" I asked her. The day before, when she'd been playing official guide, we'd grabbed a seat in the corner, but a girl like Vivvie had to have friends, as alien as that concept felt to me.

Vivvie's eyes went Bambi wide, the smile freezing on her face. "Well," she hedged, "sometimes I eat in the art room? And sometimes I just find a place outside?" She said every sentence like it was a question—and like she fully expected me to reconsider sitting with her.

"Outside works for me," I said. There were too many people in the cafeteria, and I truly did not want to know which of the onlookers would turn out to be my next wannabe "client."

Vivvie practically bounced with relief and began to lead the way. "I know you're probably wondering, about the whole 'sometimes I eat in the art room' thing."

"You're an artist?" I guessed.

Vivvie nibbled on her bottom lip and shook her head. "Not so much. I mostly draw stick figures." She paused. "They're not very good ones," she confessed.

Open book, thy name is Vivvie. "I get eating lunch alone," I told her. "You don't have to explain."

"It's no big deal," Vivvie assured me, in a way that told me that for her, it was. "It's just . . . Hardwicke is a small school. At least half of us have been here since preschool. I know everyone, but my best friend moved away a couple of months ago. We were kind of a pair. There are people I could sit with. I just . . . I don't want to bother anyone." She offered me another tentative smile. "I'm kind of an acquired taste."

Something in the way she said those words made me think they weren't hers. "Says who?" I asked darkly.

Vivvie came to a halt in the courtyard, her eyes going round.

"What?" I said. She didn't reply, so I turned to follow her gaze to the Hardwicke chapel. Or, more specifically, to the chapel's roof. There was a single octagonal window at the base of the steeple. Standing just in front of that window—thirty feet off the ground—was a boy. His toes were even with the very edge of the roof.

There was no one else outside. Just me and Vivvie and the boy on the roof. I stepped past Vivvie, wondering what he was doing up there. Wondering if he was going to jump.

"Go get someone," I told Vivvie.

The boy held his hands out to either side.

"What are you going to do?" Vivvie asked me.

I took a step toward the chapel. "I don't know."

The door to the chapel roof was propped open and marked with a sign that read DO NOT ENTER. I stepped through it. One more ladder, and I was on the roof.

The boy was still standing at the edge. I could only see the back of his head. He had auburn hair—a deep, rich red that girls would have killed for, but that looked strange, somehow, on a boy. Now that I was up here, standing just a few feet away from him, I wasn't sure what to do.

"Top of the morning to you," the boy said without turning around. I took a step forward. He lifted one foot off the roof and held it out—nothing but air and the ground below.

"It's not morning," I replied, inching my way out toward him. The roof was steeper the farther out I went.

The boy glanced back. "I'm not Irish," he said, a hint of a smile dancing around the corners of his lips. "In case you were wondering."

I was wondering what this guy was doing on the roof of the chapel—because suddenly, I was certain that he wasn't here to jump.

"It's the red hair that makes people think I might be," the boy continued. "And my habit of saying things like *top of the morning*. And the fact that I took up Irish folk dancing for two weeks when I was fourteen." He sighed. "It was a beautiful two weeks. Kathleen and I were very happy."

"Kathleen?" I asked.

"Girlfriend number seventeen," the boy replied. "Before Sophie and after Sarah."

"You'd had seventeen girlfriends by the time you were fourteen?" I asked.

"The ladies," he replied with a shrug. "They love me. It's because I'm so charming."

"You're balancing on one leg on the roof of a chapel. You're not charming. You're an idiot."

"Tell me what you really think," he said, grinning.

"I think you should come away from the edge of the roof before a teacher sees you," I told him.

The boy peeked over the edge of the roof. "Too late, fair lady. That ship has sailed and sailed again."

I rolled my eyes and started back toward the door. I'd thought he needed help—but clearly, what he really needed was a swift kick. Given that we'd met all of two minutes ago, I didn't feel particularly obligated to be the one who delivered it. He could do the hokey pokey up here for all I cared.

As I hit the top of the stairs, he fell in beside me, that stupid grin still on his face.

"You're new," he said.

I didn't reply. I'd made it to the door of the chapel when he spoke again, more quietly this time. "I was just enjoying the view."

I turned back toward him, ready to smack the smile off his face, only to discover that he wasn't smiling anymore. Seriousness didn't fit with his features.

"The view?" I asked, still annoyed with myself that I'd misread the situation so badly.

"The view," he replied. "The higher up you go, the smaller they get."

"Who?" I asked.

He held his hands out to each side, the same way he had on the edge of the roof. "Everyone."

The second I stepped outside, I realized that the boy hadn't been exaggerating when he'd said the "get down before a teacher sees you" ship had sailed and sailed again. I wasn't sure if Vivvie had actually gone for help, or if someone else had caught sight of the boy, but there were *two* teachers in the courtyard now, along with a handful of students—including Emilia Rhodes, who had a distinctly pained expression on her face.

"Did you haul him down?" Vivvie asked me in a whisper. "You forcibly hauled him down, didn't you?"

"Ms. Kendrick!" A teacher broke through the crowd to reach me. "Are you okay?"

"I'm fine."

"Care to explain what you were doing in there?" The teacher narrowed his eyes at me. Behind him, Vivvie began to gesture emphatically. She was freakishly skilled at charades. Following the gist, I glanced up at the roof. From where we were standing, you could see the edge of the roof, but you couldn't see farther back, where I'd been standing.

"It's a chapel," I said, turning back to the teacher. "What do you think I was doing in there?"

The teacher was flummoxed.

I shrugged. "When you have to pray, you have to pray." The teacher opened his mouth to reply, and I cut him off. "The Hardwicke chapel *is* open to students of all religious beliefs and affiliations," I said. "Isn't it?"

"Errr... yes," the teacher replied. "Of course." The man adjusted his tie, then zeroed in on a different target. "Mr. Rhodes!" he boomed.

The boy from the roof smiled charmingly. "Mr. Collins! Just the man I wanted to see."

"Did you also hope to see Headmaster Raleigh?" the teacher countered. "Because if you did, you're in luck."

"I'm always in luck," the boy—whose last name was apparently Rhodes—replied. "I think I got some really good shots up there." As I processed the fact that *this* must be Emilia's brother, the boy in question held up a camera, which he had most decidedly not been holding on the roof.

"You're telling me you were up on the roof of the chapel taking pictures?" the teacher asked skeptically.

I gave the boy—Asher—a look. This was never going to work.

Asher met my eyes, and his own sparkled. I could practically *hear* him thinking, *challenge accepted*.

"I was digesting what you said in your lecture on perspective in photography," he told the teacher. "You told us to think outside the box." He tilted his head to the side. "I feel so... *edified*..."

I snorted. Audibly.

"Asher, do you think I'm stupid?" Mr. Collins scowled at him.

"Not at all," Asher replied. "Do you think I'm edified?" He grinned. Beside me, Vivvie grinned. The smile was catching.

Mr. Collins shook his head. "Stay off the roof," he ordered. Then he paused. "Stay off *all* the roofs."

The fact that he felt he had to make that clarification told me a great deal about Asher Rhodes.

"Sir, yes, sir," Asher replied. And then, to my shock, Mr. Collins left it at that. The other teacher didn't say a word to Asher. It was like someone had just flashed the words *nothing to see here* on a neon sign. The crowd dissipated, and Asher met my eyes and arched a brow.

"What just happened here?" I asked Vivvie, bewildered.

Vivvie shrugged.

"People like me," Asher informed me helpfully. "I'm very likable."

"No, you aren't."

Asher grinned like I'd just professed my love for him. He lifted the camera up and snapped a picture of me. "Give it a couple of days," he told me ominously. "You'll see."

CHAPTER 13

It didn't take long for word to get around that I'd taken on Emilia's case. Forget the fact that I *had not taken on Emilia's case*. And the fact that random high school juniors didn't just declare themselves in business and start "taking cases." To the Hardwicke student body, the fact that I'd been with Asher and he'd managed to evade trouble was evidence enough that I was embracing my fixer title.

Like it or not, I *wasn't* a random high school junior. I was Tess *Kendrick*. And between Anna Hayden and Emilia Rhodes, people were starting to think that meant something.

It was just my luck that Asher was in my World Issues class. He greeted our classmates by name and accepted a wide variety of high fives on his way to the seat next to mine. He blessed me with a goofy, beatific smile.

Kill me now.

"Congratulations," Dr. Clark called out at the front of the room, clapping her hands together. "As a reward for being my last and favorite class of the day, you get to turn in your internet censorship essays!"

A round of groans went around the room. Once we'd handed in our assignment, she turned on a flat-screen television at the front of the room—to CNN.

"Prepare wisely," Dr. Clark said.

Prepare for what? I wondered.

"Debates," Vivvie told me helpfully.

"We are at the mercy of the daytime cable news channel gods," Asher elaborated, twirling a pencil in his fingers like a miniature baton. "Whatever issue the pundits are discussing, we're discussing."

All around the room, people were taking furious notes. I had no idea what the people on the screen were talking about. Five minutes in, I stopped even trying to decipher it, until the show cut one of its hosts off midsentence.

"Breaking news," the television declared. A wave of unease went through the room as the news feed cut to a man in a military uniform, issuing a statement. All eyes in the room went immediately to me.

No. Not to me, I realized. *To Vivvie.*

It took me a moment to process the fact that the caption under the man's name listed his rank (major), his position (White House physician), and his last name.

Bharani.

"It is with great sadness," the man on-screen said, "that I inform you that Chief Justice Theodore Marquette died on the table a little over an hour ago. This was our second attempt to fix a blockage in the justice's heart, and there were unforeseen complications with surgery."

Beside me, Vivvie was sitting very, very still. Asher stiffened. The rest of the room broke into murmurs.

On the screen, Major Bharani continued. "This country has lost a great man today. We ask that you respect his family's privacy in this time of grief."

CHAPTER 14

Justice Marquette's death was big news at Hardwicke. From what I could gather, the still-absent Henry Marquette was well liked—and he'd lost his father the year before. Add to that the number of Hardwicke parents who were politicians, journalists, lobbyists, or otherwise entangled with the Powers That Be in Washington, and a dead Supreme Court justice wasn't just news. It was a game changer.

It was personal.

"Tea?" The question snapped me from my thoughts. Ivy poured herself a cup as she waited for a reply.

"No," I bit back. "Thank you."

Ivy took a sip of her tea, her eyes never leaving mine. "We could order something else if you'd like."

Somehow, my sister had taken my *I don't want your cookies* speech the day before to mean *I would prefer to go out for afternoon tea.*

"I'm fine," I told her through gritted teeth. All around us, women chatted with each other over delicate pastries. I could practically taste the gentility in the tea room air.

Ivy picked up a delicate silver spoon and stirred her tea contemplatively. "Scone?" she asked.

I just stared at her. "What are we doing here?"

"I'm eating a scone," Ivy replied. "When I figure out what you're doing, I'll let you know."

I got the feeling that I could hurl obscenities at her, and she'd just keep on sipping her tea.

"What do you want?" After the day I'd had, I was too mentally frayed to beat around the bush.

"I want you to give DC a chance." Ivy waited for those words to sink in before continuing. "I won't ask you to give me one. I'm not sure I deserve it. But you do, Tessie. You deserve to have a life here."

"I *had* a life," I told her sharply. "I was . . ." *Happy?* I couldn't make my lips form the word. "I was fine."

"When I left you there," Ivy said, "three years ago, when I left you with Gramps, I thought I was doing the right thing. For you."

Then why did you invite me to live with you in the first place? I refused to say the words out loud. When I was thirteen, I'd tried to ask her why. I'd called, and she hadn't answered. I'd called again and again, and she hadn't answered. A month later, she'd called to wish me a happy birthday, like nothing was wrong.

After that, I stopped calling her, and I stopped asking why.

Across from me, Ivy began applying clotted cream to her scone. "What do *you* want, Tess?"

"Not tea and crumpets," I muttered. "That's for damn sure."

An older lady at the table next to us shot me a dirty look. I stared down at the lace tablecloth.

"I didn't ask you what you don't want," Ivy informed me. "I asked what you *do* want. Don't think of this as a heart-to-heart. Think of it as a negotiation. I want you to give this arrangement a chance." Ivy's voice never changed—not in volume, not in tone. "Tell me what you want, and I'll see what I can do."

I wanted to go home. I wanted *Gramps* to come home. But even the great Ivy Kendrick couldn't turn back the clock. She couldn't *make* him well.

"Have you heard from the doctors?" My voice sounded dull to my own ears.

"I got an update this morning." Ivy set her tea down. "He's got some cognitive impairment, disorientation, mood swings."

I thought of Gramps yelling, demanding to know what I'd done with his wife.

"He has good days," I told Ivy.

Her voice was gentle. "They're going to get fewer and farther between. There are some treatment possibilities. A clinical trial, for one."

"I want to talk to the doctors." I swallowed, pushing down the lump in my throat. "I want them to explain the different options. And I want to talk to Gramps."

I'd tried calling but hadn't been able to get through yet.

"I'll get you the doctor's direct number," Ivy promised. "What else do you want?" She paused. "For *you*?"

I didn't reply.

"I want you to give yourself a chance to be happy here, no matter how angry you are with me." Ivy leaned forward. "What do you want?"

She wasn't going to stop asking until I answered. I gritted my teeth. "No more afternoon teas."

Ivy didn't bat an eye. "Done. What else?"

She wants a negotiation. Fine. I locked my eyes on hers. "I want a car."

Ivy blinked. Then she blinked again. "A car?"

"I don't care if it's used," I told her. "I don't care if it's borrowed or barely functional. I want transportation."

I didn't like depending on other people. I needed to know that if push came to shove, I could take care of myself.

"Driving in DC isn't like driving in Montana," Ivy told me.

"I can learn." My words sounded strangely loud. For a moment, I thought I'd raised my voice. Then I realized that I hadn't—I was talking at the exact same volume; it was the rest of the restaurant that had changed.

It was silent.

I glanced to my right. The old women sitting at the table next to us were gone. And so were the women at the table beside them. *The sorority sisters on the other side, the mother with the three little girls . . .* They were all gone.

The entire restaurant was empty, except for us.

Ivy took in the silence, the empty chairs, and she sighed. Then she picked up her tea and took another drink, waiting.

For what?

The back door to the restaurant opened. A man wearing a suit stepped through. He had an earpiece in one ear and a gun strapped to his side.

"Mark," Ivy greeted him.

He nodded to her but didn't say anything. A second later, a woman stepped through the door. She was in her early sixties but could have passed for a decade younger. She had blond hair that had gone only slightly silver with age, perfectly coiffed around her heart-shaped face, and wore navy blue like she had invented the color.

A second armed man followed her into the room.

"Georgia," Ivy said. "It's nice to see you."

"Don't lie, darling," the woman replied. "It doesn't suit you." She crossed the room and pulled a chair over to our table. Then she turned warm hazel eyes on me. "You must be Tess."

CHAPTER 15

When the First Lady of the United States sits down next to you and asks you if you would like a scone, you say yes.

"*Now* you want a scone?" Ivy said, sounding somewhat disgruntled.

"Tea?" Georgia Nolan ignored Ivy and focused on me.

I smiled, no lips. "Tea would be lovely."

"Lovely?" Ivy repeated incredulously. "You don't think anything is *lovely*."

"Hush," the First Lady told her. I'd never seen anyone hush Ivy before. It was almost enough to make me forget the fact that there were two Secret Service agents watching our every move.

"You cleared the room," Ivy commented.

"There have been some threats," Georgia replied, passing me some jam for my scone. "Apparently, some radical groups blame me for my husband's foreign policy decisions."

Ivy snorted. "Imagine that." She paused. "Is that why you're here?"

"I'm here because Bodie told me that you would be," Georgia replied.

"Bodie's fired," Ivy said.

Georgia waved a hand. "Bodie is always fired. And to answer your question, no, I'm not here about the threats. I'm here because I understand that a mutual friend paid you a visit."

Georgia Nolan was Southern—very Southern. I had a feeling she used the word *friend* loosely.

"And," the woman added, "I'm here to meet Tess." She turned to me. "I asked Ivy to bring you by the White House. She politely declined."

"I wasn't that polite," Ivy muttered.

I wasn't sure what surprised me more—the fact that the First Lady was apparently one of Ivy's clients, or the fact that Ivy didn't treat her like a client.

She treated her like family.

"I was very sorry to hear about your grandfather, Tess." Georgia Nolan reached over and squeezed my hand. "From what I hear, he is a good man."

I stared down at my tea. She'd used the present tense. *He is*, I thought, clinging to that one word. *He is a good man. He is tough and smart and more like me than either one of us would ever admit.*

I could feel Ivy's eyes on me. I swallowed back the rush of emotion I'd felt at the First Lady's words. "Justice Marquette has—had—a grandson who goes to Hardwicke," I said, still staring at the rim of my cup. Better to talk about anyone else's grandfather than my own. "That's why you're here, isn't it?" My eyes flitted back up to the First Lady's hazel ones. "Ivy fixes problems. A dead Supreme Court justice is a problem."

"No," the president's wife replied, her voice never losing its warmth. "Theo Marquette's death is a tragedy." She studied me for a moment, then continued, "And, quite frankly, it's an opportunity, tragic though it may be." She set her tea down. "And speaking of," she said, turning her attention back to Ivy, "I'm guessing that's why William paid you a visit?" Georgia gave a small, close-lipped smile. "He has thoughts on the nomination and wants your whisper in this administration's ear."

William. It took me a second to process the name. *As in William Keyes.*

"Georgia." Ivy gave the older woman a quelling look and then darted a meaningful glance toward me. The First Lady held Ivy's gaze for a moment, then inclined her head slightly.

"Tess," Georgia said, "could you give us a moment?"

When the First Lady of the United States asks you to give her a moment, you give her a moment. I went to the bathroom. When I came back, she and Ivy had finished discussing whatever they were discussing.

Georgia stood. She reached over and laid a hand on Ivy's shoulder. "I'll let you know which way Peter is leaning on nominees," she told her, giving Ivy's shoulder a squeeze. "In the meantime, do keep your ear to the ground." Then she smiled. "And when things settle down, you and Tess *are* coming over for dinner."

CHAPTER 16

This was what my life had become: on Tuesday, the First Lady insisted I simply *had* to dine at the White House at some point in the near future; on Wednesday, I sat by myself at lunch. Vivvie was absent. I probably could have leveraged my fledgling reputation to obtain a seat at someone else's table, but I was used to eating lunch alone.

Solitude didn't bother me nearly as much as the idea of cementing my status as a person to know at Hardwicke.

So I ate outside. By myself. I did the same thing the next day, when Vivvie still didn't show up for school. And the day after that. After three days of self-segregation—and a half-dozen declined requests for "fixing"—the message was finally starting to sink in with the rest of the student body. I wasn't a miracle worker. I wasn't looking to make friends.

I just wanted to be left alone.

On the third day of eating lunch by myself, I got company. And not the good kind.

"If it isn't my favorite little psychopath." The boy whose phone I'd confiscated my first day at Hardwicke slid into the seat across from mine. A quick survey of my surroundings told me that his friends weren't far off. In the past few days, more and more students had moved to eating lunch outside. There were three or four small groups and one larger one.

A few students cast glances our way, but Emilia Rhodes was the only one whose gaze lingered.

"I can't help but notice you're looking a little lonely these days." The boy across from me smiled. It wasn't a friendly smile. "Your fifteen minutes of high school fame over already?"

He was like a predator, going for the antelope that had been cut off from the rest of the herd. I'd threatened him, embarrassed him. He'd steered clear until it became obvious that I wasn't going to grab at a place near the top of the Hardwicke hierarchy.

Now he'd apparently decided I was fair game.

"If you need a friend . . ." He leered at me, his eyes raking over my body in a way designed to make me feel exposed. "I can be a very good friend."

"Keep telling yourself that," I said. If he was looking for a reaction other than skepticism about his prowess as a "friend," he wasn't going to get one.

"You think you're really something, don't you?" He was tall and athletic, with perfect teeth and perfect hair. I wasn't sure what bothered him more—the idea of being rejected, or the fact that in a staring contest between the two of us, we both knew he'd be the one to look away first. "Your sister's nothing but a political ambulance chaser," he spat out. "The flavor of the month. To people like my father, she's the hired help."

He wanted me wondering who his father was.

Want away, Boy Wonder, I thought. I wasn't up on the *Who's Who?* of DC, and I didn't care to be.

"I could make things very difficult for you here." He clearly meant that as a threat.

I snorted. "And I could have a nice chat with your father about the fact that out of all the girls at this school that you could choose to terrorize, *you* chose the vice president's daughter."

I had no idea who this guy's father was. He might or might not have been the type of man who cared about the way his son treated girls. But judging from said son's attitude about power—who had it, who didn't—I was guessing Daddy Dearest might care quite a bit about the idea of his idiot son making enemies in high places.

For a split second, the idiot in question blanched. I stabbed my fork into my salad and started bringing the bite to my mouth. Without warning, the boy's hand snaked out, grabbing my wrist. From a distance, the expression on his face would have looked perfectly friendly, but up close, I saw the glint in his eye.

"Fine day we're having, isn't it?" Asher Rhodes slipped into the seat next to mine, picked up my spoon, and stole a bite of my cupcake. "I hope I'm not interrupting anything."

The boy with the glint in his eye dropped my wrist. He laughed. "Just kidding around with Tess here."

Asher snagged another bite of my cupcake. "Such a kidder, that Tess," he said jovially. "A constant riot. Keeps me in stitches, she does."

The boy blinked several times. "You two are . . ."

"Friends," Asher declared. He tried for another bite of my cupcake. I blocked his hand with my fork, a little harder than necessary.

I didn't need rescuing.

"We're not friends," I told Asher.

"Our bond goes far beyond friendship," Asher agreed pleasantly. "Epics will be written. Bards will sing." He turned back to the boy across from us. "Any interest in playing the role of the bard?"

Not surprisingly, the answer to that question was *no*. The boy made a hasty exit. He and his hangers-on retreated to a table near Emilia's. She turned around and went back to holding court at her own table, head held high.

"John Thomas Wilcox," Asher told me quietly. "His father's the minority whip."

I wasn't sure what one was supposed to say in response to that, so I said nothing.

"I see you're the strong and silent type," Asher said sagely. "I never shut up, so we're going to get along smashingly."

"I was fine," I told him. "You could have stayed with your friends."

Despite his "best friend" being absent, Asher seemed to have had no shortage of companionship the past few days. He ate lunch at a different table every day, like a king spreading the wealth among his people.

"It wasn't *you* I was worried about," Asher returned easily. "There was murder in your eyes, and, let's face it, John Thomas's face is too pretty for the maiming I'm sure he so richly deserved."

Emilia had tried to hire me to keep her brother out of trouble for a few days. I wondered if she'd figured out yet that I was the last person anyone should think was qualified for *that* job.

Trouble always had a way of finding me.

CHAPTER 17

Five minutes before the final bell cut us loose for the day, I got pulled into the headmaster's office.

"Tess," he said. "Can I call you Tess?"

"Knock yourself out."

He folded his hands in front of him on the desk. "I'm afraid we've received some complaints."

I waited for him to elaborate. He waited for me to say something. I was better at waiting than he was.

"Serious allegations have been made. Bullying. Blackmail. Theft."

Again, the headmaster paused, and again, I said nothing. The only person who had reason to accuse me of theft was John Thomas Wilcox. The idea of him reporting *me* to the administration for anything was pretty rich. He must have been betting on the fact that I wouldn't report him in return.

Unfortunately, that was a good bet. If Anna Hayden had wanted the administration involved in her situation, she would have gone to them herself.

"Now, you're new here," the headmaster continued. "And I believe in giving students the benefit of the doubt, but it would help us put this unfortunate business behind us if you would allow us to search your locker."

"For what?" The cell phone? Did John Thomas really think I was stupid enough to keep it on the premises?

The fact that I'd finally broken my silence seemed to energize Headmaster Raleigh. "I'm not at liberty to share the details of the allegations. In an effort to discourage bullying, Hardwicke has an open-door policy. We encourage students to report any trouble they're having and guarantee confidentiality during investigations."

In theory, that might have been a good practice. In reality, it was a system ripe for abuse.

"I despise bullying," I told the headmaster. "And bullies. You might say that's something my sister and I have in common."

Invoking Ivy had exactly the effect I had thought it would. Headmaster Raleigh's jaw clenched slightly. If his last interaction with Ivy was any indication, he had a healthy amount of fear of my sister's reach. Either she already had dirt on him, or he was afraid she'd dig some up.

The headmaster offered me a peppermint, then forced a smile. "If you would just allow me to conduct a simple search—"

"No," I said. "I don't think I will."

Behind the headmaster's desk, there was a photo. As a vein in his forehead began to throb, I counted the number of people in it: three in the back row, two in the front, one off to the side. Headmaster Raleigh was standing between a balding man in his fifties and a slightly older man with a shock of white hair. I recognized the older man instantly.

William Keyes.

"I don't need your permission to search your locker." The headmaster's tone drew my attention back in his direction. This, I inferred from the rise in volume, was supposed to be the voice of authority.

If you didn't need my permission, I thought, *then why did you ask for it?*

"I thought Hardwicke respected the privacy of all of its students," I said. That was what he'd told Ivy. The wealthy and politically elite sent their children here because it was secure and discreet. I had a feeling that random locker searches wouldn't sit well with the Board of Trustees—and unless Raleigh had something more solid than a vague, anonymous complaint, it would be easy enough to make any search he conducted of my locker look random.

"Maybe you should call Ivy." I dropped my sister's name a second time. "I'm sure we can sort this whole locker-search thing out."

The headmaster fidgeted with his tie like it was choking him. "I don't think that will be necessary."

"Neither do I."

Raleigh and I both turned toward the doorway. Adam stood there, looking every inch his father's son. His gaze was steady, his presence commanding. "Adam Keyes," he introduced himself, crossing the room to shake the headmaster's hand. "I'm here to pick up Tess."

"Keyes, did you say?" If anything, the headmaster looked slightly paler than he had a moment before. "And what is your relation to Tess?"

Adam's lips twisted their way into a smile that looked more like a threat. "Family friend," he replied. "If you have any concerns about her behavior, I'd be glad to pass them along."

"No," the headmaster said hurriedly. "No concerns. I am sure this is just a misunderstanding."

"I'm sure that it is." Coming from Adam, that sounded like an order. "You ready to go, Tess?"

I stood. "Headmaster," I said, meeting his eyes. "Always a pleasure."

"Do I want to know what he would have found if he'd searched your locker?" Adam asked once we hit the parking lot. His brows pulled together in what was either disapproval or amusement—I couldn't tell which.

"As far as I know, nothing." I'd taken the battery out of John Thomas's phone to prevent anyone from tracking it. I certainly wasn't stupid enough to keep pilfered goods in my locker.

"So you objected on principle?" The edges of his lip twitched slightly. *Amusement*.

"On the principle the person who made the anonymous complaint might also have planted something in my locker," I corrected. Adam gave me a long, assessing look, and I shrugged. "I've been making friends."

"You don't say." Adam didn't sound surprised. He unlocked what I assumed to be his car. I headed for the passenger side, and he stopped me, holding out the keys. "Ivy said you wanted to learn to drive in DC."

In the three days since my tea with Ivy, she hadn't said a word about my request for transportation. I'd assumed she'd forgotten or decided to ignore it.

"How did you get stuck teaching me about big-city driving?" I asked Adam.

"I didn't get stuck with it," he corrected. "I volunteered." He looped around to the passenger side, his strides even and brisk. "I don't trust Bodie to hold you to the speed limit, and no one trusts Ivy behind the wheel."

"She's a bad driver?" It was comforting to think that my sister might be bad at *something*.

"The worst," Adam confirmed. "She's never actually hit another car, but there's not a trash can, streetlight, or mailbox safe within a forty-mile radius. There's a reason she hired a driver."

I decided to let Adam pretend Bodie was *just* a driver and climbed into the car.

"First rule of defensive driving," Adam told me as he directed me out of the parking lot, "watch out for the other guy. Drivers here are more aggressive than you're used to. There's more traffic, and that means more frustrated drivers doing stupid things to shave three minutes off their commute."

"Watch out for the other guy," I repeated. "Sounds like a motto for life."

Adam's blue eyes flicked briefly over to mine as he directed me to turn onto a major street. Once he was satisfied that I could, in fact, turn without causing my car—or any car in the near vicinity—to explode, he allowed himself to actually converse. "You don't trust people?"

"Not to hit my car, or not to screw up my life?"

"Either."

That seemed like more of an answer than a question, so I didn't reply.

"How are you liking Hardwicke?" Adam tried another topic of conversation. "Setting aside any and all incidents with the headmaster."

"It's school," I said. More homework, more affluent student body—but at the end of the day, high school was high school, and my goal was to make it through relatively unscathed. "It's okay," I amended, taking pity on Adam, who deserved *something* for taking time out of his afternoon. "My classes aren't horrible."

"Not horrible," Adam said dryly. "That's high praise."

From me, it kind of was.

After several seconds of silence, Adam switched topics. "Theo Marquette's funeral is tomorrow," he said. He paused. "Your sister will want to be there."

I wasn't sure how he expected me to respond to that.

"Theo was a friend," Adam continued. He measured his words, his calm, knowing eyes slanting toward mine. "Funerals are hard for Ivy." There was something in the way Adam said my sister's name—like things that hurt her hurt him.

I kept my eyes locked on the road. I didn't have to ask why funerals were hard for Ivy. Ivy had been twenty-one when we lost our parents. Old enough to remember every last detail of the aftermath.

"Are you going to the funeral, too?" I asked Adam. He cared about my sister enough that he was here teaching me how to drive. He hurt when she hurt. I had no idea if there was anything more than friendship between them, but it seemed like a reasonable question.

Adam's jaw clenched slightly. "It's better that I sit this one out."

He didn't elaborate. I didn't ask him to. For twenty minutes, the two of us rode in silence, except for the occasional admonition from Adam for me to watch out for the other guy and keep my eyes on the road. As we pulled up to Ivy's house, I started to feel the weight of the silence.

"So what do you do when you're not teaching random teenagers to navigate the big, bad streets of DC?" I asked.

I put the car in Park. Adam unbuckled his seat belt, squaring his shoulders slightly as he replied. "I work for the Department of Defense. Before I was assigned to the Pentagon, I flew for the Air Force."

"Why the Pentagon?" I asked.

"That's where I was assigned." Adam stiffened, the muscles in his neck the only noticeable tell. His tone reminded me of the fight I'd overheard him having with Ivy.

Adam—whose father *made things happen* in DC—had gone from an assignment he enjoyed to working at the Pentagon.

"Your father wanted you in DC?" It was a stab in the dark.

"My father is very family oriented." Adam's voice was completely flat. He looked like a soldier standing at attention, eyes forward, never flinching. "He's also very good at getting what he wants."

"So is Ivy." Those words slipped out before I'd thought them through. "Not family oriented, obviously," I clarified. "Good at getting what she wants."

Adam was quiet for several seconds. Finally he said, "Your sister is nothing like my father, Tess."

I hadn't meant to bring up Ivy.

"She would do anything for you," Adam told me, angling his head to catch my gaze. Even blue eyes stared into mine. "You know that, right?"

"Sure." That was what he wanted to hear.

"She won't ask you to go to the funeral with her." The set of Adam's features was neutral, carefully controlled. "But I'm not going, and Bodie doesn't do funerals. He'll drive her there, but that's it." He let that sink in. "It would mean a lot if she didn't have to go alone."

A lot to Adam, or a lot to Ivy?

"Your father stopped by earlier this week to talk to Ivy." I needed a subject change, and that did the trick. Adam's jaw ticked slightly. An instant later, he wiped all trace of emotion from his face: not a hint of a smile, not a hint of a frown.

"You didn't know," I realized. I'd assumed that Ivy would have told him.

"Did you and my father meet?" Adam almost managed to keep his voice level, but I caught the tension underneath. He wanted me to tell him that the answer was no. He wanted me kept away from his father. I turned that over in my mind and thought of Bodie catching sight of William Keyes and ordering me to stay in the car.

"No," I told Adam, noting the relief that flickered briefly across his face. "We didn't."

CHAPTER 18

The next morning, I put on a faded black dress and went downstairs to wait for Ivy.

"Going somewhere?" Bodie asked me.

I didn't quite meet his eyes. "Justice Marquette has a grandson who goes to Hardwicke." As far as excuses went, that was a flimsy one. "He's a friend of a friend."

That was stretching the truth, given that I didn't have much in the way of friends at Hardwicke.

Bodie raised an eyebrow at me. "So you're going to the funeral."

"Yes."

"For the grandfather of a friend of a friend," Bodie reiterated.

I shrugged and headed for the car. "It feels like the right thing to do." I wasn't talking about my tenuous connection to Henry Marquette, and we both knew it.

Maybe Adam was right. Maybe Ivy needed me. Or maybe she didn't. But no one should have to go to a funeral alone.

"Theodore Marquette served this country long and well." President Peter Nolan stood at the podium. He had a weighty presence and a powerful speaking voice. As he eulogized, Ivy's hand found its way into mine. She didn't keep hold of it for long. But even that fleeting moment of physical contact told me that I'd been right to come.

I knew in my gut that she was thinking about our parents' funeral. My own memories of it were fuzzy.

I remember it was summer. My dress was blue. A pale baby blue that stuck out among a sea of black. I remembered being passed from arm to arm. I remembered eating food. I remembered being sick all over the floor. *I remember Ivy carrying me upstairs. I remember my head against her chest.*

"Most of us go through the day unaware of the impact we have on each other, the mark we leave on this world—but not Theo. He felt that responsibility, on the bench and in his daily life, to leave this world a better place than he'd found it. It sounds pat to say that he was a good man, a wise man, a fair man." The president paused for a moment. "I'm going to say it anyway. He was a good man." The president's voice reached every corner of the chapel. "He was a wise man. He was a fair man."

Stained glass cast colored light onto the casket, which had been wrapped in an American flag, like the flags that flew at half-mast throughout the country in Justice Marquette's honor.

"Theodore Marquette was a husband who'd buried his wife." The president's voice rolled over me. Even giving a eulogy, its tone said *trust me, listen to me, follow me.* "A father who'd buried his son. He was a fighter who never gave in to grief, to opposition, to the days and the nights and the months and the years when life was hard. He played a mean game of pool. I know from experience that the only way the man could sing 'Happy Birthday' was at the top of his lungs."

There was a scattering of chuckles.

"Theo was a proud grandfather, a devoted civil servant." The president paused and lowered his head. "He left this world a better place than he'd found it."

There were other speakers, hymns, prayers.

I remember it was summer. My dress was blue.

The pallbearers came forward: five men, a woman, a boy. I recognized the woman and realized that she and the men were Justice Marquette's colleagues, justices who'd sat beside him on the bench. It didn't matter whether they'd found themselves siding with or against him in court; there was grief etched into their faces as they walked in perfect step to carry the casket down the aisle.

The last pallbearer was my age. He was biracial, with strong features made stronger by the terse set of his jaw. *The justice's grandson.* It had to be. I watched him, his stare locked straight ahead as he and six Supreme Court justices carried his grandfather's casket out into the sun.

"Come on, Tess," Ivy said softly as the funeral goers began to push out of the chapel. We made our way to the end of the pew. As Ivy stepped into the aisle, someone took her arm.

Adam's father.

I froze, but as the crowd pushed gently forward, I snapped out of it and stepped into the aisle behind them.

"William," Ivy greeted him coolly. She didn't attempt to pull away from his hold. As they walked side by side, I found myself wondering who was leading whom.

"Lovely service," William Keyes commented. "Though I found the eulogy to be somewhat so-so."

I looked around to see if anyone else had heard him, but it appeared the words had only reached Ivy's ears—and mine. Near the front of the chapel, Georgia Nolan stood next to her husband. She caught sight of me looking at her and smiled slightly. Her eyes stopped smiling when she saw the man on Ivy's arm.

"Have you given any thought to our little chat?" William asked Ivy as we inched toward the exit.

"You and I don't chat." Ivy's voice was matter-of-fact. William held the door open for her. Once Ivy stepped through, he turned back. To me.

"After you," he said. I recognized the chess move for what it was—a way to get under my sister's skin. "And who is this young lady?" he asked Ivy.

I would have put money on it that he already knew the answer.

"My sister." Ivy answered his question, her voice pleasant, her eyes glittering with warning. "Tess."

William Keyes smiled and laid a hand on my shoulder. "It's nice to meet you, Tess."

I barely managed to check the urge to roll my eyes. "Right back at you."

William was not deterred by my intentional lack of social graces. "I understand you're a student at Hardwicke?"

I stared him directly in the eye. "Guess word around here travels fast."

"William." A man about the same age as William Keyes initiated a handshake with him, causing Adam's father to remove his hand from my shoulder. "Good to see you."

"Royce," William returned heartily. "How's Hannah?"

I took that as my cue to make an exit. Ivy did the same. She didn't say a word about William Keyes, but I could tell the encounter had shaken her. That made me wonder: just how dangerous *was* Adam's father?

As we made our way down the steps, my sister slipped into a line that had formed in front of the justice's surviving family.

"Pam," Ivy greeted a tall, thin African American woman, taking the woman's hand in hers.

"Thank you for coming."

I wondered how many times Mrs. Marquette had said those words today. I wondered if they'd started to sound like gibberish to her yet.

Ivy gave the woman's hand a firm squeeze before letting it go. "What do you need?" she asked.

"We're holding up." That, too, sounded like a rote reply, recited over and over again in hopes that it might somehow become the truth.

Ivy caught the other woman's gaze and repeated herself, her voice soft. "What do you need?"

A little girl burrowed into the woman's side. The woman's hand wrapped reflexively around the girl, her hand stroking the little one's hair. "There's a wake," she told Ivy. "At Theo's house, after the burial."

Ivy gave a slight nod. "I can head straight there."

"You don't have to do that," the woman said quickly. "The burial . . ."

"I can head straight there," Ivy reiterated. "Whatever you need, Pam, consider it done." The woman looked like she might object. "If Theo were here, he'd have told me to skip the funeral and go straight to the house."

Mrs. Marquette smiled wryly. Apparently, she couldn't argue with that.

"Mother?" The justice's grandson appeared at his mom's side. "Everything okay here?" Henry Marquette spared half a glance for me and seemed to decide I was worth neither his interest nor his concern, before he turned piercing mint-green eyes on Ivy.

"Ms. Kendrick was just offering to help with the wake," Mrs. Marquette told him.

"I'm sure that won't be necessary." Henry's posture was perfectly erect, his tone polished. "The arrangements have been taken care of."

By you, I thought. Seeing Henry Marquette standing slightly in front of his mother, like he could shield her bodily from grief, I felt a flash of recognition. I knew what it was like to be the one who took care of things. The one who had to be strong.

"Thank you for coming." Henry gave Ivy a pointed smile that wasn't a smile at all, then ushered his mother away.

We'd been dismissed.

CHAPTER 19

Justice Marquette's house was on the Virginia side of DC. Bodie didn't ask why we were going there. Ivy didn't elaborate.

Once we arrived, it took my sister all of ten minutes to get rid of the press camped out on the street.

"How does she do that?" I asked Bodie, watching from a distance as she said something to send the last hanger-on running.

"Witchcraft," Bodie deadpanned.

By the time the Marquettes arrived from the burial, the house was quiet, the food was warm, and a discreet security team had been established around the perimeter.

If the funeral service had been full of dignitaries and officials, the wake was a more personal affair: neighbors, family, friends. As soon as Ivy was distracted, I ducked out of the house. I didn't belong here. This wasn't my grief.

Outside, the air smelled like fresh-cut grass and forthcoming rain. The justice's house was easily as large as Ivy's, but he had more land. Staring out at it, I tried the number Ivy had given me for my grandfather. A nurse answered and put me on with Gramps.

It wasn't a good day.

When I eventually said good-bye and hung up, it felt like leaving him all over again. I started walking, aching with a constant, uncompromising sense of loss. I didn't realize how far away from the house I'd wandered until I noticed that I wasn't alone.

"Where are we going?"

I turned to see the little girl who'd been glued to Mrs. Marquette's side at the funeral. Her dark hair had been liberated from a headband. She was wearing a black dress.

"Aren't you supposed to be back at the house?" I asked her.

Her chin jutted out. "This is my grandpa's house. I get to go wherever I want."

"Fair enough." I stared at her for a moment, then kicked off my shoes. "You want to ditch yours?"

"We can do that?" She sounded skeptical.

"It's your grandpa's house. You can do whatever you want."

Accepting my logic, she sat down in the dirt and peeled off the Mary Janes.

"You're supposed to tell me you're sorry about my grandpa," she told me.

"Do you really want me to?" I asked her.

She pulled at the tips of her hair. She was older than I'd originally thought—maybe eight or nine. "No," she said finally. "But you're supposed to anyway."

I said nothing. She plucked a blade of grass and stared at it so hard I thought her gaze might set it on fire.

"You got a pond around here?" I asked her.

"Nope. But there are dogs. Two of them," she added, lest I mistakenly think she'd said *dog*, singular.

I nodded, which seemed to satisfy her.

She plucked another piece of grass before casting a sideways glance at me. "What would we do with a pond?"

I shrugged. "Skip rocks?"

Twenty minutes later, Thalia Marquette had mastered the art of skipping invisible rocks across a nonexistent pond.

"If it isn't two lovely ladies, off by their lonesome."

I turned, surprised to see Asher here—until I remembered that Emilia had attempted to hire me to keep him out of trouble *until* his best friend got back to school to take over the job.

His best friend, Henry. As in Henry Marquette.

"We're skipping rocks," Thalia informed Asher. "This is Asher," she told me. "He's okay." She smiled.

Undeterred by the lack of either rocks or a body of water on which to skip them, Asher plopped down beside us on the ground. "I," he said tartly, "am a master rock skipper."

Ten minutes later, the cavalry arrived. The cavalry did not look particularly pleased to see us sprawled in the grass.

"You're not very good at this, Asher." Thalia was blissfully unaware of her brother's arrival. Asher shot Henry a lazy grin as he skipped another imaginary stone.

"Five skips," he declared archly.

I leaned back on my palms. "Two," I countered. Thalia giggled.

"Surrounded by vipers on all sides," Asher sighed. He turned to Henry. "Back a fellow up here, my good man."

Asher's "good man" looked as if he was considering having the lot of us committed.

"Henry, watch!" Thalia ordered, unaware of—or possibly used to—the dour expression on her brother's face. She flicked her wrist.

"Excellent form," Asher commented. "It's too bad the stone got eaten by an alligator after the second bounce."

Thalia slugged him. "It did not!"

"Sadly, it did."

"Henry! Tell him it didn't."

There was a beat of silence. "I see no alligators," Henry allowed.

"Et tu, Henry?" Asher held a hand to his chest. Henry didn't bat an eye. He was clearly used to the dramatics.

"You're not wearing shoes," he told his sister. His gaze went to Asher's bare feet and then, briefly, to mine. "Why aren't you wearing shoes?"

"We took them off," Thalia clarified helpfully. Asher's lips twitched slightly.

"Why did you take them off?" Henry went with a more specific question this time.

"Does a person really need a reason to take off their shoes?" I asked.

Henry's head swiveled toward me. *Yes*, his disapproving eyebrows seemed to say. *Yes, a person does.*

"Tess," Asher said with a flourish, "meet Henry. Henry, meet Tess."

"We've met." Henry clipped the words. I thought *met* was a pretty generous description of our encounter outside the church.

"I appreciate your sister's assistance," Henry told me stiffly, "but I think it's time for the two of you to go." Henry Marquette clearly didn't want Ivy here—and just as clearly, he didn't want me near his sister. He inclined his head slightly, staring down at me. "Don't you agree?" The words were issued more like an order than a question.

I stood, brushing the grass off my legs. "You know, I think I do."

I'd expected the crowd inside to have thinned, but if anything, it had gotten bigger. I found Ivy in the kitchen.

"Everything okay?" she asked me.

"Fine."

"Bodie can drive you home," Ivy offered. "I'll stay through cleanup, but there's no reason you have to."

I nodded. Ivy might have needed me this morning, but now that she had a mission, she was fine. Within seconds, she had her cell in her hand, calling Bodie to pick me up. I made my way to the front door. When I opened it, I caught sight of a man on the front porch, clothed in formal military dress.

"Don't. Embarrass. Me." The man's words weren't meant for my ears. They were meant for the teenage girl standing next to him.

Vivvie.

She looked smaller, somehow, than she had the last time I'd seen her. Her eyes were bloodshot, her shoulders hunched, like her body was trying its best to collapse in on itself.

"Vivvie?" I said.

Her eyes—and the man's—snapped up to mine. His face changed utterly, morphing into a solemn mix of sympathy and kindness.

Bedside manner, I thought, recognizing him from the news and remembering that he was a doctor—the White House physician. The man who'd treated Justice Marquette.

"Tess." Vivvie struggled to smile. On anyone else, the expression might have looked natural, but Vivvie's features weren't made for small smiles. "Dad," Vivvie continued, "this is Tess Kendrick. I told you about her. Tess, this is my father."

Major Bharani gave me a quick once-over. "Of course," he said smoothly. "It's nice to meet you, Tess, though, of course, I wish the circumstances were better."

Major Bharani told me good-bye and slipped inside. Vivvie started to follow him, but I stopped her.

"Are you okay?" I asked her quietly.

"That's my line." She managed another weak smile.

"Where were you this week?" I asked.

Vivvie looked down, then away. "I've been a little under the weather."

Too sick to come to school, but not too sick to attend a wake? And not too sick for her father to order her not to embarrass him, like Vivvie was some kind of liability. Like she was something to be embarrassed about.

"Are you sure you're okay?" I asked Vivvie.

"I should go." She couldn't meet my eyes. "Don't worry about me. I'm fine."

All I could think as she disappeared into the house was that Vivvie was a miserable liar.

CHAPTER 20

That night, I did an internet search on Vivvie's father. He was a decorated soldier, a former trauma surgeon in Afghanistan and Iraq. From what I could tell, he'd been the head of the White House medical clinic—and the president's personal physician—for just over two years. Unable to get the image of Vivvie's haunted expression out of my mind, I clicked on the video of Major Bharani's statement to the press.

"*It is with great sadness that I inform you that Chief Justice Theodore Marquette died on the table a little over an hour ago.*" Now that I knew to look for it, I could see a resemblance—a faint one—between Vivvie and her father. "*This was our second attempt to fix a blockage in the justice's heart, and there were unforeseen complications with surgery. This country has lost a great man today. We ask that you respect his family's privacy in this time of grief.*"

Nothing in the twenty-second clip told me what was wrong with Vivvie. I thought back to World Issues, when I'd seen the clip for the first time—the stares directed at Vivvie, the way she'd gone stiff in her seat.

Her father had operated on one of our classmates' relatives, and now Henry Marquette's grandfather was dead. Did she think people would blame her?

Don't. Embarrass. Me. The words Major Bharani had hissed at Vivvie echoed in my mind.

"Everything okay in here?" Ivy poked her head into my room.

"You're home," I said.

"I am." She paused. "I wanted to say thank you. For coming today."

I looked down at my keyboard. "No big deal."

I could feel her wanting to make it a big deal, wanting to take the fact that I'd gone with her as an indication that the two of us were going to be okay.

"I sent you an e-mail," she said, instead of pressing the topic further. "With treatment options."

For Gramps. I weathered the impact of that blow.

"There's a chance we could get home care, hire nurses either here or in Montana." Ivy presented the option calmly and neutrally. "Or there's a clinical trial. He'd stay in Boston, but they have an assisted living facility, so it wouldn't be inpatient exactly."

She was waiting for me to say something. I'd asked to be involved, but now that the information was in my inbox, my mouth was dry. *It wasn't a good day today.* I willed my eyes to stop stinging.

"Thanks," I said, staring holes in my keyboard.

"Take a look. Then we'll talk."

I managed to force my eyes up as far as my computer screen. The image of Vivvie's father stared back at me.

"Do you know the White House doctor?" I asked Ivy, as much to change the subject as because I couldn't rid my mind of the look in Vivvie's eyes.

"Major Bharani?" Ivy replied. "I know he's got the patience of a saint. According to Georgia, the president makes a horrible patient." She leaned against the doorjamb. "Why do you ask?"

Why *was* I asking?

"His daughter was assigned to show me around at Hardwicke." That wasn't an answer, not really.

"Vivvie, right?" Ivy said. If I was surprised she knew Vivvie's name, I shouldn't have been. Ivy offered me a small smile. "Washington is a small world. And Hardwicke *is* Washington."

I was beginning to get that sense. Vivvie's father was the White House physician. Henry Marquette's grandfather had sat on the Supreme Court. I'd just been to a funeral where the eulogy was given by the president of the United States.

"How did you know him?" I asked Ivy. "Theo Marquette?"

There was an almost imperceptible shift in Ivy. She stood a little straighter, the set of her features completely neutral. "I worked a job for him. We stayed in touch."

Ivy was the master of answering questions without really telling me a thing.

"Justice Marquette had a problem," I said, studying her expression, looking for some clue as to what that job had been. "You fixed it."

Ivy met my gaze, poker face firmly in place. "Something like that."

CHAPTER 21

Vivvie still wasn't at school on Monday. Henry Marquette, however, was. At lunch, he sat at Emilia's table. His posture was straighter than the others', his default expression more intense. Every once in a while, his gaze flickered over to mine.

He stared straight through me, every time.

"What are we doing?" Asher helped himself to a seat at my table.

"*We* aren't doing anything," I told him bluntly.

"My mistake. I thought we were brooding in Henry's general direction. Like so." He adopted a stormy countenance, then gestured to me. "Yours is better."

"Go away, Asher."

"You say 'go away', I hear 'be my bosom buddy.'" He gave an elaborate shrug. "Seriously, though: friendship bracelets—yea or nay?"

I wasn't sure what game he was playing. I'd been at Hardwicke for a week, and even that was enough time to ascertain that Asher Rhodes was well liked. Popular, even.

"What do you want with me?"

Asher didn't bat an eye at the question. "Maybe I'm tragically bored and horribly lonely and looking for love in all the wrong places."

I rolled my eyes.

"Or maybe," he said, leaning forward and placing his elbows on the table, "I'm tired of everyone liking me all the time and it's liberating to be around someone with no expectations. Or maybe you just looked like you could use a friend." He didn't give me a chance to respond. "Diet Coke?" Asher had two cans. He politely offered me one.

"No."

"Mentos?" He held out a roll.

"Don't Diet Coke and Mentos—"

"—explode?" Asher supplied. He opened one of the sodas. "I have a passing fondness for explosions."

That was concerning on so many levels.

"I'm starting to see why your sister thinks you need a keeper."

Asher rolled one of the Mentos contemplatively around the edge of the Diet Coke can. I reached over and flicked the candy at him. It pelted him in the forehead.

"I'm going to take that as a yes on the friendship bracelets," he informed me.

Emilia had said that when Asher got bored, things got broken. *Laws, standards of decency, occasionally bones.* He was probably sitting here, at my table, for the same reason he'd gone up on the chapel roof.

I was *interesting*.

"Have you spoken to Vivvie at all?" Asher attempted to sound casual, but there was a stray note of seriousness in his tone.

"No." I studied him for a few seconds. "Should I have?"

Asher's eyes drifted to the table where Henry was sitting. "She kind of had a breakdown. At Theo's wake."

Vivvie. My gut had told me then that something was wrong—but wrong enough for her to break down? My stomach twisted sharply. *What are the chances that her father found that breakdown embarrassing?* I knew very little about Vivvie's dad. He was a war hero. A doctor. But I couldn't keep from thinking about the way his face had morphed when he went from talking to Vivvie to talking to me.

I stood and picked up my tray. *She hasn't been at school for four days.* Back in Montana, my guidance counselor had been concerned when I'd missed five. Total.

"You look like someone who's about to do something highly inadvisable." Asher caught up to me as I dumped my trash. "And God knows, if there's something inadvisable going on, I want in."

"Go away."

"You say 'go away', I hear 'wreak havoc by my side.'"

I didn't reply. In all likelihood, Vivvie was *fine*. She probably had some kind of flu.

In all likelihood, the sinking feeling in the pit of my stomach meant nothing.

"Tess?" Asher raised an eyebrow at me. "Anything I can do?"

I glanced at the building. Fifth period was starting soon. After a moment, I turned back to Asher. "Do you have a car?"

We found Vivvie's address in the Hardwicke directory. Asher drove.

"Nice car," I told him, trying to distract myself from the fact that I was skipping school to follow up a hunch I couldn't even articulate.

"Why, thank you," Asher replied. "It's Emilia's. Mine met with an unfortunate accident involving a toaster and a squirrel."

I didn't really know where to start. "You stole your sister's car?"

"Is it still stealing if she loaned it to me once and I made a copy of her keys?" The question was clearly meant to be rhetorical.

"Yes," I told him. "Definitely still stealing."

"And so begins a life of crime," Asher said with a morose shake of his head.

"Your sister is going to *kill* you," I told him. Skipping school. Stealing her car.

Asher waved away my words, unconcerned. "If Emilia was predisposed to fratricide, I wouldn't have made it past kindergarten," he said. "I am, however, somewhat concerned that she might kill *you*."

When we arrived at Vivvie's house half an hour later, I got out of the car, then hesitated. I hadn't thought this far ahead. What was I doing here? I had no plan. I wasn't even entirely certain why I'd come.

It's probably nothing. Vivvie's probably fine.

I didn't believe that, and I didn't know why. I made my way to the front porch. Asher followed. No one answered the first time I rang the bell. Or the second. But the third time, the door opened a crack.

"Tess?" Vivvie's voice was hoarse. Like she'd been yelling, or crying—*or*, I told myself, trying to be rational, *like she has strep throat and* that *is why she hasn't been at school.*

"Can I come in?" I asked.

Vivvie looked past me and registered Asher's presence.

"I was worried about you," I told her. She didn't reply. "Tell me I shouldn't be."

Vivvie summoned her voice. "You shouldn't be."

Liar. The door was open wider now. She looked like she hadn't slept since the last time I'd seen her.

"I'm going to stretch my legs a bit and let you two ladies talk." Asher set off on a stroll around the neighborhood, leaving Vivvie and me alone.

"Can I come in?" I asked.

Vivvie shook her head, but she also stepped back, allowing me entry. I crossed the threshold into the foyer. For a few seconds, Vivvie looked at everything but me: the floor, the ceiling, the walls. Eventually, her gaze found its way to mine. The oversized sweatshirt she was wearing slipped off one shoulder. The skin underneath was darker near her collarbone. *Bruised.*

She tracked my gaze to the bruise and froze.

"Did your father do that?" I asked softly.

Vivvie jerked her sweatshirt back up. She shook her head—more than once. "He's not like that." She still had a hold on her sweatshirt, like she couldn't coax her hand into letting go. "It was an accident." Now she was nodding, as if she could *will* that into being true.

"Okay," I said. But we both knew that it wasn't okay. *She* wasn't okay.

"My dad and I had a fight. After the wake." Vivvie's grip on her sweatshirt tightened. Her free arm wrapped itself around her torso in a fierce self-hug. "The kind of fight where you yell," she clarified. "Not the kind where you . . ."

Not the kind where the bigger person hits the small one, I filled in, unable to keep from thinking about that bruise.

"We were just yelling," Vivvie reiterated fiercely. "That's how we fight. He yells. I cry. He gets flustered because I'm crying."

This was Vivvie talking about what *a* fight with her father was like. Not *the* fight she'd had with him after the wake.

"This time was different," I said. I kept my voice low and stayed away from questions. Questions required answers. I was stating facts.

Vivvie slowly unwound her hand from her shirt. "This time was different," she echoed, her voice barely more than a whisper. "He grabbed me. He didn't mean to." She paused. "I know what that sounds like, Tess. I do. But it's been just the two of us for years, and he's *never* . . ."

We were still standing in the foyer. The house was immaculate: everything in its place.

"You weren't in school today." I stuck to statements—nonthreatening ones—as best I could. "You weren't in school most of last week, either."

"I'm not hiding any more bruises," Vivvie said quickly. She could see how this looked. "Last week, my dad and I weren't even—we weren't fighting. I just told him I was sick, and he let me stay home."

She'd *told* him she was sick. But she wasn't.

"You have to come back to school eventually," I said gently. What I didn't say was: *Who or what are you avoiding?*

What I didn't say was: *What were you and your father fighting about?*

"I'll come back to school tomorrow," Vivvie told me. "I swear." I could feel the nervous energy rolling off her. She was starting to panic about what she'd told me—even though she hadn't said much at all.

"I need some air," I told her. We both knew that I wasn't the one who needed it. "You want to go for a walk?"

After a long moment, her head bobbed in something I took as a nod. She slipped on a pair of shoes, and we started walking: out the front door, down the sidewalk, around her neighborhood. Neither of us said a word. I could feel Vivvie trying to reel it in. *Trying to be strong.* This was a girl who didn't want to *bother* classmates she'd known her entire life by asking to sit at their tables for lunch. No matter how badly she needed my help, she wouldn't ask for it.

She *couldn't*.

Matching the rhythm of my steps to hers, I willed my presence to do the talking for me. *You are not a bother. You are not alone.*

One block. Two. Eventually, Vivvie's arms wrapped their way around her torso again.

"Are you okay?" I asked her. I met her eyes. "I know that's your line. I was just trying it out."

She managed a small smile. We fell quiet. In that silence, she must have reached a tipping point, because she was the one who spoke next.

"Have you ever known something you desperately wished you didn't know?" Vivvie's voice was rough in her throat, like she almost couldn't choke out the words. We kept walking, slow and steady, as I processed the question.

She was asking me to tell her that she wasn't alone.

"Yes," I said, my own voice coming out almost as rough as Vivvie's, "I have."

I thought of my grandfather—of knowing beyond a shadow of a doubt that there was something wrong with him, and knowing that if I told anyone, I would be betraying him in the worst possible way. The weight of that had been a constant: there when I woke up in the morning and there when I went to bed at night. There with every breath.

I swallowed. "The worst part was knowing that it wouldn't stay a secret forever." I was generally better at listening than I was at talking, but I thought that maybe, if I let myself show weakness, she'd show me hers. "I knew that everything would come out eventually, but I thought if I just fought hard enough . . ."

Vivvie stopped walking. "What if that wasn't the problem?" she asked, a desperate note in her voice. I could feel her hurtling toward the point of no return, the words pouring out of her mouth. "What if the problem was that the thing you knew *would* stay secret? Forever. No one would ever know. Not unless you told them."

Vivvie knows something. That much was clear. *And whatever it is—it's killing her.*

"Tell me," I said. "You need to tell someone, so tell me."

Vivvie went very still. I could see her thinking, *I can't, I can't, I can't*.

I didn't let her say it. "You can tell me, Vivvie. Haven't you heard? I'm Tess Kendrick. Worker of miracles. Resident Hardwicke fixer."

I wasn't any of those things. I didn't *want* to be any of those things. But this was Vivvie, who'd offered to cheer me up by recapping her favorite romance novel (and/or horror movie), and she was crumbling in front of me.

"I can't." Vivvie sucked in a breath of air.

"It's about your father, isn't it?"

Vivvie couldn't bring herself to tell me her secret. That didn't mean I couldn't guess.

"You know something about your father," I said, making it a statement instead of a question. "Something about your father and Theo Marquette." Vivvie had broken down at the wake. She hadn't been back to school since the day we saw the announcement about Justice Marquette's death on the news.

As far as guesses went, it was an educated one.

"Maybe you think it was your dad's fault," I continued. Now I was just stabbing in the dark. "He was the justice's doctor. His surgeon. And Justice Marquette died from complications with surgery."

I was reaching the limit of what I knew. And still, Vivvie said nothing.

Think, I told myself. "Maybe you think your dad did something wrong." No reaction from Vivvie. "Maybe he operated tired, or inebriated, or maybe you just think he made a mistake."

Vivvie broke then. "He didn't make a mistake," she said fiercely. "My dad doesn't make *mistakes*. He—" She cut herself off, then started back up again, terrified but determined. "He didn't just let Henry's grandfather die, Tess." Vivvie bowed her head. "I'm pretty sure he killed him."

CHAPTER 22

Vivvie thinks her father murdered the chief justice of the Supreme Court. There was no amount of processing that could make something like that sink in.

"I know it sounds crazy," Vivvie told me haltingly. "Believe me, I know. And it's not like I have the world's most stellar track record for teenage sanity—freshman year, dark time, there may have been some Prozac involved. But this . . ." She bit her bottom lip. "I would give anything for this to all be in my head."

I could barely keep up with the words as they tumbled out of her mouth.

"I asked him about it," Vivvie continued. She thought her father was a murderer, and she'd asked him about it? "He grabbed me. And he shook me, and he told me that if I really believed what I was saying, then maybe I needed professional help."

He'd threatened her. Told her she was crazy. But what he hadn't done was taken her to see a doctor. He'd let her stay home from school. Alone.

Those weren't the actions of a concerned father.

"I heard him, Tess. Whenever he has to give a speech, he practices. In front of the mirror. Every word, every pause, every emotion."

I thought of the press release. Major Bharani hadn't been reading a script. He'd looked straight at the camera. He'd been authoritative, calm.

"I heard him practicing." Vivvie forced herself to breathe, forced her voice to stay low. "The shower was running. I wasn't supposed to be there. I'd left for school, but I circled back to ask him something—I don't even remember what. I was getting ready to call out, and that was when I heard him." She held my gaze, her brown eyes steady. "Practicing."

Practicing what? I was afraid that if I said those words out loud—if I said anything—she might stop talking.

"'It is with great sadness,'" Vivvie whispered, "'that I inform you that Chief Justice Theodore Marquette died on the table a little over an hour ago.'"

I recognized the beginning of the statement Dr. Bharani had issued at the press conference.

"He practiced his statement," I said, not quite seeing where she was going.

"Tess, he practiced it that morning." Vivvie's voice caught in her throat. "Justice Marquette died that afternoon."

I processed what Vivvie was saying. Her father had prepared a speech announcing the justice's death from *unforeseen complications with surgery* before the surgery had ever taken place.

"That's not all." Vivvie started walking again. I strode to catch up with her. Midday, the neighborhood was nearly empty.

On the opposite sidewalk, there was a woman walking a dog. Vivvie kept her voice low enough that I had to struggle to hear her.

"I stayed home sick the next day. I'd convinced myself that I'd misheard, or misunderstood, but then I heard my dad talking on the phone, which was weird, because *his* phone was on the kitchen counter. He wasn't on the landline, either."

Vivvie was babbling now, and I had to fight to find the meaning in her words.

"I think it might have been a disposable. Why would my dad have a disposable cell phone?"

My mouth felt dry. "Who was he talking to?"

"I couldn't make out most of what he was saying." Vivvie's voice was very small. "All I heard . . ." She swallowed. "He was reading a number."

"Like a phone number?"

Vivvie shook her head. "Like an account number."

The president's doctor knew that Justice Marquette was going to die. He had a speech prepared. And the day after the justice's death, that doctor was on a disposable cell phone giving an account number to whoever was on the other end.

"We have to tell someone," I told Vivvie. "The police, my sister, I don't even know, but—"

"We can't, Tess." Vivvie reached out to grab my arm. "*I* can't. I know it looks bad." That was an understatement. "But, Tess, he's my dad."

Vivvie had to have known, when she'd told me this, that I couldn't just turn around and pretend that nothing had happened.

"You said you were a miracle worker," Vivvie whispered, weaving her fingers together and holding them clasped in front of her body. "I want a miracle."

I couldn't go back and change what she'd heard. I couldn't wave a magic wand and alter the facts. "What do you want me to do, Vivvie?"

She was quiet for several seconds. "I want proof," she said finally. "Not just suspicions, not just something I overheard. I *want* to be wrong. But if I'm not . . ."

She didn't want it to be her word against his. She didn't want to be the one to tear her family apart at the seams.

"Proof?" I repeated. "What kind of proof?"

Vivvie toyed with the bottom of her shirt. "If I can get you the phone," she said, "can you figure out who he was talking to?"

That was so far outside my skillset I didn't even know where I would start. "I can try."

Vivvie blew out a long breath, then nodded. "Okay," she whispered. Then she turned and started walking back toward her house.

"Vivvie," I called after her. "Are you sure you're going to be okay at home? With your father?"

"He won't hurt me." Vivvie had to believe that. She wanted me to believe it, too. "He doesn't know that I know about the phone. After the wake, all I told him was that I'd heard him practicing his speech."

And look how that ended.

"You don't have to do this. You can come with me. We'll . . ."

"No, Tess." Vivvie forced a smile. The painstaking upturning of her lips hit me like a knife to the gut. "I just told you that I think someone paid my father to kill a Supreme Court justice. I asked you not to tell anyone about it until we have proof. So, yeah, I kind of *do* have to do this." She started walking back toward her house again. This time I let her go and stood there on the sidewalk, feeling like I'd fallen into some kind of parallel universe.

"Funny story."

I turned to see Asher Rhodes rounding the corner.

"Vivvie's voice carries," he said. "And I have freakishly good hearing."

CHAPTER 23

Asher and I stared at each other for several seconds. *He heard*. I racked my mind, trying to remember what, exactly, Vivvie had said in the last thirty seconds of our conversation.

I just told you that I think someone paid my father to kill a Supreme Court justice . . .

"Henry's my best friend." Asher's tone was conversational, but quieter than normal. "In the first grade, he was the one who strongly advised me against roller-skating off my roof." There was a beat of silence. "He was also the one who taught me to write left-handed when I broke my right arm. When we were nine, I inadvertently-possibly-on-purpose insulted a sixth grader. The kid would have pounded me into the ground, but Henry stepped forward and *challenged him to a duel*. Because he was into knights and honor and standing up for best friends who were too stupid to watch out for themselves." Asher shook his head, his voice still quiet, intense. "I can still remember when Thalia was born. Henry spent the night at my house, and I woke up in the morning and found an itemized to-do list, focused on his duties as a big brother."

The image of a tiny Henry Marquette making a big-brother to-do list was all too easy to picture.

"He's been my best friend for almost as long as I can remember, Tess. When his dad died . . ." Asher shook his head and didn't finish that thought. "Henry and his grandfather were close. Theo was the closest thing to a father Henry had left."

My stomach twisted sharply. It was too easy to put myself in Henry Marquette's shoes, to imagine how I would feel if I woke up tomorrow and Gramps was gone. It was a short jump to imagining what it would be like to know that my grandfather's death hadn't been an accident.

I would have been out for blood.

"You can't tell Henry what you just heard," I told Asher.

Asher gave me a look. "I knew you were a little crazy, Tess. It's there, in the eyes." He gestured in the general vicinity of my face. "But I, too, have been in possession of the Crazy Eyes on occasion. I get it. If you want to go head-to-head with John Thomas Wilcox, or take up permanent residence in the guys' bathroom, or skip out in the middle of the school day, I will happily go along for the ride."

But you won't keep this from your best friend, I filled in.

"How do you think Henry will respond to this news?" I asked. Asher's expression darkened. "My guess would be not well," I continued. "And right now, even if he knew, there wouldn't be anything he could do about it. He could try going to the police. But if Vivvie gets spooked, if she *recants* . . ."

All we had was Vivvie's word.

"We're talking about the president's physician, Asher." I wasn't sure what kind of background checks working at the White House involved, but if the Powers That Be were willing to put the president's life in Vivvie's father's hands, he obviously wasn't considered a security risk. Or a threat.

"Darn you and your infernal logic." Asher ran both hands through his hair, mussing it to ridiculous heights. "Fine," he capitulated. "But I want in. Whatever you're planning to do about this, whatever Vivvie's doing, I want in."

It went against every instinct I had to agree. But based on the mutinous set of Asher's jaw, I didn't see that I had much of a choice.

"Fine," I said sharply. I scuffed my shoe into the ground. "Any chance you know someone who can get information off a disposable phone?"

Asher drove me back to Ivy's. I texted Bodie to let him know that he didn't need to pick me up from school. A moment later, I got a text back: *Call from school. Skipping classes? HRH not pleased.*

So Ivy wasn't happy with me. Right now, that was the least of my problems. Belatedly, I translated Bodie's code for Ivy. *HRH: Her Royal Highness.* I snorted.

Asher glanced over at me from the driver's seat. "Care to share with the class?"

"Ivy's driver," I replied, like that was explanation enough. For Asher, it turned out that it was.

"And by *driver*, I'm assuming you mean *bodyguard*."

"That's a thing?" I asked.

Asher turned onto Ivy's street. "At Hardwicke," he replied, "that's definitely a thing."

Of course it was. I'd been in DC a week, and I'd already met the First Lady, crossed horns with the minority whip's son, and gone to the funeral for a Supreme Court justice. Ivy had said it herself: Hardwicke *was* Washington. For every student like Asher, whose parents were dentists, there was someone like Henry or Vivvie.

Or me. As Asher pulled into Ivy's driveway, I was reminded of the fact that I wasn't as removed from the power players in this town as I felt. There was a limo parked in the drive.

Asher eyed it. "Just another afternoon at Ivy Kendrick's house?"

The car had shaded windows, with glass that I deeply suspected was bulletproof. *One of Ivy's clients*, I thought. With any luck, maybe she would be busy enough that she wouldn't have time to cross-examine me about why I'd skipped school—or where I'd spent the afternoon. I unbuckled my seat belt and opened the car door.

"Thanks for the ride," I told Asher. What I was really thinking was, *Don't tell anyone what happened. What Vivvie overheard. What you* heard.

Asher inclined his head slightly and gave me a smoldering look. "Until tomorrow."

I slammed the car door before Asher could say anything else. I'd nearly made it to Ivy's front door before I realized the entrance was blocked. A man in a dark-colored suit stepped forward, gesturing for me to stop. It took me less than a second to get a read on him: suit, sunglasses, gun holstered at his side. *Secret Service.*

"My sister lives here," I told him. "Light brown hair, about yea tall? Is probably in there talking to the First Lady right now?"

The agent raked his eyes over me.

"Seriously," I said. "I live here."

The agent glanced from me to the street. He watched Asher pull away from the curb and tracked his progress until the car disappeared. I was about to reiterate the fact that I *resided in this house* when the front door opened. *Bodie*. He walked out and whispered something into the Secret Service agent's ear, letting the door close behind him as he did.

"Tess," Bodie said, turning his attention to me. "Meet Damien Kostas. Kostas, this is Ivy's sister, Tess."

The Secret Service agent made no move to allow me into the house. I was about to suggest that he ask the First Lady if *she* thought I was a threat when Ivy's front door opened again. Another agent stepped outside.

Behind the agent was the president of the United States.

Not the First Lady, I thought, my brain scrambling to catch up as President Nolan glanced over at Bodie and the Secret Service agents before his gaze settled on me.

Ivy stepped up beside him, her eyes locking onto me. "You're home," she said.

"By some definitions," I replied, trying not to stare at the president.

The leader of the free world offered me a smile. "Tess," he said. "Short for *Theresa*, isn't it?"

I managed to nod but couldn't summon up a verbal reply.

"It's nice to meet you, Theresa." President Nolan was in his late sixties. He had an easy smile and—unlike his wife—not even a hint of an accent. "I've heard a lot about you—a bit from Ivy, but mostly from Georgia. She said something about a dinner?" The president gave me another trademark smile. "My wife has an uncanny knack for getting her way," he said. He eyed Ivy. "Something she and your sister have in common."

"Mr. President," one of the Secret Service agents prompted, glancing down at his watch.

The president nodded. "No rest for the weary," he told me before turning back to Ivy. "You'll do some digging?"

Ivy worded her response carefully. "I doubt I'll come up with anything your people missed."

The president wasn't dissuaded. "You're resourceful. If there's a skeleton in his closet, I want to know."

Whose closet? I wondered. I flashed to the First Lady saying that Justice Marquette's death was *an opportunity, tragic though it may be*. Was the president already working on digging up information on possible replacements?

"If there are skeletons," Ivy said coolly, "will I be burying them or exposing them?"

This time, Peter Nolan gave *her* his most presidential smile. "Let me have a chat with the party leadership," he said, "and then I'll let you know."

And just like that, the president was gone.

Unfortunately, it didn't take Ivy long to turn the full strength of her attention on me. "You want to tell me why you skipped your afternoon classes?" She crossed one arm over the other and tapped the tips of her fingers against her elbow, one by one. "Or where you went?"

I went to see a girl who thinks her father murdered Justice Marquette, I thought. Out loud, I opted for: "Not really."

Ivy pressed her lips together, like if they parted, she might say something she would regret. "You know that you can come to me, right?" she said finally. "With anything, at any time."

Maybe I believed that, and maybe I didn't. With Ivy, it was always the maybes that hurt me most. *Vivvie asked me to keep this secret*. I concentrated on that. *Until she's sure. Until we have proof.*

There was no maybe about that.

"Are Supreme Court justices normally treated by the White House physician?" I asked.

Ivy blinked once, twice, three times at the change of subject. The question had caught her off guard. "No," she said finally. "They're not. But Theo wasn't just a justice. He was a friend."

Not just Ivy's friend. The *president's* friend, treated by one of the military's most highly decorated physicians.

"Is everything okay?" Ivy asked me.

I pushed past her into the house, my heart pumping like I'd just run a marathon. "Sure," I told her, lying through my teeth. "Everything's fine."

CHAPTER 24

The next day, Vivvie was back in school. Her hair was pulled into a high ponytail on her head. Makeup covered the bags under her eyes. She did a fighting job of looking normal, like everything was fine.

I wondered how blind the rest of the school had to be not to realize that she wasn't.

The two of us didn't have a chance to talk before classes started. In English, she kept her eyes locked on the board. She wouldn't even look at me. In physics, we were assigned to work in partners.

"We're supposed to calculate the coefficient of friction," Vivvie said, busying herself with pulling metal discs out of a plastic bag. "We'll need the angle of the ramp . . ."

"Vivvie."

She looked up at me. I held her gaze but didn't say anything, willing her to remember that, for better or worse, she wasn't in this alone.

"I got the phone." She said those words so quietly, I almost couldn't make them out. "He'd thrown it out. I went through the trash."

Her hand shook as she set one of the metal discs on the scale. On the other side of the room, Henry Marquette was doing the same thing. Vivvie tried very hard not to look at him, but she couldn't keep her gaze down. I reached out and steadied Vivvie's hand.

"You're okay," I told her.

She reached into her bag and slipped out a flip phone. Her hand wrapped around it so tightly that her knuckles strained against her skin. "Nothing is okay." For a moment, she pulled the phone close to her body, but then, like someone ripping a bandage off an open wound, she thrust it across the table toward me, forcing her grip to relax, finger by finger. I closed my own hand around the phone, feeling the weight of it.

"Girls." The teacher stopped by our table. "No phones."

I dropped the phone into my blazer pocket before he could move to take it from me. "What phone?"

The teacher pointed his index finger at me. "Exactly."

The class passed torturously slowly. We did the work. But all I could think about was the phone in my pocket and the fact that on the other side of the room, Henry Marquette kept sending narrow-eyed glances at Vivvie and me.

"As it turns out," Asher told me, slipping behind me in the lunch line, "it is possible that I do know someone who might be able to get information off a disposable cell phone."

"Even if the phone has been wiped clean?" In between classes, I'd checked the call log and contacts. Both had been cleared.

"My contact is ... let's say, *resourceful*," Asher told me. "Nothing electronic is ever truly deleted."

"Asher." Henry Marquette cut between the two of us. "Any chance you're actually intending *not* to skip out on your remaining classes today?"

"That's Henry's way of saying he thinks you're a bad influence on me," Asher informed me. "Given the high bad influence standards set by yours truly, I'm pretty sure that's a compliment."

Based on the steely expression on Henry's face, I was pretty sure that it wasn't.

If only he knew. Asher excelled at acting natural. From his tone, you would have thought he and I had been plotting a high school prank, not discussing how one went about pulling deleted information off a disposable phone.

Henry had no idea just how bad an influence I was.

"I'll meet you in the computer lab during free period," Asher told me.

I started making my way to the courtyard.

"Tess," Henry called after me. On his lips, my name sounded like a nonsense word, one he'd condescended to saying and thought about as much of as *flapdoodle* or *flibbertigibbet*. "A moment?"

What if he knows? My heart announced its presence in my chest, beating viciously against the inside of my rib cage. *Of course he doesn't know*, I told myself. There was no way he could.

"Yeah?" I said.

Henry came to stand next to me. "I understand Emilia hired you to keep Asher out of trouble in my absence."

Emilia. Not Vivvie. Emilia. The knots in my stomach relaxed, just slightly.

"Emilia *tried* to hire me," I corrected, forcing myself to respond to what he was saying instead of what he wasn't. "She also tried to bribe me, and I'm pretty sure that threatening me into compliance might have eventually been on the table."

Henry took his time with his reply, spacing his words apart, giving each its own weight. "Regardless, as it happens, I am no longer absent." His green eyes narrowed slightly. "Whatever you're doing with Asher, you can stop."

Henry Marquette hadn't wanted Ivy at his grandfather's wake. He hadn't wanted me around his little sister. And he didn't want me *fixing* Asher.

"Hate to break it to you," I replied, "but Asher's a big boy. He can make his own decisions about who to hang out with and who's a liability."

At the word *liability*, Henry's expression shifted slightly. He hadn't expected me to see things from his perspective so clearly. "I know what your sister does, and I know the kind of destruction she leaves in her wake." Henry's voice was perfectly pleasant, but the glint in his eyes was anything but. "If you want to fashion yourself into some kind of high school fixer, fine. But stay away from Asher."

I probably should have been insulted that Henry was so convinced that he needed to protect Asher from me, but given what Asher and I had planned for that afternoon, I couldn't help wondering if he was right.

CHAPTER 25

Asher's contact met us in one of the smaller computer labs. She seemed about as surprised to see me as I was to see her.

"You have *got* to be kidding me." Emilia gave her brother a *look*.

"Is this my kidding face?" Asher asked her.

Emilia glared at him. "It's the only face you have."

"And what a face it is," Asher agreed jovially. "Now, about that memory card reconstruction . . ."

"Do I even want to know where you got a burner phone?" Emilia asked. Asher opened his mouth to reply. "Don't answer that," she told him before swinging her attention over to me.

"Can you do it?" I asked Emilia flatly.

"Can I?" she repeated. "Yes. Girls qualify as an underserved minority if you're applying to a STEM field." At my blank look, she rolled her eyes. "Science, technology, engineering, math? Have you even thought about college applications?" She held up a hand. "Don't answer that, either. I *could* do this. That doesn't mean I will."

She folded her arms over her waist. "I told you I'd owe you if and only if you agreed to keep my brother out of trouble for just a few days. Let's do a brief accounting, shall we?" She began ticking items off on her fingers. "In the time since he's made your acquaintance, Asher has skipped school, committed grand theft auto, and threatened to rearrange John Thomas Wilcox's face."

I turned to look at Asher. He hadn't threatened John Thomas in my presence. Asher shrugged and then turned back to his twin. "Tess did get me off the chapel roof," he volunteered helpfully.

"For which she has my undying gratitude." Emilia's voice was dead dry. "Now, if you'll excuse me, some of us like to use our study period to actually study."

She turned. Asher gestured at me to say something.

"I'll owe you." Those words grated, but they had the desired effect. Emilia turned back to face us.

"One favor, no questions asked, whenever and wherever I ask it of you." Emilia gave me her sweetest smile and held out a delicate hand. "Deal?"

Gritting my teeth, I took her hand, feeling like I'd just signed on the devil's dotted line. "Deal."

Half an hour later, Emilia handed the phone back to me. "Voilà, and you're welcome—in that order."

I took the phone and pulled up the restored call log. All the ingoing and outgoing calls were linked to the same two numbers.

"Any way to tell who these numbers are registered to?" I asked.

"Unless the owner of that phone is a complete moron," Emilia replied, "I'm guessing those numbers belong to other disposable cell phones."

"One way to find out." Asher plucked the phone from my grasp, and before I could stop him, he'd hit *call*. He switched the cell to speaker and set it on the counter.

This is a bad idea. I reached for the phone, just as a computerized voice filled the air. The number had been disconnected.

I shouldn't have been surprised. If Vivvie's dad had been smart, he would have destroyed this phone—not just thrown it away.

Emilia stood up and stretched slightly, like a gymnast preparing to tumble.

"Tess?" Asher nodded to the phone in my hand. "There's still one more number."

This is still a bad idea. But putting myself in Emilia's debt had also been a bad idea. Letting Vivvie fish this phone out of her father's trash had probably been a very bad idea. Not going straight to my sister with Vivvie's accusations almost certainly was.

I brought my thumb to the phone's keypad, scrolled down, and hit *call* before I could change my mind. This time, the phone rang. Once. Twice. Three times. I didn't put it on speaker. My hand tightened around it with the fourth ring. I could feel my heart beating in my stomach.

No one is going to answer. Whoever Major Bharani was talking to on this phone, they're long gone. That was what I told myself, right up to the point when someone picked up.

"I told you, you'll get your money when I get my nomination." The voice was male, deep and velvety with an American accent I couldn't quite pinpoint. Whoever he was, he wasn't happy. "Don't call this number again."

The line went dead.

"Any answer?" Emilia asked, unable to keep the curiosity from her tone.

I cradled the phone in my hand for a moment, then flipped it closed. "No."

Asher met my eyes over his sister's head. He wasn't buying that answer. I didn't expect him to.

You'll get your money when I get my nomination. The words were burned into my brain. I'd wanted Vivvie to be wrong. I'd wanted this to be a mistake.

Clearly, however, it wasn't.

CHAPTER 26

"The process for appointing a judge to the Supreme Court is an involved one. It starts with the president and his staff vetting candidates for the nomination. Who can they get past the Senate? Who best serves the party's needs?" As Dr. Clark lectured, I thought of the president telling Ivy to dig for skeletons in someone's closet.

I tried not to think of the voice on the other end of the phone line.

You'll get your money when I get my nomination.

"Eventually, the president selects a nominee, typically one who shares his broader ideological viewpoint. Once appointed, the only way a justice can be removed from the bench is impeachment—and no justice has been so impeached since 1804. As a result, Supreme Court appointments have the potential to dramatically change our legal and political landscape for *decades*."

As the class wore on, we got a brief overview of some of the biggest cases the Supreme Court had ever taken on. *Voting rights. Segregation. Women's health.*

"The president's nominee eventually goes before the Senate Judiciary Committee," Dr. Clark continued. "During the hearings that follow, the nominee is questioned on everything from their record to their personal life. The committee then issues an assessment. A negative evaluation might send the president's team scrambling for a new nominee. Eventually, to get a confirmation, the would-be justice will have to be confirmed by a majority vote of the Senate."

Dr. Clark leaned back against her desk. "It probably won't come as a surprise to most of you to hear that long before the nomination goes to the floor, lobbyists and special interest parties will already be attempting to sway votes, one way or another."

Lobbyists. Special interest. She was speaking a language that was foreign to me, but for many of my classmates, it was their native tongue. I understood only that there were a lot of reasons for different groups to want—or not want—a person on the Supreme Court.

I tried not to think about the fact that there were probably just as many reasons to want a Supreme Court justice dead.

There were two numbers on the phone's call log. I couldn't stop the gears in my mind from turning. One of the numbers had belonged to the man I'd talked to. And the other?

That one was a giant question mark.

"For the next two weeks, you and your partner will be playing the role of the president." Dr. Clark began handing out an outline of our assignment. "You'll be researching candidates, putting forth your own nominee. Think of it like March Madness, but instead of putting together a bracket, you have your eye on the prize, and instead of winning a championship, the appointee instantly becomes one of the most powerful individuals in our country."

I took the sheet someone passed me and stared down at it. There were dozens of names on this list: possible nominees to research.

"Mr. Marquette." Dr. Clark lowered her voice as she came to Henry. "If you would prefer an alternative assignment . . ."

"No," Henry said, his posture almost supernaturally straight, his face giving nothing away. "This will be fine."

"You know something," Vivvie said the second we settled in the back corner of the room to "brainstorm" for our project. "I know you know something. You have that look on your face."

I tried to think of a way to catch Vivvie up to speed without hurting her. That way didn't exist.

"There were two numbers on the phone." I stuck to the facts, as bare-bones as I could make them. "We called both of them."

"We?" Vivvie leaned toward me, her eyes wide and panicked. "Who's *we*?"

Her voice carried. Several other students—and Dr. Clark—turned to look our way. Vivvie lowered her voice again. "Who's we?"

I broke it to her that Asher had overheard her—and that his twin had been the one to retrieve the call log for us. Vivvie weathered that blow, pressing her lips together and bowing her head.

"What happened when you called the number?" she asked quietly, looking up at me through impossibly long lashes. She must have known, from the expression on my face, that the answer wasn't good. She gripped the paper in her hands so hard I thought she might tear it.

"The first number was disconnected," I said, pitching my voice as low as I could.

"And the second?"

I told Vivvie what the person who'd answered had said, verbatim.

"So we're dealing with what? A person who's hoping to get the nomination himself? Or someone who has a candidate in mind?" Vivvie stared down at the paper in her hands—the list of names.

"How are we doing here, girls?" Dr. Clark came to stand beside us.

Vivvie forced herself to snap out of it. She smiled brightly, an expression so sweet it could make your teeth ache, and so utterly artificial that I wanted to cry. "We got distracted," she said, sounding like a copy of a copy of the happy, chattering girl I'd met that first day. "But, hey, procrastination is the mother of invention, right?"

Dr. Clark bit back a grin. "I believe that's *necessity*," she said, studying Vivvie a bit more closely. "Are you sure you're okay, Vivvie?"

"Great," Vivvie replied forcefully. It hurt me just to hear her say it.

"In that case," Dr. Clark said, "I'm going to suggest you two switch partners. Procrastination, I am afraid, is the mother of nothing but more procrastination."

Before I could object, Dr. Clark had steered Vivvie in the direction of a new partner and brought someone else back to work with me.

"Do you two know each other?" Dr. Clark asked.

Henry Marquette looked about as happy with this development as I was. "We've met."

CHAPTER 27

Partnering with Henry Marquette on a project devoted to choosing a replacement for his grandfather, while harboring suspicions that his grandfather had been murdered *so that he could be replaced*, was not what one would call a highlight of my day.

I was pretty sure it wasn't the highlight of Henry's day, either.

"So we're in agreement," he said, his voice crisp. "I'll take the top half of the list. You take the bottom."

Your grandfather's death was planned. I said that silently, because I couldn't say it out loud. *There were at least two people involved. Maybe three.* My mind went to the other number on the phone—the one that had already been disconnected.

"I know you and Asher are up to something." Henry's words snapped me back to the moment. "Emilia, too, God help us all."

He said Emilia's name the way one might reference a force of nature—a tsunami, perhaps, or a hurricane.

"I don't know what you're doing." Henry gave me a look. "I'm fairly certain that I don't want to know."

He really, really didn't.

"If this is the part where you warn me away from your friends," I told him, putting on my best poker face, "why don't we just skip straight to you making veiled comments about my sister, and me telling you that I'm not her."

Henry stared at me, a detached observer taking mental notes on my features for later reference. I had no idea what was going on inside his head.

"Actually," he said finally, "this is the part where I tell you that you don't want to be anything like your sister." The bell rang as he gathered his books. "Take it from someone who knows."

Vivvie caught up to me outside of the classroom. "What did you say to Henry Marquette?" she asked, unable to keep the note of urgency from her tone. I pulled her into the girls' restroom and checked the stalls. Empty.

"I didn't say anything. Not about your father, not about what we found."

It took Vivvie a moment to absorb that information. "Sorry. I just . . . you two were working together . . . and . . ."

"Breathe, Vivvie."

She leaned back against the bathroom door. "Maybe you misunderstood," she said quietly. "Whatever you heard the person on the phone say, maybe you misunderstood. Maybe I misunderstood. Maybe none of this is what it looks like."

She sounded so hopeful, so desperately hopeful that my body ached with the force of that hope. I knew what it was like to want so badly to be able to *believe* something into being true.

He's not sick. He's just confused. How often had I told myself that, back in Montana? I knew what it was like to teeter on the edge of the truth, to squeeze your eyes closed with everything you had and hope that when you opened them, things would look different.

I also knew that they never did.

"We have to tell someone," I said softly. "You know we do, Vivvie."

"Who?" Vivvie shot back, her hair spilling down her chest. "Your sister? This time last week, you didn't even know what she did for a living." Vivvie's lips trembled. "Clearly the two of you are *close*."

Ouch.

Vivvie pressed her hand to her mouth, hard. "I'm sorry," she stammered through her fingers. "I didn't mean that. I'm the one who asked you for help. I asked you to do this. I'm not allowed to hate you for it." Her arms encircled her waist, her head bowed. "I know I can't ask you to keep this a secret." Dark brown eyes met mine. "I know that, Tess."

But she was. Asking.

"If we knew," Vivvie said quietly, "if we were *sure*, if we could figure out who he was talking to . . . it would be different."

It was never going to be different. Her dad was always going to be her dad. Based on what she'd said the day before, he was the only parent she had.

"Would you recognize the voice?" Vivvie asked me. "If you heard it again, would you recognize it?"

I thought of the list Dr. Clark had handed out. Potential Supreme Court nominees.

"I might."

CHAPTER 28

That night, I went through the list on Dr. Clark's handout. Attorney generals. Circuit court judges. Law professors.

I'll take the top half. You take the bottom.

Somehow, I doubted this was what Henry Marquette had in mind. I was supposed to be finding basic biographical data on each of our dozens of potential nominees. Instead, I was searching for videos and audio clips. Halfway through the list, I still hadn't heard the voice I was looking for.

"Hey, kid." Bodie knocked on my door and stuck his head into my room a moment later. "Pizza's here. Her Royal Highness is locked in her office," he added before I could ask. "When she gets her teeth into something, it's impossible to pry her away."

Downstairs in the kitchen, I helped myself to a slice. "You guys still working on digging up the skeletons in some potential nominee's closet?" I asked.

Bodie choked on his own piece of pizza and narrowed his eyes at me. "You have *got* to stop doing that."

"I heard the president tell Ivy to go digging," I said, rolling my eyes. "It's not exactly rocket science to figure out why he might be asking her to go looking for someone's dirty little secrets *now*." I took another bite of my pizza. "Besides," I said, "our assignment in World Issues is to come up with the perfect nominee ourselves."

"Of course it is," Bodie muttered. "Because heaven forbid Hardwicke just teach American history." Bodie reached over and grabbed the pizza box.

"Where are you going?" I called after him as he strode out the door.

"You're a Kendrick," he called back. "You figure it out."

He was making sure Ivy ate—because that, along with driving and bodyguard duty and breaking the laws that Ivy wouldn't, was Bodie's job. I followed. Not because I wanted to see Ivy. Not because I hadn't seen her all day.

Because when I got stuck on something, when things were too much, I started walking.

Bodie didn't bother knocking on the door to Ivy's office. He just slipped in, leaving the pizza positioned strategically and temptingly on the end of Ivy's desk.

My sister's voice carried out into the hallway. "Thank you for taking the time to speak with me, Judge Pierce. As I'm sure you understand, this little video conference is completely off the books."

It occurred to me, then, that knowing who Ivy was investigating for the president might let me skip straight to the end on the World Issues assignment. *It's not cheating if I—*

"Of course, Ms. Kendrick." The reply to Ivy's words cut my thoughts off with the force of a blade. "You've been doing your homework on me. And that means you know I'm discreet."

My muscles tensed, one by one. That voice was deep. Velvety. *Familiar.*

You'll get your money when I get my nomination.

Bodie looked up and saw me standing in the doorway. Leaving the pizza box where it was, he nudged me away from the door and shut it behind him.

"Who's Ivy talking to?" My words came out in a rushed whisper, my throat closing tight around them. "Is it about the nomination?"

Say no.

He didn't.

"She called that man 'judge.'" I forced out the words. "Is he the one the president . . ."

The one the president was considering nominating.

"He is, isn't he?" I said, dread mounting inside of me.

"You saw nothing," Bodie ordered. "You heard nothing. Ivy would kill us both."

Kill. Ivy would kill *us both*, I thought dully, my mind focusing on one and only one word in that sentence. *They killed Justice Marquette. They killed him, and now the president is considering nominating that man for the Supreme Court.*

"I need to talk to Ivy." I reached for the door. Bodie caught me.

"Easy there, kitten."

"You don't understand, Bodie. *I need to talk to Ivy.*"

"Tess?" Bodie must have heard something in my voice. He rarely called me by my given name. It was always *kitten* or *kiddo* or *kid*. Before I could respond, the doorbell rang.

Bodie arched an eyebrow at me. "You expecting visitors?"

I shook my head. The bell rang again. Bodie went to answer it. I stayed, staring at the closed door to Ivy's office. *I have to tell her*.

"Tess?" Bodie called. "Company." His voice was calm. Talking-a-jumper-down-from-a-ledge calm.

I walked toward the foyer, my shoes clicking against the marble floor. The closer I got, the faster I walked. When I rounded the corner, Bodie was standing between me and the front door, blocking my view of the porch.

"I should go."

I recognized Vivvie's voice. She was here. At night. I pushed past Bodie just as Vivvie turned to leave.

"Wait," I said. Vivvie froze where she stood, but didn't turn back to face me. I walked out onto the porch and looped around her, so that we were facing each other. Her head was bowed, her dark hair dangling in her face.

"Vivvie?"

She angled her head up to look at me. Her lip was bleeding. Her left eye was swollen shut.

CHAPTER 29

Vivvie was shaking. Gently, I raised a hand to her arm. She stepped back.

"My dad knows," she whispered, her voice cutting through the night air. "About the phone. He knows I took it. He must have had second thoughts about the way he disposed of it, because he went to get it back."

And it was gone. Bile rose in the back of my throat.

"I've never seen him like that, Tess." Vivvie shook her head. She couldn't stop shaking it, her body saying *no*, *no*, *no*, again and again. "He was . . ."

She couldn't finish the sentence. My heart beating viciously inside my chest, I did it for her. "Angry."

"Scared," she said softly. "He was so scared. I told him I didn't know what he was talking about, but he didn't believe me. He kept saying that I had to give him the phone."

Vivvie didn't have the phone. I did. She couldn't give it to him, and I was looking at the result.

I knew. I knew he might hurt her. I knew—

"I'm so sorry, Vivvie." I choked out the words. I was sorry I had let this happen to her, sorry I hadn't told Ivy the second I realized the major had laid hands on his daughter to begin with.

"He gave me ibuprofen for the swelling." Vivvie's voice shook.

He hit her, then gave her something for the swelling. Fury churned in my gut.

"Tess?" Ivy's voice had a tendency to carry. She came to stand on the front porch, and I realized I'd followed Vivvie out into the street.

"We have to tell her, Vivvie."

Vivvie shook her head again.

"I know who your father was talking to. I know who hired him."

Vivvie's head stopped shaking, but her body still trembled. "Tess—"

"The president asked Ivy to look into a potential nominee." I searched my memory for the details. "Judge Pierce. Ivy was on a video conference with him." My throat was dry, each word hard-won. "I recognized his voice." That statement—and all its implications—hung in the air. Vivvie said nothing. I couldn't stop talking. "If we don't do something, *that man* might be the person the president nominates to replace Justice Marquette."

I could hear Vivvie's breath go ragged. On the porch, Ivy was still staring out at the two of us. Vivvie pressed her lips into a line. Her breath evened out. And she said one word.

"Okay."

• • •

Vivvie and I sat on the sofa. Ivy was sitting across the coffee table from us. As soon as we'd started talking, she'd called Adam. He stood behind her now.

"Here." Bodie handed Vivvie a fresh bag of ice. Vivvie took it but didn't press it to her face.

"You're sure about what you heard?" Ivy asked Vivvie. There was no judgment in her voice. This wasn't a leading question. She wasn't trying to make Vivvie second-guess herself.

Still, I stiffened. "She wouldn't be here if she wasn't."

"I'm talking to Vivvie, Tess." Ivy barely spared me a glance. The moment she'd realized that Vivvie wasn't just now coming to me with this, that I'd known and said nothing, a visible change had come over my sister's body. It was like she'd been submerged in a tub of freezing water and steeled herself against the cold.

Sugar and spice and everything nice, right up to the point where she wasn't.

"I'm sure." Vivvie turned the bag of ice over in her hands. "I know it sounds crazy. It doesn't make any sense that he would do something like this, but . . ." Vivvie swallowed back whatever words or tears wanted to come. When she spoke again, her voice was detached. "He's not himself right now."

The father Vivvie knew wouldn't have killed someone. But the father Vivvie knew wouldn't have hit her. *Hurt* her.

"Vivvie's father isn't our only problem." I drew everyone's attention from Vivvie to me. "She mentioned the cell phone she heard him talking on. What she didn't say was that after she fished it out of the trash, she gave it to me."

Ivy's gaze slowly shifted from Vivvie to me. I felt the weight of her stare.

"She gave you the phone, and you didn't bring it to me?" Ivy asked sharply. Behind her, the frown on Adam's face deepened. Beside me, Vivvie shivered.

Let them focus on me, cross-examine *me*. "She gave me the phone. I had a friend retrieve the call log."

"You *what*?" The iciness in Ivy's tone gave way to heat.

"I called the numbers."

Ivy ground her teeth together. I could feel her, silently counting to ten.

Bodie didn't make it that far. "Of course you did," he muttered. "Because why *not* call the number of someone you think might have bankrolled an assassination?"

"Bodie," Adam ground out. "You're not helping."

Ivy must have reached ten, because she leaned forward, reducing the space between us by half. "You called. Someone answered." She didn't phrase it as a question.

"Someone answered," I confirmed. I told her what that person had said, the same way I'd told it to Vivvie: verbatim.

"You still have the phone?" Adam asked. I nodded. "Get it," he ordered. "Now."

I did as I was told. The moment I placed it in his hand, his fingers closed lightly around mine. "You're done," he told me. "I have people I can take this to at the Pentagon. Your sister can loop in the White House. But you're done."

It was suddenly very easy to see the soldier in Adam. The one who was used to giving orders and having them obeyed.

"There's one more thing," I said. I glanced over at Vivvie. Her hair fell into her face, obscuring her fat lip and most of her swollen eye. Her fingers gently kneaded the bag of ice in her lap.

"The person on the other end of the phone line? The one who said that the doctor wouldn't get his money until *he* got his nomination?" I looked from Adam to Bodie and finally to my sister. "I recognized his voice."

CHAPTER 30

Once they'd squeezed every last drop of information out of us, Ivy, Adam, and Bodie retreated downstairs to Ivy's office. By that time, it was almost midnight. There was never any question that Vivvie was spending the night—Ivy had set her up on the sofa. Vivvie crawled under the blanket and just lay there.

Sometime around two in the morning, I went to bed. I couldn't sleep, knowing that downstairs, Ivy was . . . I didn't even know what she was doing. Had Adam called his contact at the Pentagon? Was Ivy on the phone with the president right now?

"Tess?"

I sat up in bed. It took a moment for my eyes to adjust to the dark, but once they did, I could make out the outline of Vivvie's body in the doorway.

"You okay?" I asked. What a stupid question. Of course she wasn't okay.

"Can I . . ." Vivvie trailed off. She had a blanket draped over her shoulders.

"Can you what?"

Vivvie hovered in the doorway, like there was some kind of barrier physically keeping her out. "I just . . . *I don't want to be alone.*" Her voice was barely more than a whisper.

I propped myself up on my elbows. "Do you want to sleep in here?" My bed was big enough for both of us. "It's okay," I said when she didn't move. "There's plenty of room."

Vivvie shuffled to my bed. She climbed up on it, lying on top of the covers, still wrapped in her own blanket.

She wasn't the only one who didn't want to be alone.

Vivvie's eye was black the next morning. There was no way she could go to school, and there was no way I was leaving her alone with Ivy. My sister fixed problems *for a living*. I couldn't help thinking that if I left Vivvie here, I might come back to find her gone. Boarding school, maybe. Someplace safe. Someplace out of the way.

I lent Vivvie a set of clothes. When she went to shower, I went in search of Ivy. Downstairs, my sister had a cup of coffee in her hand and a phone pressed to her ear. I seriously doubted she'd slept the night before. "You owe me," she was telling the person on the other end of the phone line. "We won't go into the *how* and the *why*. Suffice it to say, you will get me what I need." A sharp smile cut across her features.

It wasn't a friendly smile.

"I knew we'd see eye to eye," she said. "Tell Caroline hello for me." Without waiting for a response, Ivy hung up. She turned, saw me, and studied me for a moment, cataloging my expression, the dark circles under my eyes. "How did you sleep?"

"Better than you."

Ivy put her phone in her back pocket and herded me into the kitchen, where she poured herself another cup of coffee, then poured me a glass of milk.

"I'd prefer the coffee," I said.

She gave me a look. "And I would have preferred it if you'd come to me."

So we're doing this now. The night before, she hadn't yelled at me. She hadn't dragged me over the coals.

"I did come to you," I said.

"Don't give me that, Tess." Ivy set her coffee down on the counter, a little harder than necessary. "The second Vivvie told you what she'd overheard, you should have come to me. What were you *thinking*?"

I was thinking that Vivvie had confided in me, not Ivy. I was thinking that if I told Ivy—if I told anyone—Vivvie might take it all back.

"I promised I'd help her figure out what was going on." I stared at the rim of my glass. "I keep my promises."

"And I don't," Ivy said softly. She turned away from me. I could see the tension in her shoulders, her back. "That's what this about? You're punishing me?"

For leaving me in Montana three years ago. For cutting me out. For never telling me why.

"This wasn't about you," I insisted.

"The hell it wasn't." She turned back around. "Do you have any idea what could have happened? To Vivvie? To you, calling that number?"

"You told me I could come to you," I said lowly. "With anything." I swallowed. "So I came to you. Maybe not the way you would have wanted me to, maybe not as soon as you wanted me to, but, Ivy, I came to *you*."

Those words hung in the air between us.

"Have you talked to the president yet?" I asked.

"I'm not discussing this with you." Ivy crossed to my side of the counter and stood directly in front of me, too close for comfort. "You have no part in this. Is that clear?"

Crystal.

Ivy wasn't done yet. "You can't tell anyone what you told me, Tess. Neither can Vivvie. Until we've got a handle on it, until we know exactly who's involved, we can't risk drawing attention to either one of you."

"Who's involved?" I repeated. "You think it wasn't just Judge Pierce and Vivvie's dad. You think there might be someone else." I paused. "The other number on the phone . . ."

Vivvie's father had made sure that Justice Marquette didn't leave the hospital alive. Pierce had paid him—or was going to pay him—to do it. What did that leave?

"The heart attack," I said, thinking out loud. "For the plan to work, they had to get Justice Marquette into surgery to begin with."

"I'm not doing this with you, Tess." Ivy caught my chin in her hand and forced my eyes to hers. "If there's something to be found here, I promise you that I will find it. I will keep you safe. I will keep Vivvie safe. I will make this okay. But I need you to stay out of it."

"Have you told the president?" I asked again.

"What part of 'I'm not doing this with you' was unclear?"

"You haven't told him, have you?" What was I supposed to read into that? "Vivvie's father is the president's doctor," I said sharply. "Don't you think he has a right to know the man might have homicidal tendencies?"

"I spoke with the Secret Service." Ivy clipped her words. "Major Bharani is no longer assigned to the White House."

The set of her jaw told me that was all she was going to say. When Ivy shut the door on something, it stayed shut.

"What's going to happen to Vivvie?" I asked. That, at least, she might tell me.

Ivy's face softened slightly. Her hand dropped to her side. "I'm working on it."

"Working on what?" Vivvie appeared in the doorway. Her hair was wet, her face a mottle of bruises, but she held her head back, her shoulders out.

"Just the girl I wanted to see." Ivy offered her a far friendlier look than the ones she'd been giving me. "If you're up to it, I have a couple of questions for you."

Vivvie's eyes flickered briefly over to mine. "I'm up to it."

"Tess?" Ivy arched an eyebrow in my direction. It took me a moment to realize that she was waiting for me to leave.

"But—"

"Theresa." Ivy didn't raise her voice, but the use of my full name spoke volumes.

"Go," Vivvie told me.

"If you want me to stay . . . ," I started to say.

"It's fine," Vivvie said quietly. "Just go."

CHAPTER 31

Vivvie wouldn't tell me much about what she and Ivy had talked about. "Your sister's just trying to establish a timeline," Vivvie said when I asked her. "How my father got involved, when he got involved, how he and Pierce know each other, *if* they know each other."

"And?" I said.

"And," Vivvie hedged, "I answered her questions."

She wouldn't say anything else. My sister wanted me out of this. Ivy Kendrick excelled at getting what she wanted.

That night, Vivvie slept in my room again. The next morning, I woke up alone. *She's probably just downstairs*, I told myself. I threw on clothes. No Vivvie in the living room. No Vivvie in the kitchen, the foyer . . .

"She's not here."

I turned toward the sound of Bodie's voice. " 'She' as in Ivy, or 'she' as in Vivvie?"

Bodie took in the expression on my face. "Your sister's out," he said, hooking his thumbs in the pockets of his jeans. "Little Viv's gone."

"What do you mean, *gone*?"

Bodie held up his hands in a mea culpa. "Bad choice of words. She's fine. She's just not here."

"Where is she?" I asked flatly.

"Viv's in good hands, kiddo," Bodie said. "Scout's honor."

In other words: this was need-to-know, and I didn't.

"Where's Ivy?" I asked. She'd found someplace to stash Vivvie and left Bodie to break the news to me.

"She and Captain Pentagon had an errand to run." Bodie's answer was cryptic. I tried to figure out what kind of "errand" Adam and Ivy might be running this early in the morning, but came up empty.

"Catch." Bodie tossed his cell phone at me. I caught it. "Number's already cued up. If you're worried about Little V, call it."

I took that to mean that Bodie would rather clue me in on Vivvie's location than Ivy's. I stored that fact away for future reference, then made the call.

Vivvie answered. "I'm fine," she said, instead of *hello*. "Ivy didn't want me to wake you."

What Ivy wanted, Ivy got.

"Where are you?" I asked Vivvie. "What did Ivy do?"

"She found someplace for me to go."

Vivvie had an aunt. Her father's younger sister. Vivvie had never even met the woman until this morning. Now she was living with her.

Courtesy of Ivy.

"Don't do anything I wouldn't do." Bodie made an attempt at levity as he pulled past the Hardwicke gates to drop me off. "For that matter, you might want to stay away from about ninety percent of the things I *would* do, too."

Vivvie wasn't coming back to school until Monday—time for her bruises to heal, and time for her to get to know the relative Ivy had summoned up out of nowhere, like a magician pulling a rabbit out of a hat.

I didn't have the option of staying home from school another day. My sister wanted me out of the way. She wanted me *safe*. And as it so happened, Hardwicke was more secure than most consulates.

Bodie pulled up to the curb. I was out of the car before he could impart any more words of wisdom. He rolled down his window. "Hey, kid?"

I turned back to look at him. His lips parted in a smile, but there was a serious glint in his dark eyes. "Mum's the word."

In other words: *Don't tell anyone about Vivvie's dad. Or Judge Pierce. Or Justice Marquette.*

Unfortunately, *anyone* hunted me down before my first class.

"What happened?" Asher asked, falling into step beside me. "Where were you yesterday? Where was Vivvie?" When I didn't reply immediately, Asher tried another tack. "True or false: you're going to tell me what happened."

"False," I said.

He gave me a morose look and lowered his voice to a stage whisper. "The correct answer was *true*."

Asher sounded like he was joking, but my gut told me he wasn't. This wasn't some lark to him. It was personal, and if I tried to shut him out, he would do something about it.

Like tell Henry.

Mum's the word.

"Short version?" I told Asher as we approached the classroom. "My sister knows. About Vivvie, about the phone, about everything."

"And the long version?" Asher asked.

"Vivvie's father found out about the phone." That much I could tell him without compromising Ivy's investigation—whatever that investigation entailed. "She showed up at my place two nights ago with a fat lip and the beginning of a black eye."

"Is she—"

"She's going to be fine," I said. "Physically. But Vivvie and I are done. Out of it. Off the case." I entered the classroom with Asher on my heels. I could feel him getting ready to pounce—another question I couldn't answer, another look that told me he *knew* I was holding back. Then Asher's eyes landed on Henry, sitting near the front of the room, his head bowed over a book.

Asher wouldn't keep asking questions in earshot of his best friend.

I slid into the seat next to Henry, all too aware that Asher knew exactly what I was doing.

"True or false," he whispered into the back of my head as he took the seat behind me. "We aren't done talking about this."

I could almost hear him thinking that of all the people in the world who Henry Marquette might trust to find out what had happened to his grandfather, my sister wasn't near the top of the list.

In fact, it was a good bet that Ivy wasn't on that list at all.

CHAPTER 32

"I assume you've made progress with your half of the assignment?" Henry Marquette sat opposite me in World Issues, a thick file folder open on the table between us. Clearly, he'd done *his* half of the assignment.

"You know what they say about assumptions," I said.

Henry quirked an eyebrow at me. "Tell me, Kendrick, what *do* they say about assumptions?"

"It's Tess."

"Is that your way of telling me that you did *not* screen the candidates on your half of the list?" Henry asked me. "*Tess*."

"Actually," I said. "I looked into them." He didn't need to know what exactly I'd looked for—or why I'd been looking.

"And?"

And there's reason to think Judge Pierce paid to have your grandfather killed.

"And," I said, "I wasn't really that impressed."

Henry's lips ticked slightly upward. "I get the sense that you might be a hard girl to impress."

That almost sounded like a compliment.

Henry seemed to realize that, too. "In all likelihood," he said abruptly, thumbing through the file he'd compiled and tearing his eyes away from mine, "we're looking for someone on the court of appeals—DC circuit is most likely, but I wouldn't rule any of the others out."

My mind went immediately to Judge Pierce. Was he on the court of appeals?

Ivy told me to stay out of it, I thought. But she could hardly blame me for doing a school assignment, now, could she? As Henry briefly outlined the credentials of his top couple of candidates, I pulled Pierce's information up on my laptop. I stared at the photograph that popped up. He was balding, in his early fifties. He stared back at me from the screen: deep-set eyes, solemn expression, a face you could trust.

You'll get your money when I get my nomination.

I forced my eyes away from the photo and read. Pierce had a seat on the Court of Appeals for the Ninth Circuit. Prior to that, he'd served as the attorney general for the state of Arizona.

"Pierce." Asher came up behind me and peered over my shoulder. "An interesting choice, to be sure."

I forced my face to stay perfectly neutral. Asher was clearly fishing for information—and not about the assignment. I closed the window.

"Don't you have your own project to be working on?" Henry asked Asher mildly.

"Indeed I do," Asher replied, his eyes still on me. "Sadly, however, my partner is absent. Woe be to the Asher who is forced to work on his own."

"I mourn for you," Henry said dryly.

"So what *do* we know about Pierce?" Asher ignored Henry's sarcastic tone and helped himself to the chair next to mine. He leaned over, plunking his elbows down on my desk.

"Nothing," I said, reaching for one of the papers in Henry's file.

Asher gave me a look. "Somehow, I find myself doubting that's true."

I felt Henry's eyes on us then. I gave Asher a *look*.

"Vivvie Bharani has been absent for over a week." Emilia didn't bother with a hello. She slid into the seat next to Henry's. "Last year, she was the only person in our grade other than me to have perfect attendance. Am I the only one who finds that strange?"

"Is that an expression of concern?" Asher asked his twin, arching an eyebrow at her.

"I can be concerned," Emilia told him, sounding almost insulted. "I'm a very empathetic person."

Asher and Henry exchanged a glance over her head. Clearly, empathy had *never* been Emilia's strong suit.

"I heard Vivvie's father got fired," Emilia continued bluntly.

I darted a glance at Asher.

"And where might you have heard that?" he asked.

"From a freshman whose mom works at the *Washington Post*."

The idea of people knowing that Vivvie's father had lost his position at the White House made me queasy.

"I mean, technically, he wasn't fired," Emilia clarified. "He was reassigned. But precision of language has never been the gossip mill's forte, and I guess anything's a pretty big step down after the White House."

Henry stood up abruptly. "Whatever position her father has or does not have, can we agree that has little to nothing to do with Vivvie?"

Emilia blanched as if he'd slapped her. "I thought you'd want to know."

"Why would I?" Henry replied. His voice was calm, but I could see the tension in his neck. He had to have noticed the timing: Vivvie's dad getting demoted shortly after operating on his grandfather.

Henry came around to my side of the table and slammed a piece of paper down in front of me. "My choice for nominee." Without waiting for a reply, he turned and stalked toward the front of the room. I heard him ask Dr. Clark for permission to go to the bathroom.

Emilia shot Asher a bewildered look. "What was that?"

I moved to follow Henry. At my Montana high school, teachers guarded bathroom passes like they were the keys to the proverbial kingdom, but Hardwicke didn't even *have* passes. Dr. Clark just let me go.

I caught up to Henry just as he reached the bathroom door.

"Can I help you?" he asked without turning around.

I didn't reply immediately. Henry stood there, perfectly comfortable with the silence, until I broke it. "Thank you," I said. "For standing up for Vivvie."

Henry looked distinctly uncomfortable with my thanks. "It is possible," he admitted, his voice taut, "that I know what it is like to have your family be the featured story on Hardwicke's gossip circuit."

If what we suspected was true, if it got out, Henry and Vivvie wouldn't just be the subject of gossip at Hardwicke. Their families would be front-page news.

"It is also possible," Henry continued, his back still to me, "that I suspect you might have had something to do with Vivvie's father's demotion."

Henry was connecting the dots—too much, too fast. *How?* "Not everything is my fault," I told him.

"Believe it or not, that wasn't meant as criticism." Henry turned to face me. "My mother breakfasts at the Roosevelt Hotel." He waited for those words to register, but they meant nothing to me. "She thought she saw Vivvie there. This morning."

It took me a moment to read between the lines. If Henry's mother had seen Vivvie, she'd seen Vivvie's bruises.

"I knew something was wrong. At the wake." Henry's jaw tightened. "I just didn't know what."

He'd seen Vivvie break down. Maybe he'd noticed her absence since.

"I knew something was wrong," he said again, "and I did nothing. I was so focused on my own grief—"

"Pretty sure that at a wake for a loved one, you're allowed to be focused on your own grief," I told him.

I could feel him rejecting that logic. She was a classmate. She'd needed help. He'd missed it. Henry Marquette wasn't a forgiving person—especially of himself.

"It is possible," Henry said, his voice still sounding oddly formal, "that I might have misjudged you, Tess."

He knew Vivvie's dad was abusive. He thought I'd helped her. He thought I was the reason her father was no longer the president's doctor.

That's not even the half of it. I couldn't tell him. It made me angry that I wanted to. It chafed that I *cared* that he'd misjudged me—and, more than anything, I could feel guilt nipping at my heels, ready to devour me whole for keeping the truth from him, for forcing his best friend to keep it from him.

"It's possible," I told him sharply, pushing down the mess of emotions churning in my gut and pulling back from the boy who'd caused them, "that I don't really care whether you misjudge me or not."

CHAPTER 33

That night, Ivy left me to my own devices. It was like she thought that by avoiding me, she could somehow make me magically forget everything I already knew about Justice Marquette's death.

Fat chance of that happening.

Hardwicke was a small school. There were fewer than a hundred kids in my entire grade. I couldn't turn around without seeing Henry. Vivvie's empty seat in English class the next morning was just another reminder.

I dredged my way from English to physics and from physics to Speaking of Words, trying not to think about the big questions.

Who did the second number on the disposable cell belong to?

Why hadn't Ivy gone straight to the president with our suspicions?

"Tess." The Speaking of Words teacher zeroed in on me within moments of the bell's ringing. "Do you have something prepared for us?"

It was Friday. I'd been at Hardwicke for two weeks. It was probably too much to hope that the teachers would continue skipping over me indefinitely.

"Almost," I lied through my teeth. Mr. Wesley—who was sixty if he was a day—didn't call me on it. He just gave me a long, assessing look, then asked for a volunteer.

The assignment was an eight- to ten-minute "persuasive speech" on a controversial topic. Icelandic, never-turns-down-a-dare Di volunteered to go first, followed by a boy whose name I didn't know, followed by Henry. The last speech of the day came from John Thomas Wilcox. He'd rigged a projector to throw pictures onto the whiteboard as he talked. His topic was stem cell research. I wasn't paying much attention until he flashed a picture of my grandfather up on the board.

"Alzheimer's disease is progressive, debilitating, and ultimately fatal."

I stopped breathing and had to force myself to start again.

The picture was maybe five years old. I couldn't tell where it was from, because John Thomas had cropped the photo close up on the face. *Hazel eyes. Lips set in a firm line.* My grandfather's skin was tan and weatherworn. No one but me would have seen the softness in his expression: the warmth in his eyes, the humor dancing around the edges of that nonsmile.

"Let me tell you about this man," John Thomas said. As he continued, each word sliced into me, like a dull knife forcibly carving up flesh.

We'd been told to personalize our arguments, to appeal to emotions, as well as reason. From an outside perspective, that was exactly what John Thomas was doing. He was using a real human example to make his audience care.

This man was degenerating. *This* man was losing his memory. *This* man was going to continue losing cognitive capacity and parts of himself until he died.

John Thomas took us through it in excruciating detail. And the entire time, he was staring straight at me. "Imagine the pain of knowing that someone you loved was going to degenerate to the point where they would lose the ability to walk, to talk, to communicate in any meaningful way." John Thomas's expression was so solemn, so impassioned, but his eyes—his eyes gleamed. "Now imagine the months—or maybe even years—leading up to that. Imagine someone you loved forgetting you, not even recognizing you, *blaming* you . . ."

At first, I thought the room was shaking. Then I realized that I was. I couldn't tear my eyes away from my grandfather's picture. I'd known, objectively, that his condition was going to get worse. I'd *known* that—

My fingers dug into the sides of my desk.

"Stem cell research won't provide a cure for Alzheimer's," John Thomas was saying. "But it might allow for treatments that stave off the inevitable brain cell death. And if it can buy precious days, months, even years with a loved one . . ." He changed the picture on the screen.

Gramps, with his arms around me.

"I'd say it's worth it. Wouldn't you?" John Thomas mimicked compassion perfectly as he nodded toward me—as if I'd known he was doing this, as if he'd done this *for* me instead of *to* me.

My ears rang. I barely heard Mr. Wesley dismissing the class. I bowed my head as I gathered my things, my jaw clenched so hard it hurt. I pushed my way out of the classroom. I made it to my locker, opened it, and leaned forward, shutting out the noise. *Degeneration. Inevitable. Fatal.* I couldn't block out those words.

"My father told me about your grandfather." Without warning, John Thomas was there beside me, his expression morose. He crowded me, bringing his face down to mine. "I hope you don't mind that I did a little internet sleuthing for some photos. The visuals really make the presentation." I tried to back away, but there was nowhere to go. He leaned into me, his lips so close to my ear that I could feel his breath on my face as he whispered, "*My condolences.*"

I could hear the smile in his voice.

Something inside me snapped. My hand balled itself into a fist, but just as I started to swing, there was, without warning, nothing to swing *at*. John Thomas wasn't where he'd been standing a second before.

It took me a second to register the fact that he was on the floor, and another second after that to realize that the person who'd helped him onto the floor was Henry Marquette.

"My apologies," Henry said. The expression on his face was oh so proper and oh so polite, considering he'd just knocked the other boy's legs out from beneath him. "I didn't see you standing there, John Thomas." He reached down and offered John Thomas a hand. "Let me help you up."

He held on to John Thomas's hand a little longer than necessary—and, I was guessing from the expression on John Thomas's face, a little *harder* than necessary.

Once he had his hand back, John Thomas gave Henry a look that was just as proper, just as polite. "You, too?" he said. "I knew Tess here was, shall we say, *servicing* Asher, but I had no idea she offered a two-for-one deal."

For one horrifying moment, I thought Henry might actually punch him. "I'd defend your honor, Henry," I cut in, "but he's not worth it."

Henry gave a curt nod. "His own father would be the first to tell you—he's not worth much."

John Thomas's veneer of control evaporated the moment Henry said the word *father*. He lunged at Henry, slamming him back into the locker. This time I really did come to Henry's defense.

Some people just *need* to be flying tackled.

"Would any of you care to explain your behavior to me?" Headmaster Raleigh glared at the three of us from the other side of his desk. I was sitting to his left, John Thomas to his right. Henry was in the middle.

"I believe someone must have spilled something in the hallway," Henry said. "It was terribly slippery."

He had quite possibly the best poker face of anyone I'd ever seen.

"You expect me to believe you fell?" the headmaster said.

"Well, first John Thomas fell," Henry said diplomatically. "Then I helped him up. Then I fell. I think that must have thrown Tess off balance." Henry offered the headmaster the same polite smile he'd given John Thomas. "She fell last."

"Ms. Kendrick?" Headmaster Raleigh raised an eyebrow at me.

I adopted an expression that mirrored Henry's. "I do believe Henry is right. I fell last."

The headmaster was not amused. He turned his attention to John Thomas. "If you would prefer we talk alone . . . ," he started to say.

"No." John Thomas's voice was stiff. "There must have been something on the floor. We slipped."

John Thomas Wilcox might have been a psychotic jerk, but he was a psychotic jerk who didn't want any blemishes on his permanent record.

The headmaster clearly did not believe us, but just as clearly, he didn't seem to fancy the idea of dealing with any of our parents. So instead, he launched into a lecture on personal responsibility, which I tuned out approximately five seconds in.

My eyes drifted to the photograph on the wall behind him—the same one I'd noticed the last time I was here. Six men: three in the back row, two in the front, one off to the side. I recognized William Keyes. But this time, I also recognized the man standing beside Headmaster Raleigh. *Balding. Early fifties. Deep-set eyes.*

Judge Pierce.

And in front of Pierce stood Vivvie's father.

CHAPTER 34

I needed to get another look at that picture. *The president's physician. An appeals court judge from Arizona.* The idea of them being in the same place at the same time, in that small of a group . . .

Your sister's just trying to establish a timeline, Vivvie had told me. *How my father got involved, when he got involved, how he and Pierce know each other,* if *they know each other.*

I wanted to know when that picture had been taken, where it had been taken. I wanted to know who else was in it. And I wanted to know what Adam's father had been doing there.

And that meant that I needed to arrange another visit to the headmaster's office.

"You look like someone who's thinking deep thoughts." Asher slid in beside me at lunch. "Deep thoughts about telling me what you've spent the past two days *not* telling me, perhaps?"

Asher probably wasn't expecting an answer, but I gave him one. "When I called the second number on that phone, someone answered. I know who it was, and I might have found a clue that could tell us how that person and Vivvie's father know each other."

"This new, forthcoming Tess is a strange and wonderful thing," Asher remarked. "Should I be suspicious?"

I answered his question with a question. "How good are you at getting sent to the headmaster's office for something that won't actually get you expelled?"

Asher smiled beatifically, as if he'd been waiting his whole life for someone to ask just that question. "How would you feel about some Mentos and Diet Coke?"

As it turned out, the Hardwicke administration was not terribly fond of explosions. Asher and I sat outside the headmaster's office, awaiting judgment.

The headmaster's assistant shook her head at the two of us. "Weren't you just in here a few hours ago?" she asked me.

I did my best to look ashamed—and probably failed miserably. She turned her attention to my companion. "Asher Rhodes. What are we going to do with you?"

"Win me over with patience and gentle correction?" Asher suggested.

In retrospect, I probably should have taken the fall for this particular explosion myself, but I needed to get a good look at the photo on Raleigh's wall, and that meant that I needed someone to distract the headmaster while I did it.

"Mr. Rhodes?" Headmaster Raleigh appeared at the door to his office. "I'll see you first."

Asher and I glanced at each other. The plan required us to go in together.

"Ladies first," Asher said. "I insist."

The headmaster sighed. "All right," he capitulated. "Ms. Kendrick, I'll see you first."

"Don't you think that's kind of sexist?" I asked the secretary. She froze.

"I'm sure it's not," she said, not sounding sure in the least.

"Chivalry isn't sexist," Asher told me.

"If you're suggesting that females need special treatment *because* they're female," I replied, "it kind of is."

Headmaster Raleigh still hadn't quite recovered from the accusation of sexism. "Asher," he started to say. Then he changed his mind. "Tess." He scowled. "Both of you, my office, now."

The headmaster turned around. Asher winked at me, then followed the man into his office. I entered the room last and closed the door behind us. Immediately, my eyes found the picture I was looking for on the wall.

William Keyes. Judge Pierce. Major Bharani. A glare off the picture frame made it difficult for me to see any of them clearly.

"Ms. Kendrick, are you listening to me?" Headmaster Raleigh asked.

Not in the least. "Yes, sir." The *sir* seemed to appease him somewhat.

"We have a zero tolerance policy for weapons here at Hardwicke," the man continued.

"Can it really be considered a weapon if you can eat it?" I asked.

"Or drink it," Asher added.

"If it explodes, it's a weapon," the headmaster declared. "I'm afraid the two of you have put me in a very difficult position."

"I can only imagine," Asher said consolingly. "You'll probably have to suspend me from the lacrosse team."

The headmaster hesitated slightly.

"And," I added, "I'm sure you're going to want to talk this incident over with my sister."

"You'll probably have to field all kinds of answers about the contents of Hardwicke's vending machines," Asher continued solemnly. "If only we'd considered the ramifications before deciding on this as our Yates Fellowship entry."

"Yates Fellowship?" the headmaster repeated.

"I came in second last year," Asher replied. "They appreciate the ability to walk the line between scientific exploration and performance art—but this was really inexcusable. I *thought* setting up outside would be enough to mitigate any administrative concern, but clearly, I should have checked with someone."

"Yes," the headmaster said sternly, "you should have."

Asher and I sat quietly.

"Do you think they'll have to review security protocols?" I asked meekly. "If you consider the Mentos *weaponized* . . ."

"Oh God." Asher turned to me, wide-eyed. "What if the media gets ahold of it?"

The headmaster stood suddenly, as if sitting had become severely uncomfortable. He walked toward the window and stared out, clearly aggrieved. Asher gestured to me, and I nodded, slipping my phone out of my bag. I took a picture of the photo on the wall. A quick glance at my phone told me the glare was a problem. I glanced over at the headmaster.

"I'm a reasonable man," Headmaster Raleigh said, still staring out the window. "I hope I've impressed upon you how serious this is . . ."

I leaned to the side and tried to get a picture from a different angle as the headmaster droned on. The glare was still there. I rose up slightly on the balls of my feet, my butt leaving the chair, as I leaned over farther.

The second after I snapped the photo, the headmaster started turning back to face us. I thrust my phone into my pocket and tried to retake my seat. Asher thought fast and opted for a distraction: he leaned back in his chair and toppled over, yowling like a cat in a tub full of ice water.

Headmaster Raleigh startled. I leapt to Asher's side.

"Don't sue!" I yelled.

"Sue?" Raleigh repeated in horror.

"Where am I?" moaned Asher.

Mission complete.

CHAPTER 35

Ivy picked me up after school, which I took to be a bad sign. Worse, she'd driven herself.

"Probation?" she said, the second I got in the car. "You've been at the school less than two weeks, and you're already on probation?"

She started to pull out of the parking lot, and I hastily buckled my seat belt, remembering what Adam had said about her driving.

"What were you thinking?" she demanded.

Somehow, *I was gathering intel on a political conspiracy you told me to stay away from* didn't slide right off the tongue.

"You know what's going on right now, Tess. You know what I'm working on. Do you really think I have time to be dealing with some teenage discipline problem?"

That cut deeper than I would have expected. "I wasn't trying to be a problem."

"Can you at least tell me why?" Ivy's voice was terse. "Is it because you feel like I'm ignoring you? Are you angry about the way I took care of Vivvie's situation?"

"It wasn't about *you*."

"I have been trying *so hard*, Tess." Ivy's voice was softer now. "And I thought—" She cut herself off, then cut someone off in traffic. A horn blared behind us. "I thought we were doing okay. I thought you were starting to trust me. I thought . . ."

My eyes stung. I wasn't sure if the tears were because she was acting like I'd crossed some uncrossable line or because a big part of me couldn't help *wanting* to get somewhere with Ivy, *wanting* things to be like they used to be.

Wanting them to be better.

"Sorry if I'm complicating your life." I stared out the windshield, my eyes on the road. *It only hurts if you let it*. I pushed back against the emotions building inside of me.

"Tessie," Ivy said.

I stared down at my lap, willing myself not to care. *It's Tess*.

Ivy's grip tightened around the steering wheel. "Nothing is more important to me than you are."

I felt like she'd slammed a knife into my gut. I pressed my palms flat against my stomach. I couldn't do this. Not with her. We sank into silence like a drowning man sinks into water. Neither one of us could come up for air.

"I love you." Ivy chose those three words to break the silence. "Whether you believe that or not, whether you even hear me saying it or not, I do. You're my . . ."

Sister, I thought, the muscles in my throat clenching. For so long, that word had come tangled with meanings.

"You're my family, Tess. And family isn't something I have ever been good at. I wasn't a good daughter. I haven't been a good granddaughter. But I am trying to be the kind of sister you deserve." Ivy pulled onto her street and slowed. "Consider yourself grounded."

"Grounded?" I repeated incredulously.

Ivy pulled into the driveway. "Don't plan on going anywhere for the next two weeks." By the time she finished that sentence, her attention was clearly elsewhere. I followed her gaze to a dark-colored sedan across the street.

"Stay in the car," she told me, unbuckling her seat belt.

A second later, she was standing in the driveway, and William Keyes was striding toward her, like this was his house and she was the visitor.

My hand went to the door handle. *Ivy told me to stay in the car.* I pulled the handle and cracked the door open. *She never said I couldn't listen from here.*

William Keyes had the kind of voice that carried. "We need to talk."

"You need to leave." Ivy's voice went up on the last word.

"I thought we'd reached an understanding. When the president came to you for your thoughts on Edmund Pierce, you were supposed to back him."

Keyes wants Pierce to get the nomination. My mind raced. I thought about the photo on my phone. William Keyes had been there—wherever *there* was—with Pierce and Vivvie's father. My hand curled tighter around the door handle.

"I never agreed to anything," Ivy told the older man calmly. I wondered if she suspected him of being involved. I wondered if *Adam* suspected him.

"You were supposed to get your president in line." Keyes clearly meant those words as an indictment.

"He's your president, too," Ivy replied.

"No," Keyes barked out. "He is not, nor will he ever be, *my* president. You're the one who put him in that office."

"He won both the electoral college and the popular vote."

Keyes scowled. "You *got* him the electoral college and the popular vote!" He balled his hands into fists. His index finger escaped, and he pointed it at Ivy. "I taught you everything I knew, I lifted you up from nothing, I treated you like a *daughter*, and you thanked me by putting a man I despise in the White House."

Ivy adopted an icy countenance. "We came down on the opposite sides of a primary, William. You're the one who told me not to come back if I left. You don't get to come here now and ask me for favors."

"I damn well do!" Keyes shook his fist, like he was pounding a phantom table.

A car door slammed nearby, and they turned in unison.

"The front lawn?" Georgia Nolan stopped several feet from them, flanked by Secret Service. "That's the location you choose for this discussion? Really, William?"

For a moment, William Keyes was struck silent. His gaze lingered on Georgia. I craned my neck, trying to get a look at her face.

They know each other. It was there, in the way he looked at her. *They know each other very well.*

"We both know the Judiciary Committee will look more kindly on Pierce than some of his contemporaries." Keyes recovered his voice. It was quieter than the one he'd used with Ivy, but just as authoritative.

"Thank you," Georgia said, her tone dripping honey, "for your advice and counsel. We will certainly take that into consideration."

That was a dismissal, as clear as if Georgia had ordered him off the lawn.

Keyes straightened his tie, then issued a parting shot. "It's a pity about the doctor," he said. "When a man kills himself over being removed from his position at the White House, that doesn't look very good for the administration."

"It is a tragedy," Georgia said tersely. "Our thoughts are with Major Bharani's family."

I felt the blood rushing out of my head. My hands went numb. *It's a pity about the doctor.*

"Major Bharani is dead?" Ivy said. "When?"

Neither the First Lady nor Adam's father answered. Their eyes were locked on to each other.

Vivvie's father is dead. He killed Justice Marquette, and now he's dead.

Keyes finally ripped his eyes from Georgia's and turned to Ivy. "You never did have the stomach for this business," he told her.

Then he walked away—past her, past Georgia, past the car.

I leaned into the car door, pushing it open. One second I was inside the car, the next, I was standing beside it, separated from William Keyes by the body of the sedan and nothing else. When his eyes landed on me, they opened wider.

He hadn't realized I was here.

Neither had the First Lady.

"Tess, dear," Georgia started to say, but my gaze was locked on Keyes.

"How did he die?" The words came out in a whisper. *Vivvie's father killed Justice Marquette, and now he's dead.* My hand tightened around the door, like my grip was the only thing keeping me vertical.

"William," Ivy and Georgia said in one voice, Ivy stepping toward me, Georgia toward Keyes.

Keyes looked at them, then back at me. "He put a bullet in his own head."

CHAPTER 36

I was still standing there, my fingers digging into the metal door, when Keyes got into his car and drove off. Then Ivy was next to me, her hand on my shoulder.

"I'm sorry you had to hear that," she said.

Vivvie's dad was dead. He was dead. *He put a bullet in his own head.*

"Vivvie's dad killed himself." There was no filter between my brain and my mouth—only that sentence, repeated in stereo. "We did this."

Ivy reached out and placed her own hand on the door near mine. I didn't realize until she steadied it that both the door and my hand had been shaking.

"This is not our fault," she told me, her voice steady. "It's not yours. It's not mine."

Wasn't it?

"He must have known," I said, my throat clenching. "That we were on to him. That things were going to get bad." I couldn't stop picturing Vivvie. *Smiling Vivvie, beaming at me over bagels the first day.*

I couldn't stop picturing her father, picking up that gun.

"We'll talk about this later," Ivy said quietly.

"Vivvie," I said, barely hearing her. "I need to call Vivvie. She's the one who told us about her father. She's going to think this is her fault."

A few feet away, Georgia Nolan turned her head slightly to one side, her eyebrows arching upward as she processed our exchange. "I get the very real sense that I am missing something here." Georgia stepped toward us. "Did you have something to do with Major Bharani's reassignment, Ivy?"

It hit me then why Ivy wanted to talk about this *later*. Georgia didn't know—about Vivvie's dad, about Judge Pierce. About any of it. Ivy hadn't told her.

You can't tell anyone what you told me, Tess. Ivy's warning echoed in my mind. *Until we've got a handle on it, until we know exactly who's involved, we can't risk drawing attention to either one of you.*

I thought of Georgia saying that Justice Marquette's death was an *opportunity, tragic though it may be*.

"There was a situation with Bharani's daughter." Beside me, Ivy was answering Georgia's question. "I intervened."

She's not telling Georgia about Justice Marquette. She's not telling her about Pierce.

"Ivy?" My voice shook with everything I wasn't saying: *Why aren't you telling Georgia everything? Why didn't you tell the president the second we told you?*

"This was a mistake." Ivy ran a hand roughly through her hair as she took in the look on my face. "Your life here was supposed to be normal, Tess." And then, more to herself than to me: "Adam was right. I never should have brought you here."

I didn't realize until she said those words that I'd been waiting to hear her say them since the moment I saw the bedroom she'd saved for me. Nausea rose in the back of my throat.

Vivvie's father was dead, and my sister was keeping secrets from the president and the First Lady, and Ivy thought bringing me here was a mistake.

Just like that, I was thirteen years old again. *She asked me to live with her, and then she left.* I tried so hard not to let myself remember. I tried so hard not to hurt—to push against any weakness, to *fight* it, to go numb.

I can't be here. I can't do this.

I couldn't let Ivy see me cry.

I bolted—down the driveway, past Georgia's Secret Service escort. I heard Ivy calling after me, but I just kept running. My feet slapped the pavement. I needed out. I needed *away*. Ivy still had the First Lady to deal with. She couldn't follow me.

I ran faster. Wind-in-my-hair, nothing-can-touch-me, muscles-burning *faster*.

I had no idea where I was going. I ran until I couldn't run anymore, and then I bent over at the waist, heaving in and out, my breath scalding my lungs. My cell phone rang from inside my pocket.

I realized on some level that the phone had *been* ringing. I pulled it out, but didn't answer. Eventually, it stopped ringing. I waited for it to ring again. Instead, it informed me that Ivy had left me a message.

I started moving again, concentrating on the rhythm of my steps, the push and pull of my muscles.

I didn't want to listen to Ivy's message. What could she say? That we *needed to talk*? That she had her reasons for keeping everyone, even the president and Georgia, in the dark? That bringing me here *hadn't* been a mistake?

That Vivvie's father hadn't killed himself because of something we'd done?

Feeling numb, I turned my phone over in my hand. For the longest time, I just stared at it, and then my clumsy fingers found their way to the keypad. I called the number Bodie had given me the day before—for Vivvie.

It rang until the voice mail picked up. I couldn't find any words, certainly not the right ones.

I hung up.

An hour passed. Maybe two. Every once in a while, the phone rang. *Ivy. Adam. Bodie.* And then, finally, a number I didn't recognize. I hesitated. Probably, it was Ivy. Probably, I should just let it ring.

But what if it was Vivvie?

I answered. "Hello?" My throat was dry, and my voice sounded it.

"Tess!" It took me a minute to place the voice. "Tessssss." The second time Asher said my name, he stretched it out.

"Asher?" I raised my eyebrows at the phone. "Are you drunk?"

"High on life," he declared. "And possibly piña coladas." Then he murmured something incomprehensible. There was a tussling sound on the other end of the phone line. I heard Asher yelp, and a second later, a new voice came on the line.

"Asher is a bit indisposed at the moment."

Henry.

"Isn't it a little early in the day to start partying?" I asked, hoping Henry couldn't hear the hoarseness in my tone.

"Asher has . . . ups and downs." Henry chose his words carefully. I thought of Asher, telling me he'd climbed to the top of the chapel because the higher you were, the smaller everyone else got. "Are *you* all right?"

So much for hoping I could pass for normal. "I'm fine."

Henry was too polite to call me a liar. His silence did that for him. "Your sister called Asher's phone," he said finally.

"She what?"

"She called to see if he'd seen or heard from you. We gathered that you'd pulled a bit of a disappearing act." He paused. "Or rather, I gathered, and Asher serenaded her with some kind of eighties medley."

I tried not to think too hard about any part of that statement.

"She gave Asher your number. God knows how he managed to remember it."

"Tess?" Asher was back on the phone, sounding slightly— though not significantly—more sober. "Was your sister calling about The Thing?" I heard him stage-whisper to Henry, *"There's a thing."*

Henry's grandfather was dead. So was Vivvie's father. My sister thought bringing me to live with her was a mistake, and Asher was getting ready to let the cat out of the bag with Henry. Everything was unraveling—most of all me. I felt useless. Helpless and useless and *weak*.

"Vivvie's dad killed himself." My mouth seemed set on saying the words out loud—like saying them proved something. Like if I forced myself to *feel* this, it might give me some level of power over the pain.

"Poor Vivvie," Asher mumbled. "First her dad kills Theo, then he kills himself."

It took exactly three seconds for Henry to take the phone back from Asher.

"Tess," he said, his voice straining against his vocal cords. "What is Asher talking about?"

My mouth opened, but words wouldn't come out.

"Tess?"

This time, I managed to form a coherent sentence. "Henry, can you pick me up?" My heart thudded against my rib cage. "We need to talk."

CHAPTER 37

Henry Marquette drove a hybrid. When he pulled up to the curb next to me, Asher was sprawled across the backseat, leaving me no choice but to crawl into the front. As I shut the door, I caught sight of my reflection in the window. My hair was falling out of its ponytail, flyaway pieces stuck to my forehead with sweat. I couldn't make out enough of my face to tell if it betrayed how close I'd come to crying.

No more. I was done with this. Tears were useless. Crying was useless. I focused on Henry—and the unalterable fact that I was *screwed*.

From the second I saw the set of Henry's features—the tense jaw, the down-turned lips, the eyes that betrayed the mix of emotions swirling in his chest—I knew that I wouldn't be able to lie to him. Henry wasn't a *problem*. He wasn't a fire to be put out, or a situation to be handled.

He had a right to know.

"Someone once cautioned me against making assumptions," he said. He had a death grip on the wheel, his eyes locked on the road. "So you're not going to make me assume, Tess. You're going to tell me if that was just the piña coladas talking, or if Asher . . ."

Was telling the truth. My brain finished his sentence as if it were my own.

I swallowed, then summoned my voice. "Four days ago," I said quietly, "Vivvie Bharani told me that she thought her father had killed a patient."

"My grandfather." Henry's Adam's apple bobbed in his throat.

I nodded, even though he wasn't looking at me—*wouldn't* look at me.

"Talk," Henry said roughly. "Every detail, every suspicion, every single thing you know, Tess."

The phone. The voice on the other end. That voice's identity. I told Henry everything. Not just for him. For me. I kept picturing Vivvie's father lifting a gun to his temple. I kept picturing his blood splattered on a wall.

Secrets came at a cost.

So I told Henry. Maybe a part of me wanted his anger. I wanted him to lash out. I wanted him to blame me, the way I blamed myself.

"Asher knew?" Henry almost choked on those words. I glanced back at Asher—self-destructive, *loyal* Asher, who'd been Henry's best friend since they were kids.

"He wanted to tell you."

I could see Henry thinking, *But he didn't.* "I don't suppose it occurred to any of you—or to your sister, for that matter—to take this to the police." That wasn't a question. It was an accusation.

"Ivy's working on it." That was all I could say, all she'd told me.

"You might trust your sister to *work on* this," Henry said, his voice soft, with a lethal thread of steel. "But I most certainly do not."

A fuller understanding of what my telling Henry meant slammed into me like a semitruck broadsiding a car. Henry despised Ivy's occupation. He believed that when she "fixed" things, she left destruction in her wake. I'd known he wouldn't be able to sit on this information. I'd *known* that, and I'd told him everything anyway.

Because I had to.

"Do what you have to do," I told Henry, "but remember that if it wasn't for Vivvie, none of us would know what really happened. She's the only reason there's anything to *work on*, and it cost her everything."

Her father. Her home. The naive certainty that there were people in this world that you could count on not to blacken your eyes.

I leaned forward, so that I could see all of Henry's face, so that out of his peripheral vision, he might catch a hint of mine. "Whatever you do with this information," I told him, "whoever *you* trust with it, you better make sure they can protect her."

Ivy hadn't even told the president. To protect Vivvie. To protect me.

Henry absorbed my words. "You said there were two numbers on the phone?" he asked after an extended silence.

He *would* catch that.

"The other number was disconnected." I wondered if Henry was coming to the conclusion that I had reached: that in order for

Vivvie's dad to kill his grandfather, someone had to get Justice Marquette into surgery first.

Did they poison him somehow?

"Do you know where your grandfather was that morning?" I asked Henry. "Or the night before?"

Without warning, Henry pulled the car over to the shoulder of the road. He killed the engine, his fist wrapped tight around the keys. "I can find out," he said, and then, moving briskly, he got out of the car and slammed the door behind him. I stared after him as he walked a few feet away, his head bowed, every muscle in his shoulders and back tensed beneath his shirt.

"Henry's not big on public displays of emotion." Asher followed that statement with a noise halfway between a whimper and a moan. I turned to face him. I waited for a rush of anger at him for blabbing, but it didn't come.

"You would have told him eventually," I said. I'd been living on borrowed time.

Asher pressed the heel of his hand to his head and made another moaning sound. "I'm the screwup in the Henry-Asher friendship. Always have been."

I wasn't sure if Asher thought he'd screwed up by telling Henry or by keeping it from him in the first place.

"So what you're saying," I said, in an attempt to bring some of the old light back to Asher's eyes, "is that Henry is used to having to rescue you from your own drunk self."

Asher shook his head, then winced, clearly regretting that action in his current condition. "I'm not normally an imbiber," he said. "But there was a lot going on. Oblivion sounded nice." He closed his eyes, but apparently there was no oblivion to be found. "Vivvie?" he asked.

"Haven't heard from her."

The driver's side door opened, and Henry climbed back in. He took in the fact that Asher was awake, but didn't comment on it.

"My grandfather didn't have a history of heart problems," he told me instead. "We need to figure out what, if anything, can mimic the symptoms of a heart attack."

"Are we thinking *what* as in *what poison*?" Asher asked.

Henry didn't reply. I couldn't tell if that was because he wasn't speaking to Asher, or if he just had nothing to say.

"We?" I asked finally. They'd both used the word.

Henry answered my question with a seemingly unrelated statement. "It wasn't a good plan." Everything about him was hyperfocused, intense—it just took me a moment to figure out what he was focused on. "If the plan was to kill my grandfather so that Pierce could assume his spot on the Supreme Court, it wasn't a good plan." He curled his fingers into a fist, then uncurled them. I wondered if he even realized he was doing it. "You saw the handout Dr. Clark gave us," he continued. "There are dozens of potential nominees. The only way this plan makes any sense— the only way it could even potentially be worth the risk—is if Pierce had reason to believe he'd get the nomination."

You'll get your money when I get my nomination.

"And the only way," Henry continued, "that Pierce could possibly be *that* sure was if he had someone on the inside."

The inside of the nomination process.

The inside of the White House.

"Ivy hasn't told anyone," I said, thinking out loud. "Not the president, not the First Lady . . ."

Henry clamped his jaw down, then forced it to relax. "You were right when you said that I needed to think about who I could possibly hand this information over to, Tess. If there's even a chance that this goes as high as the West Wing, we can't trust anyone. Not the police. Not the Justice Department. No one."

"So where does that leave us?" I asked.

Henry's chest rose and fell slightly with each breath. He was completely in control of himself in a way that he hadn't been when he left the car. "I know where it leaves me. I'm going to figure out who had access to my grandfather before his so-called *heart attack*," he told me. "And you're going to go home."

CHAPTER 38

By the time I got back to Ivy's, it was dark. I let myself in the front door. The entire house was lit up like a Christmas tree, but there wasn't another person in sight.

"Hello?" As much as I just wanted to make my way up the spiral staircase and climb into bed, I doubted putting this off until morning would make the coming confrontation any easier. I'd taken off and ignored Ivy's calls for hours on end. She wasn't going to be happy about that.

"Hello?" I called a second time. I walked back toward her office. The sound of my footsteps echoed through the otherwise silent house. Ivy's office door was slightly ajar. I pushed gently on it. "Ivy?"

The door opened. The office was empty. I hovered at the threshold, like a vampire waiting for an invitation. *I should turn around and go.* But I didn't. I stepped over the threshold and walked slowly toward Ivy's desk.

It had been three days since I'd told Ivy everything I knew. She'd had three days to begin unraveling what was going on here. She'd been working, almost nonstop.

The only way this plan makes any sense—the only way it could even potentially be worth the risk—is if Pierce had reason to believe he'd get the nomination.

If Henry had come to that conclusion, Ivy must have seen it, too. What had she been doing for the past three days? What had she discovered?

What did she know?

There was a thick manila envelope sitting in the middle of her desk. I hesitated for a second or two, then reached for it. Ivy wanted to keep me out of this, but I was already in too deep. *Henry. Vivvie.* This wasn't some exercise for World Issues. It wasn't a game.

I opened the envelope.

The first thing I saw was the edge of a photo. The second thing I saw was myself. *Pictures.* My brain processed what I was seeing. *Of me.*

This wasn't evidence. It had nothing to do with the case. My breath caught in my throat. I slid the photos out of the envelope. There were dozens of them: me at twelve, my hair falling out of a thick braid; at sixteen, behind the wheel of Gramps's truck; elementary school plays; middle school dances.

I didn't even remember most of these pictures being taken. Gramps must have sent them to her. Thinking about my grandfather taking these pictures was enough of a punch to the gut. But knowing that Ivy had kept them? That realization knocked the wind out of me.

"There." In my memory, Ivy sits on the edge of my bed, and I sit on the floor in front of her. She fixes my hair into a braid. I lean back into her leg.

She'd stayed with me for a few days, after our parents' funeral. I'd almost forgotten that.

My hand is woven through Ivy's. Another memory came viciously on the heels of the first. *Ivy kneels beside me. My free hand finds its way to her face. I pat her cheek. It's wet. Why is Ivy crying? I burrow into her side. She picks me up, pressing my head to her chest, breathing in my smell.*

And then she hands me away.

"Tess?" a male voice called my name. I stuffed the pictures back in the envelope and made my way into the hallway a second before Adam rounded the corner. He was moving quickly, long strides covering the space between us in seconds flat.

"Are you okay?"

I'd been prepared to let Ivy yell at me. I hadn't expected to have Adam staring down at me, worry giving way to anger on his face.

What did he have to be angry about?

"I'm fine," I said. "I just needed some space. Where's Ivy?"

"You needed some space, so you went radio silent and took off." There was an edge in his voice. He turned his back on me for a moment and ran a hand roughly through his short brown hair. "Of course you did."

I wasn't sure how to respond to that.

"Call your sister," Adam ordered, turning back around and pinning me with a glare. "Now."

I called Ivy. She answered on the first ring. "Where are you? Are you okay? Do you need me to come get you?"

I didn't think she'd stop asking questions long enough for me to respond. "I'm at your place," I said.

"Okay." Ivy let out a breath and then repeated herself. "Okay. I'm on my way. Is Adam there?"

I glanced up at Adam, who was tracking my every move, like I might take off again any second. "He's here," I told Ivy.

She must have heard a hint of wariness in my voice, because the next thing she said was, "He's a worrier. Try not to hold it against him."

I eyed Adam, whose even features were set into an expression of uncompromising disapproval. "Roger that."

Adam narrowed his eyes at me. "What did she say?" he asked suspiciously.

"Nothing," I told him.

I could practically hear Ivy rolling her eyes on the other end of the line. "Put him on."

I handed the phone to Adam. He took it. "As far as I can tell, she's in one piece," he said, then paused. "What makes you think I'm going to yell at her?" Another pause. "I don't *yell* . . . fine. I'll be on my best behavior until you get here. I won't tell her that family doesn't just take off, or that running away never solved anything." Adam might have been talking to Ivy, but his sharp blue eyes were on me. "I certainly won't tell her that if it were up to me, she wouldn't be leaving this house again until she was thirty."

For a guy who'd met me only a handful of times, Adam did a good impression of my grandfather.

He and Bodie are Ivy's family. I didn't know how long they'd known each other, or what exactly there was between them. All

I knew was that while I'd been in Montana with Gramps, they'd been here with her—probably for years.

Apparently, from Adam's perspective, that made me family, too.

"I'm not supposed to yell at you," he informed me when he hung up the phone, the muscles in his jaw taut.

"If it would make you feel better, I don't really mind," I offered.

Adam's eyelid twitched. "Of course you don't," he said with a shake of his head. "You do realize that completely defeats the point?"

I was pretty sure there was no right answer to that question. "I was only gone for a few hours."

Adam fixed me with a look. "This isn't a good time for you to go off the grid—not even for a few hours."

I thought about Ivy telling me to keep my mouth shut, about Henry pointing out that we couldn't trust anyone—not the police, not the Justice Department, and certainly not the White House.

"Ivy hasn't told the president or the First Lady what's going on." I studied Adam's face as I said those words. "The only way any of this makes any sense is if Pierce had reason to believe that he would get the nomination."

Adam's poker face was even better than Henry's. "Don't take off again," he ordered.

He's not going to tell me anything. With a curt nod to acknowledge his words, I turned to go upstairs.

"This isn't the time to jump to conclusions," Adam called after me. His voice stopped me in my tracks. He measured his words, choosing each one carefully. "The president is rarely the most powerful person in Washington, Tess. He's part of a system, a cog in a machine."

"Are you saying you don't think the president was involved?"

"I'm not saying anything," Adam replied, "because Ivy told you to stay out of this. *I* am telling you to stay out of this." The warning was clear in his voice. If he had to *make* me stay out of this, it wouldn't be pleasant. "But if I *was* saying something, it would be that this isn't simple. Power is currency in Washington. And you don't always know who's holding the cards."

He was saying that the president wasn't the only one we should be wary of. He might not even be the most likely suspect.

Not when there were people out there who *made things happen* behind the scenes.

People like Adam's father.

That night, as I plugged my phone in to charge, I remembered the photo from the headmaster's office. I pulled up the shots I'd taken on my phone. The first two were unusable, but the third one only had a minor glare. I zoomed in and studied the men in the photo: three in the back row, two in the front, one off to the side.

Major Bharani. Judge Pierce. The Hardwicke headmaster. William Keyes. The fifth man, I didn't know. And the sixth—he was standing slightly off to one side. The glare obscured his face, but the way he was standing, the general shape of his features—

Familiar.

I loaded the picture onto my computer and looked up every tutorial I could find on removing glare from photos. I cloned the picture. I adjusted the shadow. I played with the filters. The end result wasn't pretty, but it was enough for me to confirm the man's identity.

Six men. Five I recognize. I walked through them one by one. *The doctor who killed Justice Marquette. The judge who paid him to do it. The headmaster of DC's most exclusive private school. Adam's father, who makes things happen behind the scenes.*

And standing off to the side, staring straight at the camera:

President Nolan.

CHAPTER 39

I spent the night at my computer, trying to track down anything I could about the picture—where it had been taken, when it had been taken, what the relationship was between these six men.

No matter how thoroughly I searched the internet, I couldn't find any other connection between Judge Pierce and Vivvie's father. They lived thousands of miles apart. They'd gone to different schools, had different occupations. They weren't even the same age. I couldn't find evidence of the two men ever having been in the same place.

Except for the picture.

It was easier to connect Judge Pierce to William Keyes. The two men shared an alma mater. They were both on the university's board of regents.

In contrast, I couldn't find any evidence of a direct link between William Keyes and Vivvie's dad, but it wasn't outside the realm of possibility that a man who made things happen in Washington might be acquainted with all manner of White House staff.

With the president, it was the reverse—it was easy to connect him with Vivvie's father. The man was his personal physician. But Judge Pierce? All my sleuthing could turn up was speculation about who the Nolan administration's nominee for the Supreme Court might be. Pierce's name was one of many—and it rarely even came up.

The only way this plan makes any sense—the only way it could even potentially be worth the risk—is if Pierce had reason to believe he'd get the nomination. That thought dogged me until I fell asleep at the keyboard.

The next morning, I printed out a copy of the picture and folded it in half, then in half again. I put it in my back pocket, then went downstairs. Ivy and Bodie were in the kitchen. Ivy had a cup of coffee in one hand and a small overnight bag in the other.

"Going somewhere?" I asked her.

"Arizona." She downed the last of her coffee. "I hear it's nice this time of year."

Arizona. Judge Pierce was from Arizona. I wanted to ask what she would be doing there but knew she wouldn't answer.

"I'm sorry to leave," she said. "After yesterday—"

"It's okay."

"No," Ivy told me. "It's not. The way you heard about Vivvie's dad was not okay. What Vivvie is going through right now is not okay. The fact that I'm asking you not to tell anyone about any of this is *not okay*. I know that, Tess, and I'm sorry. I'm sorry about yesterday, I'm sorry I got you involved in any of this."

"Technically," I said, "I got *you* involved in this."

"You Kendricks," Bodie cut in. "You love your technicalities."

Ivy ignored him. "Bodie will be here all weekend," she told me. "And if you need anything, you can call Adam."

Adam, whose father was in that picture.

I glanced at the bag in Ivy's hand, then punched a button on my phone and pulled up the photo. "Before you go," I said, "there's something you should see."

Ivy confiscated my phone. An hour later, Bodie handed me a new one. He'd inputted his number, Adam's, and Ivy's. I tried calling Vivvie, dialing the number from memory, but there was no answer.

Ivy hadn't been happy to discover the real reason behind my trip to the headmaster's office. She wouldn't discuss the men in that picture—or what, if anything, she thought it meant that Vivvie's dad and Judge Pierce had apparently been in the same place at the same time. She just flew off to Arizona, taking the evidence with her. I was left with an empty house, a "driver" who kept one eye on me at all times, and a printed copy of the photograph, folded into quarters in my back pocket.

Being grounded gave me lots of time to think.

Monday morning, when I dialed the number for Vivvie's phone, I didn't really expect her to answer. When she picked up, my voice fled. I couldn't even force out the word *hello*. Vivvie was on the verge of hanging up when I finally recovered.

"It's me," I said. Once I started talking, words poured out. "I'm so sorry, Vivvie. I—"

"Stop." Vivvie spoke over me. "Just stop, Tess."

I stopped, then waited for the first blow to fall.

"I'm not mad at you."

I could picture her face fighting against those words. I wasn't sure if she believed them or not.

"Are you . . ." I wasn't sure how to finish that question. I certainly wasn't going to ask if she was okay.

"We're burying him this morning." Vivvie let those words drop and said nothing in the silence that followed them.

"Do you want me to come?"

There was another long pause after my question.

"It's supposed to just be me and my aunt," Vivvie said. "And the honor guard. It's a military funeral, but they want it quiet. Because suicides don't look good."

Suicides don't look good. The brutality of that statement made my stomach lurch.

"I keep telling myself that I did the right thing." I could hear Vivvie suck in a breath of air. "I keep telling myself that, Tess, and I almost believe it, but I need to know that this isn't—" She cut off. "That it's not just going to . . ." She couldn't finish that sentence, either. "I need to know that my going to your sister matters, that it made a difference, that it wasn't for *nothing*."

"It wasn't." I wished I could make this better for her. I wished I could give her something more than that. "Ivy flew to Arizona today. She wouldn't say why, but it has to have something to do with Pierce."

On the other end of the phone line, Vivvie was quiet for so long that I thought she might have hung up.

"What if my dad didn't kill himself, Tess?" Vivvie's question caught me off guard. "Ivy said this was dangerous. That's why she wanted to keep you out of it." The full force of her pent-up emotions crept into those words. "What if someone realized Ivy was looking into things? What if someone found out that she knew about my dad? If my dad could identify the people he was working with, he was a threat to them."

"Vivvie—"

"Or what if my dad told someone he was worried about getting caught? What if he got freaked out that the phone was missing, and he *told someone*? Pierce, or . . . or . . ."

Or whoever else was involved.

It had been easy for me to believe that Vivvie's father had killed himself. With the phone missing, he had to have known things were unraveling. He'd lost his job at the White House. Maybe he even hated himself for hurting Vivvie.

What I hadn't thought about was the fact that Vivvie's father wasn't the only one who stood to lose something if he got caught. I hadn't thought about the fact that he might have been able to identify the other people involved.

He put a bullet in his own head, William Keyes had said, staring straight at me. And maybe Vivvie's father had.

But now that Vivvie had raised the issue, I couldn't help thinking that maybe—*maybe*—he hadn't.

CHAPTER 40

I got to school late. In English, I could feel Henry's eyes on me across the room. In physics, he sat down at my lab table. The day's experiment was on centripetal force.

"You asked if I could find out where my grandfather was the night before his heart attack." Henry's attention seemed one hundred percent focused on the knot he was tying around a tennis ball. His expression gave nothing away: the very portrait of the dedicated student. "He was at a fund-raiser for the Keyes Foundation."

Keyes. As in William Keyes. Adam's words echoed in my head. *The president is rarely the most powerful person in Washington.*

"There were over four hundred attendees," Henry said, testing the security of his knot. "Not to mention the waitstaff. It wouldn't have been that difficult to slip something in my grandfather's drink."

Poison the justice. Send him to the hospital. Have the White House physician declare it a heart attack. Have him operate. Twice.

By the time the justice died, the poison would have been out of his bloodstream.

The perfect murder.

In my mind, I could still hear Vivvie telling me that she needed having gone to Ivy with her suspicions about her father to have made a difference. To *mean* something.

"Any idea who those four hundred attendees were?" I asked Henry, my eyes locked on the instructions for our lab.

"My mother got me a list." Henry's eyes flickered toward mine, only for a second. "She doesn't know why I requested it."

He won't tell her, I thought, reading his expression. *Not until he knows more.* In his position, I probably would have done the same thing.

There were times when I thought Henry and I were a lot alike.

Glancing up to make sure that we hadn't attracted the attention of the teacher—or anyone else—I reached into my bag and pulled out my copy of the photograph from Raleigh's office. After a moment's hesitation, I slid it across the table to Henry.

Ivy had told me to stay out of it. But Ivy had told me a lot of things over the years.

Henry had a right to know.

Across from me, he unfolded the picture and studied it for a few seconds, then set it aside and returned his attention to our project.

"Any idea where it was taken?" he asked.

"No. I can identify five of the men." I indicated which five.

Henry weighed the tennis ball and made a mark in his notebook. "The one next to the president is John Thomas Wilcox's father."

That made six.

"And how many of those men are on the list you got from your mother?" I asked Henry. *How many of them might have had the opportunity to poison Theo Marquette?*

Henry didn't have to consult his list. He held up two fingers.

I considered the men in the photograph, setting aside Vivvie's dad and Pierce. *The Hardwicke headmaster. The minority whip. The president. The man behind the scenes.*

"Which two?" I asked.

Henry arched an eyebrow at me, and I answered my own question. Looking down at the photograph, I pointed first to one man, then the other.

William Keyes. That was easy. Given that we were talking about a Keyes Foundation gala, that went without saying.

My heart beat viciously in my chest as I slowly moved my finger to my second guess. *Not the headmaster. Not John Thomas's father.* My finger hovered over the president's face-you-could-trust. After a long moment, I pressed my finger down.

I wanted Henry to tell me that I was wrong.

He didn't.

CHAPTER 41

At lunch, Henry was nowhere to be seen. He wasn't at his usual table. Asher hadn't seen him. Even my short acquaintance with Henry Marquette was enough for me to know that he operated according to a series of predictable algorithms. He did what he was supposed to do. He was reliable. Responsible.

Missing.

I found him in the computer lab. The door closed behind me seconds after I stepped into the room. Henry barely glanced away from the screen.

"I'm trying to narrow down a time frame on the photograph," he told me. "Look at this." He pulled up two digital images. "Congressman Wilcox shaved his mustache off last spring, so wherever the picture you found was taken, it's recent. Six months ago or less."

I processed that. Six months ago or less, Judge Pierce and Vivvie's father had been in the same place at the same time.

Six months ago or less, the president and William Keyes had been there, too.

"It might not mean anything." I wanted to be the voice of reason, but I didn't *feel* reasonable. I felt like we were standing on the verge of something cavernous and unthinkable and *real*. "The picture. The guest list for that party. It might not mean anything," I continued, grappling for objectivity like a climber trying to hold on to the edge of a cliff. "We don't know for sure that someone poisoned your grandfather at the gala that night, let alone if it was someone in that picture. The fact that the president and William Keyes were the only ones in both places could be a coincidence."

"I don't believe in coincidences, Tess. Sometime in the last six months, the man who killed my grandfather and the one who paid him to do it had a little sit-down. I've looked for another connection between Bharani and Pierce. I skipped my morning classes to look, Tess, and I couldn't find anything. The only connection is this photo. This meeting, whatever it was."

I was surprised that Henry Marquette had skipped class. I wasn't surprised that his next move had been the same as mine: to look for connections, to figure out what—besides the murder—tied the judge and Vivvie's father together.

"There was another number on that disposable phone." Henry was implacable. "That means there is at least one other person involved."

Someone with access to the justice. Someone who could get close enough to poison him. Someone who could make sure Pierce was positioned to be nominated in his place.

"We don't know a lot of things, Tess." Henry's voice was curt. I was starting to recognize that tone as an indication that he was clamping down on his emotions, refusing to let them gain control. "We don't know if Pierce approached Vivvie's dad or the other way around. We don't know who masterminded this whole thing." He paused. "We don't know who your sister is working for now."

That took me off guard.

"We don't know what her endgame is," Henry continued forcefully.

My mouth felt like it had been filled with sawdust. "What are you saying, Henry?"

"Your sister solves problems. Professionally. Whoever the other number on that phone belonged to, I'd say they have a pretty big problem right now, wouldn't you?"

I'd underestimated just how much Henry mistrusted my sister. It had never occurred to me that he might believe that instead of working to uncover this conspiracy, Ivy might be working to cover it up.

"Your grandfather and Ivy were *friends*. She would *never*—"

"What do you think fixers do, Tess?" Henry's voice was maddeningly calm. "They cover things up. Even if there's a cost. Even if they have to break a few laws to do it."

"You have no idea what you're talking about," I said fiercely.

"Vivvie's father's suicide didn't make the papers," Henry continued. He was like a train chugging its way toward a tunnel at a steady pace. Never slowing down. Never stopping. "Someone kept that away from the press."

I thought of Ivy, wrangling the press outside Justice Marquette's wake. If my sister wanted to keep something like that out of the papers, could she?

Yes.

"Everyone knows your sister works for Georgia Nolan," Henry said. "Can you honestly tell me she doesn't troubleshoot for the president, too?" He didn't give me a chance to answer. "And William Keyes? He's rich. Rich enough to pay her whatever it takes for her to protect him and his image."

"She's not working for Keyes." It took everything I had not to raise my voice. "They don't even get along."

"Then why did his son pick you up from school last week?" Henry arched an eyebrow at me. "Word travels fast at Hardwicke, Tess. Whether you like it or not, you have to accept that there's at least a possibility that your sister may have a conflict of interest here. And the side she comes down on may not be the right one."

Ivy had told me not to tell anyone. *To protect me*, I thought desperately. *She did it to protect me. And Vivvie.*

"Tallyho, friends of Asher!" Asher had impeccable timing. He waltzed into the room and hopped up on the computer table, his legs dangling down, like he didn't have a care in the world.

Like the tension in the room wasn't thick enough that you could have cut it with a knife.

"Am I interrupting something?" he asked blithely.

Just Henry telling me he thinks my sister might be working to cover up his grandfather's murder. Henry must have read something in my expression, because a hint of remorse flashed across his features.

"You're not interrupting anything." Henry pulled his gaze from mine and turned to Asher. "Tess and I were just having a bit of a debate." His green eyes found their way to mine again. "I may have pushed my case a little too hard."

"You?" Asher said, feigning shock. "Never."

As Asher launched into a story that seemed to involve a cupcake and a remote-controlled airplane—clearly meant to dissolve the tension—I had to fight the urge to stare at Henry until I knew exactly what he was thinking.

What had Ivy done to convince him she was capable of something like this?

I turned my head away from Henry. I could just barely make out our reflection in the glass pane that separated the computer lab from the hall: Asher constantly in motion, and Henry and I sitting still as statues, neither of us looking at the other.

Movement on the other side of the pane forced my attention away from the reflection.

Emilia. She opened the door to the lab a second later. I saw the moment she registered the fact that Henry, Asher, and I had gone silent at her entrance.

Her chin jutted out, her perfect posture going even more erect.

"Did you need something, Em?" Asher asked.

"Not from you." Emilia's tone when she addressed her brother was a mix of comfortable and blunt. Henry stood up, obviously expecting Emilia to address him, but she just gave him an icy look, then turned to me.

"I need to talk to you." Emilia had a knack of issuing statements like orders. I was going to ask her if it could wait, but something in her eyes made me hesitate.

She took a step forward. "It's about Vivvie."

That was all it took for her to have my complete attention.

"She's in the bathroom," Emilia said softly. "She looks . . ." Emilia bit her bottom lip. I hadn't pegged her for the lip-biting type. "She's not okay."

"Vivvie's here?" I interrupted.

"Listening comprehension," Emilia snapped back, looking more like her usual self. "Yes, she's here. And something's wrong."

"Which bathroom?" I asked, a feeling of dread taking up residence in my stomach. Vivvie had buried her father this morning. Why would she have come to school? And how bad must she have been for Emilia to come get *me*?

"Downstairs," Emilia replied. "East corridor."

I started walking before she even finished talking. Henry and Asher followed. When I got to the bathroom, there was no one else inside. I'd expected to find Vivvie in one of the stalls, but she was just sitting on the floor.

"Vivvie." I knelt down next to her.

"Sorry," she said roughly. "I'm sorry. I'm fine."

"What's wrong?"

"You weren't in the courtyard," Vivvie said. "It's stupid. I came to find you, and you weren't in the courtyard, and—"

"Breathe."

Vivvie breathed. Then she thrust something toward me. It took me a second to realize it was a newspaper, and another after that to realize that she wanted me to take it.

I took it. Slowly, I unfolded it. Then I understood instantly why Vivvie had come.

PIERCE FRONT-RUNNER FOR SUPREME COURT, the headline declared. My mind whirred. This wasn't an op-ed piece, and it wasn't some two-bit newspaper. This was the front page of the *Washington Post*.

There was a knock at the door.

"Everything okay in there?" Asher called. "I ask in the most unobtrusive possible way!"

I looked down at the paper in my hand.

"You can show him," Vivvie told me, pushing herself to her feet. "He's going to see it anyway. Everyone's going to see it."

I reached out and squeezed Vivvie's shoulder, and then we made our way out into the hall. Asher was standing next to the door. Henry was behind him. Wordlessly, I held up the article.

PIERCE FRONT-RUNNER FOR SUPREME COURT. The headline was just as disturbing the second time, but not as disturbing as the subheading. *Sources say the president is moving toward nomination at an unprecedented rate.*

"What sources?" Henry asked the question before I could. I had no answers. All I could do was move a step closer to Vivvie and take her hand in mine.

Her father had died on Friday. She'd just buried him—and now the *Washington Post* was announcing that some anonymous source had gone on record saying that the president was preparing to nominate the man who'd hired her father to commit murder.

"They can't do this." Vivvie found her voice again, her hand squeezing mine until it hurt. "Tess, the president can't nominate Pierce. He can't." She pulled her hand away from mine and stepped back. "What if they killed him, Tess? What if Pierce and whoever he's working with killed my father, just like they killed . . ."

Vivvie's eyes darted to Henry's. Her words dried up, and the two of them were suddenly caught up in the kind of staring contest that nobody wins. Neither one could look away.

"Henry." Vivvie swallowed. "I . . ."

"I know," Henry said softly. "About my grandfather. About your father."

Vivvie flinched. She waited for him to lash out.

"You could have kept quiet." Henry was so focused on Vivvie that I felt like I was eavesdropping, like neither Asher nor I had any place in this moment. "You didn't," Henry continued, his voice just as soft. "You spoke up."

Vivvie's eyes filled with tears.

Henry reached out and laid a gentle hand on her arm. "I owe you for that."

"I'm sorr—"

"Don't." Henry's voice was implacable. "Don't apologize. Not now, not ever, not to me." He turned back to me. "We need to know if the article is true."

Was the president really on the verge of nominating Pierce? And if he was—what did that mean?

The president was at the gala. The president is in the picture. The president has the power to see this nomination through.

"Maybe Ivy knows something," I said, turning the situation over in my mind, trying to come at it from a different angle. "She won't give me details, but I can ask."

"Right." Henry's voice went cold. "Because talking to your sister will make everything better."

Vivvie looked from Henry to me. "Tess?"

Vivvie trusted Ivy—and she *needed* to trust someone.

"Henry," I bit out. "A word?"

We retreated slightly from the group. "Vivvie's been through hell, and right now, Ivy is the one person she is counting on to make this right." I willed Henry to hear me. "You can't take that away from her."

"Vivvie didn't come to your sister for help on this." Henry's tone was unapologetic. "When she saw that article in the paper, she came to *you*."

I swallowed, trying not to feel the weight of that. "She trusts Ivy."

"Maybe she shouldn't."

I took a step closer to him. "This isn't about whatever unforgivable sin my sister committed to get on your bad side—"

Henry closed what little space remained between us. "My father didn't die in a car accident." Henry lowered his voice, whispering those words directly into my right ear, his lips brushing against the side of my face as he did. "He killed himself, and my grandfather hired your sister to cover it up."

I froze. I'd read articles about Henry's dad's death. His *accident*.

"Your sister staged the wreck," Henry continued. "She greased the right palms, and she put out the right story. My mother doesn't know." Henry was still so close that I could feel his breath against the side of my face. "I wasn't supposed to know, either. But I do, Tess. *I know*."

I thought about what it must have been like to carry a secret like that, to watch his family mourning his father, knowing that the man had taken his own life.

"I get up every day, and I lie to everyone I care about in this world. I don't get to be angry. I don't get to ask why. I'm complicit. She made me complicit."

He had a problem, I'd said to Ivy, of Theo Marquette. *You fixed it.* Her reply had been *Something like that.*

"I told you," Henry said, taking a step back. "Fixers are experts at covering things up. Your sister's practically an artist."

Vivvie's father's suicide hadn't made the papers.

"Whatever Ivy did," I said, my throat tightening around the words until I thought I wouldn't be able to get them out, "your grandfather was the one who hired her to do it."

How could he hate Ivy and not the old man?

Because it's easier. Because he'd just lost his father. Because he needed someone to blame.

"My grandfather and I never discussed it," Henry said tersely. "And now we never will."

CHAPTER 42

I made it through the rest of my classes like a sleepwalker drifting blindly down a hall. My mind was a mess, tangled with questions I didn't want to ask and thoughts I couldn't banish.

The photo. The gala. The president moving toward nominating Pierce. Ivy.

Five minutes into my last class, I was called to the headmaster's office. If I'd done anything to deserve his attention, I wasn't sure what it was. I half prepared myself for this to be another round of John Thomas Wilcox Tries to Get Tess's Locker Searched, but I couldn't bring myself to really care about John Thomas or Headmaster Raleigh or my continued enrollment at Hardwicke.

"Tess, dear." Mrs. Perkins greeted me with a smile. "They're waiting for you. Go right on in."

They? I barely had time to process that before the door to the headmaster's office opened, and Headmaster Raleigh stepped out. "Tess," he said. "Excellent."

Excellent? That wasn't exactly a response I'd ever provoked from the man.

"Come in, come in," he said. The moment I stepped into his office, I realized why the headmaster had changed his tune.

"Tess." Georgia Nolan greeted me with a kiss on the cheek. I stiffened. In the corner of the room, a Secret Service agent looked on, his expressionless face never wavering. "I am sorry for surprising you," Georgia continued, "but I was scheduled to meet with Headmaster Raleigh about the upcoming Hardwicke auction, and I wanted to check in and see how you were doing." She squeezed my arm. "You had a bit of an upset last week."

I cast a glance at the headmaster, who seemed altogether pleased with himself for being able to accommodate the First Lady's request. He probably would have tied me up with a little bow if he'd thought there was a chance of ingratiating himself further.

"I'm fine," I said, turning my attention back to Georgia. She clucked her tongue.

"You really do resemble your sister," she said. "Ivy all over again, don't you think?" she asked the headmaster.

"Certainly." The slight strain in the headmaster's voice told me that he wasn't quite as fond of the resemblance as the First Lady was.

"Would you mind giving us a moment, Chester?" Georgia had a way of issuing requests, sweet as honey, but rhetorical nonetheless. The headmaster was out of the room before he knew it. Georgia nodded to the Secret Service agent, and he positioned himself just outside the door.

Georgia shut it, leaving the two of us alone.

"How are you really, Tess?" she asked once it was just us. "Ivy told me that Vivvie Bharani is a friend of yours. I can only imagine what she's going through."

I didn't want to talk about Vivvie, but Georgia looked content to stand there indefinitely until I said something. "They buried her father this morning."

"I regret not being able to attend." Georgia studied me for a moment. "Ivy indicated that Ms. Bharani and her father were having some problems before his death?"

Why do you want to know? I caught those words in the filter between my brain and my mouth. When she realized that I wasn't going to respond, Georgia let out a light, airy sigh, then leaned back against the headmaster's desk. "I know when I'm being kept in the dark, Tess," she said. "Quite frankly, there's not much that goes on in Washington that I don't know."

The president is rarely the most powerful person in Washington. Standing across from Georgia Nolan, I suddenly found myself wondering where she stood in that hierarchy.

"I know your sister flew out to Arizona this weekend. I understand she's due back today. What I don't know is what, precisely, she is doing there." Georgia's Southern drawl softened every word she said, but there was no mistaking the thread of steel underneath. "In the past week, it's become perfectly clear that William Keyes is pushing for Pierce's nomination. Hard. William's calling in a lot of chips on this one. I have known the man for a very long time, Tess. He excels at getting what he wants. And when he doesn't get it, well, let us say that the man holds a grudge." She clicked her nails lightly along the surface of the desk. "If Ivy is in Arizona looking for information to discredit Pierce, it would be in everyone's best interest if I were prepared to deal with the fallout. Believe me when I say that I can deal with William Keyes if and only if I am forewarned."

She wanted to know what was going on, why Ivy was in Arizona, what Ivy was looking for. I felt the pull to tell her what I knew, but resisted.

"Your husband asked Ivy to dig for skeletons in Pierce's closet," I said instead. "I'd guess that's why she's in Arizona."

"Would you?" Georgia mused.

"Ivy's very thorough."

"Thorough," Georgia repeated. "And that's why she had Major Bharani removed from duty at the White House when she discovered the altercation with his daughter. Because she's thorough."

Georgia didn't *sound* skeptical, but I knew suddenly, studying her warm hazel eyes, that she was. The First Lady knew Ivy well enough to know that there was something else going on here.

The question was: Did she know what that something else was?

The president was there when Vivvie's dad and Judge Pierce met, I thought. *The president was at the gala.* And the First Lady had said that there wasn't much that went on in Washington that she didn't know.

"Your sister isn't the type to ask for help, Tess." Georgia pushed off the desk and began slowly pacing the room, her hands clasped in front of her body, like a bride carrying a bouquet. "Our

Ivy is, I'm afraid, better at solving other people's problems than allowing them to assist with her own."

That had the ring of truth to it. Ivy had swooped into my life and taken charge in an instant, but she'd always shut me out of her own.

"I would like, very much," Georgia continued, "to know if your sister requires my help now."

If whatever Ivy discovered in Arizona led her somehow to the third party involved in the chief justice's murder—if that third party was either of the men I suspected—Ivy would need all the help she could get.

But one of those men was Georgia Nolan's husband.

"Is it true, what they said in the *Post*?" I asked. Georgia had been pumping me for information. Turnaround was fair play. "Is your husband really getting ready to nominate Pierce?"

Georgia waved away the question with one hand. "Peter would hardly move on anything until he hears back from Ivy. You mustn't believe everything you read, Tess."

"So the reporter's sources were wrong?" I asked. That wasn't what she'd said—not exactly—and I knew it.

"I'd be willing to bet his source, singular, is nothing more than an intern looking to forge some connections, and quite frankly, Tess, it isn't worth my time to track it down. The reporter is unlikely to reveal his source, and even if he could be persuaded to do so, he would want something in return." Georgia returned to stand directly in front of me. "In politics, Tess dear, you're rarely given something for nothing."

I wondered if she knew those words sounded like a warning.

I wondered if she meant them that way.

"Well," Georgia said, seeming to realize that she wasn't going to get anything else out of me. "Thank you for speaking with me, Tess. It has been illuminating. And I do hope you know that when I inquired about your well-being, I meant it. Ivy is not much older than my own sons, and I've grown to care about her very much. You matter to her, and that matters to me."

Even with everything else going on, it hurt to hear that I mattered to Ivy. Turning away from Georgia before she could see the effect her words had on me, I took a few steps toward the far wall. My eyes landed on the picture behind the headmaster's desk, and in the split second that followed, I knew that I wouldn't get an opportunity like this again.

"How does your husband know the headmaster?" I asked, gesturing toward the photo like I'd seen it for the first time. I could feel my heart beating in my chest, hear it in my ears.

Georgia glanced at the photo from a distance, not paying it much mind. "Our youngest went to Hardwicke," she said. "We try to donate something to the auction each year. Last spring, there was some water damage to the school. They were in need of big-ticket items, so we arranged for a weekend retreat at Camp David. The Presidential Retreat," she clarified. "It's occasionally open to the public, you know."

A weekend at Camp David.

"Was the president's attendance part of the prize?" I asked.

"Heavens, no," Georgia said. "But William won the auction and invited Peter along. My husband, I'm afraid, has never been able to back down from one of Will's challenges."

I forced myself to pretend like there was nothing to read into those words. Like there was no reason, in particular, that I had asked.

But as Georgia and I parted ways and I left the administrative building, I couldn't stop thinking that if William Keyes had won the auction, if he'd been the one to issue the invitations, then he was the one who'd brought the men in that picture together.

Including Judge Pierce and Vivvie's father.

CHAPTER 43

"You're quiet." Bodie issued that statement with no small amount of suspicion.

"I'm always quiet."

As Bodie pulled the car past the gates and out onto the street, he glanced at me just long enough to smirk. "And I'm always perceptive. This quiet is a different quiet."

My mind was awash in the day's events. *Georgia's visit. Vivvie and the article on Pierce. The two names from Henry's list. Adam's father being the one who had arranged the get-together in that photograph.*

"I'm fluent in all varieties of Kendrick silences," Bodie declared. "And you and your sister both stare very intently at *absolutely nothing* when the wheels are turning in here." He lazily reached over and tapped the side of my head. I swatted his hand away.

"I have a lot to think about."

"And would some of that *lot* concern a certain First Lady with sweet, Southern manners and the mind of Machiavelli?"

I snorted at that description of Georgia.

"How did you guess?" I asked Bodie.

"I didn't." He merged onto the highway. "I caught a glimpse of Mark pulling away as I pulled in."

"Mark?" My brow wrinkled in confusion.

"Mark Maddox," Bodie said. "He's one of the agents on Georgia's detail."

"You're on a first-name basis with the Secret Service?"

"I make it a point to learn names. Half of the time, the Secret Service wants to be noticed. Their presence is a deterrent."

"And the other half of the time?" I asked.

"They fade into the background. They try not to engage, not to interfere. If you're not careful, you forget they're there."

"Unless you know their names," I said.

"Unless you know their names." Bodie reached over and tapped the side of my head again.

"What was that for?" I asked disgruntledly.

"That," he replied, "was for trying to distract me from the fact that when I asked you about Georgia, you didn't answer."

I was still processing my interaction with the First Lady. I wasn't used to processing out loud. Bodie reached over and flicked my ear. Clearly, unlike Adam, he didn't believe in driving with both hands on the wheel.

"Fine," I said, before he could escalate further. "Yes, I'm thinking about the First Lady. She had a meeting with the headmaster today, supposedly."

"Supposedly." Bodie didn't turn it into a question, but I responded like he had.

"She had me pulled out of class. Just to check on me, see how I was doing."

"Of course," Bodie said dryly.

"Of course." This time, I didn't make him press for more information. "She was fishing for details about what Ivy's doing in Arizona."

Bodie snorted. "I told Ivy we'd have to loop Georgia in sooner, rather than later. What did you say?"

"I told her that Ivy was just doing what the president asked—looking into Pierce's background." I paused. "And I asked her if her husband was really moving at an accelerated rate toward nominating Pierce."

Bodie glanced over at me. "You saw the article in the *Post*?"

I nodded. "Vivvie came to school today. Her father's funeral was this morning, and she came to school to find me, to show me the newspaper."

"And what did Miss Georgia have to say about that article?" Bodie asked, drumming his fingers along the edge of the steering wheel.

"She said the source was probably some intern."

Bodie snorted. "Doubtful." He glanced over at me, then fixed his gaze back on the road. "There are two reasons to leak a story like that, kid." His voice was casual, like he wasn't imparting wisdom that neither Ivy nor Adam would have shared. "You either do it in hopes that it becomes a self-fulfilling prophecy, or you do it to sink the potential nominee's chances by putting him in the spotlight too soon."

Help Pierce get nominated, or hurt his chances.

"Did Ivy leak it?" Twenty-four hours ago, I wouldn't have asked that question.

"This time?" Bodie asked with an arch of one brow. "No."

This time. He wasn't saying that Ivy wouldn't strategically leak a story like that. He was saying that she *hadn't*.

"The day we found out about Vivvie's father, I heard William Keyes say something to Ivy." I caught my bottom lip in my teeth. Now I really was thinking out loud. "He said that he'd taught her everything she knew."

Once upon a time, Ivy had worked for Keyes. He'd taught her how to manipulate the system. How to *make things happen*.

"He could have leaked the story." I turned that possibility over in my mind. "The First Lady said Keyes is pushing Judge Pierce for the nomination." I could have stopped there, but I didn't. "That photo I gave Ivy—the one that connects Vivvie's dad and Judge Pierce—was taken at Camp David. According to the First Lady, Keyes was the one who arranged the retreat. That means Keyes brought Vivvie's dad and Pierce together. And the night before the chief justice died, he attended a fund-raiser for the *Keyes* Foundation."

Bodie drove one-handed, the other resting on his threadbare jeans. He cast a lazy glance toward me. "I seem to recall something about you staying out of this."

"You're the one who just told me that there are only two reasons to leak an article like that," I said.

Bodie put his free hand back on the wheel. "I was making conversation."

"If there's any chance Adam's father might be the one who—"

"He's not."

The certainty in Bodie's voice made my stomach twist. *If it's not Keyes . . .*

"The president?" I asked softly.

Bodie gave me an incredulous look. "You think the president might be behind this, so you asked Georgia about that picture *and* the article in the *Post*?"

I decided that was probably a rhetorical question.

"Keyes is in the clear," Bodie told me. "So are both of the Nolans."

I blinked. Twice. "The president and William Keyes were the *only* people in that photo who—"

Bodie didn't let me finish. "They were the first people Ivy cleared."

The first people Ivy *cleared.* Somewhere, in the back of my mind, I could hear Henry: *Your sister solves problems. Professionally. Whoever the other number on that phone belonged to, I'd say they have a pretty big problem right now.*

"How did she clear them?" I heard myself ask.

Bodie's answer—if he was going to answer me at all—was cut off by the sound of a siren. His eyes flicked toward the rearview mirror, and he cursed under his breath.

That was when I noticed the flashing lights.

"Speeding?" I asked Bodie as he pulled his car to the side of the road.

"That," Bodie said, "or things are about to get interesting." He cut the engine and turned to face me head-on. "Stay calm. Do exactly what they say. Don't answer questions without a lawyer present."

He rolled down his window.

I caught his arm. "Bodie, what's going on?"

Before he could answer, an officer approached, gun pulled. "Get out of the car!"

CHAPTER 44

We got out of the car.

When the officer threw Bodie down on the hood to frisk him, Ivy's driver said two things. The first was: "Well, this should be fun." The second—aimed at me—was: "Call your sister."

Two hours later, as I sat at the front of the police station, that was what I did.

I'd followed Bodie's instructions to a T. I'd stayed calm. I'd done what I was told. I hadn't answered any questions, other than the basics: *my name; my age; Bodie was my sister's driver; he was just driving me home from school.*

I'd played shell-shocked and scared. It went against every fiber of my being, but sometimes the best defense was letting yourself seem defenseless. I didn't lash back. I didn't demand answers. And they didn't take my phone. Eventually, the poor defenseless girl was plunked down out front while one of the officers made some phone calls and the other questioned the suspect.

Answer. Answer. Answer. My hand tightened around my cell as I made a call of my own. *Come on, Ivy.*

"Tess."

A breath escaped my lungs when I heard my sister's voice. "Bodie and I got pulled over," I said.

There was a beat. "Was he arrested?" Ivy asked. Then she rephrased the question. "Did they read him his rights?"

I thought back. "No." They'd thrown him down on the car. They'd frisked him. They'd shoved him in the back of a police car—but they hadn't made an arrest. "Ivy, what's going on?"

I could practically hear Ivy grinding her teeth on the other end of the line. "Someone's making a point," she said.

I didn't get a chance to ask who would do this—or what kind of point they could possibly be making.

"Hey." One of the officers saw me on my phone. "You can't be on that in here."

My capacity for playing small and defenseless snapped. "I was told I had to wait here until an adult could pick me up. I'm not allowed to call my legal guardian?"

The cop—a female officer whose acquaintance I hadn't yet had the pleasure of making—frowned. "Someone will make that call on your behalf."

"It's been two hours," I replied. "Why hasn't someone already made that call?"

"Tess." Ivy had been listening from the other end of the phone line, but now she spoke up. "Give the officer the phone."

I handed the woman the phone. Five seconds into the call, her lips pressed themselves into a thin line. Ten seconds into the call, she paled.

That was about the time that Social Services showed up.

Even from the other side of a phone line, Ivy took charge. By the time the door to the police station opened and Adam walked in a half hour later, the social worker had been dispatched and a woman in a thousand-dollar suit had arrived, pronouncing herself Bodie's lawyer.

"Adam." I stood up the second I saw him. "Is Ivy—"

"She's on her way back," he replied, before turning his attention to the officer who'd taken charge of me. "Adam Keyes," he introduced himself. "Department of Defense."

He was dressed in uniform. I had a feeling that wasn't an accident.

"You should have received faxed confirmation that I'm authorized to take custody of Tess until such time as her sister arrives," Adam continued. His tone didn't invite a response.

"I've been instructed to hold the girl until—"

Adam cut her off. "You'll want to review those instructions. I'm sure Tess's sister has already told you she'll be filing a complaint. I suggest you not compound the situation."

Without waiting for a reply, Adam put a hand on my shoulder and steered me out the door. Once we'd put some distance between us and the building, I let myself ask: "Ivy called you?"

"She did." He gave my shoulder a light squeeze, then dropped his hand to his side. "Are you okay?"

"I'm fine." As we hit the parking lot, my brain caught up with me, and I came to a halt. "Bodie—"

"Ivy will take care of it." There wasn't an ounce of uncertainty in Adam's voice. "Maybe a few hours behind bars will improve Bodie's disposition."

I almost managed a smile at the deadpan with which Adam issued that statement.

Almost.

"What's happening?" I asked point-blank. "Why did they bring Bodie in for questioning? Questioning about *what*?"

Adam seemed to be weighing the chances that I would let this go. He must have decided they weren't good, because he answered. "It appears some evidence has come to light linking Bodie to an unsolved crime."

Adam didn't specify what the evidence was—or what the crime was. I waited until we were situated in his car, me in the passenger seat and him behind the wheel, before I spoke again. "When I asked Ivy what was going on, she said someone was trying to prove a point. What point?"

A tick in Adam's jaw was the only tell to the fact that my question had hit a nerve. "What point?" he repeated. "That he can get to Bodie." Adam stared out the windshield, the muscle in his jaw ticking again. "That he can get to you. That there are costs to *being difficult* and standing against his wishes."

"Your father." I didn't phrase it as a question. The First Lady had said that William Keyes could hold a grudge, that there would be fallout if he thought Ivy was going to challenge his pick for the nomination.

If Georgia Nolan knows that Ivy is in Arizona looking into Pierce, what are the chances that Adam's father knows the same?

I thought of the way the cop had thrown Bodie onto the hood of the car—harder than necessary. I thought about the fact that the police had called Social Services to pick me up instead of Ivy.

"So this is what?" I asked. "Payback?"

The muscles in Adam's neck tensed. "This was a warning shot," Adam corrected tersely. "My father collects things: information, people, blackmail material. He wants Ivy to remember what he's capable of."

Bodie had insisted that Ivy had cleared William Keyes of involvement in the justice's murder, but—

Keyes wants Pierce to get the nomination. He organized the retreat where Pierce and Major Bharani met.

"Ivy will take care of it," Adam told me for a second time. His eyes darkened as he pulled out onto the road. "And I'll take care of my father."

CHAPTER 45

Ivy arrived home that night. I'd just gotten out of the shower when she knocked on my door. Running a towel over my hair, then tossing it aside, I answered the knock.

From the look on Ivy's face, I had a pretty good idea what she wanted to talk about.

"Let me guess," I said. "You want to chat about my little adventure this afternoon?"

Ivy inclined her head slightly. "Can I come in?"

I stepped back from the doorway. "Knock yourself out." I combed my fingers through my wet hair, working out kinks as I went.

"Here," Ivy said, sitting down on my bed. "Let me."

At first, I had no idea what she was talking about, and then she picked a brush up off my nightstand.

Ivy sits on the edge of my bed. I sit on the floor in front of her. The memory hit me just as hard this time as it had the last. *Ivy murmuring softly to me. Ivy's fingers deftly working their way through my hair.*

"You used to braid my hair." I hadn't meant to say that out loud.

Emotion danced around the edges of Ivy's features. "Mom preferred pigtails," she said. "High on your head." She shook her head slightly, a soft smile coming over her face. "Even when you were tiny, you'd never met a pair of pigtails you couldn't demolish. A braid was a little sturdier."

"You stayed with me," I said, the words catching in my throat. "After the funeral, you stayed with me."

"For a few weeks," Ivy replied, her voice difficult to read. "Then Gramps came, and . . ."

And she'd given me away. I couldn't blame twenty-one-year-old Ivy for that—and I wouldn't have given up the years I'd had with Gramps, not for anything.

"I've been thinking," I said. "About the clinical trial."

My throat went dry, just saying the words. It was easier, in a twisted way, to think about murder and politics and what Vivvie and Henry were going through than to think about my own situation.

About Gramps.

"If the results are promising . . ." I trailed off, thinking of John Thomas Wilcox, rattling off the stages of my grandfather's illness, the losses—one after another—we'd be facing down the road. "Maybe it's a good idea."

"Maybe it is," Ivy returned. She studied me for a moment, then continued.

"I know this is hard for you. If you ever want to talk—"

"I don't," I said. The words came out more abruptly than I meant for them to, so I softened them slightly. "I'm not much of a talker."

Ivy accepted that with a nod. The two of us fell into silence, then she gestured to the floor in front of her with the brush. "Sit."

I sat. She began gently working the brush through my hair. For a minute, maybe two, she said nothing as she brushed. "I'm sorry about this afternoon. Bodie and Adam said you handled it well."

"Is Bodie okay?"

"I took care of it." That was all Ivy said. How she'd taken care of it, what precisely the situation had been—she clearly wasn't in a detail-sharing mood.

"I heard Georgia ambushed you at school," Ivy said. She kept brushing as she changed topics. "I'm sorry about that, too. It won't happen again."

Based on the tone in Ivy's voice, I was guessing that she had already had or would soon be having a rather pointed conversation with the First Lady.

"She asked what you were doing in Arizona," I told my sister. "She seemed to think that William Keyes might take exception to your digging into Pierce."

Given what had happened *after* school, I expected that to provoke some sort of response in Ivy, but she just continued working the tangles out of my hair.

"You haven't told the First Lady that Justice Marquette was murdered." I laid that out on the table. "I'm betting that means you still haven't told the president, either."

"I have my reasons," Ivy replied. The rhythm of her brushing never changed.

"Bodie said you don't suspect the president."

Ivy paused in her brushing, just for an instant. Then she caught herself and resumed. "The president has nothing to do with this," she said. "That's not why I've kept it quiet, Tess."

"And William Keyes?" I asked.

"What about him?"

"He had Bodie dragged in for questioning on who knows what kind of crime, just to prove he could! Adam said that was just a warning shot—"

"You don't need to worry about William Keyes," Ivy told me. "I can handle it."

"He wants Pierce nominated." I let those words hang in the air. "He wants him to get the nomination badly enough that he's willing to have Bodie arrested to scare you into compliance."

"Bodie wasn't arrested." Ivy's voice was maddeningly calm. "He was just taken in for questioning. And I'm not scared."

The only way this plan makes any sense—the only way it could even potentially be worth the risk—is if Pierce had reason to believe he'd get the nomination. Henry's words came back to dog me for the hundredth time.

"He's good at getting what he wants, isn't he?" I asked Ivy. "Adam's father?"

"I'm better."

That wasn't what I'd been asking. "How many people, other than the president, have enough power to sway a Supreme Court nomination?"

That question took Ivy by surprise. She was quiet long enough that I wasn't sure she was going to reply. "Men like William Keyes," she said finally, "they're called kingmakers. They have money. They have power. For any variety of reasons, they're not viable political candidates themselves, but when it comes to elections, they can sway things one way or another."

The president is rarely the most powerful person in Washington . . .

I tried to turn around to look at Ivy, but she turned me back around.

"Bodie said that clearing the president and Adam's father was the first thing you did." I tried a different tactic.

Ivy set the brush down and ran a hand over my hair. Without a word, she started braiding.

"Ivy?"

"Bodie talks too much."

If she hadn't had a hold on my hair, I would have turned around to face her again. "I have a right to know. *Vivvie* has a right to know."

Ivy reached the bottom of the braid. She held on for a moment, then fixed it in place. "You're going to have to trust me just a little bit longer on this, Tess."

Trust. That one word was enough to put a mile of distance between us. I stiffened, and Ivy stood. I didn't realize until she'd taken a step away that I'd been leaning lightly against her.

"You don't know what it's like," I told Ivy, standing up myself and walking over to the mirror. With my hair tied back, I could see the similarity in our features. Part of me wanted to tear out the braid. "You don't know what it's like," I said again, "to be told over and over to just sit back, while other people make decisions that affect you. Vivvie is *my* friend. She came to *me*. And whatever you're doing, it's not helping her! Keeping her in the dark, keeping me in the dark—it's not helping, Ivy." I lowered my voice. "It just makes us helpless."

Ivy came to stand behind me. I turned to face her so that I didn't have to look at our reflections side by side in the mirror.

"I know what it's like to feel helpless," Ivy told me quietly. "I know what it's like to have other people making *your* decisions. I do, Tess." There was emotion in her voice—but I couldn't pinpoint it any more specifically than that. She was feeling *something*. About me? About this case?

"I never want you to feel like that, Tessie. I don't. But you truly don't need to know what I'm doing. This job?" Ivy never raised her voice, but each word was delivered more intensely than the last. "I get to make a difference. I get to help people, but that comes at a cost."

My father killed himself. I could see Henry's face, as clear as if he were standing here in front of me. *She covered it up.*

"I don't want that for you," Ivy said. "Can you understand that? I have to keep you separate, Tess. I won't let you be part of the cost."

"The First Lady is making social calls," I retorted. "Vivvie is dying inside. I'm not *separate*, Ivy." I didn't give her a chance to respond. "I know there's a third person involved—someone other than Vivvie's father and Judge Pierce. If Pierce supplied the money and Vivvie's dad made sure the justice didn't leave the hospital alive, then what was the third person's job?" I cut Ivy off before she'd gotten a word out. "I'm guessing that person either slipped the justice something to get him to the hospital, or they were in charge of making sure Pierce got the nomination. Either way, the two individuals you 'cleared' first seem like pretty good suspects."

"There were cameras on the president," Ivy said curtly. "Practically the whole evening." That Ivy was volunteering information at all should have been comforting. But it wasn't.

"Practically," I repeated.

Ivy was starting to look like she was losing her patience. "Tess," she bit out.

"And Keyes?" I plowed on before she could say more. "How did you clear him?"

There was a long pause. "I collect information," Ivy said finally. "Details that might prove useful down the road. Given that William does the same, it is always in my best interest to have something on him. And right now, what I have on him tells me that Theodore Marquette is the *last* person he would have wanted to see removed from the Supreme Court."

Like that wasn't cryptic.

"Keyes is working to get Pierce nominated," I insisted. "The president is the one who actually does the nominating. They were both there the night before Justice Marquette's heart attack. They were both in that picture I gave you—"

"Let *me* worry about this," Ivy interrupted.

"The picture was taken at Camp David," I continued. Maybe, if I kept pelting her with information, I could get something—anything—out of her in return. "A retreat. I think that's where Vivvie's dad and Pierce met. We know there's a third party involved. And the president and Keyes were the only ones there who were also at the gala that night."

"No," Ivy said sharply. "They weren't."

I frowned, an argument on the tip of my tongue.

"I know where that picture was taken, Tess. I knew before you did. This is *my job*. It's what I do. I trade in secrets and information. I solve problems. You brought this one to me, and so help me God, you are going to let me fix it."

"What do you mean the president and Adam's father weren't the only people in both places?" I asked.

Ivy threw her hands up in frustration. "Did you ever wonder who took the picture? Who might be standing right outside the frame? You have a *fraction* of the story, Tess. Don't confuse that with the truth."

Who took the picture? Ivy was right. I hadn't wondered that.

"You said that you already knew the picture was taken at Camp David." The words almost got stuck in my throat. "How?"

Ivy stared at me for a few seconds, then answered. "Because I was there."

When I'd given her the photograph, she hadn't said anything about recognizing it. She hadn't allowed so much as a flash of recognition to cross her face.

Fixers are experts at covering things up. Henry's words wouldn't leave me alone. *Your sister's practically an artist.*

"I'm going to help Vivvie, Tessie. I'm going to find the truth here. You just have to let me." She tucked a stray piece of hair back into my braid.

The second she called me Tessie, my throat started to sting. "You can't let the president nominate Pierce."

"I won't."

"The article in the *Post* said—"

"I won't," Ivy repeated, her voice louder this time, more final. She turned to take her leave but glanced back at me. "For what it's worth," she said, "you can tell Vivvie that I wouldn't pay much attention to that article."

Bodie had said that there were two reasons for leaking a story like that—to help Pierce's case or to hurt him.

"Are you going to track down the source?" I asked Ivy.

I'm not having this conversation with you. I could practically see her bite back those words. Instead, she lifted her chin slightly. "Trust me, Tessie, it's not worth checking out."

CHAPTER 46

By the end of the week, a slew of opinion articles had come out in Pierce's favor. In World Issues, we had to watch people debate his merits on TV.

And with each day, I became more convinced that whoever had leaked that article had done it to help Pierce's chances, not hurt them.

It's not worth checking out. Ivy's words rang in my ears as I watched Henry Marquette take a seat across the courtyard at lunch. He hadn't spoken to me once since he'd told me about his father. Asher cast a glance at me but took a seat next to Henry.

"Has Ivy found anything?" Vivvie asked me. It was just the two of us at our table—the way it had been before all this had started.

"I don't know." I wished I had something to tell her, but Ivy had spent the past few days locked in her office, going over files she'd brought back from Arizona. I had no idea what kind of files they were. All I knew was that she'd brought boxes of them back—and I'd barely seen her since that night in my room.

"I need to do something." Vivvie's voice was quiet, but it vibrated with an intensity of emotion that told me that *need* wasn't an exaggeration. "I need for *us* to do something."

"What?" I asked.

"Something," Vivvie insisted. "Talk to your sister again, or set up a meeting with the First Lady, or . . . or . . . *something*."

It had been four days since her father's funeral. A week since he'd killed himself. Eleven days since she'd told me what she'd overheard.

So much had happened. And now it felt like *nothing* was happening. Nothing except the media practically paving Pierce's road to a nomination with gold. Because of that article in the *Post*.

Because of some anonymous source.

"Okay," I told Vivvie.

Her eyes grew round. "Okay *what*?"

"Okay," I said. "I have something we can do."

Step one: Waylay Emilia Rhodes on her way to class.

"Oh," she said. "It's you. Turned anyone's twin even more delinquent than usual lately?"

I took that as a cue that I didn't need to bother with niceties. "The day you told us that Vivvie's dad had been fired, you mentioned that you'd heard it from a freshman whose mom works for the *Washington Post*."

Emilia arched an eyebrow, waiting for me to get to the point.

I obliged. "Which freshman?"

Step two: Make nice with the freshman.

Vivvie took the lead on step two. She was better at being nice than I was. Eventually, she dropped my name, and the freshman was all too happy to call in a favor with "Uncle Carson"—the man who'd written the article—in order to put herself in *Tess Kendrick*'s good graces.

Word of Georgia Nolan's impromptu visit had spread, and that only served to remind people that my sister had some very powerful friends. What money was at most schools, power was at Hardwicke. It wasn't about who had the nicest car or the biggest house. It was about who had the best *connections*. Through no fault of my own, I'd edged my way back onto the A-list—a problem I'd deal with later. For now, all I needed to do was prepare for my meeting with good old Uncle Carson, who thought he was being interviewed for some kind of school project.

"What's step three?" Vivvie asked me, just before the final bell. Dr. Clark cast a warning look at us, but a second later, the bell rang. Vivvie and I made our way into the hallway.

"Step three," I said, "is finding some leverage."

When the reporter met with me, he probably wouldn't be happy to find out that I'd arranged the meeting under false pretenses. He definitely wouldn't be in the mood to volunteer his source's identity.

Even if he could be persuaded to do so, I could hear the First Lady saying, *he would want something in return.*

And that meant that I needed something the reporter wanted.

And that meant that I needed Henry Marquette.

CHAPTER 47

Henry wasn't just ignoring me. He was avoiding me. When he saw me coming his way, he made his excuses to the group he was talking to and ducked into the boys' bathroom.

Presumably, he thought that I would not follow him.

He obviously did not know me very well.

Henry cast a glance at the door when it opened behind him, then did a double take when he realized it was me.

"Really?" he said dryly.

I leaned back against the door, blocking his exit.

"Get out of my way, Ms. Kendrick."

"Ms. Kendrick," I repeated. "We're not even on a first-name basis anymore?"

He didn't reply. I didn't know how much of his avoiding me was because he was angry at me for being Ivy's sister, for trusting her, even a little, and how much of it was him being angry at himself for telling me about his father.

"Must we do this?" Henry asked, his voice painfully polite.

"I'll get out of your way once you've listened to what I have to say," I told him. "Otherwise, we can stay here and stare at each other."

He glared at me. I offered him a lazy smile in return. He snapped.

"Talk," he ordered crisply.

"I've got a plan for trying to figure out who leaked the story about Pierce."

Henry's face didn't move a muscle, but he couldn't quite squelch the flicker of interest in his eyes. "I thought the sum total of your plan was to let your sister do her job."

Now that I knew where Henry's feelings about Ivy came from, I couldn't steel myself against them in the same way. Objectively, maybe Ivy had done the Marquette family a favor by making Henry's father's death seem like an accident, but I couldn't expect Henry to be *objective* about something like that. He was the one who had to live with the secret. His father wasn't here. His grandfather wasn't here.

Ivy was the only one left to blame.

"My sister has been otherwise occupied," I said, choosing my words carefully. "She doesn't think this is a lead worth following up on." A hint of interest sparked in Henry's eyes. I pushed on. "I do."

Henry cracked the barest of smiles. "And you have a plan."

"It's not really a plan," I said, "so much as a gamble."

Someone attempted to open the door to the bathroom, and I leaned back against it harder.

Henry cleared his throat. "Would it be possible to talk about your gamble in a slightly less inappropriate location?"

"If you really want to." I eased off the door and opened it, ignoring the stare of the boy on the other side. Now it was my turn to arch an eyebrow at Henry.

"After you."

I texted Bodie that Vivvie and I needed to work on a project after school. To add credence to that story, Henry and I met the reporter at Vivvie's—or, more specifically, in the lobby of the Roosevelt Hotel, where Vivvie and her aunt were staying until her aunt could find more permanent lodging. Vivvie watched from a nearby coffee shop. Her aunt was with her but had her back to us.

Let's hope it stays that way, I thought.

I looked at my watch. The reporter from the *Post* was supposed to meet us here any minute.

"Tess Kendrick?" A red-haired man with a reddish brown beard approached. His eyes flicked over to Henry, and I saw a spark of recognition.

Good.

"Carson Dweck?" I said. He nodded.

"I hear you need to talk to a reporter for a school project." The man's lips curved up slightly. "Hardwicke—very big on projects, aren't they?"

I wondered if he would have said yes to his honorary niece's request if I hadn't gone to Hardwicke. And then I wondered if he would have said yes if my last name hadn't been Kendrick.

"You wrote the piece on Edmund Pierce," I said, deciding it wasn't worth beating around the bush. "The one that said Pierce was a shoo-in for nomination and the president was moving at an unprecedented rate toward seeing that nomination through." Whatever the man had been expecting me to say, it wasn't that.

"Kendrick," he said, turning the name over in his mouth. "As in Ivy Kendrick?"

Like he just figured that out, I thought.

"And you're Henry Marquette," the man continued, turning an eagle eye on the boy standing next to me. "My condolences on the loss of your grandfather."

Henry gave a brief nod. "Thank you."

The reporter held Henry's gaze a moment longer, then turned back to me. "This is about the Pierce piece?" he said. "Annika led me to believe you needed input on some kind of school project."

"Let's call it a school project on the Pierce piece." I bared my teeth in something vaguely resembling a smile. "You cited an anonymous source, saying that the decision was all but made. I'm wondering what made you think this information was legit."

"You're wondering who my source was," the reporter translated. He was starting to look like a man who wanted a drink. "You might want to look into shield laws," he said. "For your project. Or"—he flicked his eyes over to Henry—"you could look up what the Supreme Court has to say about the somewhat narrow circumstances in which a reporter can be compelled to give up a source."

"That would be of interest," Henry said politely, "if we were attempting to acquire the information via a legal subpoena or in conjunction with state or federal government."

Carson Dweck huffed, stuffing his hands into his pockets. "Look, kids, all I can tell you is that my source wishes to remain anonymous, but that the facts I was given have since been verified."

I had a feeling he'd delivered a slightly less condescending version of that statement to multiple people in the hours since the article had gone up.

"What if we had something you wanted?" I asked pointedly. "Could you point us in the right direction then?"

Those words seemed to take the man by surprise. He smiled slightly. "And what is it that you have that you think I would want?" he asked in a tone that told me he was humoring me.

"An exclusive with Justice Marquette's grieving grandson." I saw a flash of interest in Dweck's eyes. Theodore Marquette's death was big news, and Henry wasn't just a tragic figure—he was young, handsome, wealthy, *and* tragic.

"Sounds like more of a *People* magazine piece than something for the *Post*," the reporter commented. But he didn't say no.

"Does that mean you're not interested?" I asked point-blank.

"It means," Dweck replied, "that I'm not going to violate journalistic integrity for a fluff piece."

"What if it wasn't a fluff piece?" Henry countered.

I stared at him. What was he doing? This—whatever *this* was—hadn't been part of the plan.

"No offense, son, but what could you possibly have to tell me that could get me a Pulitzer?"

A warning bell went off in my head. *He wouldn't*, I thought, horrified. I tried to catch Henry's eye.

"Off the record?" Henry ignored me, his attention focused solely on Carson Dweck. The reporter nodded.

"I have reason to believe my grandfather was murdered. And," Henry continued, "I have reason to believe that the White House is covering it up." He took a step forward. "Now," he said, his eyes glittering, "who's your source?"

CHAPTER 48

Twenty minutes later, the reporter was gone, and I was considering *ending* Henry Marquette.

"You," I started to say, but that was all I could manage. "*You*," I said again.

"I went public," Henry supplied calmly. "You got what you wanted, and I insured that your sister is not going to be able to sweep this under the rug."

Ivy was going to kill me. And I was going to kill Henry.

"That wasn't the plan," I told him, poking him in the chest with my index finger.

"That wasn't *your* plan," he replied. "I never said that I didn't have one of my own."

Apparently, his plan involved taking everything we knew—the fact that Vivvie's father had been implicated in Justice Marquette's death, the doctor's subsequent suicide, the existence of the burner phone, the suspected involvement of other players with powerful political connections—to the press. And the kicker was that I'd helped him do it. I'd set up the meeting *myself*.

"They won't print anything on your word alone," I told Henry.

"Which means," he emphasized, "that your sister isn't going to be the only one looking into this. Our friend at the *Post* is already thinking of this as his Watergate."

Henry had a rare gift for sounding reasonable no matter *what* he was saying.

"If you're done silently judging me," Henry commented, "might I turn your attention to the information we got in exchange for what I was willing to barter?"

I pictured myself actually wringing his neck. It was therapeutic, but possibly not productive. Begrudgingly, I thought back over what Carson Dweck had told us about his source for the Pierce story.

"I'll tell you what I told your sister," he'd said, pointing a finger at me. *"The tip came from inside the West Wing, and that's all I'm going to say."*

Fighting back a sinking feeling in my stomach, I tried not to think about the first half of that sentence.

"Inside the West Wing." I focused on that part, saying the words out loud. That revelation shouldn't have been surprising. Where else would a tip about the president's plan for nominating a Supreme Court justice have come from?

I thought he was going to tell us the tip came from William Keyes. I hadn't even realized that was what I'd expected to find until we'd heard differently. Keyes was the one who'd attempted to coerce Ivy into supporting Pierce. He was the one who'd arranged the Camp David meeting.

"Inside the West Wing," Henry repeated. "That means we're talking about the president and his immediate staff."

I was fairly certain that meant we *weren't* talking about an intern.

"Even if we knew who in the West Wing had leaked the information," Henry continued, "we couldn't rule out the possibility that the order to leak it came from President Nolan."

In Henry's mind, this was damning. The president had been at Camp David with Pierce and Vivvie's father. The president had been at the Keyes Foundation gala the night before Justice Marquette's so-called heart attack. The president's office had leaked a story designed to build momentum for Pierce's nomination.

"Ivy cleared the president," I said abruptly. Henry and I hadn't had this conversation yet. He'd been too busy ignoring me for the past few days for me to tell him what Ivy had said. "If someone poisoned your grandfather at the gala that night, it wasn't the president. There were cameras on him practically the whole time."

Henry latched on to the same word in that sentence that I had. "Practically."

I glanced over at the coffee shop. Vivvie was staring over at the two of us. Sooner or later, I'd need to fill her in on what was going on.

A second later, Vivvie's aunt turned to look our way.

I grabbed Henry's arm. "Look natural," I told him, turning my head and pasting a smile on my face.

His hand curved around my shoulder in response. "I always look natural."

We started walking. Vivvie's aunt turned back around, but Henry didn't drop his arm from my shoulder. "Did it ever occur to you," he said to me, his voice low and pleasant, "that the president might not have to do his own dirty work? Even if you believe that he didn't poison my grandfather, that doesn't mean he didn't have it done."

The same logic could apply to William Keyes—or to anyone else in that photograph, or anyone else at Camp David that weekend *not* pictured in the photograph.

I said as much.

"Who else was there?" Henry asked me.

I didn't know how many other people had been there—but I knew that Ivy had been. I couldn't tell Henry that. Not with the way he felt about my sister.

"It occurs to me," Henry said, his voice still sounding so reasonable, so *calm*, "that according to our dear reporter friend, your sister got to him before we did." Henry finally dropped his arm and stopped walking. "Everything we know, she knows."

"That's not a bad thing," I said, but all I could think about was Ivy telling me to trust her, Ivy telling me that the reporter wasn't worth checking out.

"My sister is not a part of this," I told Henry, shutting out those thoughts. "She's on our side."

Henry reached out for me again, his touch light against my skin. "She may be on your side," he said quietly. "She's not on mine."

On the other side of the lobby, Vivvie and her aunt stood, getting ready to leave the café.

"Am I on your side?" I asked Henry. "Or am I the enemy, too?"

He'd used me to set up this meeting, and the whole time, he'd had a plan of his own. I couldn't blame him for that. If it were my grandfather who'd been killed, I might have done the same thing.

"You aren't the enemy," Henry said, dropping his arm to his side once more and taking a step back. "That doesn't mean our goals are aligned."

CHAPTER 49

The next day was Saturday. I was still grounded—*school projects* aside—which apparently, in Ivy's book, meant that my job was sitting around the house doing nothing while she was out doing who knows what. I had the vague sense that the case had taken a turn, but what that turn was, what she knew, what she was *hiding*—I had no idea.

I'd caught Vivvie up on what I knew. She'd caught me up on the fact that her aunt had recognized Henry but not me. Apparently, the woman had assumed that I was Henry's girlfriend. *Because that's not disturbing.*

My cell phone rang at half past three. I answered it, glad for the distraction.

"It's your favorite person," Asher informed me.

"No," I said, leaning back against my headboard. "You're not."

"I won't embarrass you by proving I am," Asher replied, unfazed. "We have bigger problems."

"Problems?" By Asher's definition, that could mean any number of things.

"More like problem, singular," Asher amended. "I just talked to Henry. He's planning to go with his mother to a state dinner tonight."

That seemed like something Henry would do. "And?"

"*And*," Asher said emphatically, "Henry is planning to go with his mother to a state dinner tonight." He paused, presumably for an audible reaction on my part.

He got none.

"Henry avoids white-tie events like the plague," Asher elaborated. "His mom gets invited to these things all the time—her family is, shall we say, *well off*, with a lot of international holdings. But no one would expect her to put in an appearance this soon after Theo's death." Asher finally paused for a breath. "My spidey senses tell me that Henry's mom was not overcome by a sudden desire to honor the queen of Denmark."

"You don't have spidey senses," I told Asher automatically.

"I *do* have a Henry sense," Asher said firmly. "And I'm telling you, he was acting super shady when I talked to him. I think he actually convinced his mother to go tonight. That means he's willingly donning a tailcoat and bow tie and venturing into a bedazzled crowd of people, all of whom will tell him how sorry they are for his loss."

I thought *bedazzled* was probably overstating things a bit, but focused on the rest of what Asher was saying. "You really think going to this thing with his mom was Henry's idea?"

"I do," Asher pronounced. "I just can't figure out why."

Unfortunately, I *could*. "Who attends state dinners?" I asked with a sinking feeling.

"Three hundred of the president's closest colleagues and friends." Asher paused, thinking. "Members of the cabinet and staff, the vice president and his family, assorted governors, donors, lobby firm executives, Hollywood celebrities, professional athletes, philanthropists, congressmen, and a half-dozen partridges in a governmental pear tree."

I paused for a second. "What's Henry's phone number?"

After he gave it to me, I hung up, glared at my phone, then made the call.

"Hello." Henry answered the phone with trademark calm.

"What *exactly* do you think you're doing?" I asked him, without bothering to identify myself. He must have recognized my voice, because he didn't ask who it was.

"Currently, I'm reading *The Economist*."

"You're going to a state dinner?" I gritted out.

"I take it Asher called you?"

"What's your endgame here, Henry? Why are you going?"

"My mother needed an escort." Henry was a good liar. But not good enough.

You aren't the enemy. That doesn't mean our goals are aligned. Henry had a goal. He had an agenda. He had a reason for going tonight that had nothing to do with his mother.

"You have a plan," I said. "And given that it's a plan that involves rubbing elbows with several hundred of the city's most politically powerful people, I'm not feeling very comforted at the moment."

"Rest assured, Tess. I can take care of myself."

Until he told me that he could take care of himself, it hadn't occurred to me that whatever he had planned for tonight might be dangerous.

"What are you going to do?" I asked softly.

"I'm just going to show up. See people. Be seen."

Be seen. Why would Henry want to be seen?

"Henry, either you tell me exactly what you're doing, or I'll tell my sister you're up to something."

The silence on the other end of the phone line grew decidedly chillier. "Fine," he said stiffly, glaring at me through the phone. "I'm simply interested to see if Carson Dweck has gone back to his source in the West Wing for information on my grandfather's murder, and if that source is at all curious about how Carson got his information."

It took me a few seconds to process that statement. Henry had told the reporter everything we knew. I'd taken him at his word when he'd said that he'd done it so that Ivy wouldn't be the only one looking into this.

But if the reporter went back to his source, if his source was in any way involved in the conspiracy . . . My mind raced.

"You're trying to draw the third player out," I realized.

I wanted to believe that Dweck wouldn't reveal Henry as the source of his information about the justice's assassination. I wanted to believe that hadn't been Henry's plan all along.

"So that's it?" I said. "You start making noise, then parade around at a state dinner and see who takes the bait?"

"I assure you, I have no intention of parading."

"I assure *you*," I replied, "that this isn't going to work. Even if our missing conspirator has heard that you're asking questions, even if he or she thinks you know too much, they're not going to make a move in front of three hundred of the president's closest friends."

I could practically hear Henry's subtle, pointed smile in response to those words. "Then you don't need to worry about me," he said. "Do you?"

I hung up the phone. I took a second to tamp down on my temper, to think this through. In a crowd, with security, Henry would probably be fine. But I couldn't help thinking that Henry's grandfather might well have been poisoned at an event just as posh and secure as this one.

Biting the bullet, I did the only thing I *could* do. I called Ivy. No answer. I called Bodie. No answer. Where *were* they? I called Adam. No answer. Ivy again. No answer. I kept calling.

It was four o'clock. A quick internet search told me the state dinner, honoring the queen of Denmark, started at 7:30 p.m.

Another call. Still no answer.

Henry was going to do this. I wasn't going to be able to stop him. *Fine*, I thought darkly. I called him back.

"I'm going with you." My words came out equal parts promise and threat.

"As whose date?" Henry asked. "Unless your sister is willing to rustle you up a last-minute invitation—and I think we both know she is not—you have no way in the front door."

He was right. Sneaking into a state dinner wasn't like sneaking into a movie. It was probably a felony.

"This is a big mistake, Henry."

He was quiet for a moment. "I suppose," he said finally, "that is the only kind of mistake I make."

He hung up the phone. I tried Ivy again. Bodie again. Adam again. *Where were they?*

Finally, I called Asher back. "We have a problem."

"I won't say I told you so," Asher replied. "But let's just take a moment of silence to think about the fact that I was right."

I didn't have time to acknowledge the quip. "What does a person wear to a state dinner?" I asked.

"Why?" Asher said. "Are we invited?"

"You aren't," I told him. "But with a little luck, I might be."

"I'd tell you that was pretty much impossible," Asher replied, "but you're Tess Kendrick. My spidey senses tell me that impossible is kind of your thing."

After I got off the phone with Asher, I tried Ivy one last time. Wherever she was, whatever she was doing, she still wasn't picking up. I'd written down a phone number Asher had gotten for me, and I pulled the trigger and called it.

"Hello?"

"Anna?" I said. "It's Tess Kendrick."

"Tess!" The vice president's daughter sounded delighted to hear from me. "What's up?"

I walked to the window and stared out at Ivy's front lawn. "I need a favor."

CHAPTER 50

Asher was supposed to bring me something to wear. Instead, he brought me his twin.

"I'm not doing this for you," Emilia told me, thrusting a trio of garment bags at her brother, who obligingly took hold of them. "Asher seems to think your presence at this state dinner is essential for Henry's continued well-being." She eyed the foyer, seemingly decided it would not do, then marched up the spiral staircase. She set up camp in my bedroom and pulled out my desk chair. "Sit."

I cast a pained look at Asher, then sat.

"We don't have much time," Emilia told me, opening what was apparently *not* a toolbox, but some kind of makeup kit. "Don't flinch."

Over the next hour and a half, I came to the conclusion that Emilia Rhodes was either the devil incarnate or the second coming of Coco Chanel.

She suggested the second option herself.

Emilia threw Asher out of the room around the time she had me start trying on dresses.

"You're lucky Di goes to a ton of these things," she told me. "And that she's about your size."

I was not lucky, however, when it came to the ambassador's daughter's views on cleavage. After I'd nixed a second dress for being too low-cut, I thought Emilia might exact vengeance with an eyelash curler, but she just nodded to the third garment bag.

"It's that one or nothing," she told me.

The dress was sapphire blue, dark enough that I could almost tell myself it was navy. It was full-length, with a fitted bodice and flowing skirt. I eyed the neckline.

"Here." Emilia slipped it off the hanger and ordered me to turn around. She helped me step into the gown, then fastened it up the back. I glanced down at my chest, and seeing it tucked firmly away, allowed myself to be turned toward the full-length mirror.

The sheen off the sapphire fabric made it look almost like flowing water. There were gathers at my waist, and the bottom half of the dress rippled to the floor, arcing out around me in a full skirt that swayed slightly as I turned. The bodice fit perfectly, clinging to every hint of a curve my body had to offer. A light scattering of beadwork caught the light just so.

"Well?" Emilia said.

I forced myself to stop staring at my reflection. "This will work."

Emilia stepped in front of me and examined her handiwork. She reached a hand out to rearrange a tendril near my face.

"Why are you doing this?" I couldn't help asking the question.

Emilia gave me a look I couldn't quite read. "Asher's the nice twin. He's the one people like." She paused. "I'm the one who gets things done." She handed me a tube of lipstick. I stared at it like she'd handed me a snake.

"In case you need to reapply," she said briskly. Clearly, she'd shared as much of her motivation as she was going to share. The doorbell rang downstairs. I took a deep breath.

On my way out the door, Emilia's voice stopped me. "If I asked you what was going on, would you tell me?"

I glanced back at her.

"That's what I thought," she said, averting her eyes. "Don't worry about it. Asher's the one people confide in, too." The doorbell rang again, and Emilia walked past me. "Whatever you're doing," she told me, "don't mess it up."

I managed to walk down the stairs without killing myself, but it was a near thing. Emilia hadn't brought shoes, so we'd borrowed a pair of Ivy's. Luckily, my sister seemed to have a fairly elaborate collection.

When I reached the front door, Asher opened it for me. A man in a navy suit stood there. He held out a card to me.

"Special delivery," he said. "Courtesy of Vice President Hayden."

The invitation was engraved on white linen paper. At the top, there was a gold seal, an eagle surrounded with stars, so intricate in detail that it looked as if it had been painted on by hand. Below that, black-inked calligraphy declared, *The President and Mrs. Nolan request the pleasure of the company of Theresa Kendrick at a dinner in honor of Her Royal Highness, Queen* . . .

I stopped reading when I reached the word *Queen*.

The man who'd delivered my invitation gestured toward the car he'd driven here. "Miss Hayden also thought you might appreciate a ride."

I glanced back at Asher and Emilia.

"Like I said," Asher told me, slinging an arm over his sister's shoulder, "impossible is kind of your thing."

CHAPTER 51

Walking in heels while wearing a ball gown was, as it turned out, more difficult than finagling an invitation to a state dinner. I made it past White House security without incident but had to fight to keep my balance. Head held high and trying not to grind my teeth, I strode past the photographers documenting the arrival of the president's guests, my heels clicking audibly against the marble floor and my heart thudding inside my rib cage. The gown swished lightly around my legs as I was ushered into a long hall lined with massive columns. A red carpet the length of Ivy's house separated me from my destination. Crystal chandeliers hung overhead.

No pain, I thought, *no gain*.

I walked the length of the carpet, one step after another, my eyes on the prize. When I stepped into the expansive receiving room at the end of the hall, few of the president's guests marked my entrance—but one who did went ramrod stiff.

To say that Henry Marquette was surprised to see me would have been an understatement. As the shock wore off, he began making his way toward me, weaving through the designer gowns and tuxedos, a polite smile on his face and murder in his eyes. I took possession of the card with my table assignment on it and awaited his arrival.

I didn't have to wait long.

"What are you doing here?" he asked me sharply. I took his arm as if he'd offered it to me—partially to irritate him and partially for balance.

"I told you I wasn't letting you do this yourself," I replied, my smile just as perfunctory and polite as his own. "I'm at table twelve. Where are you?"

He walked me along the edge of the vast, oval-shaped room. "I do not even want to know how you managed this," he said. Dressed in a long-tailed tuxedo, his resistance to using contractions didn't seem as out of place as it would have in the halls of Hardwicke.

A waiter came by and offered us appetizers. I spotted the president and First Lady on the other side of the room, near a quartet of windows that looked out over the White House lawn. They were standing next to an older woman wearing a sash and crown, who I could only assume was the queen of Denmark.

"I deeply suspect this is a bad idea," I told Henry.

He executed an elegant shrug. "The room is crawling with Secret Service. What could possibly go wrong?"

Before I could answer, his mother approached the two of

us, clothed in a deceptively simple black gown with sleeves that hugged her shoulders. "Tess," she said. "We thought that was you. Is your sister here?"

She looked around, as if Ivy might materialize at any second.

"No," I said. "A friend from school was supposed to come, but she got sick at the last minute, and she thought I might enjoy taking her spot." I couldn't help looking back to the president and First Lady. "Apparently, I'd already been cleared to visit the White House."

"Of course you had," Henry said dourly.

Across the room, the Nolans spotted us and began making their way through the crowd. I tried not to read anything into that but found myself taking a step closer to Henry.

The president stopped in front of Henry's mother. "Your Highness," he said to the older woman on his arm, "may I present to you Pamela Abellard-Marquette?"

The queen peered at Henry's mother. "I believe I know your father," she said in faintly accented English. "Louis Abellard, yes?" She saw Henry and processed Mrs. Marquette's married name. A fleck of sorrow crossed her eyes.

Henry's mother saw it, too. Appreciation flickered briefly across her features as she offered a curtsy so naturally that it didn't even strike me as odd. "And this is my son, Henry," she said, "and his friend Tess."

Georgia Nolan looked at Henry and me with a gleam in her eye. "The Marine Band will be playing later," she told Henry. "You and Tess will have to dance."

Those sounded more like the words of a matchmaker than someone who, in any way, considered Henry or me a threat.

The president didn't address either of us at all. As the Nolans continued greeting people, I exchanged a glance with Henry.

Either they're excellent actors, I thought, *or they have no idea that we went to the press.*

Henry read my expression, then arched an eyebrow slightly in return. *Wait*, I could almost hear him saying, *and see*.

Soon, we were herded toward the Grand Staircase. The president and First Lady, as well as Her Highness, were announced. Slowly, the rest of us descended into the State Dining Room, like Cinderella walking into the ball.

After dinner, there was indeed dancing in the East Room. Music echoed off the twenty-foot ceilings, a trio of chandeliers casting light on the gathered Washington elite below. I caught sight of a graying A-list actor leading his philanthropist wife out onto the dance floor. As others followed suit, a somewhat reluctant Henry offered me his hand.

"I don't dance," I said flatly.

"You do," he replied, "if you want to get a three-hundred-and-sixty-degree view of the room with no one the wiser."

I gave him my best thousand-yard stare. He was undeterred. "Henry," I bit out his name.

"Yes?"

I gave in to the inevitable. "Would you like to dance?"

Henry walked me onto the floor. He settled one hand near the small of my back and used his other hand to take mine. After a moment's hesitation, I wrapped my free arm around his waist.

As we began to move, I tried my best not to step on his toes. He went left. I went right.

"Just follow my lead," he said.

I got the sense he wasn't just talking about the dancing. Slowly, we found our rhythm.

"What are we looking for?" I asked as we spun.

"Anyone who's watching us," Henry replied.

I caught sight of the Nolans again. The president's arm was around his wife's waist. Behind them, I saw a trio of Secret Service agents doing their best to fade into the background. A dozen yards away, William Keyes was talking to a man in his early forties. Every once in a while, Keyes cast a subtle glance away from the conversation he was having, but it wasn't to look at Henry and me.

Each glance was aimed at the president and the First Lady.

"Smile," Henry murmured into my ear. A photographer snapped a photo of the two of us, then moved to get the money shot: the president leading the First Lady out onto the floor. For a couple in their sixties, they moved with easy grace.

"What now?" I asked Henry as he led me off the floor.

"Now," he said, "I go for a little walk."

Before I could respond, Henry was ducking through the crowd, toward the balcony. He'd made sure we'd been seen, and now he was removing himself from the crowd.

Making himself a better target.

I started after him but didn't make it three steps before I was intercepted—by William Keyes. He looked dapper in his tuxedo. Powerful, but harmless.

Looks could be deceiving.

"Ms. Kendrick," he said. "Tess, wasn't it?"

You know my name. You're the one who had the police bring Bodie in for questioning. You're the reason they called Social Services about me.

"Yes," I told Keyes, meeting his gaze head-on. "It's Tess."

I looked past him and tried to find Henry, but couldn't.

"I understand you've been spending some time in the company of my son." Adam's father had a disconcerting stare. His eyes were hazel, close in color to my own, but there was an uncanny awareness in them—like he knew what you'd had for breakfast that morning and how you would sleep that night.

"Adam volunteered to teach me how to drive." Even as I said the words, I sensed that there was something to this conversation that I was missing. It was like the two of us were playing chess, except I didn't know the rules of the game.

What do you want? I thought, on guard and on edge.

Keyes gave a small shake of his head. "My son always did have a weakness for your sister."

The song wound down. The first couple finished with a flourish, the president dipping his wife. The crowd applauded, and then the Nolans melted back into the masses. I tried to track them, both of them, my attention temporarily distracted from Adam's father.

Where was Henry?

"Would you favor an old man with a dance?" Keyes asked, beginning to lead me to the floor without waiting for a reply.

I tried to resist, but he was polished and smooth, and that was when I realized—Henry's plan had been to make noise.

Come here. See who approached. For the first time, it occurred to me that if the reporter *had* gone back to his White House source, if someone *had* put two and two together and started looking for the person who'd tipped the reporter off about Justice Marquette's death, they might not have ended up with the conclusion that it was Henry.

The reporter's appointment was with me.

"Excuse me." I tried again to pull away from the grip Keyes had on my arm. "I need to go."

"I don't bite," the old man promised, his voice low enough for only me to hear. "No matter what your sister may have led you to believe."

This time, I ducked the old man's grasp a little more firmly, trying not to draw attention to either of us. As I slipped into the crowd, a man in a suit approached me. It took a second for me to recognize him.

Secret Service. Remembering Bodie's advice, I searched my memory for a name. He'd been the one on the front porch the day the president had come to see Ivy.

"Is everything all right here?" he asked me, eyeing Adam's father.

"Kostas, right?" I said. A slight change in the man's expression told me that Bodie was right. It paid to learn names. "Everything's fine."

I started walking toward the balcony. I needed to find Henry. He'd been gone for too long. There were too many people to keep track of. *The president. Georgia. William Keyes.* And who knew how many others.

How many people here work in the West Wing? I wasn't sure I wanted to know the answer to that question.

I'd made it three steps when I ran smack into someone heading in the opposite direction with the same speed and force of purpose. *Ivy.* I registered her presence an instant before she registered mine. She'd reached out instinctively to steady me when we'd collided, but now her hand tightened around my arm.

"What are you doing here?" I asked her. She hadn't been present for appetizers or dinner.

"What am I doing here?" Ivy asked, her voice dangerously pleasant. "What am *I* doing here?" The second time, even the veneer of pleasantness began to slip from her tone. "What are *you* doing here?"

I was grounded and this was a high-security, invitation-only affair. It was a fair question, but all I could think was that I'd lost track of Henry.

"Tess." Ivy shook me slightly.

"I tried calling you." I stepped toward her so that I could whisper without fear of anyone overhearing. She loosened her grip on my arm—slightly. "Henry Marquette knows. Everything I knew, he knows, and he went to the press. He told the reporter who wrote the Pierce article everything."

Ivy went pale as a sheet. An instant later, a mask of calm slid over her face, her lips held in a soft smile that sent a chill down my spine.

"Henry's been making noise about his grandfather's death," I reiterated, afraid to stop talking. "And then he came here."

Understanding shone in Ivy's brown eyes. "He hoped someone was listening."

"I have to go." I tried to push past Ivy.

She brought her free hand up and grabbed my free arm. She held me out in front of her, one of her hands on each of my shoulders.

"He went off by himself a few minutes ago. I should have gone with him, but Keyes stopped me." I kept talking as I tried to pull out of her grasp. "I have to find Henry."

"No. *I* have to find Henry," Ivy replied tightly. "*You* are going to go introduce yourself to the Icelandic ambassador and tell him you go to school with his daughter. Don't leave his side. Don't say anything to anyone. *Do you understand?*"

Before I could say a word, she'd whisked me over to Di's father, who vigorously shook my hand and seemed to have no intention of letting go. Ivy disappeared into the crowd, and I was left trying to extract myself from a very enthusiastic Icelander, who seemed intent on educating me about the relations between Iceland and Denmark.

By the time I managed to shake him, Ivy was long gone.

I started off in the direction I'd seen Henry go. The edges of the room were crowded. The farther I walked, the harder it became to make my way through the ball-gowned masses without giving in to the urge to throw some elbows.

"Tess." A light hand was laid on my shoulder. "Is everything all right?"

Georgia. I tried to step back, but suddenly the hand on my shoulder wasn't so light.

"I understand from your sister that we have a situation," Georgia said. She gave every appearance of someone chatting about the weather as she linked her arm through mine and turned me back toward the dance floor. "It's important that we stay calm and trust the proper authorities to get to the bottom of this... unfortunate situation."

Authorities? What did she know? What had Ivy told her?

"What situation?" I asked out loud.

"The situation," Georgia repeated. "With the reporter."

CHAPTER 52

The reporter, I thought. *The First Lady knows Henry and I talked to the reporter.*

Ivy was nowhere in sight. I hadn't laid eyes on Henry in at least five minutes. When I scanned the room, I didn't see the president, either.

Stay calm. Think. I had to get out of here. I had to find my sister, or Henry, or both.

The First Lady studied me with eyes every bit as knowing as Adam's father's.

Just as she opened her mouth to say something, Ivy reappeared beside us. She said something to Georgia, too low for me to hear, then steered me out of the room.

I tried to turn around and look at my sister, and found myself turned forcibly back to face forward. "Henry—"

"Henry is fine," Ivy said calmly. "At least, he will be until his mother finishes with him."

We passed two security teams on our way out of the White House. As we stepped out the East entrance, I tried again. "What happened back there?" I asked, my body dwarfed by massive columns that reminded me that this was the *White House*. The center of power for the entire country—by some definitions, the world. "Georgia knows about the reporter."

"She knows," Ivy said sharply, "that the reporter is *dead*."

"Dead?" The word got caught in my throat. The man we'd talked to the day before—the one Henry had tipped off about his grandfather's death—was *dead*?

"The police found his body in an alleyway." Ivy's words were remarkably unemotional given the content of what she was saying. "Someone slit his throat."

Bodie pulled the car up. Before I could say anything, my sister had forcibly deposited me in the backseat and climbed into the front.

"What's she doing here?" Bodie asked Ivy, nodding toward me.

"Tess and Henry Marquette decided a state dinner was a good place to play bait." Ivy's answer was laced with barely contained fury.

My brain wouldn't stop racing, couldn't stop racing. *Someone killed the reporter. Is the killer here? Does he know about us?* My skin felt clammy all of a sudden. I felt my fingers digging into the seat beneath me.

"Reagan National," Ivy told Bodie. He turned and shot her a look I couldn't quite read from the backseat, but she was already on the phone. "Adam," she said. "I need a favor. Can you go by the house and pack a bag for Tess?"

What?

On the other end of the line, Adam must have asked a similar question, because Ivy responded.

"Yes, I'm sure, Adam." She paused, listening, and then spoke again. "Indefinitely."

"Indefinitely?" I overcame my inability to form coherent words. "What do you mean, *indefinitely*? Why is Adam packing me a bag?"

Ivy didn't answer. I turned my attention to Bodie.

"What is Reagan National?"

Bodie met my eyes briefly in the mirror. "Airport," he answered.

Airport. Bag.

"I'm not going," I said, feeling a ball of panic slowly unfurling inside me. "I'm not going anywhere. Ivy!"

She wasn't listening to me. As soon as she got off the phone with Adam, she placed another call. "Stetson," she said, a smile in her voice that I knew, without being able to see her, was not reflected on her face. "Ivy Kendrick. I need a favor."

It soon became clear that when Ivy said *I need a favor*, what she really meant was *I need a plane*.

Less than an hour after she'd removed me from the White House, she was putting me on that plane. Standing on a private airstrip, being ordered onto a private plane, I didn't have time to wonder when, exactly, I'd become a girl who wore ball gowns and had access to jets.

"Ivy," I said for probably the fortieth time. "What is going on?"

This time, she answered. "*What's going on*," she said, her voice cutting through the wind around us like a red-hot knife through butter, "is that Carson Dweck was murdered this afternoon."

Less than twenty-four hours after talking to Henry and me.

"*What's going on,*" Ivy continued, "is that I have every reason to believe the person who killed him was there tonight." Ivy's gaze was focused entirely on me, with an intensity that scared me. "*What's going on* is that I came to the White House to fill the president in on the situation, and I found *you.* *What's going on*, Tess, is that you have drawn an enormous target on your own forehead, and I am getting you out of here." She glanced back at her driver. "Bodie will go with you."

Bodie gave a brief nod in response.

"You're sending me away." That wasn't a question. I wasn't sure why I'd said the words out loud. My chest was tight, each breath hard-won. "Ivy, I didn't mean to—"

Ivy took a step forward, closing what little space there was between us. "Right now, I don't care what you meant to do, Tess. I asked you to do one thing. I asked you to *keep your mouth shut.*" Her lips trembled slightly, then pulled back to reveal her teeth. "I asked you to *trust me.*" She turned her head, like she couldn't stand to look at me. "Maybe I should have known that was asking too much."

I felt like she'd knocked the breath out of me.

"Ivy, I—"

"Give me your phone." She wasn't going to listen to me. She'd shut down. She was shutting me out.

I handed it to her. She popped the battery out, dropped the phone onto the tarmac, and crushed it underneath her heel.

"Ivy."

Ivy stared at the crushed phone for a moment, then looked back up. "You won't need this," she said. She turned to Adam. "You have her bag?"

Adam held it out to me. I stood with my hands to my side. If I didn't take it, this wasn't real.

"You can go with your things," Ivy told me calmly, "or you can go with nothing but the clothes on your back, but I swear to you, Tess, you are getting on that plane if I have to order a sedative and knock you unconscious."

Adam put a hand on Ivy's shoulder. She took in a ragged breath. I looked over at Bodie, who was standing a few feet away.

"Get on the plane, kid," he said gently.

"You can't do this," I said. I was talking to Bodie and to Ivy and to Adam, who hadn't said a word since he'd gotten here.

"I can," Ivy said, "and I am." For a second, I thought she'd leave it there, but she didn't. "I'm the adult here. I make the decisions. You're the kid." She brought her hand gingerly to my cheek. "You're my kid."

"Ivy." That was all Adam said—just her name—but she responded like he'd said something else.

"No, Adam. If she's never going to trust me, if she's set on hating me forever, she might as well hate me for the right reason."

I don't hate—

I couldn't even finish the thought, because suddenly, Ivy was talking again, and it was very hard to breathe.

"You're my kid." She repeated the words. "Mine, Tess."

I told myself that she meant that I was her responsibility now.

"I'm not your sister." Those words were harder to understand. "I was never your sister."

I don't understand.

I don't want to.

"I was seventeen." Ivy's arms encircled her waist. "He was young, too, recently enlisted. It was the first, last, and only time I'd ever really let go. And then, when I found out . . ."

Found out. Found out. Found out. The words echoed in my mind.

"I was your age, Tess. I was a kid, so when Mom and Dad decided that the best thing would be for them to raise you, I said yes." She repeated herself then. "I said yes."

I remember my parents' funeral.

I remember my sister carrying me up the stairs.

I remember my head on Ivy's chest.

Except Ivy was saying that they weren't my parents. They were *her* parents, and she wasn't my sister.

She was my mother.

"I am going to keep you safe," Ivy told me, her voice shaking. "I have to."

I stood there, staring at Ivy, a hundred thousand thoughts and memories and moments rushing through my head.

And then I got on the plane.

And then I shattered.

CHAPTER 53

For the longest time after the plane landed, I just sat there, staring straight ahead, feeling like a hitchhiker in someone else's body. My limbs had grown unbearably heavy. I felt like I might never move again.

I was seventeen, Ivy had said.

I didn't want to replay the words. I didn't want to picture Ivy at my age. I didn't want to think about the one year we'd lived in the same house, before she'd gone off to college and it had been just Mom and Dad and me.

Not my mom. Not my dad.

It wasn't fair. It wasn't fair that they'd died, and it wasn't fair that Ivy had taken the few memories that I had and twisted them until I didn't recognize them anymore.

My parents died when I was little. How many times had I said those words? But it wasn't true—none of it was true. I wasn't an orphan. I'd never *been* an orphan. The woman who'd given birth to me wasn't dead. And my father?

He was young, too, recently enlisted.

Six words—and that was all I knew.

My parents were never my parents, I thought, forcing my brain to actually form the words. *And my grandfather . . .* I thought of Gramps forgetting that I existed and mistakenly believing that I was Ivy and that Ivy was his daughter.

Gramps knew, I realized suddenly. *Of course he knew.* He'd lied to me.

They all did.

I closed my eyes, memories flooding over me. *I remember the funeral. I remember Ivy carrying me up the stairs. I remember sitting on the floor in front of Ivy while she brushed my hair. I remember Ivy kneeling down next to me. I remember patting her wet cheek.*

I remember Ivy crying, then giving me away.

Having your entire life rewritten in a heartbeat was an impossible thing.

"You can't sit there forever, kid." Bodie had given me my space, but now I felt him slide into the seat next to mine. I couldn't bring myself to open my eyes to look at him, because I didn't want to see the way he was looking at me.

Like he felt sorry for me.

Like I was broken.

The minutes ticked by before Bodie spoke again. "She saved that ranch of yours, you know."

She as in *Ivy*. My eyes stung under my eyelids. I swallowed, trying to shut out what he was saying.

"She hired someone to look after things, checks in on it herself every day." Bodie's tone was casual, like he wasn't effectively reaching into my chest and ripping out my heart with each word.

Ivy had saved the ranch. Ivy, who was my—

"Stop," I said. My tongue felt thick in my mouth. I forced my eyes open. "Why would you tell me that now?"

Bodie propped one leg up against the seat in front of him. "Got you to open your eyes, didn't it?"

I couldn't argue that point. "Where are we?" I asked flatly.

Bodie rested an arm on the back of my seat, but kept his gaze focused straight ahead. "Welcome to Boston."

Boston.

My grandfather looked exactly as he always had. In the three weeks I'd been in DC, I'd tried calling him a half-dozen times. We'd spoken twice. He'd only recognized my voice once.

But today was a good day.

"You're looking like something the cat dragged in, Bear." Gramps sat at a small table near the window. The suite was private—more condo than hospital room—but there was no kitchen, no stove, and the nurses were right down the hall. "Got a hug for an old man," he said gruffly, "or were you raised in a barn?"

It was an old joke, because, of course, I *had* been raised, at least in part, in a variety of barns. I managed a small smile and was blindsided with one emotion after another: *longing* and *gratitude*; *loneliness*, *emptiness*, *hope* I knew better than to let myself feel. *Hurt* and *betrayal*. *Anger* that he'd lied to me for so long. *Fear* that if I let myself be angry, I might somehow be wishing away one of his last good days.

Swallowing down the lump rising in the back of my throat, I walked over to the window. I willed my arms to wrap themselves around him, but they were dead weight by my side.

Gramps was here, and he was himself. I loved him. He was in me and part of me, he'd made me—but I couldn't make my arms move.

"How are they treating you?" I asked, my voice rough.

"It's not the Four Seasons," Gramps replied. "But it'll do."

"I tried," I said, the words working their way out of the pit of my stomach. "I tried to keep you at home." If I could focus on that—the older hurt—I didn't have to deal with the new one.

"You're a fighter," Gramps commented. "Always have been."

Always. Always. Always. He'd always been the one person I could count on.

Always. Always. Always. He'd been lying to me from the beginning—snapping pictures of me and sending them to Ivy.

Pictures she'd kept.

I didn't realize until I felt a sharp pain in my hand that I was digging my nails into my palm.

"You look skinny." Gramps pushed himself to stand—slowly, painstakingly. "Doesn't your sister feed you?"

I wrapped my arms around my middle, when all I wanted was to wrap them around him. "She's not my sister."

He saved me the work of reaching out to him by pulling me forward and into his arms. His callused hand stroked the back of my head. "I know."

CHAPTER 54

That first day in Boston was my grandfather's best day, like the universe had seen fit to give him clarity where I had none. The next day wasn't as good. The day after that was worse.

Sometimes, he knew who I was.

Sometimes, he didn't.

One day, we played checkers. He won. The next day, we played chess. I won. I could almost pretend that coming to Boston had been my decision, that the fact that Bodie slept by the door and paid for our motel room with cash meant nothing.

But.

But then I would think about Henry and wonder if he had someone watching out for him. I would think about Vivvie and whether anyone had explained to her why I had to go.

I didn't let myself think about Ivy at all.

I filled my days with chess and checkers. My nights filled themselves with nightmares and phantoms—throats slashed and bullet holes and the president and the First Lady dancing a waltz.

On our fourth day in Boston, I was futilely attempting to assemble a full deck of cards so Gramps and I could play poker, when someone turned the television in the community room from an old Clark Gable movie to the news. I tuned it out as background noise until I heard someone say the name *Edmund Pierce*.

My fingers closed around a card—the nine of spades—and my eyes shot to the television screen.

"Supreme Court hopeful Edmund Pierce was found dead in his Phoenix home this morning."

Pierce's picture stared out at me from the screen. *You'll get your money when I get my nomination.* I could hear Pierce saying those words. I could *see* it.

"While no official word has been released in Judge Pierce's death, early reports suggest an aneurysm." The news anchor on the screen had a naturally serious expression, perfect for delivering this kind of news. "Pierce was rumored to be the front-runner for President Nolan's nomination to the Supreme Court following the death of Chief Justice Theodore Marquette earlier this month. No word from the White House yet on how this might . . ."

Someone changed the channel, and just like that, we were back to Clark Gable. I set the card in my hand down and made for the lobby and the closest exterior door. Bodie saw me go by and followed me out.

"Pierce is dead," I told him, waiting until the door had slammed shut behind me and I'd sucked in a breath of fresh air to force out the words.

Bodie narrowed his eyes. "Heart attack?" he guessed, his eyes darkening.

"Aneurysm."

Bodie pulled a pack of cigarettes out of his back pocket. He took a cigarette out of the package, rolling it back and forth between the tips of his fingers.

This is too much of a coincidence, I thought. I could tell from the look on Bodie's face that he was thinking the same thing: in all likelihood, Pierce hadn't died of an aneurysm any more than Justice Marquette had died because of unforeseen complications during surgery.

"Vivvie thinks her father might have been murdered," I said, studying Bodie's reaction to those words.

"Vivvie's a smart girl," Bodie replied. In other words, he thought she was right.

"I need to call her," I said. "I need to call Henry."

"Easy there, slugger."

"This isn't a joke, Bodie."

He threw the cigarette down on the ground and crushed the tip underneath his toe. "I ain't joking."

I knew that. "Who's doing this?" I asked him quietly.

"Your sister would tell you to stay out of it."

She's not my sister.

"But as far as I can tell," Bodie continued languidly, "you'd take being told to stay out of it as an invitation to frolic gaily in a field full of *it*. All *it*, all the time. You and Ivy are too much alike."

I turned into the wind, determined not to flinch.

"Who's doing this?" Bodie repeated my question. "If you assume the good doctor's death wasn't a suicide—and I think, at this point, that's a safe bet—I'd say we're looking for someone with military training. Special Forces, most likely, possibly military intelligence."

Bodie's phone rang. *Ivy.* I knew it was her, the way you know the protagonist of a horror movie really shouldn't go down into that basement. Bodie took the call, then nodded at me to go back inside.

I made my way back down the hall toward my grandfather's room.

I'd say we're looking for someone with military training.

I thought about the fact that Ivy had been at Camp David that weekend. She'd pointed out just how much I didn't know—who'd taken the picture, who'd been standing right outside the frame.

Who else was there the day Bharani and Pierce met? My breaths got slightly shallower. *Was Adam?* Adam's father was the one who'd organized the retreat.

Had Adam been at the Keyes Foundation gala?

I'd say we're looking for someone with military training. Bodie's words dogged my every step. *Special Forces, most likely, possibly military intelligence.*

Adam was Air Force. Adam worked at the Pentagon.

No. I rounded the corner. There was an orderly outside my grandfather's room, his arms stacked high with blankets. *Adam isn't involved. He's not.* One of the blankets tumbled off the orderly's stack. Trying not to think about Adam—or Ivy or Pierce or any of it—I bent to pick up the blanket.

"Here—"

The orderly surged forward, slamming blankets into my face, cutting off the flow of air to my lungs as he pulled me tight against his body. *Not an orderly.*

Not Adam. That should have been a relief—but it wasn't. *Too big to be Adam. Too tall.* I struggled. *Too strong.* I couldn't see, couldn't *breathe*. The man who wasn't an orderly was going to kill me. I was going to die, smothered to death feet away from my grandfather's door.

I tried to kick my heel into my captor's shin. Then I felt a pinch in my neck.

And then everything went black.

CHAPTER 55

I woke with no feeling in my wrists and a throbbing at my temples. At first, all I could see were my own feet, bound at the ankles with transparent zip ties. My shoes had been removed.

So had my clothes.

That realization shocked me into full and unforgiving consciousness. I was wearing some kind of loose cotton shift. The knowledge that someone must have removed my clothes—that while I'd been unconscious, hands had *undressed* me—made me shiver violently.

Nausea racked my body. I lurched forward, as far as the ties that bound me to the metal chair would let me. My hair fell into my face and my stomach emptied itself onto the concrete floor. Unable to even wipe the back of my hand across my mouth, I coughed.

Floor, I thought, fighting to pay attention to the details and using them to ground me in the here and now. *Concrete floor.*

I was inside. The expanse was large—possibly a basement of some kind. No windows. There was a collection of electrical wires at one side. The space was dimly lit, but even that dim light made my head pound harder.

The orderly drugged me. I remembered the pinch at my neck, the darkness that followed. Maybe the headache was a side effect, but that raised the question: *A side effect of what?*

What had the man injected into me?

Poison? I tried not to think about the likelihood that Judge Pierce hadn't died of an aneurysm. I tried not to think about the fact that someone had poisoned Justice Marquette.

Not just someone, I thought. I tried to summon up an image of the orderly, but I couldn't. I hadn't been paying attention. *Dark hair. Tall.* That was it. All I'd seen. All I knew.

I struggled against the ties, jerking my body to one side, then the other as hard as I could. All that achieved was knocking my chair over sideways. My head hit the ground. Hard.

I have to get out of here. Knowing that didn't make it achievable, any more than trying to picture the orderly helped me summon up his face. *He's going to kill me. He knows what I know. He's going to kill me.*

Ivy had sent me out of DC, but she hadn't sent me far enough.

Focus. My cheek rested against the cold ground. *Think.* I knew, on some level, that planning wouldn't do me any good—but what other choice did I have?

Bodie said we were looking for someone with military training. I couldn't think about the future. I couldn't think about what might or might not happen to me in this basement. So I thought about the man who'd brought me here. Had there been something familiar about him?

Think, Tess.

I thought about everything I knew—about Pierce and Vivvie's father and the reporter who'd gotten his throat slashed.

The tip came from inside the West Wing, and that's all I'm going to say.

Inside the West Wing. Military training.

How many people were on the president's staff? How many of them were there at the gala the night Theo Marquette was poisoned?

How many of them had William Keyes invited to Camp David?

The president was there. My mind defaulted to that. I couldn't get it to stop. *The president was there. The president was there.*

But the president of the United States hadn't slammed those blankets over my mouth. The president of the United States hadn't slipped a needle into my neck and knocked me unconscious.

The president was there.

The tip came from inside the West Wing.

We're looking for someone with military training.

I remembered, suddenly, the conversation I'd had with Ivy about the Camp David picture. She hadn't just told me that she'd been there that weekend. She hadn't just hinted that there were other people there.

She'd asked me if I'd thought about who was standing just out of frame.

The president was there. This time, the thought took on different meaning in my mind. *The president was there, at Camp David. The president was there at the gala.*

"Who was standing just out of frame?" I said the words into the concrete, my muscles screaming in objection to the angle at which my body was held. I translated the question, ignoring the pain.

Who was standing just a few feet away from the president?

Who went with him—to Camp David, to the gala? Who works inside the West Wing *because the president works inside the West Wing?*

Who had I overlooked?

Who specialized in fading into the background?

I heard the footsteps coming behind me. I renewed my struggles, but it did no good. I wasn't going anywhere—and the steps were getting closer.

I make it a point to learn names. Bodie's voice was clear in my ears as my captor stepped into view.

Who went where the president went? Who had the training to kill?

The Secret Service agent knelt down next to me and examined my wounds. "Look what you've done."

CHAPTER 56

Damien Kostas. I'd met him for the first time on Ivy's front porch. He'd approached me at the state dinner. After Henry and I had talked to the reporter, we'd tried drawing out the killer. Kostas had approached me, *and I hadn't even noticed*.

Just like it hadn't occurred to me that the president of the United States never went anywhere alone.

Nimble fingers probed the side of my head. I winced. Kostas brushed my hair out of my face, then in one smooth motion, he righted my chair. "You should be more careful," he told me.

Seriously?

My brain-to-mouth filter failed me entirely. "Seriously? You brought me here to kill me, and you think I should be more careful?"

He straightened, assuming his full height. "Whether or not I brought you here to kill you remains to be seen."

I wanted to grasp at even the smallest possibility that I might get out of this alive, but I'd seen his face. I knew who he was. "I'm supposed to believe you might just let me go?" I said, my stomach roiling and my throat closing around the words as I choked them out.

My captor was silent. He had a naturally serious expression, uncompromising and weighty. I remembered how little luck I'd had getting him to respond to me that day on Ivy's front porch.

"What do you want?" I asked, knowing the question was probably futile.

He made no move to reply, walking over to a bag at the side of the room. He removed a towel and unfolded it. Then his hand disappeared back into the bag, and he set a collection of needles on the towel, one by one.

Oh God. What were the needles for?

"What do you want?" I asked again. I pictured him picking up a needle. Was this how torture started? Was he going to force me to tell him what I knew? Would he torture me until I told him *who* else knew?

Vivvie. Henry. Ivy. No matter what he did to me, I couldn't tell him.

The Secret Service agent picked up one of the needles and walked toward me. I thought I might throw up again, but there was nothing left to expel from my body. Kostas took my head firmly in one hand. I tried to jerk back, but he tightened his grip, then pressed the needle into my neck.

I gasped.

He emptied the syringe into my body, pulled the needle out, then let go of me. I waited.

Nothing. No blackness. No pain. No throbbing in my head.

"It counteracts the effects of the sedative I dosed you with." Kostas didn't look at me as he spoke. "I may have given you a bit too much for a girl your size. You've been out for over twelve hours."

Twelve hours. I'd been missing for twelve hours. Ivy would be looking for me. Bodie would have discovered me gone within minutes of my disappearing, and my sister—my *whatever-Ivy-was*— would be tearing Boston apart piece by piece, looking for me.

"What do you want?" I asked a third time. My voice was higher pitched, on the verge of hysterics.

Kostas stared at me for a moment. "I have a problem. It is my understanding that your sister specializes in problems."

This isn't about what I know. This is about what Ivy does. It took me a moment longer than that to fully realize the implications. I wasn't a liability to be disposed of. I was a *hostage*.

"You want Ivy to make this go away. You want her to get you out of this, and if she doesn't, you'll . . ."

Kill me.

"No." The response was simple and swift. "I'm not walking away from this. I don't expect to." He paused. "I don't deserve to. But I have a problem, and your sister is going to fix it."

He'd killed three men—and helped to kill Justice Marquette. That made him a monster. The fact that he didn't sound like one wasn't comforting.

Neither was the presence of the other needles on the towel.

He doesn't expect to walk away from this. I tried desperately to concentrate on something else. *He's not wearing a mask, because he doesn't expect to walk away from this. He doesn't care if I know who he is.*

That should have been a relief, but all I could think was that if Kostas had resigned himself to being caught, I was being held by a man with nothing to lose.

A phone rang. He walked back to his bag and removed a flip phone. *A disposable?* I wondered. He stared at it for a few seconds, then returned it to its place, ignoring the call.

"You said you have a problem," I said quietly. "What is it? What do you need Ivy to fix?"

He didn't answer. This was the man I'd met on Ivy's front porch—quiet and still as a guard at Buckingham Palace.

"You killed Judge Pierce." Maybe I should have stopped talking—maybe I should have just sat there and waited for him to decide whether I was going to live or die—but I *couldn't*. "You killed the reporter."

"The reporter was regrettable." Kostas cast a brief glance back at me, then the phone in his bag rang again. This time, he let it ring, but still, he didn't answer.

"What about Major Bharani?" I asked, thinking of Vivvie. "Was he *regrettable*?"

My captor's face betrayed just a hint of surprise. That I knew that he'd killed Vivvie's dad? That I cared?

"Your sister should have kept you out of this," he commented, in the tone of someone who was confident that if I'd been his responsibility, he *would* have kept me out of it.

"Major Bharani had a daughter my age," I told him.

"He hit her."

"Are you telling me you killed one of your co-conspirators because he hit his daughter?"

"I killed him because he was becoming a liability," Kostas replied, a hint of annoyance entering his voice. "I don't feel bad about it because he hit his daughter. He's a doctor who premeditatedly killed one of his patients. He was not an honorable man."

And what do you call a Secret Service agent who murders three people to cover up the fact that he helped kill a Supreme Court justice?

"The doctor killed for money," Kostas told me as the phone started ringing again. He picked the phone up and, with one sharp movement, snapped it between his hands.

Special Forces, I thought dully, wondering if he could snap my neck just as quickly. Just as easily.

"You didn't kill for money." I repeated back what he had—essentially—told me.

I was tied to this chair. There was no way out. The only advantage I had was that my captor did not seem to want to kill me. Understanding him and playing off that might be the difference between life and death.

"I get why you killed the doctor," I said, struggling to keep my voice even and calm. "He was a liability. So was the reporter. But what about Judge Pierce?"

No reply.

"I guess Pierce wasn't very honorable, either." Still nothing, so I pressed on. "What about Justice Marquette? Wasn't he an honorable man?" No response. "Why would you get into bed with Major Bharani and Judge Pierce? It wasn't money."

Kostas retrieved a new disposable cell, still in the package, from his bag. He ripped the package open and began dialing the phone.

"Why would you agree to poison a good man?" I let the question hang in the air.

Kostas looked up, his face terrifyingly neutral, like I wasn't having this one-sided conversation tied to a chair, like he wasn't mentally preparing himself to kill me if the need arose.

"My problem," Kostas answered abruptly. "Pierce was made aware of my problem. He was in a position to fix it."

There was a hint of emotion in his voice when he talked about his *problem*. It wasn't a money problem. My gut told me it wasn't about power, either. This was a man who was tasked with protecting the life of the president. It was his *job* to take a bullet for President Nolan, and looking at him now, I could almost believe that he would have done it.

What could Pierce possibly have offered this man—what problem could Kostas possibly have—that he was willing to throw his life away for? Willing to kill for?

"Pierce came to you," I said. "He offered to solve your problem. He arranged this whole thing."

Kostas stilled. An expression I couldn't quite read flitted over his features. A moment later, it was gone. "You talk too much," he said abruptly. Without warning, he crossed the room to stand in front of me, too close for comfort.

I clamped my mouth closed.

He finished dialing, then held the disposable phone up to my ear. "Talk to your sister."

"Ivy?" My voice cracked halfway through her name.

"Tessie?" Ivy's voice didn't crack. It didn't break. But somehow, that one word was enough to tell me she was already broken.

"He has me in a basement somewhere," I said, rushing the words out. "A big building. There's electrical wiring to one side—"

Kostas took the phone from my ear. "You asked for proof of life," he said. "You have twelve hours to get me what I need."

He hung up the phone—and didn't say another word to me for eleven hours.

CHAPTER 57

I had one hour left to live. Ivy had one hour to give Kostas what he wanted—whatever that was.

I tried talking to him, even though my throat was like sandpaper, even though he'd stopped replying hours ago. If Kostas was going to kill me, he could do it while I was speaking to him. He could watch the life go out of my body and know that *he* had no honor.

I'd moved past the denial stage of things. Now I was pissed.

"It's my life. I'm the one who's going to die if Ivy doesn't solve your problem. The least you can do is tell me what it is you need her to do."

He didn't say a word. It was like he didn't even hear me. Like he was steeling himself, already, to do what needed to be done.

I don't want to die. It was a stupid thought, a cliché one, thought by everyone who was about to die, ever.

"I don't want to die." I said it out loud. "I don't want to—"

"I heard you." Kostas broke his silence. "For what little it is worth, I don't want for you to die, either."

"But you will kill me."

He didn't reply. That silence was answer enough. He *would* kill me.

I'm no good to him dead. I clung to that thought. If he killed me, he lost his leverage.

That was the moment when I started wondering what else was in his bag. I started entertaining the possibility that he might not kill me immediately. He might hurt me first.

A finger. An ear. Would he send pieces of me to Ivy? What was in those syringes? Would he anesthetize me before sending her something to show he was serious? Would he put me down like a dog if it became clear that she couldn't do the job?

I tensed against the bindings on my wrist. The plastic cut into my skin. I ignored the biting pain and struggled harder. Blood trickled down my wrists, warm and sticky against my skin.

Slick.

I let the pain roll over me. I felt it. I clung to it. I tried to pull out of the bindings, greased up with my own blood. I tried. I *tried*—

"Stop." Kostas followed the order up by picking up one of the needles.

"No," I said. "Please, *no*. I won't try anything. I won't—"

"It's a sedative," he told me. "To calm you down."

I felt panic rising up inside me like bile in the back of my throat. *I don't want to be calm. I don't want—*

Footsteps sounded outside the door. My captor straightened and slipped the sedative into his back pocket, then picked up another syringe. This one was empty.

The sight of an empty syringe shouldn't have made me shiver, but as he crossed the room to stand next to me, I felt like someone was sliding a shard of ice up my spine.

A female voice called out three words: "I came alone."

Ivy. My heart jumped into my throat. *Ivy's here. She came.* My arms tensed against the bindings. My body lurched forward of its own accord.

Kostas pressed the needle into my neck, into a vein. I hissed slightly. "Do not move," he told me, his voice low.

I could feel my heart beating in my throat, pulsing against the sharp, uncompromising pressure of the needle.

"I didn't tell anyone I was coming here," Ivy kept talking as she came around the corner. She didn't pause at the door, didn't hesitate when she saw the man poised with a needle at my neck. "I can get you what you want, Damien."

"That's far enough," Kostas told her.

I couldn't move my head, couldn't so much as lean toward her.

"I'm here," Ivy said, her voice authoritative and calm. "We can all get what we want, but not if you don't step away from the girl."

"I get what I want," Kostas replied, "or I press down on this." He indicated the needle in his hands. "She will not survive an air bubble to the heart."

In. Out. In. Out. I forced myself to breathe. *He's going to kill me.*

"I'm not armed. No one knows I'm here. I came alone." Ivy wasn't looking at me—only at him. "You need to let her go, and then we can talk."

I felt Kostas tense beside me. "That wasn't the deal." The Secret Service agent's free hand slid to the far side of my neck, then tightened. I couldn't twist away from the needle. I couldn't move. "No talking," he told Ivy. "You get me what I want, and you get your sister back."

I could feel my heartbeat in my neck, tensing against my skin. I could feel it, pounding back against my captor's hold.

"I can't summon up a presidential pardon on a whim, Kostas," Ivy said.

"You said you had what I wanted."

Breathe in. Breathe out. In. Out. In—

"I said I could get you what you want. And I can. But first you have to let her go."

A low, inhuman whine reached my ears. It took me a few seconds to realize that it was me.

"If I let her go," Kostas bit out, "I have nothing to bargain with."

He wants to let me go. He wants to, I thought, desperation twisting in my gut, *but he won't.*

Ivy took a single step forward. "You'll have me. The president won't bargain for my sister's life. But he might bargain for mine."

I realized then what she was saying. My throat tightened, my arms tensing against the bindings so hard the pain should have brought tears to my eyes. "Ivy," I said, my voice escaping my throat in a hoarse whisper. "No."

I could picture her, that day on the tarmac. *You're my kid. Mine, Tess.*

"You're that valuable to him?" Kostas asked Ivy, his grip on my neck tightening slightly.

Don't, Ivy. My mouth wouldn't form the words. *Don't do this.*

"Keeping me alive is that important to his administration." Ivy's voice never wavered. "In my line of work, it pays to have an insurance policy. I know where the bodies are buried. I know every skeleton in every closet. If I didn't have some method of ensuring that it was to my clients' benefit that I stay alive, eventually someone would decide that the only way to make sure their secrets stayed buried was to bury me, too."

Stop it, Ivy. Stop talking. I willed her to listen, willed her to stop before it was too late, but she didn't. She *wouldn't*.

"If I go off the grid, a program is initiated, and all those secrets—everything I've learned, everything I know, everything I've buried—are released. Online. To the media."

"You worked on the president's election campaign," Kostas said. "You've worked for him since."

"I have."

"You're saying he has secrets."

"I am."

"You're saying that if I hold *you*—"

"He might give you what you want," Ivy supplied. "If you have *me*."

I'd spent my whole life as an orphan. I'd mourned the parents I'd never even gotten the chance to know. Now Ivy was here, doing this, and I couldn't push down the voice inside me that said that I was going to lose her, too.

I felt numb. I felt like I was lying on my back in a dark hole, and there was someone at the top, throwing dirt down on top of me. Burying me.

"You'll stay," Kostas ordered, his gaze sharp on Ivy's. "Contact the president."

"No," Ivy replied, her voice taut. "I won't. Not unless you let Tess go."

That was the first time she'd said my name. My stomach twisted sharply. *Don't do this, Ivy. You can't—*

"You do not make the rules here." Kostas removed one hand from my neck. A second later, he had a gun aimed at Ivy. "Come here."

"No. Me for her," Ivy said, nodding at me. "That's the deal."

You're my kid. Mine, Tess.

"Ivy," I rediscovered my voice, my eyes and throat stinging, my whole body fighting against the bindings that held me in place. "No."

"Yes," she said fiercely. "*Me for her*," she told the Secret Service agent again. "Otherwise, you might as well put a bullet in my head right now and say good-bye to that pardon, because without me, you don't stand a chance."

She was doing this. There was no talking her out of it, no going back. She was doing this. *For me.*

Kostas removed the needle from my neck. I could feel a trickle of blood against my skin as he stepped back and aimed the gun at my right knee. "Come here," he told Ivy. "Do not make me hurt her."

"Let her go."

He stared at her. He pulled the trigger. The bullet went into the ground, less than an inch from my foot.

Oh God.

"You come here," Kostas repeated, his eyes narrowing. "Now. Or the next one goes in her leg, Ms. Kendrick."

Ivy put herself between him and me. "You don't need her," she said. "You need me."

"I need her to make you cooperate."

"She's not my sister." Ivy looked him straight in the eye as she said those words. "She's my daughter. I was seventeen. Too young. You know what that's like."

Even tied to a chair, even with Kostas aiming a gun at Ivy, even *now*—I couldn't keep from reacting to those words. Kostas's gaze flickered briefly toward mine. I ducked my head, pressing my lips together. What was Ivy doing? Why tell him this? *If he thought I was good leverage before . . .*

"Let her go," Ivy said, her voice wavering. "There's no trick here. Let her go, and I will call the president. I will tell you exactly what to say, exactly how to handle this situation. But first, you have to let her go."

Kostas lowered the gun. He knelt down in front of me and took out a knife. My breath caught in my throat. He brought the knife to my legs and cut the bindings between my ankles. As he walked behind me to do the same thing to my wrists, my eyes found Ivy's.

She has a plan, I told myself. *She's not going to stay here. She's not going to risk her life . . .*

But as her lips curved slightly upward in a soft, sad smile, I knew—there was no trick. No trap. No plan. This was a trade. Ivy for me.

"*No*," I said, louder this time. "No, Ivy. You can't."

I was four years old again, throwing up at my parents' funeral. I was lying against Ivy's chest as she carried me up the stairs. I was patting her wet cheek as she handed me away.

I was walking into the room she'd saved for me in her house. The room she'd never decorated, never used, her favorite room in the house—

Kostas finished cutting my bindings. I lunged from the chair, falling to the ground on limbs that weren't ready to support my body yet. Ivy was beside me in an instant. She knelt next to me, her hands on my shoulders.

"You're the kid," she said. "I'm the adult."

You're my kid. She didn't say it this time, but I heard it all the same. I saw it in her eyes.

"I love you, Tessie. When you get out of here, go to Adam. He'll take care of you, okay? Bodie, too."

That sounded too much like good-bye.

"You do what they say," Ivy told me. "Exactly what they say."

"I'm not leaving you here." My eyes stung with tears. My face was warm with them. Breathing hurt. Looking at her hurt.

"I'm sorry," Ivy told me. "About everything. I'm sorry for never being what you needed. I'm sorry for doing it all wrong. I'm sorry for lying to you, and I'm sorry for telling you the way I did. I'm so sorry, baby, and I love you, and *you are leaving*."

She'd never called me *baby* before.

No. This wasn't happening. I wasn't leaving. She wasn't crying. I wasn't crying. This wasn't—

She pressed her lips to my forehead, then stood. She glanced at Kostas. "You'll want to knock her out," she said.

"Ivy, I—" I was going to tell her that I loved her, that I *hated* her, that I wasn't leaving her, that I *couldn't*, but for the second time in twenty-four hours, there was a pinch at my neck.

And everything went black.

CHAPTER 58

Something dripped onto my face. *Liquid. Cold.* My head tilted to one side. *Another drop.* Awareness hit me like a sledgehammer. My eyes flew open. *The Secret Service agent. Ivy.*

I scrambled backward, jamming the heels of my hands into the pavement. It took me a moment to register the fact that I was alone. Outside. *Safe*, I thought, choking on the realization.

Ivy wasn't safe.

My cheeks were wet—with tears, with drizzling rain. It was dark out—nighttime. *How long?* I pushed myself to my feet, my heart thudding. *How long was I out for?*

Kostas had Ivy. And if the president didn't give him what he wanted, he was going to kill her.

I stumbled out of the alley, pausing when I reached the street. Looking up, I could see the outline of a tall, thin building rising to a point in the distance. *The Washington Monument.* I was in DC.

Ivy's not. He has her. Where does he have her? My brain wouldn't slow down. It wouldn't stop stacking questions, one on top of the other.

"Miss?"

I almost couldn't hear the word over the cacophony in my head. *Kostas has Ivy. She traded herself for me. I'm safe. Safe. Ivy's not. He has Ivy—*

"Miss." A man reached out to grab my arm.

I jumped back, my hands held out in front of my body, a last line of defense against whatever might come. "Don't." The word that exited my mouth barely sounded human.

Calm down, I thought.

He has Ivy.

Calm down.

Have to find Adam. Have to find Bodie. He has Ivy.

Calm down.

"Are you all right?" the man asked.

I slammed the door on the rush of thoughts beating a rhythm against the inside of my skull. I took a deep breath, forcing myself to put together a coherent sentence. "Can I borrow your phone?"

Of the people I knew in DC, there was only one whose number I had memorized—Vivvie's. I called. She answered. Words came out of my mouth—not the right ones, not enough to make sense—but somehow, she was able to tell her aunt where I was.

Her aunt was able to tell Adam.

And Adam came for me. As he ushered me into his car, I told him about Ivy, Kostas—all of it, in stilted sentences and streams of words that came too fast and blurred together. I told him everything, and when he tried to take me to the hospital, I said no. He must have decided that it wasn't worth it to argue with me, because the doctor ended up coming to us.

Adam had a one-bedroom apartment, small and hyper-organized. After the doctor had checked me over, after I'd told Adam and then Bodie everything I knew—told them again and again until I had no more words left inside me, until there was nothing left to say—Adam steered me gently toward his bathroom. He turned on the shower, handed me a towel, and laid one of his USAF T-shirts and a pair of sweatpants out for me.

Then he left me alone.

As the shower steamed up behind me, I stood in front of the mirror. I was still wearing the cotton shift. My face was dirty. There was the beginning of a bruise on one side. *I woke up in a room with concrete floors and no windows.* Even now that there was no one left to tell, I couldn't stop going over the facts. *There was some kind of electrical wiring on the wall.* I couldn't stop hoping, somehow, that I'd remember something, some detail, no matter how tiny, that might tell me where Ivy was.

That might help us get her back.

Kostas is going to use Ivy to try to blackmail the president into pardoning someone. The surface of the mirror began to steam up, obscuring my face. I swiped my hand across it and stared at my reflection, like it might have the answers I was looking for.

Ivy's eyes are brown, I thought. Mine had flecks of green, like moss amid the mud. Our faces had a similar shape to them. I had her lips, somebody else's nose.

It doesn't matter, I told myself. Dragging my eyes from my reflection, I undressed and stepped into the shower, letting the hot water beat against me. *Get it together, Tess.*

I didn't have the luxury of falling apart. Not now. Ivy had told the rogue Secret Service agent that she had a program that started releasing her clients' secrets if she went missing for forty-eight hours. I wasn't sure if she'd been telling the truth or not, but either way, if the president didn't agree to pardon *somebody* before that time period had elapsed, this situation was going to escalate.

I wanted to believe Kostas wouldn't kill Ivy.

I wanted to believe that, but I didn't.

I got out of the shower and slipped on the clothes Adam had left me. They dwarfed my body. I tied the sweatpants and doubled the waistband over, then made my way back out into the world.

Adam and Bodie were still in the living room. I saw a healthy amount of caution in two sets of eyes as they turned to look at me.

"What's the plan?" I asked. "How are we going to get Ivy back?"

"We've got people looking for her," Adam said. "FBI, Homeland—"

"And some less law-abiding types," Bodie added. "I'll head back out once . . ."

He trailed off.

Once you have me settled, I finished. "I'm fine. I can take care of myself. Go, do whatever you need to do. Find Ivy. He'll kill her if he doesn't get what he wants."

I realized then that they hadn't pressed me for details—about Kostas, about what he wanted. "You weren't surprised when I said Kostas wanted the president to pardon someone,"

I said slowly. "Or when I told you that Kostas was the one who took me."

"Ivy suspected from pretty early on that we were looking for someone in the Secret Service or intelligence." Adam was sitting on the couch, his hands in his lap, his gaze fixed on his hands. "We just didn't know who."

"How—" I started to say.

"Ivy went to the Secret Service," Bodie cut in. "First thing after you and Vivvie told us everything, Ivy went to the Secret Service and asked them to bar Vivvie's father from the White House."

I remembered Ivy saying something to that effect.

Ivy talks to the Secret Service about Vivvie's father. Vivvie's father is immediately taken out of the picture. I saw the connection with hindsight. Ivy must have seen it from the beginning.

"She suspected it was a Secret Service agent, and she didn't tell the president?" I asked.

"She didn't tell the president *because* she suspected it was a Secret Service agent," Adam replied. "The president is a difficult man to get alone, and even if she managed to pass the message along in private, she was fairly certain that the person we were looking for *knew* that we were digging. If Ivy met with the president and his behavior changed *at all* . . ." Adam shook his head. "That wasn't a risk Ivy was willing to take."

"What about the pardon? You weren't surprised when I said Kostas was the one who took me, and you weren't surprised when I said he asked for a pardon."

Adam and Bodie were silent.

"A pardon for who? For what?" As the questions left my mouth, I became more and more certain that they knew the answers.

"He took *me*," I said slowly. "Ivy is *my*—she's my family, and he has her." I felt like my body might start shaking, but my voice was steady, fierce. *Like Ivy's.* "You don't get to keep me out of this," I said.

After a moment, Adam stood and left the room. When he came back, he had a thick file in his hand. "Ivy flew down to Arizona to look for a connection between Judge Pierce and someone in the Secret Service—or the intelligence community. She came back with detailed information about Pierce's docket. Cases he'd heard. Cases he was scheduled to hear. Appeals."

"She found a connection?" I knew, even as I asked the question, that the answer was *yes*. She was Ivy Kendrick. Of course she found the connection.

Adam handed me the file. "It's a death penalty case. Defendant was nineteen when the crime was committed, with a history of traumatic brain injury. There's a question about whether he was mentally competent to stand trial at all."

I opened the file. The defendant's name didn't ring any bells, but when I saw his picture, my breath caught in my throat. *The eyes. The set of his features.*

"Kostas?" I asked.

"His son," Bodie confirmed. "From what we can tell, Kostas didn't even know the kid existed until the mother came to him for help with legal fees."

I thought of Kostas saying that Vivvie's father had no honor. I thought of the way he'd spoken of people who killed for money, or for power. I'd wondered what he had killed for, and now I knew.

"He let me go," I said, my throat tightening. "He wasn't going to, but when Ivy told him I was her *daughter*—"

She'd asked him, one parent to another. And he'd let me go.

"Pierce was supposed to hear the son's case?" I tried to focus on the file.

"Best as we can figure," Bodie told me, "Pierce offered to set aside the son's sentence if Kostas helped assassinate the chief justice. Once the deed was done, the judge failed to fulfill his end of the bargain."

Pierce reneged, and Kostas killed him. I felt sick.

"Ivy said she had a program." I thought of the promises *she* had made. "She said that if Kostas held *her* captive, the president might bargain."

"He might," Adam said after several seconds. What he didn't say was: *He also might not.*

He has to, I thought. *He* has *to.* But we were talking about the president of the United States. He didn't *have* to do anything.

"We need to find her." I was back to that, back to the ticking clock and the certainty that if we didn't find Ivy, she might not make it out of this alive.

"You need to get some sleep," Adam corrected. He stood and walked over to me, setting a hand on my shoulder. "The president has been filled in on the situation. He wants to find Ivy as badly as we do. Everyone who could be looking for her *is* looking for her."

At that, Bodie nodded at Adam and took his leave.

"Aren't you going, too?" I asked Adam. I could accept that there might not be anything I could do. I didn't like it. I certainly wouldn't be able to sleep. But I could accept that a sixteen-year-old girl probably wasn't as qualified to look for Ivy as the people who were *actually* looking for her.

But Adam worked for the Pentagon. He *could* do something.

"You're not the only one who loves her," Adam said softly. "But I know where your sister would want me, and that's here. With you."

I swallowed. "You called her my sister."

"Force of habit." He looked like he might stop there. "She wanted to tell you, Tess. Years ago, as soon as she was set up here, as soon as she was in a position to take care of you, she wanted to tell you the truth. She wanted you here."

"And then she changed her mind." The words escaped my mouth before I could bite them back. Ivy was missing. She was *gone*, and I was so angry at her—for doing this, for leaving me.

Again.

"She stopped visiting. She barely even called." I closed my eyes. "She never told me why. I don't know what I did, why she left—"

"Hey," Adam said, capturing my chin in his hand. "You didn't do anything, Tess."

I believed that. But the thirteen-year-old inside me couldn't. Ivy had left me. She was my *mother*, and she'd *chosen* to leave.

She chose to stay with Kostas. I should have been grateful for that. She'd traded herself for me, she'd saved me, she *loved* me. But there was nothing I could do to keep from feeling like she'd thrown me away, all over again.

"Your grandfather asked her to go." Adam's voice broke into my thoughts. His words knocked the breath out of me. "He said she was being selfish. That being a parent wasn't about what *she* wanted. That she had to think about what was best for *you*." Adam cupped my face in his hand. "He sent her away, Tess, and she came back here, and something happened that convinced her he was right."

What happened? I didn't ask the question out loud. It didn't matter. Gramps might have sent Ivy away, but she'd gone. She was the one who hadn't said good-bye. She was the one who'd stopped calling.

"There was never a day, not one," Adam said softly, "that she didn't think about you."

She should have been there. I closed my eyes, more to keep them from tearing up than because I was tired. *She should be here now.*

"Come on," Adam said. "You need to rest." He steered me toward his bedroom, toward the bed. Adam waited until I'd actually sat down on the edge of the mattress before retreating.

Sleep never came.

Every second, every minute, every hour that passed was time I wouldn't get back. Time *Ivy* wouldn't get back.

In the dead of the night, I started pacing: the bedroom, the hallway right outside, the bathroom. As I came to the living room, I paused in the doorway.

Adam was awake. He was bent over his desk, looking at something. *A note? A photograph?* Whatever it was, he tucked it back into a drawer. He looked up but didn't see me. From the expression on his face, I was willing to bet he didn't see anything at all.

CHAPTER 59

The next morning, I had a visitor. Vivvie hovered in the doorway to Adam's room. It felt like a lifetime ago that she'd stood outside the door to my room, wrapped in a blanket, wanting to come in, not wanting to ask.

I looked down at my hands, unable to meet her eyes. My wrists were still angry and red. The raw skin looked how I felt.

"I don't want to be alone," I whispered. The second those words left my mouth, Vivvie flew across the room. She hugged me like hugging was a contact sport.

"Are you okay? Last night you sounded . . . not okay. And before that, you were just *gone*. Asher told me you went to the state dinner last weekend. Henry said your sister was there, and that she took you away, but we couldn't figure out *where*, and you weren't answering your phone—"

"Vivvie."

Belatedly, she realized that she still had me in a death grip and relaxed her hug, her arms falling to her sides.

"Ivy sent me away," I said, saying Ivy's name the way a cutter might press a blade to skin. It hurt. It was supposed to. "She did it to protect me," I continued. That was what Ivy did. She didn't ask me what I wanted. She didn't give me a choice.

She left me, and she sent me away, and she gave up her own life for mine, and it wasn't fair. It wasn't fair that she could do this to me, and it wasn't fair that I was the one who had to live with the results.

It wasn't fair that I was here, and she wasn't.

"Ivy told my aunt to get me a bodyguard," Vivvie said, pulling me out of my thoughts. "For protection. He's waiting in the hallway."

It occurred to me then to wonder how much Vivvie knew. Telling her—about Ivy, about Kostas, about what had happened to me—seemed insurmountable.

"You don't have to," Vivvie said quietly. "If you're not ready to talk about it yet, you don't have to."

"Yes," I said. "I do." I swallowed, then pressed on. "Your father didn't kill himself."

I wasn't sure how long we were in my room, but by the time I finished, Vivvie knew everything except the truth about Ivy's relation to me.

"You aren't *listening*!" Adam's voice cut through the walls. He was yelling.

For a split second, Vivvie and I sat there, frozen, and then our eyes met. I slipped off the bed and out of the room.

Ivy was missing. Whoever Adam was talking to, whoever *wasn't listening*, I had a right to hear it.

"My answer is no."

I stopped just outside the door to the living room. From this angle, I could see just a hint of the person who'd just spoken.

Adam's father. The man who'd had Bodie hauled in for questioning, just to prove a point to Ivy.

My answer is no. I wondered what the question was, and why those words made my stomach feel like it had been lined with lead.

"You know," Adam said, each word issued with quiet force, "that I would never ask you for anything, if the situation weren't—"

"Desperate?" his father supplied. "Believe me, Adam, I'm well aware of what you think of me. You have made it abundantly clear that you have no interest in taking your place in this family."

"No interest in politics," Adam corrected.

"You were born for this. If you retired from the military, we could have you on the road to the Senate in a matter of months. A decade from now, you could be a contender for the White House."

"You really think this is the time for this discussion?" Adam asked tersely.

"You're the one who invited me here," William countered.

"Because I wanted your help." Adam said those words like the act of speaking them was physically painful. "Ivy—"

"That girl crawled under your skin years ago." As intense as Adam's tone was, William's was casual. "I've never understood the hold she has on you. If she's gone, I won't shed a tear."

My fingers curled themselves into fists. Without meaning to, I took a step forward. Adam's father saw me a second before Adam did.

"Tess," Adam said, his voice tight. "Could you give us a minute?"

"That won't be necessary," Keyes said, matching Adam's tone. "I was just leaving."

I beat the older man to the front door. The fact that Adam had asked him for help meant that Adam thought he *could* help. If William Keyes wanted to walk away from this—from his own son—he could go through me to do it.

"Tess." The tone in Adam's voice told me that he wanted me out of this room, away from his father. It was a tone that, in other circumstances, I would have obeyed.

"It's my understanding," I said, trying to force Keyes to look at me again, "that my sister has some kind of insurance policy. If something happens to her, a lot of very powerful people will be very unhappy. Including you."

A flash of something in my adversary's eyes told me I'd guessed right on that last point.

"Your sister always has a contingency plan," William Keyes said, his voice perfectly modulated. "But I'm the one who taught her that." He brushed past me and out the door.

"Stay here," Adam ordered as he followed.

After a pregnant pause, Vivvie stepped into the room. "That was . . ."

"Adam's father," I supplied. "He's not Ivy's biggest fan."

He could help, but he won't. He'll let her die. I didn't want to imagine myself at Ivy's funeral. I didn't want to think about the fact that she was all I had left. I didn't want to feel like someone had carved out my insides, like I was empty and hollow and crumbling apart.

No. I couldn't do this, couldn't go down that rabbit hole. *Ivy's going to be fine. I'll hate her forever if something happens to her. She's going to be fine.*

I walked the length of the living room. Around the futon. Around the desk, and then I stopped, thinking of Adam sitting at the desk the night before. I tested the drawer, expecting it to be locked.

It wasn't.

Inside, I found a neat line of pens, printer paper, and a photograph, tucked into the side. I gingerly pulled it out and turned it over.

Ivy and Adam.

Her hair was in a messy ponytail. His was buzzed close to his head. They were young. Ivy couldn't have been more than nineteen or twenty.

She had my smile, I thought, forcing myself to stare masochistically at the curve of her lips. On the heels of that crippling thought came a second one. *Ivy knew Adam when she was young.*

And then I remembered Ivy's words the day she put me on the plane: *He was young, too, recently enlisted.* I reached out to the desk to steady myself, my fingers digging into the wood.

There was never a day, Adam had said, *not a single one where she didn't think of you.* He'd said those words like he *knew*—what it was like for Ivy, thinking of me every single day.

What if he wasn't just talking about Ivy?

I could see Adam in my memory, standing behind Ivy, his hand on her shoulder as she told me the truth. I could see Adam, sitting in the passenger seat of his car as he taught me to drive.

I could see Adam, reading me the riot act, telling me that family doesn't run off when things get hard.

I could see Adam the first time he'd ever seen me, looking at me like I was something precious. Like I was a ghost.

Vivvie came to stand behind me. "Your sister," she said, looking at the photograph. "And Adam. They look so young."

That girl crawled under your skin years ago. Adam's father's voice echoed through my head. *I've never understood the hold she has on you.*

"She's not my sister." I was staring at the photograph—at a college-aged Ivy and a younger Adam—so I didn't get to see the expression that crossed Vivvie's face in response to my words. "She's my mother. I didn't know." My eyes blurred with tears. I blinked them away and kept staring at the photo. "She was a teenager when she had me. She said my father was military."

Adam was military.

You're not the only one who loves her, he'd told me the night before. *But I know where your sister would want me, and that's here. With you.*

I hadn't questioned why Ivy would want Adam with me. *Adam*, not Bodie, even though Bodie was the one I saw every day.

I hadn't questioned the way that Adam, Ivy, and Bodie all seemed so intent on keeping me away from Adam's father.

I thought it was because he was powerful and dangerous if crossed. But what if that wasn't it? *My father is very family-oriented.* Adam had said those words in a way that wasn't complimentary.

"Tess?"

It took me a moment to realize that Adam was the one who'd said my name, not Vivvie. He walked over to me and saw the photograph in my hand.

"You and Ivy have known each other a long time," I said, my throat tightening around the words. "Are you ... Are you and I ..." *Say it, Tess. Just say it.* "Are you my—"

"Vivvie, your aunt is downstairs." Adam interrupted my question. "And my father's visit has put your bodyguard on edge."

With one last glance in my direction, Vivvie was out the door, leaving Adam and me alone. I stared at him, searching for similarities in our features, the way I'd looked at my own reflection, searching for Ivy.

Adam's hair was brown. His eyes were blue, but there was something familiar about the shape.

"Adam." I forced his name out. "Ivy said my father was young. She said he was in the military. You two have known each other for a very long time." My mouth felt like cotton. My tongue felt too thick for my mouth. "When I first got here, I heard you say that Ivy shouldn't have brought me to DC because she wasn't on good terms with your father. You didn't want me to meet him." I paused, then corrected myself. "You never wanted him to meet me."

No response. Adam wasn't telling me I was wrong.

"Ivy's missing," I said, choking on the words, "and you're *here*. With me." I ripped off the bandage, rushing out the words. "Are you my father?"

"Tess." Adam's voice was thick with emotion.

That wasn't a no.

"Ivy's the one who should be having this conversation with you," Adam said. "We'll tell you everything, I promise, just—"

Just let us get her back, I finished.

"And what if we don't get her back?" I asked. "What if we never get her back?"

What if, what if, what if—

Before Adam could answer, there was a knock. Moving briskly, Adam steered me to the side of the room. His hand went to his side as he went to answer the door, and I realized that he was wearing a gun.

Another knock. Adam looked through the peephole. Then he opened the door.

"Captain Keyes," President Nolan greeted him. "We need to talk."

CHAPTER 60

The president had two Secret Service agents with him. After my experience with Kostas, the president's security detail would never fade into the background for me again.

"Mr. President." Adam led the group into the living room. I eased out from my spot behind the wall.

"Have a seat, Captain," the president said, taking a seat himself.

Adam sat, every muscle in his body taut. I stayed standing. The president removed something from his jacket lapel and handed it to Adam.

"You might want to ask the girl to leave the room," he said, the words residing somewhere between an order and a suggestion.

It probably said something about Adam's mental state that he chose to interpret it as a suggestion. He didn't tell me I could stay, but he didn't tell me to leave, either.

It probably said something about my mental state that I chose to interpret that as an invitation to come closer.

The folder the president had handed Adam didn't have much in it: a single photograph. Ivy was holding a newspaper—today's newspaper. There was a single strip of duct tape over her mouth.

And strapped to her chest was a bomb.

"When?" Adam said. That was all he got out, one word.

"It arrived via e-mail this morning," the president replied. "We have our top analysts working on it. We'll find her."

"And if you don't?" I asked, taking a step forward.

A photograph like that would have been accompanied by a ransom demand. A deadline. A threat.

"Kostas told you what he wants," I said, trying not to think about how *I* had felt, strapped to a chair, watching the time *I* had left slip away. "He wants you to pardon his son."

President Nolan neither confirmed nor denied my statement. He kept his gaze trained on Adam. "What Ivy's captor does or does not want is immaterial, Captain Keyes. We're taking care of this."

The use of Adam's military title was a reminder that we weren't on even footing in this room. This was the president, and when it came to how he dealt with threats, this *wasn't* a democracy.

We didn't get a vote.

"We'll find Kostas," the president said. "We'll find Ivy. The important thing, in the meantime, is for you to back off. Whoever Bodie has working on this, I want them out. Now. This has become a matter of national security."

"If anything happens to Ivy," Adam began.

"It won't," the president said, in that voice that said *Trust me, believe me, follow me.*

I didn't trust him. I didn't believe him. I wasn't following, not if it meant sitting back and waiting for that bomb to go off.

"If anything does happen to Ivy," Adam said, "it won't be good for this administration." He paused. His tone was respectful. It was the pause that made it seem like a threat. "If Ivy doesn't get to a computer in the next twenty-four hours, it won't be good for anyone."

The president stood. "We're working on that, too."

Meaning what? I thought. *That he's working on finding a way to dismantle Ivy's fail-safe? To make sure that whatever secrets her program is set to release don't get released?*

"Have you even looked at the case?" I asked the president. I could hear the strain in my own voice. "Kostas's son," I said, forcing myself to continue. "Have you looked at his appeal? Adam said he had a brain injury—"

"Miss Kendrick," the president said. "Tess." His expression was grave. "I care for your sister. So does my wife. You have this administration's sympathy, our regrets, and our promise that we are doing everything we can to get Ivy home."

Not everything.

His next words proved that. "But the United States does not negotiate with terrorists—and neither do I."

CHAPTER 61

If push came to shove, if the president couldn't *find* Ivy before time ran out—he wasn't going to negotiate. He was going to let Kostas blow her up.

It should have been me. I should have been the one Kostas was holding captive. Ivy should have been the one standing here with Adam, trying to find a way around the president's hard line. *It should have been me. It was supposed to be me.*

"Go," I told Adam, swallowing back the urge to say all of that out loud. "I can't do anything, but maybe you can."

What Adam was—or wasn't—to me could wait.

Ivy's the one who should be having this conversation with you, he'd said. *We'll tell you everything, I promise—*

"Go," I told Adam again, my voice sharper this time, louder.

"I'm not leaving you here alone," he said.

"So don't leave me alone," I said, trying not to replay the president's words over and over again in my mind. "I hear Vivvie has a bodyguard now."

• • •

Vivvie's suite at the Roosevelt Hotel was impressive. There were massive bedrooms, a sitting room, a living room, a state-of-the-art kitchen.

"What does your aunt do?" I asked Vivvie, ignoring the elephant in the room. Or maybe the elephants, plural.

"I'm not really sure," Vivvie replied. "She works overseas. Or worked. Or . . ." Vivvie punctuated that sentence with a shrug.

I wondered if Vivvie was thinking, like I was, of my first day at Hardwicke, when I'd had to ask her what Ivy did for a living.

Ivy with a bomb strapped to her chest. The memory of that image came over me with no warning. It felt like someone had thrust a hand into my chest, like there was a vise around my heart. I couldn't think, and I couldn't breathe.

"Hey, Tess?" Vivvie said. I forced air into my lungs. Vivvie's face was shadowed with the toll the past few weeks had taken. I wanted to push her away, but I couldn't, because we were the same.

"Yeah?"

Vivvie reached out and grabbed my hand. "The offer about my favorite romance novel and/or horror movie," she said, her voice hoarse with all the things neither one of us could bear to say. "It still stands."

Adam didn't come for me that night. I slept on the sofa, even though Vivvie offered to share her king-size bed. It felt wrong for me to be with people when Ivy had no one but the man who might kill her for company. It felt wrong to even be lying on the sofa when Ivy had a bomb strapped to her chest.

If I'd thought it wouldn't raise questions, I would have slept on the cold, hard floor.

If I hadn't gotten snatched, if I'd been more suspicious when I'd seen an orderly outside my grandfather's room, if I'd fought back harder, if I'd been stronger—

If, if, if, then Ivy might be okay.

The next morning came and went. I couldn't bring myself to get up.

If I hadn't gone to the state dinner, Ivy wouldn't have flipped out and sent me to Boston. And if I hadn't gone to Boston, I would have been at my more-secure-than-most-consulates private school instead of outside my grandfather's room.

If, if, if . . .

Vivvie tried to get me to sit up, but I couldn't move, couldn't take my eyes off the clock, masochistically watching the minute hand crawl along, closer and closer to Ivy's final hours.

At some point, Vivvie went to the door. I heard murmuring, but my gaze stayed fixed on the clock.

"Tess." I could tell by the tone in Vivvie's voice that she'd said my name more than once.

I blinked. In addition to Vivvie's bodyguard, we now had three other visitors: Asher, Henry, and a woman who was almost certainly *Henry's* bodyguard.

Asher sat down on the sofa beside me. I couldn't even summon the energy to shove him off the sofa.

"Vivvie told us." Henry didn't specify what she had told them.

If, if, if . . .

"I am sorry about your sister," Henry told me. "For what it's worth, I have to believe she has a contingency plan of some sort."

A rush of anger went through my body, and with it, came my voice. "You're the authority, aren't you? On Ivy? *She can't be trusted* and all that?"

"Tess." Henry knelt next to me. "You have to know, I never would have wanted—"

"Wouldn't you?" I sat up, then stood, all in one motion. He could stay kneeling for all I cared. "You did this," I told Henry. "If you hadn't opened your mouth with the reporter, if you hadn't *insisted* on going to that state dinner, then I might have been here, in DC! I might not have gotten taken, and Ivy would never have had to trade herself for me. You did this," I told Henry.

Henry stood and took a step back.

"Hey!" Asher objected, but I barely heard him.

"We did this," I said, my eyes still locked on to Henry's. "She's going to die. I did that. I did—"

"You were right the first time," he said. "Blame me. If you have to blame someone, blame me."

If, if, if . . .

"She didn't even let me say good-bye." I sounded small and broken and weak. I didn't know how to sound any other way.

"No." That word burst out of Vivvie with the strength of a small whirlwind. "You don't get to blame yourself," she told me, her voice vibrating with emotions I recognized all too well. "Blaming yourself is easy. Blaming other people is, too. You think that I don't think about the fact that if I hadn't said anything, if I'd just kept my mouth closed, my father might still be alive? You think it wouldn't be easier to hate myself for that? To hate you? To hate *Ivy*? You have a choice, Tess, and you don't get to make the easy one, because if *you* give up, if you can't make it through this—what chance do I have?" Her eyes shone with tears, but she didn't shed them. "You don't get to check out. You don't get to give in. You can't."

My eyes were drawn back to the clock again. How many hours did Ivy have left? "I don't want to give up," I said softly, "but I don't know what else to do."

"What would your sister do?" Asher's question hurt, but instead of shrinking from it, I absorbed the pain. I let myself feel it, and then, I made myself *use* it.

What *would* Ivy do?

"She'd find a way to fix this," I said, my voice hardening. *But how?* If Ivy had been able to take care of the situation, she would have taken care of it when I got kidnapped. What chance did I have, if even DC's most prominent problem solver hadn't been able to come up with an answer that didn't leave her own head on the chopping block?

"I can't change the president's mind," I said, thinking out loud, trying to channel Ivy, trying—in vain—to *be* like her, to prove that there was something of her in me. "I could try to talk to the First Lady, but I doubt I could even get a hold of her. Everyone's out looking for Ivy."

"What does that leave?" Henry asked quietly.

I blew out a long breath of air. "Who besides the president can issue a pardon?"

Asher raised the index finger on his right hand. "The governor of the state in question."

I glanced at Vivvie. "I don't suppose anyone at Hardwicke has an uncle who's the governor of Arizona?"

She shook her head.

"What about William Keyes?" Henry asked. "My mother refers to him as the kingmaker. His support can make or break a political career. If the governor is looking to curry favor—"

"Adam already asked him to help," I cut in. "Keyes has a grudge against Ivy. He won't lift a finger."

My father collects things: information, people, blackmail material. Adam's voice echoed in my mind. He wouldn't have asked his father for help unless he'd believed the man could actually deliver.

"In my experience," Asher said thoughtfully, "sometimes *'there is no way I am doing that for you, Asher'* just means *'make me a better offer.'*"

I got the distinct feeling he was talking about Emilia, but set that aside. *What does Keyes want?* What could I possibly offer him? He'd wanted Pierce on the Supreme Court, but Pierce was dead. I racked my mind for everything I'd overheard William Keyes say in his conversation with Adam.

He wants Adam to retire from the military and run for the Senate. I rolled that over in my mind. *He thinks Adam could be president someday.*

Ivy had said that a kingmaker was someone with enough money and power to affect the outcome of elections, but who—for whatever reason—wasn't a viable candidate himself. I didn't know why William Keyes couldn't—or wouldn't—run for office, but I did know that he wanted more than being the person who called the shots behind the scene.

He wanted his son to do what he couldn't.

William Keyes wanted a legacy.

A plan began to take hold in my mind. Maybe Adam had been going about this all wrong. Maybe he shouldn't have been *asking* his father for help.

Maybe he should have tried blackmail.

CHAPTER 62

William Keyes lived in Virginia. His residence—and I doubted it was his only one—was nothing short of palatial. The guard out front hadn't wanted to buzz me through the gate, but I could be very convincing.

Ultimately, William Keyes had a weak spot, and I could tap into it with just four words: *It's about your son*.

The others waited outside. Fifteen minutes after I'd been let into the Keyes house and seated in some kind of formal library, the old man joined me.

"You," he said after a moment, "surprise me."

It wasn't clear from his tone whether that was a compliment or a complaint.

"I haven't surprised you yet," I replied. "But I'm about to."

Despite himself, the old man looked slightly intrigued. "Your sister wouldn't approve," he said, coming to stand closer to me. I got the feeling that he liked towering over me, that it didn't matter that physically, I was small.

An enemy could always be made smaller.

"Ivy is being held captive by a rogue Secret Service agent," I said, not beating around the bush. "President Nolan has received a ransom demand."

"He won't negotiate." The corners of Keyes's lips twitched. It wasn't a smile, but it wasn't a grimace, either.

"She's got a bomb strapped to her chest." I kept my voice calm but couldn't tamp down the intensity in it. "If you can't get the governor of Arizona to issue a pardon, she's going to die."

After exactly three seconds of silence, William Keyes took a seat across from me. "What makes you think I have any sway over the governor of Arizona?"

"If you don't, you know someone who does."

This time, he did smile. "You," he said, lingering on the word, "are very much like your sister."

I could hear, in those words, that he'd been fond of Ivy once. Keyes stiffened, like he'd heard the same thing and didn't appreciate the reminder.

"Unfortunately," he continued, leaning back in his chair, "your sister is no longer my concern. She put Nolan in office. Clearly, she prefers his judgment to mine."

Whatever bad blood there was between Keyes and the president, the man sitting across from me would never forgive Ivy for helping Peter Nolan make it to the White House.

Luckily, I hadn't come here to beg forgiveness.

"She's not my sister." I let those words sink in, knowing they weren't what he'd expected—knowing that *I* wasn't what he'd expected. "She's my mother, and I don't think you want anyone figuring out who my father is."

Keyes was on his feet again in an instant. "What precisely are you trying to say, young lady?"

"I'm saying that Ivy got pregnant at seventeen. I'm saying that the man who got her pregnant was young and recently enlisted. I'm saying she hid the pregnancy and gave me to her parents to raise, and I am saying that from the moment I stepped foot in this town, Ivy has done everything she can to keep you from looking too hard at me."

Keyes was staring at me now, as if he could see into my cells and disassemble my DNA, piece by piece.

"How long have Ivy and Adam known each other?" I asked him. I didn't wait for an answer as I pelted him with question after question. "Did you know he's teaching me how to drive? Or that the first time he ever saw me, he looked at me like the bottom had dropped out of his stomach?"

The old man came to stand behind the chair he'd been sitting in moments before. His hands closed over the back of it, his grip turning his knuckles white.

"Did you know," I said slowly, "that I heard Adam tell Ivy that bringing me to DC was a mistake because she'd made an enemy of you? I heard you say that Ivy had gotten under Adam's skin, that you had no idea how she'd done it. I have a theory."

Keyes took a step forward. "You think Adam is your father."

There was a ferocity in his voice when he'd said those words, like it took every ounce of determination and power he had just to choke out that one statement.

"I asked him," I said. "He didn't deny it. We'd need a DNA test to know for sure, but a DNA test might raise some questions."

I paused. "You're still hoping that someday, Adam might retire from the military and go into politics."

William Keyes had barely interacted with me, but I'd watched him. I'd heard him talking. I knew, instinctively, how to go straight for his heart.

"You have a plan for Adam," I said, "and I doubt that I am part of that plan."

"Are you attempting to blackmail me?" Keyes said. If I hadn't known better, I would have thought he sounded pleased.

"I prefer to think of it as a negotiation," I said. "You want to see your son in the Oval Office someday, and I want the governor of Arizona to issue either a pardon or a permanent stay of execution for Damien Kostas's son."

Now that the cards were on the table, I saw how easily this could go either way. William Keyes might not give me what I wanted. Adam might not even *be* my father.

I needed this to work.

Ivy needed for this to work.

"When were you born?" Keyes issued the question like a demand. Those four words—and the laser-sharp focus with which he assessed my features—told me that he wasn't dismissing my claims outright.

I can do this. I have to do this.

I told him when I was born, and then where. I told him, again, what Ivy had told me: my father was young and recently enlisted.

"Adam joined the military after college." William's grip on the back of the chair relaxed slightly. "He met your sister when he was home on leave. She'd just turned twenty."

I felt like a balloon that had been scratched with a knife. There was one moment of tightness in my chest, like I might explode, and then I felt the fight drain out of me. This was supposed to be my Hail Mary pass.

This was supposed to be me saving Ivy.

Adam met Ivy after I was born. As I forced myself to process that fact, I realized that I hadn't just thought Adam was my father, I hadn't just believed it—I'd wanted it to be true.

If Keyes was telling me the truth, Adam couldn't be my father. I wasn't anything to him but Ivy's daughter.

I stood up and turned sharply to the door.

"I suggest you sit back down."

I stopped in my tracks but didn't sit.

"Tess, isn't it?" the older man said, coming around to stand in front of me. "Is that short for Tessa?"

I wondered what game he was playing.

"Theresa," I said finally.

Keyes studied me, eyes sharp. "My late wife's name was Theresa."

The game had changed—but I wasn't sure how.

"I never quite figured out how Adam and Ivy met," William Keyes continued. "She was at Georgetown. He went to see her. I've wondered, over the years, if there was something romantic between them." He paused. "I see now that there's not. That there couldn't be."

He walked over to a shelf on the opposite side of the room and returned with a picture. In it were two young boys. The older one had a serious expression on his face. *Adam.* The younger boy—he had dark hair, a shade too light to be black. He was laughing, smiling.

His eyes were hazel, a familiar mix of brown and green.

"You look like him," William Keyes said. I had no idea what he was feeling. I couldn't tear my eyes away from the picture—away from the boy.

"Adam said he had a brother," I said slowly. The memory washed over me. "The first time we met, Adam said he had a brother."

He'd said that his brother had never cared for school, that he had preferred to spend his time outside.

Like me.

"You know what I think, Tess?" Keyes said, putting the picture down. "I think that my youngest met Ivy during basic training. I think they were young and stupid and, if we want to be generous, maybe even in love. Tommy was like that. If he fell, he fell hard."

Was, I thought dully. *Tommy* was *like that*. The past tense hit me with an almost physical force.

"I told him not to enlist. I told him to go to college. He could have been an officer—but he didn't listen." Keyes ran a hand roughly through his hair. "Adam thinks I pushed Tommy away, pushed him into joining up by forbidding him to go. Tommy died. I lost both sons." The kingmaker's sentences got shorter and curter. "And then there was Ivy."

Adam's father—*Tommy's* father—began to pace. I watched him, hyperaware in that moment that it was almost like watching myself. I'd looked at Adam, wondering if there was any of him in me, and now I knew.

It wasn't Adam.

It was never Adam.

"Adam must have known Tommy was seeing someone," Keyes continued, his voice raising a decibel or two as he paced. "And somehow, he found out about you."

Me. The pieces fell into place in my mind. All of those times I'd felt like Adam was looking at me like I reminded him of someone—I'd assumed I reminded him of Ivy.

But what if I was wrong?

What if, when he yelled at me, when he told me that family didn't bolt just because things were hard—what if those had been the times when I'd reminded him of his brother?

His dead brother. I'd lost so much in the past few weeks: *Gramps, my home, my identity, who I thought my parents were, Ivy.* I'd read a poem once in English class, about what it meant to master the art of losing.

I was an artist.

And now—now I would never know my father. I would never get to meet him, never know if he would have looked at me and seen pieces of himself, if he would have *wanted* me.

If I could have been a daughter he would have loved.

I couldn't stay here. I started for the door with no plans of what I would do when I walked out. I'd gambled and I'd failed, and now I really was going to be an orphan. Tommy was dead, and Ivy—

Kostas is going to kill her.

I tried.

"Hold it right there, young lady." Keyes barked out as my hand closed around the doorknob.

"Why?" I asked, whirling around, caught between sorrow and a smoldering anger I wasn't sure would ever go away. "If it was

Adam, I had something to offer. But my father is dead. Dead men don't win elections."

Dead men fathering illegitimate children was barely even news.

My father is dead. It hurt. All I'd ever seen of him was a picture, and it hurt. *Ivy might die.* I hadn't saved her.

Just this once, I wanted to save someone.

"No matter what Ivy and my son might have told you"—Keyes crossed the room to stand in front of me—"I'm not so heartless as to send my only grandchild away."

His *grandchild*. There was something in the way he said that word that was almost manic, as if my importance were larger than life.

My heart clenched.

"You'll do it?" I asked, terrified to hope for even a second that the answer might be yes. "You'll get the pardon?"

You'll save Ivy?

William Keyes—my paternal grandfather—put a hand under my chin. He tilted my face toward his. "That depends," he said, "on whether or not you'll do something for me."

CHAPTER 63

Back at Vivvie's place, I told the others about the deal I'd struck, and I waited. Eventually, Asher got a text from his sister. Without a word, he flipped on the news.

On the television, a pretty Asian American reporter stared directly into the camera, her hair whipping in the wind. "Again, I am standing outside the Washington Monument, where a SWAT team is closing in on what we are told is a hostage situation." The camera panned to show a blockade—and beyond that, two dozen men, armed to the teeth.

"Ivy," I whispered. She had to be okay. She *had* to be. *You have to get through this*, I thought fiercely. *You have to, Ivy. I'll never forgive you if you don't.*

I couldn't look away from the screen, the armed men.

Henry sat down beside me. "I would venture to guess that Kostas decided to make it harder for the president to ignore his demands," he said.

Ivy had promised Kostas that she would tell him exactly how to handle this situation. I wondered if she'd been the one to suggest taking the situation public.

I will hate you forever if you leave me now, Ivy, I thought, wishing she could hear me. My eyes were dry. So was my throat. I had nothing left but the words repeating themselves over and over again in my head. I'd done everything right. I'd *fixed* this. Help was coming.

She didn't get to leave me again.

On-screen, the reporter kept throwing information at us. The Washington Monument had been closed for construction. No one was sure how many people were inside, but there was a bomb.

The bomb strapped to Ivy's chest.

I looked at the clock on the wall, like it could tell me when the deal I'd struck with Keyes would come through. Even for a man known for making things happen, conjuring a governor's pardon out of nowhere took time.

Time Ivy might not have.

"We don't have to watch." Vivvie reached for the remote. I pulled it back.

"Yes," I said simply, "we do."

The four of us sat, one next to the other, our eyes locked on the screen. Vivvie's hand worked its way into mine. On my other side, Henry surprised me by doing the same.

I held on—like a person dangling from the edge of a skyscraper, like a drowning man reaching for a hand to pull him to shore.

The press couldn't get close. The Capitol loomed in the background. The SWAT team, the FBI . . . I didn't know who else was there, trying to talk Ivy's captor into releasing her, into not setting off the bomb.

If it had been just her, if it hadn't been public, would they have just let her die? Would they have swept it under the rug, covered it up? It hurt to ask myself the question. It hurt even more to know that the answer was almost certainly yes.

"John!" the woman on the screen addressed the station's news anchor excitedly. "Something is happening. Something is definitely happening."

Far away, behind the blockade, there was movement. Guns were raised. A door was opening. I couldn't make out the features on anyone's face.

My phone buzzed, alerting me to arrival of a new text. *It's done. WK.* William Keyes.

I stopped breathing. I stopped blinking. I stopped thinking. I stopped hoping.

All I could do was sit there as the reporter continued yelling at the camera, telling us that someone was coming out.

"We have confirmation that the hostage is female," the reporter was saying. "I'm hearing unconfirmed reports that there's a bomb strapped to her chest."

I couldn't see. I couldn't tell what was happening. There was a flurry of movement on-screen.

"I don't see her," I said, wheezing the words out. "I don't see her."

If the others responded, I didn't hear them. My ears rang. Suddenly, I was on my feet, but I didn't remember standing.

"The hostage is safe," the reporter said suddenly. "I repeat, John, we are hearing reports that the bomb has been disarmed and the hostage is safe."

My body didn't relax. I couldn't breathe. I couldn't risk

believing what she was telling me—then the camera panned. It zoomed in, and just for a moment, I saw her. *Ivy*.

The shot was grainy. All I could make out was her hair, a hint of her features, but the way she moved, the way she stood—it was Ivy.

I sank back into the sofa. *It's done*, the text had said. Kostas had gotten what he wanted. He'd let Ivy go. Not because of the president, or the hostage negotiators, or the SWAT team, or the FBI.

Because somehow he'd gotten word that his son had been pardoned.

Because of William Keyes.

Because of me.

"They've got her." Vivvie said the words slowly, as if she didn't quite believe them. "She's okay."

Part of me still didn't believe it. Part of me wouldn't believe it was really over until Ivy was here, with me.

"The hostage-taker is coming out," the reporter said suddenly. "I repeat, the hostage-taker is coming out."

I never saw Kostas take that first step out into the open, his hands up. The view was blocked from the cameras. I never saw him give himself up.

But I did hear the shot that rang out a second later.

I heard the screams, the chaos.

I heard confirmation that the hostage-taker was dead.

CHAPTER 64

The FBI—or the Secret Service or Homeland Security or the White House, I wasn't really sure on the details—kept Ivy in seclusion for nearly twenty-four hours. They must have allowed her access to a computer, because her insurance policy didn't rear its head, but they didn't let her near a phone.

I knew this because I knew, in the pit of my stomach, that if she'd had a phone, she would have called me.

I got a call from Bodie instead. Ivy really was okay. Kostas really was dead—shot with an exploding round before anyone had a chance to see his face. The number of people who knew his real identity could be counted on two hands—and that was why they hadn't released Ivy right away.

This, Bodie had been informed, was a matter of national security.

They wanted to get their stories straight. I deeply suspected that when the dead man's name was released, it wouldn't be a name we recognized.

Major Bharani was dead. Judge Pierce was dead. And now so was Kostas.

There was no one left to bring to justice—and no one left to tell the story, except for Henry and Asher and Vivvie and me. The White House wanted this kept quiet.

With the guilty parties dead, I wasn't saying a word—for Vivvie's sake, if not my own. Something in my gut told me that Henry would do the same. He would bury this, push it into the recesses of his mind where he kept the secrets that hurt him most. The ones with the potential to hurt the people he loved.

I wondered if he'd hate Ivy for this, too.

I wondered if Ivy had ever really been the one he was mad at.

Ivy's fine. That was the refrain I repeated to myself, over and over again. *She's fine. She's fine. She's coming home.* But no matter how many times I told myself that, I could never be more than ninety percent sure, until the moment the door to Adam's apartment opened and I saw Ivy standing on the other side.

They must have let her wash up at some point, because she looked as polished as she had the day she came for me at the ranch. Her light brown hair was pulled into a loose French braid at the nape of her neck.

She walked like she had somewhere to be.

I stood, frozen in place. Ivy stopped a few feet away from me. I was still so angry with her. I'd been so *scared*. I'd spent years telling myself that she didn't matter, that she couldn't hurt me unless I let her, that we were nothing alike. But the past twenty-four hours had washed all of that away.

She was in me. She was under my skin, and there in my smile and the shape of my face, and she would *always* matter. She would *always* be able to hurt me, and there was nothing I could do, no space I could put between us to erase that.

She's here. She's okay. She's here. The words beat out a gut-wrenching rhythm in my head. Ivy's lips trembled slightly. She took one step toward me, then another, then another, until she was right in front of me, and something in me gave. I fell—fell against her, fell into her arms, wrapping mine tightly around her. I buried my head in her shoulder.

She was shaking—or maybe I was.

But she was solid and real and *fine*. I bent, my head against her chest. She breathed in the smell of my hair. I could hear her heart beating.

"Tessie." That was all she said, my name.

I mumbled something into her shirt.

"What?" Ivy said.

I repeated myself. "It's Tess."

I slept in Ivy's room that night, curled into a tiny ball beside her on the king-size bed. In the morning, I could be mad at her. I could hate her for the secrets she'd kept, the lies she'd told—but for now, for this one night, I wasn't letting her out of my sight.

Whatever Ivy was—both in the grand scheme of things and to me—we were family. Not just in blood, not just because she was somehow responsible for half of my DNA. We were family because I would always love her more than I hated her. Because losing her would have killed me. Because I would have done anything, made a bargain with any devil, to keep her from harm's way.

We were family because she would have walked through fire for me.

For the longest time, we lay there, neither one of us asleep, neither of us saying a word, not even touching.

I fell asleep to the rhythm of her breaths.

Sometime later, I woke. Outside, pitch-black was giving way to the first hints of morning. I was alone in Ivy's bed. Panic shot through me, like ice through my veins, but I forced my heart not to pound, forced my feet onto the floor. I walked through the apartment, down the spiral stairs, and through the foyer, and saw a slant of light coming from the conference room.

The door was cracked open. I pushed it inward. Ivy sat in the middle of the conference table, staring at the wall. There were three pictures hanging there: Judge Pierce, Major Bharani, and Damien Kostas.

"Ivy?" I announced my presence because she was staring at the pictures so hard that I wasn't sure she'd marked my entrance to the room. Ivy turned to look at me. She blinked twice.

"Sometimes you look like him," she said, a soft smile playing around the edges of her lips. "Your father."

"You loved him."

"I did." She slid off the table and walked toward me. "Some days, I still do." She tucked a stray strand of hair behind my ear. I let her.

"You're not my mother." I softened those words as much as I could. "I don't know if I can . . . I don't know what you are."

Ivy met my eyes. "I'm yours."

It hurt a little less this time. It still cut to hear I mattered to her; inside I still bled—but this time, I didn't pull back. "Adam said Gramps told you to go." This wasn't a conversation I'd ever planned on having with her—but it also wasn't a conversation I'd believed I would ever again have the opportunity to have. "That summer, when I was thirteen, when you asked me to live with you—Adam said Gramps was the one who told you to go."

Ivy nodded. I started to say something, but she cut me off. "He was right to tell me to go, Tess, and the rest of it? That's not on Gramps. Not calling, not being there—that's on me." Ivy let out a long breath. "I couldn't be your sister anymore, Tess, and *that* is on me. When I got back here after that visit, I threw myself into my work. I made enemies, and I told myself that you were safer if I kept my distance."

I knew without asking who one of those enemies was. "William Keyes."

If Ivy noticed the note of apprehension in my voice when I said that name, she gave no sign of it. "We had a disagreement. He went after someone I cared about. It didn't end well, and I told myself that you would be safer if I stayed away."

"You wanted to protect me." *From my own grandfather*, I added silently. *From the man I went to in order to save you.*

"I wanted to protect you," Ivy repeated, then she closed her eyes and bowed her head slightly. "That was what I told myself. I told myself that I was doing it to protect you, but God help me, Tess, if I'm honest—with myself, with you—I think I was really protecting *me*." When she opened her eyes again, they were full of self-directed anger and grief. Whether or not I could forgive her, she'd never forgive herself for what she was about to say. "Seeing you, talking to you, *loving* you wrecked me. You said once that I didn't know what it felt like to feel helpless, to have other people making my decisions—but I do, Tessie. Because I let Mom and Dad decide, I let Gramps decide, I *let* them take you—and I swore I would never let that happen to me again."

Ivy was my age, I thought. *She was my age when she met Tommy Keyes, my age when she got pregnant with me.* I'd known that, objectively, but somehow, I'd never thought of Ivy as young or scared or fallible. She was Ivy Kendrick. She wasn't supposed to be any of those things.

"I guess I always thought," Ivy said softly, "that if I was strong enough, if I was formidable enough, if I was successful enough—I could be *enough*. For you. I thought that if I became this person who could take on the world, then I could take care of you." She shook her head—at her past self, maybe, or to snap herself out of it. "When I came to Montana that summer, Tess, I thought I was ready. I really did. I was going to give you *everything*. But Gramps called me out, *and he was right*, Tessie. I wasn't doing it for *you. You* were thriving. *You* were happy. And I . . ." The words got caught in her throat, but she forced them out. "I was your sister. I was never going to be strong enough or successful enough. There was never going to be a *right time* to tell you. You were happy. And you deserved to be happy."

I'd never heard her sound as fierce as she did saying those words. *You deserved to be happy.*

"So you left me there," I said, the emotion in my voice an echo of hers.

"I left you there, and it broke me. It *shattered me*, and I didn't know how to go back." Ivy was quiet for a moment, then forced herself to continue. "I left you there for you, but I stayed away for me. I have made so many mistakes, but that?" Ivy shook her head again. "That's the one that never goes away. I thought, when I brought you here, that I could make up for it, that I could be whatever you needed me to be."

That was my cue to say something. I was supposed to tell her that it was all right, that I understood, or that it wasn't ever going to be all right, and that I was never going to understand.

"Right now," I said instead, "all I need you to be is alive."

I knew now why she'd left. Why she'd stayed away. Eventually, we'd have to deal with that—but not tonight. After the past few days, I didn't have it in me to *feel* anything else. I was so sick of being sideswiped by emotions. Just this once, I needed something to be neat. I needed simple. I needed to just concentrate on the fact that she was alive. She was *here*.

I can't do this with you right now, Ivy.

"I thought Adam might be my father," I said abruptly. As far as subject changes went, that one was effective.

"He's not," Ivy said immediately.

I met her eyes. "His brother was."

Ivy froze for a moment. "Now I know what Bodie's always talking about," she said finally. "It *is* freaky." I thought she'd stop there, but she didn't. "Tommy was ... exciting." It took her a moment to decide on the word. "He was motion and emotion. He never stopped moving, never stopped *feeling*. He was stubborn and loyal and never once thought about the consequences of anything he did."

"So I get that from him." I meant that as a joke, but I couldn't keep from thinking the words again. *I get that from him.*

Ivy reached for me. I let her squeeze my shoulder, then turned to the photos tacked to the wall. "What's all this?" Another subject change—this one less successful than the first. Ivy's lack of response pinged on my internal radar. "Ivy?"

I gestured to the photos on the wall. *Judge Pierce. Major Bharani. Damien Kostas.* The case was over. So why was Ivy down here, staring at pictures of these three men?

"It's nothing," Ivy said, standing up and moving to take the photographs from the wall.

"Right," I said. *Nothing* wasn't keeping Ivy up at night. "Tell me."

Nothing good had ever come from Ivy keeping me in the dark. Maybe she was starting to see that, or maybe she was too worn down to fight me on this. She drew her hand back from the first photograph, leaving it pinned to the wall. A second later, she started to speak.

"After Kostas got word that his son had been pardoned, he let me go." Ivy shuttered her eyes, and I knew she was thinking back to that moment. "He was coming out. He wasn't a threat. He wasn't armed. He was turning himself in, so why shoot?" Ivy looked down at her hands. "We're talking trained hostage negotiators, Tess. There's no way they should have taken that shot."

She turned back to the wall. To the photographs. *The judge. The doctor. The Secret Service agent.* "Kostas killed Bharani when he became a liability," Ivy said. "Kostas killed Pierce when he reneged on their deal."

I heard what she wasn't saying and gave life to the question myself. "So who killed Kostas?"

Who had fired that shot? A member of the SWAT team, presumably, but—

"Who killed Kostas?" Ivy repeated, interrupting my thoughts. "Or," she added, "who gave the order?"

Ivy's gaze went to the conference table. On it, there was a notebook, and on the notebook, there was a list.

Names.

I thought back to a conversation I'd had with Henry. *There was another number on that disposable phone*, he'd said. *That means there is at least one other person involved.*

At least.

I'd thought, multiple times, that we were either looking for someone who could have poisoned Henry's grandfather or someone who had the power to usher Pierce's nomination through. It had never occurred to me that we might be looking for *both*.

"You think there might be someone else," I said. Ivy neither confirmed nor denied those words. "Kostas killed Vivvie's dad because he was becoming a liability, but once Kostas's son was pardoned..."

Kostas had told me that he didn't expect to get out of this. He'd talked about being honorable.

Kostas was a liability, I thought, unable to keep the possibility from taking root in my mind. Maybe the Secret Service agent *had* been shot by an overzealous SWAT agent. Or maybe someone on the SWAT team had instructions to make sure Kostas didn't leave that building alive.

The only way this plan makes any sense—the only way it could even potentially be worth the risk—is if Pierce had reason to believe he'd get the nomination.

Kostas didn't have the kind of power. And when I'd asked him if Pierce was the one who'd arranged this whole thing, he hadn't replied. He'd stilled, an unreadable expression on his face.

Not because he was thinking about Pierce. Because he was thinking of someone else.

"*Pierce was made aware of my problem*," I told Ivy. "That's what Kostas said to me. Not that Pierce figured it out, not that Pierce masterminded the whole thing. *Pierce was made aware of my problem*."

By who? My mind went to the phone that Kostas had snapped in two. It was a flip phone, obviously a disposable. So who had the number? Who was calling?

My eyes traveled back to Ivy's list. There were maybe a dozen names on it, but I only saw one.

My paternal grandfather's.

"You said you cleared William Keyes," I told Ivy, a feeling of dread taking up residence in my stomach. "You said Keyes was the last person who would have wanted Justice Marquette dead."

Ivy flipped the notebook closed before I could get a look at the other names. "Nothing for you to worry about," she told me, squeezing my arm again. "Let's go back to bed."

CHAPTER 65

A judge. The White House physician. A Secret Service agent.

Once Ivy put the thought in my head, I couldn't keep from coming back to it. Were all the people responsible for Theodore Marquette's death dead? And if not, who was still out there?

Judge Pierce had stood to gain a nomination.

Vivvie's father had done it for money.

Kostas had done it for his son.

If there was someone else—someone whose role had been ushering the nomination through, someone whose calls Kostas had been avoiding—what had that person stood to gain?

I didn't speak a word of those thoughts to Henry. Or to Vivvie. Our lives were slowly getting back to normal. That first Monday back at Hardwicke, the gossip mill ran full force. Ivy's name had been released as the hostage. Everyone wanted the inside scoop—but I'd managed to do a pretty good job dissuading people from asking me questions.

I was, in general, pretty good at dissuading.

I knew things were dying down when a student approached me claiming that someone was sabotaging her grades. No one outside of Vivvie, Henry, and Asher knew about my role in getting Ivy released, but there was no escaping the persistent belief that if you had a problem at Hardwicke, Tess Kendrick was the person to see.

A week to the day after my last text from William Keyes, I received a second. He'd held up his end of our bargain. It was my turn to hold up mine.

"Are you okay?" Vivvie asked me, the question taking me back to the way she'd asked, over and over, my first day at Hardwicke.

"I just received a royal decree from my grandfather that he's picking me up after school," I said. The word *grandfather* felt foreign on my lips, like maybe I wasn't saying it right. Gramps was my grandfather, but William Keyes? He was one of the wealthiest men in the country. He was a kingmaker, a powerful enemy, a powerful friend.

His name was on Ivy's list.

"What exactly did you promise the old chap?" Asher fell in beside us in the hallway on our way to the exit.

"Besides a press conference announcing my existence to the world?" I asked, giving no visible clue to where my thoughts had really taken me. "Weekly dinners, giving him a say in my education, letting him set up a trust fund for me, and—" I mumbled the rest of it.

"Did you say *changing your last name*?" Asher asked.

"You said once that your sister and Keyes didn't get along." Now it was Henry's turn to join the conversation. "I do hope that was an exaggeration." The two of us weren't friends, exactly, but we'd been through something—he'd sat by me when I'd been waiting for news on Ivy; I was the only person he'd ever told about his father.

Sometimes, when I caught him staring at me, I thought maybe he knew my secrets, too.

"Not an exaggeration," I told Henry. "When Ivy finds out I went to William Keyes for help, when she finds out what I promised him . . ."

That would have been an ugly conversation no matter what. But given that Ivy was still staying up nights, locked in her office, given that *she* thought there was another conspirator out there and my grandfather's name was on her suspect list—she was going to kill me.

We hit the front corridor. Asher pushed the door open. "Ladies," he said with a gallant half bow, "after you."

I stepped out into the sunshine and stopped dead in my tracks. There was a limo waiting at the curb, and standing just outside the limo was William Keyes. The man the First Lady said excelled at holding a grudge. The one I'd been told was ruthless and dangerous. The one who valued family, who wanted a *legacy*.

The one who looked at me, across the pavement, with a hungry look in his eyes that told me that legacy might be me.

"Will you remember us when you're fancy?" Asher asked me. I shoved him to one side. All around us, students were slowing to look at Keyes. It wasn't the limo that attracted their attention. It was the man.

Asher's sister honed in on the four of us like a missile zeroing in on its target. "That's William Keyes," Emilia told Asher. "What is William Keyes doing here?"

Henry, Asher, and Vivvie all darted their eyes toward me.

Asher was the one who broke the silence. "Have you met my friend?" he asked Emilia. "Tess Keyes."

Emilia stopped dead in her tracks. Asher had spoken just loudly enough that several people overheard him. My good old buddy John Thomas Wilcox looked like he'd swallowed a worm.

Note to self, I thought, *kill Asher*. But a second later, I had bigger things to worry about, because apparently Bodie hadn't come by himself to pick me up today.

Ivy had come with him.

"Incoming," Bodie coughed, and that was all the warning I had before Ivy swooped down, intercepting me before I made it to the limo and the man who was standing there.

"Tess," Ivy said calmly.

"Yes?"

"What is Adam's father doing here?"

I looked to Bodie, who gave me a look that said, oh so clearly, that I was on my own.

"*What is Adam's father doing here?*" Ivy repeated.

There was no way to sugarcoat it. "Apparently, he's giving me a ride home from school."

We'd acquired enough of an audience that Ivy lowered her voice. "And why would William Keyes do that?"

"Because he knows," I said. "About Tommy. About me."

Ivy had to have suspected that was what I was going to say, but that didn't keep her nostrils from flaring slightly the moment I said it.

"We needed a pardon." I said the words below my breath, so low that no one but Ivy could hear them. "I did what I had to do to make sure you came home alive."

I didn't regret it. No matter who—or what—my paternal grandfather might be, I couldn't regret it.

"Ivy." William Keyes stepped forward and greeted Ivy with a cat-eating-canary smile. "You look well."

"What are you doing here?" she asked him.

He smiled. "I'm picking my granddaughter up from school."

Ivy forgot about keeping her voice low. "I want you to stay away from her. You have no legal standing—"

"I'll stay away from her when she asks me to stay away from her," William Keyes replied.

Ivy looked at me. "Theresa," she said, her voice low. "Tess Kendrick. Tell him."

His name was on that list. But there were other names, too.

"I gave him my word," I said. This was the bargain I'd struck: the kingmaker's presence in my life in exchange for saving Ivy's.

It was a deal I would make all over again.

"In this business," Keyes told Ivy, still looking altogether too satisfied with himself, "your word is the most valuable asset you have."

He gestured toward the limo, and I stepped toward it.

"What's your endgame here?" Ivy asked the man she'd once worked for. "What do you want with my daughter?"

"The same thing I've always wanted, dear," William replied. "An heir."

Unlike the rest of us, he made no move whatsoever to lower his voice. All around us, my fellow students were buzzing.

"By the way," the man who made kings told Ivy, "her name isn't Tess Kendrick. She's changing it—to Tess Kendrick Keyes." He smiled smugly. "There'll be a lovely profile of her—and her courageous father, God rest his soul—in tomorrow's *Post*."

For once, Ivy was speechless.

Nearby, someone snapped a picture of the three of us on a cell phone. Keyes opened the door to the limo. With one last look at Ivy, I climbed in. My paternal grandfather climbed in beside me.

"Ivy's going to kill me," I said.

"You're a Keyes," he replied smoothly. "We excel at thinking five steps ahead. I'm sure you can handle it."

As the limo pulled away from Hardwicke, I could see Ivy's mind racing, looking for a way to undo this—and quite possibly plotting my immediate demise. I thought about Justice Marquette and the likelihood that there was a fourth player who'd gotten away with his part in the murder.

I thought about the fact that the person in question might be sitting beside me in this car.

And then I settled back in my seat and responded to his assertion that I could handle it. "I can try."

ACKNOWLEDGMENTS

As always, this book would not exist without the wonderful team who helped bring it into being. First and foremost, thank you to Catherine Onder, for seeing the potential in this book and working with me to make sure it lived up to that potential. I owe you a huge debt of gratitude (as do Vivvie, Henry, and Asher—not to mention the book's plot!). Major thanks are also due to Anne Heltzel, who helped me take this book from its first revision to its final draft. Anne's input was invaluable (and delivered on an extremely tight timetable to boot!).

I'm blessed to have worked with my incredible agent, Elizabeth Harding, on fourteen books now. As always, Elizabeth, I am so grateful for your help and support at every step in the process. Thank you also to Ginger Clark, whose passion for this project never failed to humble me and bring a smile to my face, and to Holly Frederick and everyone else at Curtis Brown for all their hard work!

Huge thanks to the writer friends who gave me pep talks, commiseration, and occasionally food and drink in their attempt to get me through the submission, drafting, and revision of this book! Thank you to BOB for company, day in and day out, Carrie Ryan and Rachel Hawkins for Arizona adventures, and Sarah Rees Brennan, Maureen Johnson, Cassandra Clare, Josh Lewis, and Kelly Link for Cornwall! Lastly, I cannot begin to describe how grateful I am to my Oklahoma girls, Ally Carter and Rachel Vincent, for deadline closets, Panera Thursdays, brainstorming, commiseration, and moral support. I love you guys dearly!

Finally, I am grateful for the support of my family and friends. Special thanks go to Ti30, Mom, Dad, Justin, Allison, and Anthony. And to Connor, for helping to drag Aunt Jen away from the book long enough to go to the zoo.

Kim Haynes Photography

JENNIFER LYNN BARNES

is the number one *New York Times* bestselling author of more than twenty acclaimed young adult novels, including the Inheritance Games series, the Debutantes series, *The Lovely and the Lost*, and the Naturals series. Jen is also a Fulbright Scholar with advanced degrees in psychology, psychiatry, and cognitive science. She received her PhD from Yale University in 2012 and was a professor of psychology and professional writing for many years. She invites you to visit her online at jenniferlynnbarnes.com or on Instagram @authorjenlynnbarnes.

DON'T MISS THE PAGE-TURNING SEQUEL!

CHAPTER 1

"Tess, has anyone ever told you that you're an absolute vision when you're plotting something?" Asher Rhodes shot a lazy grin in my direction.

I ignored Asher and kept my gaze fixed on the street in front of the Roosevelt Hotel. A man named Charles Bancroft had a reservation at the Roosevelt's five-star restaurant for lunch—pricey, considering Mr. Bancroft had recently convinced a judge that his child support and alimony payments should be kept to a minimum.

"Asking for a friend," Asher clarified. Then he nudged his best friend. "Henry, my good man, tell Tess she's pretty as a picture when she's preparing to unleash her wrath on the delightfully unsuspecting father of one of our classmates."

"Kendrick?" Henry Marquette said.

"Yes?" I replied without taking my eyes away from the street.

"You are utterly *terrifying* when you are plotting something."

A dark car pulled up to the curb. I smiled. "Thank you," I told Henry. Then I turned to Asher. "Get Vivvie on the phone," I instructed. "Tell her we're a go."

Vivvie and her aunt had lived at the Roosevelt Hotel for almost a month until they'd found a DC apartment. That was plenty of time for friendly-to-a-fault Vivvie Bharani to have endeared herself to the staff.

Convenient, that, I thought as I watched Charles Bancroft climb out of the backseat of his luxury sedan. Asher relayed my message to Vivvie, then put the phone on speaker.

"The eagle has landed," Vivvie said from the other end. "The bird is in the bush."

Few things in life gave Vivvie and Asher as much joy as talking in code. I didn't bother translating. One of the bellhops wheeled a cart of luggage out in front of Bancroft's car. Bancroft disappeared into the restaurant, but his driver wasn't going anywhere.

That was my cue.

I took a step forward. Henry caught my elbow. "No bloodshed," he said. "No blackmail. No obstruction of justice."

"You drive a hard bargain," I told him, stepping away from his grasp. "What are your thoughts on extortion?" Without waiting for an answer, I headed for Bancroft's car.

Henry and Asher followed on my heels.

"The cat is dancing in the catnip," Asher reported back to Vivvie. "Grumpy lion is grumpy."

"Did you just refer to me as a grumpy lion?" Henry asked Asher.

"Absolutely not," Asher promised. Then he took the phone off speaker and lowered his voice. "*Suspicious lion is suspicious*," he stage-whispered to Vivvie.

With one last glance back at Henry and Asher, I approached Bancroft's car and knocked on the window. The driver rolled it down.

"Can I help you?" he asked.

"I'm a friend of Jeremy's," I said. "I'd like to talk."

Jeremy Bancroft was a senior at the Hardwicke School, due to graduate in the spring. Or at least he had been due to graduate from Hardwicke in the spring until his father stopped payment on his tuition. From what I'd gathered, Mr. Bancroft's sole focus was making his ex-wife suffer for daring to divorce him, and he had no qualms whatsoever about using his own children to do it.

I had no qualms about lying in wait in the man's car. An hour later, I was rewarded.

"I'm telling you right now," Bancroft said, shifting his phone from one ear to the other as he situated himself in the backseat of the car, "they'll be signed on with the firm by the end of business day tomorrow. Guaranteed."

The car pulled away from the curb. I sat silently in the front passenger seat until we'd merged into traffic. Then I turned around.

"What the . . ." Bancroft hung up the phone and started barking out orders to his driver. "Mick, pull over."

"Mick had to step out," I told Jeremy's father. "Right about now, he's probably wondering where you and your car are."

In reality, Bancroft's driver had agreed to take a very conveniently timed bathroom break. He was, as it turned out, fonder of his boss's son than of his boss.

"I don't know who you are," Bancroft gritted out, "or what you want—"

"I'd like for you to stop using your children as pawns in whatever sick game you have going on with your ex-wife," I said. "But I'll settle for a rather large transfer of funds."

Bancroft stared at me in disbelief. "Who put you up to this?"

"A better question might be what I'm going to do if you don't transfer those funds."

"Do?" Bancroft sputtered. "You can't *do* anything. You're a kid."

"I'm Tess Kendrick," I said. "Keyes." The second last name was an afterthought. The combination of the two had the man in the backseat paling. "I go to Hardwicke with your son. Jeremy seems fairly convinced that you're hiding money in an offshore account to keep your child support payments to a minimum."

Bancroft showed not even a trace of emotion at the mention of his son. "Prove it," he spat out.

"I don't have to." I took my time explaining those words. "Either you *have* been hiding assets," I said, "which makes you a felon, or you're actually as broke as you claim to be, which makes you the very last person in the world whom anyone in DC should trust to invest their money." I paused. "I wonder how long it would take for news of your financial difficulties to spread."

Bancroft snorted, but his eyes gave him away. He was looking nervous. *Good*. "You think my ex-wife wants DC society to realize how broke *she* is?" the man countered. "If she was going to go public with this, she would have already."

True.

"I'm not your ex-wife." I picked up my phone and brought up the contact information for the *Washington Post*. "And as it turns out, *I* don't have a vested interest in whether people think she's broke or not." I turned the phone toward Bancroft just long enough for him to see who I was calling, then hit the *call* button, setting the phone to speaker.

It rang once.

Twice.

"Stop," Bancroft said.

I hit the button to end the call just as someone picked up. I held out the paperwork Henry had asked his family attorney to draw up. "In an ideal world," I said, "you'd amend the divorce settlement you made with your ex-wife."

A muscle in Bancroft's jaw ticked. He'd take his chances weathering damaging rumors before he'd give his ex anything she wanted.

"However," I continued, "I thought you might prefer making an anonymous donation to your children's school."

I held out the papers again. Bancroft took them. Reading them, he frowned. "A scholarship fund?"

"Donors can put whatever stipulations they would like on a donation. Your stipulations are very specific."

Jeremy and his little sister would be the recipients of scholarships that would pay their Hardwicke tuition through graduation.

"I only have two children." Bancroft looked up from the pages and glowered at me. "Why am I funding three scholarships?"

I offered him a tight-lipped smile. "Price of doing business."

A vein in Bancroft's forehead throbbed. "And if I tear up these papers, call the police, and have you arrested for stealing my car?"

I shrugged. "Technically," I said, "*I* didn't steal your car."

The car slowed to a stop at the curb of the Roosevelt, having circled the block. In the driver's seat, Henry turned around. "Technically," he said, "I did."

"Henry Marquette," I clarified for the man in the backseat. "His mother is Pamela Abellard." My smile took on a cat-eating-canary glint. "Correct me if I'm wrong, but aren't the Abellards your firm's biggest client?"

Bancroft's grip tightened over his phone, his knuckles turning white.

"We both know you're not making that call," I said. I nodded toward the paperwork in his hands.

The man's eyes went back to Henry's.

"Normally," Henry told him conversationally, "when someone asks me to commit grand theft auto, my answer is a firm no. But I have a sister." Henry's expression was perfectly polite, but his mint-green eyes flashed, striking against his dark brown skin. "My little sister," Henry continued, "is your daughter's age. Nine years old."

Bancroft signed the papers. He made a call and authorized the transfer of funds.

As I exited the car, I glanced over at Henry. "Should I call Asher and tell him we won't be needing that getaway distraction?"

Before Henry could reply, pop music reverberated off the building. Asher jogged into the middle of a large crowd and struck a dramatic pose.

"You say 'distraction,'" Henry deadpanned, "Asher hears 'flash mob.'"

Five seconds later, Vivvie danced wildly past and gave me a questioning look. I nodded.

"The possum has fallen on the nun!" Vivvie called to Asher.

Asher didn't miss a beat of choreography. He shimmied and punched a fist into the air. "Long live the possum!"

CHAPTER 2

I had exactly three hours to recover from my confrontation with Jeremy Bancroft's father before I found myself facing off against a very different opponent.

"What do you know about the War of the Roses?" My paternal grandfather closed his fingers around a black knight and then used it to remove my rook from the chessboard.

No mercy. No hesitation.

"*Wars* of the Roses," I said, countering his move. "Plural."

The edges of the old man's lips quirked upward. He inclined his head slightly—both an acknowledgment of my point and a command to continue.

"Bunch of guys in the fifteenth century fighting for the throne of England."

I kept my summary short and to the point. As in chess, every move in a conversation with William Keyes came with consequences, either immediate or down the line. He was grooming me as his heir, attempting to mold me in his own image. If I gave an inch, he'd take a mile, and I had no desire to be either molded or groomed.

Especially by a man who may or may not have conspired to assassinate the chief justice of the United States Supreme Court.

"The Wars of the Roses were a series of lethal confrontations and political maneuverings between the house of Lancaster and the house of York," Keyes corrected, sliding his bishop across the board as he lectured. "Political unrest tends to be unkind to weak and strategically impotent kings."

His gaze settled on the chessboard—on *my* king—but I knew he was thinking about another ruler and another throne.

Weekly Sunday night dinners at the Keyes mansion had cemented my understanding of my paternal grandfather as a man with many allies and many enemies. More often than not, he considered President Nolan the latter. Every bump in the road for the Nolan administration was taken as incontrovertible evidence that Peter Nolan had never been the right man for the job.

I picked up my bishop and plunked it back down. "Check."

"Bloodthirsty girl," Keyes commented. "You get that from your mother. Patience," he continued, eyeing the board, "is a Keyes trait."

This was the way it was with him, drawing lines between the Kendrick blood in me and the Keyes.

"Did you know that the term *kingmaker* was first used to refer to the role the Earl of Warwick played in the struggle between Lancaster and York?" My grandfather resumed his lecture, but I knew his eyes missed nothing—not the effect that hearing Ivy referred to as my *mother* still had on me, not the positions of the pieces on the board. "During the Wars of the Roses, Warwick deposed not one but two kings."

Kingmaker was what people called William Keyes. He wielded tremendous power and influence behind the scenes in the American political game.

"Warwick wasn't just wealthy and powerful," Keyes continued. "He was *strategic*."

Power. Politics. Game theory. This was what passed for casual conversation in this house. William Keyes had two sons. One of them was dead; the other was estranged. I was his only grandchild. In his eyes, that meant his legacy rested on me.

"I'd like to see you showing a bit more initiative about becoming a part of the Hardwicke community, Tess."

From the Wars of the Roses to high school extracurriculars in two seconds flat.

"I'm not really much of a joiner," I said. That was an understatement.

"The debate club, a sport or two," William Keyes continued, as if I hadn't spoken. "It's high time you started making your mark."

The prestigious Hardwicke School was a microcosm of Washington. The mark I'd made there, up to and including what I'd done for Jeremy Bancroft a few hours earlier, wasn't the kind you could put on a résumé—or the kind my newfound grandfather would have approved of.

"The queen," Keyes told me, returning his attention to our game, "is the most dangerous piece on the board." His index finger trailed the edge of the black queen for a moment, before moving it forward. "Check."

He was boxing me in.

I could see, already, how this was going to end. "You'll have checkmate in three moves."

The old man's lips parted in a dangerous smile. "Will I?"

He'd gone into this game fully expecting to win it, just like he fully expected me to yield to his decrees about Hardwicke.

"Luckily for me," I told him, my fingers closing around my own queen, "I'll have checkmate in two."

THE ORIGINAL BESTSELLING SERIES

THE GAMES CONTINUE IN . . .

OVER 6 MILLION COPIES SOLD

THE DEBUTANTES

'A PLOT TWIST EVERY TWENTY PAGES...
BARNES IS AT HER PAGE-TURNING BEST'

E. Lockhart, author of *We Were Liars*

A FAMILY **FORTUNE**.
A **MYSTERY** TO SOLVE.
A TOWN FULL OF **SECRETS**.

'A PROPULSIVE MYSTERY-THRILLER . . .
YOU WILL CLING TO THIS BOOK UNTIL
YOU REACH THE END.' Maureen Johnson

A FORGOTTEN PAST.
A MISSING GIRL.
A DARK SECRET.